WHERE IT HURTS

ALSO BY REED FARREL COLEMAN

DYLAN KLEIN SERIES
Life Goes Sleeping
Little Easter
They Don't Play Stickball in Milwaukee

MOE PRAGER SERIES
Walking the Perfect Square
Redemption Street
The James Deans
Soul Patch
Empty Ever After
Innocent Monster
Hurt Machine
Onion Street
The Hollow Girl

JOE SERPE SERIES
Hose Monkey
The Fourth Victim

GULLIVER DOWD SERIES
Dirty Work
Valentino Pier
The Boardwalk

ROBERT B. PARKER'S JESSE STONE
Blind Spot
The Devil Wins

STAND-ALONE NOVELS
Tower (with Ken Bruen)
Bronx Requiem (with John Roe)
Gun Church

WHERE IT HURTS

Reed Farrel Coleman

G. P. PUTNAM'S SONS

NEW YORK

G. P. PUTNAM'S SONS
Publishers Since 1838
An imprint of Penguin Random House LLC
375 Hudson Street
New York, New York 10014

Copyright © 2016 by Reed F. Coleman, Inc.
Penguin supports copyright. Copyright fuels creativity, encourages diverse voices,
promotes free speech, and creates a vibrant culture. Thank you for buying an
authorized edition of this book and for complying with copyright laws by
not reproducing, scanning, or distributing any part of it in any form
without permission. You are supporting writers and allowing Penguin
to continue to publish books for every reader.

Library of Congress Cataloging-in-Publication Data
Coleman, Reed Farrel, date.
Where it hurts : a Gus Murphy novel / Reed Farrel Coleman.
p.   cm.
ISBN 978-0-399-17303-5
I. Title.
PS3553.O47445W48   2016   2015017115
813'.54—dc23

Printed in the United States of America
1   3   5   7   9   10   8   6   4   2

BOOK DESIGN BY AMANDA DEWEY

For Paul E. Pepe Jr., Evan Lieberman, and Jeff Fisher

There is always a cause, but not always a because.
And even when there is, the dead are beyond its reach or caring.

WHERE IT HURTS

(MONDAY NIGHT)

ome people swallow their grief. Some let it swallow them. I guess there're about a thousand degrees in between those extremes. Maybe a million. Maybe a million million. Who the fuck knows? Not me. I don't. I'm just about able to put one foot before the other, to breathe again. But not always, not even most of the time. Annie, my wife, I mean, my ex-wife, she let it swallow her whole and when it spit her back up, she was someone else, something else: a hornet from a butterfly. If I was on the outside looking in and not the central target of her fury and sting, I might understand it. I might forgive it. I tell myself I would. But I'd have to forgive myself first. I might as well wish for Jesus to reveal himself in my sideview mirror or for John Jr. to come back to us. At the moment, my wishes were less ambitious ones. I wished for the 11:38 to Ronkonkoma to be on time. I should have wished for it to be early.

I checked the dashboard clock as I pulled into the hotel courtesy van parking spot out in front of the Dunkin' Donuts shop at the station. *11:30, eight minutes to spare.* But spare time was empty time and I had come to dread it because empty was pretty much all I was anymore. Two years steeped in emptiness and I still didn't know how to fill it up. My shrink, Dr. Rosen, says not to try, that I should let myself fully experience the void. That if I don't give myself permission to feel the depth of the abyss, the slipperiness of its walls, I'll never climb out. The thing is, you have to want to climb out, don't you? Even a spare minute was chance enough to relive the last two years. Took forever to live it. Takes only seconds to live it again. I had tried filling in the fissures, cracks, and cavities with wondering, wondering about the trick of time. That got me about as far as wishing. Nowhere.

I stepped out of the van into the chill night. My breath turned to heaving clouds of smoke as cold as God's love. *Hail Mary, full of shit, the Lord is with thee, not me.* I didn't really want coffee. No man who lives for sleep as I do wants coffee. But I had to sustain my waking trance until six a.m. Then I could turn the van keys over to Fredo and fall into my cool sheet-and-quilt-covered solace. When I was on the job, it was different. Everything was different. I liked the world then and the people in it. Liked the buzz of caffeine. Yeah, that was me once, the cop in a doughnut shop, reinforcing stereotypes. Now I was just occupying my mind, doing something, anything not to sit in the van marking time.

Aziza, the mocha-skinned Pakistani girl behind the counter, nodded at me. Smiled a gap-toothed smile. She no longer asked what I wanted. *Small coffee. Half-and-half. Two Sweet'N Lows.* She made it up for me. Put it on the counter. She no longer gave me the change when I paid. She dropped the change in the paper tip cup with the other careless pennies, quarters, dimes, and nickels. I liked Aziza because she expected nothing of me beyond our routine. We danced our nightly dance and then went back to being strangers. She didn't expect me to put the pain behind me or to bravely get on with my life.

Khalid, the night manager, a fleshy man with shark eyes and a suspicious face, stared at me as he always did. It was as if he could smell the taint on me. He didn't like me in the shop. Thought I might sully the place with my taint, or maybe that wasn't it at all.

I got back to the van as the 11:38 pulled into Ronkonkoma. In the eight minutes that had passed, the usual crowd had descended upon the station. Parents in double-parked SUVs, waiting to pick up their kids.

Bored-looking husbands unhappy at being dragged off their sofas into the cold night because their wives felt like doing Broadway with the girls. Cabbies outside their cars, their flannel-shirted bellies flopping over their belt lines, smoking cigarettes, talking shit to each other. I placed the coffee inside the van and took out my Paragon Hotel placard on which the words WESTEX TECHNICAL were written in black marker.

I was scheduled to pick up a party of three from Westex and bring them back to the Paragon. The Paragon Hotel of Bohemia, New York, was paragon of nothing so much as proximity, proximity to Long Island MacArthur Airport. And MacArthur Airport, an airport of three airlines, was nothing so much as an unfulfilled promise, the little airport that couldn't. The Paragon was a way station, a place to pass through on the way to or from the airport. There was the occasional foreign tourist who'd fixated on the room rate instead of the distance to New York City or had neglected to convert kilometers into miles.

The three Westex guys were what I expected, what most of my passengers were: tired, hungry, distracted. When I got back into the van after loading their bags into the rear, all of them were busy with their phones or tablets. They kind of grunted to themselves and one another. I was glad of that, happy to be ignored. I had trouble with the chatty ones, the ones who wanted to be your pal. When I was on the job, I understood nervous chatter because the uniform made people nervous. I also had empathy for the compulsively polite. Not anymore. Who in their heart of hearts really wanted to be the van driver's buddy? It was all so much bullshit, a way to pass time from point to point. I was in on the lie of passing time, so I never spoke first. Never asked where anyone was from. Never asked if they had enjoyed the city. Never asked what they did for a living, or about their families. Never asked where they were headed. I knew where they were headed. We were all headed there, eventually.

I put the van in drive, looked in my sideview for oncoming cars or the Second Coming. And not seeing either, I pulled the wheel hard left and made a sweeping U-turn west onto Railroad Avenue. As we went, I sipped at my unwanted coffee, thinking of my dead son.

The phone bleating on the nightstand woke me from a dreamless sleep, but John Jr. was my first waking thought, just as he had been my last conscious thought before I closed my eyes. It was as reflexive to me as blinking. After two years grieving him, missing him, tearing my guts out over his death, he never really left me. At least he was no longer every thought in between my first and last. There had been periods during that first year when I felt I would choke on his constant presence. When I would have given almost anything for a few minutes of simple forgetfulness. It got so oppressive that I began hating the son I had loved more than myself and then hated myself for hating him.

The TV was still on but tuned to *SportsCenter*, so it could have been any time of the day or night. I looked out the southeast-facing window of my room and saw the sun was relatively low in the sky. I felt the weariness still deep in my bones and knew I hadn't been asleep very long.

I reached for the phone.

"Yeah, what?"

Nothing.

I dozed off with the phone still in my hand. This time when it rang, I managed to press the talk button.

"Yeah."

"Gus, there's a gentleman down here asking to see you." It was Felix at the front desk, his Filipino lilt less prominent when he was speaking in front of a guest.

"What time is it?" I asked even as I stretched to see the clock radio.

"Nine seventeen."

I yawned. "This gentleman have a name?"

"He won't give me his name, but he says you have dealt with him in the past."

"That really narrows it down. What's he look like?"

Felix cleared his throat and, without a hint of guile, whispered, "Trouble."

I laughed, felt the smile on my face. It didn't used to feel so foreign. "Tell him I'm sleeping."

"Don't you think I have attempted that, Gus? He said he will wait down here all day if that is what it will take." Then Felix was whispering again. "He's a rough-looking man with tattoos and he makes me nervous."

"All right. Tell him to go wait for me in the coffee shop and I'll be along."

"When?"

"When I get there."

"Thank you, Gus."

For my part, I was in no rush to get downstairs, but I liked Felix. He didn't have much of a heart for confrontation. Then again, I had spent most of my adult life collecting scar tissue from it. It's what cops did.

I brushed my teeth, finger-combed my grief-gray hair—that's what my sister called it—and pulled on my Costco wardrobe: Kirkland jeans, black Tommy Hilfiger sweater, Kirkland athletic socks, and running shoes. My Glock and ammo were the only pieces of my outfit that I hadn't bought at Costco. Even the black leather jacket I wore had come from there.

It was a five-step stroll to the elevator from my room. The room was part of my deal with the Bonackers, the family that owned and managed the Paragon. I drove the van from six to six, three or four nights a week, and occasionally acted as house detective. Although the hotel was half-empty most of the time, the Full Flaps Lounge did big happy-hour business because of its proximity to a large industrial park and office buildings. And when it was turned into a '70s and '80s throw-back disco on Friday and Saturday evenings, things sometimes got a little hairy. Middle-aged men flexing their weekend beer muscles for drunk divorcées could get ugly, and often did. The Bonackers liked knowing that when I called the cops, they came, and fast.

The lobby of the Paragon was actually a pretty grand sight if you didn't look too closely, and if your taste ran to despair. Completed in the mid-'80s, the hotel had gone through several incarnations. The last time any serious work had been done on the place was prior to the 2008 financial collapse. It took more body blows after JetBlue declined to set up shop at MacArthur, and Southwest began shifting flights to LaGuardia. The Paragon had already changed hands four or five times when the Bonackers bought it. The rooms were cheap, clean, and available. If that wasn't enough for you, you were shit out of luck.

I nodded at Felix as I came off the elevator. He pointed his short little arm at the hotel coffee shop, poking the air with his finger. "Big man, Gus. Very big."

"I hope you take this the right way, Felix, but—"

"Don't you talk about my height again. I am the same size as Manny Pacquiao."

I took a boxer's stance and threw a shadow jab. "Too bad you don't punch like him."

"There is going to be trouble, do you think?"

"I guess we're gonna find out."

I walked into the Runway coffee shop, the walls of which were covered in murals of great moments in aviation history connected to Long

Island. Lindbergh taking off from Roosevelt Field for his flight to Le Bourget. The Grumman-built moon lander touching down in the Sea of Tranquility. The first A-10 rolling off the Fairchild Republic production line. A swept-wing Grumman F-14 swooping low over an air-show crowd at Jones Beach. For the second time in twenty minutes, I laughed. I laughed because there would be no more such great moments. Roosevelt Field was now an enormous shopping mall. Fairchild Republic was gone and Grumman, once the largest employer on Long Island, had been dismembered and swallowed up, existing now only as a feeble outpost in a sea of abandonment. I knew a little something about that.

The coffee shop was nearly empty but for the ghostly scent of fried bacon and dark grace notes of burnt black coffee. Along with the smells of breakfast, the big man was the only other thing in the place. He sat at a booth, a cup of coffee before him on the wingtip-shaped table. I didn't approach him. He looked like somebody I knew, but I couldn't quite place him. When I was on the job, I'd had a steel-trap memory, but the last two years had taken their toll. Not much was crisp or clear to me any longer. Vague familiarity was my default setting. Even the pain of John Jr.'s loss had transformed itself from the excruciating burn of a puncture wound to the dull ache of a dying tooth. There was also something in the big man's expression that reminded me of my own reflection. A distance in his moist brown eyes, a disconnection from the moment. It's hard to explain, but it was there as sure as the cup in front of him.

I was frozen in place, pinned by the resonance in the big man's expression. That was when somebody in the kitchen dumped a load of silverware onto the sorting tray. The crash and jangle of the metal utensils broke the silence. The big man's eyes refocused. He turned to look up at me, a mournful smile on his crooked mouth. Yeah, I knew him: Thomas Delcamino, Tommy D. Everybody who had worked in the Second Precinct knew Tommy D. Most of us had arrested him. Many of us, more than once.

(TUESDAY MORNING)

He stood to greet me, the sadness in his bent smile seeming to vanish. As he rose, I patted my jacket pocket to feel for my weapon. He noticed. I guess I'd wanted him to notice. On the job you hear lots of revenge tales about humps you busted coming around to pay you back, but it turns out that only a very few of those stories had any truth in them. They were meant to keep you alert and to remind you not to be too much of an asshole to the handcuffed people riding in the back of the car. A lot of guys I worked with over the years needed to hear those stories more than I did. Funny how the ones who needed to hear them never listened. When Tommy D. saw me pat my hip, the wind went out of him, the sadness returning to his expression as he shook his head at me in disappointment. Disappointing people, I did a lot of that these days.

Tommy D. looked scary enough, if he wasn't exactly the behemoth Felix had hinted at. Maybe six three at most, not a whole lot taller than me. Felix hadn't exaggerated about the tats. He'd gotten that much right. Delcamino was inked up pretty good. His hands were blue, green, and red with tattoos, many of which seemed to be continuations of designs hidden by the sleeves of his tan, dust-covered Carhartt jacket.

But it must have been the barbed-wire tat that swirled around his neck and the streaks of red-inked blood leaking out of where the prongs appeared to cut into the skin of his throat that had freaked Felix out.

Delcamino held out his big right hand. "Officer Murphy," he said. "You don't need to carry. You got nothin' to worry about from me. You always treated me with respect. More than a dildo like me deserved."

I shook his hand without much enthusiasm. He may not have been much taller than me, but he *was* bigger, broader, and thicker through the chest and limbs. His hand dwarfed mine. The skin of his palm and fingers was rough and callused.

"You behaving yourself these days, Tommy?" The words came out of my mouth by reflex. As if it mattered. As if I cared.

He lit up. "Yeah, yeah. I got a job as a laborer with a company that does masonry and paving over on Long Island Avenue in Holtsville. I live in a trailer over there, too. Watch the yard, work on the trucks. It's hard work, you know, but it pays good."

Tommy looked fierce, but he wasn't. It was a Technicolor feint, a lion's roar from an alley cat. The Tommy D. I knew would probably have preferred fading into the backdrop. The stuff I'd arrested him for was all petty shit: possession of stolen property, minor drug sales, ripping stereos out of car dashboards when that still made sense, like that. None of that is to say Tommy couldn't take care of himself. If you pushed him hard enough, he'd push back harder.

"I'm glad you got your shit straight, but why are you here, Tommy? How'd you find me?"

He thumped back down in the booth. I kept my feet. I wanted the high ground if it came to that.

Head bowed, he said, "I went to your house, like, two weeks ago and the woman renting the place told me you didn't live there no more. She said she didn't know where you lived. Nice lady. You know, you should really get your driveway redone. I can get you a real good discount. My boss—"

"How did you know my address?"

He shrugged. "The Internet. You can find anybody on the Internet."

"And here. How did you find me here? There's nothing on the net about me being here."

"I asked around."

"What the fuck does that mean, you asked around? Who'd you ask? You don't start giving answers I need to hear, I'm gonna—"

He looked up, his eyes rimmed in red. He held up his palms in surrender. "Sorry, Officer Murphy. I didn't mean no harm. I swear."

"I didn't ask for apologies or explanations."

"Just around. Then last Friday night a guy I grew up with was in the dance club here. He was telling me about it and mentioned you was working the door. He recognized you, is all. If he didn't say nothing about it to me yesterday, I guess I never woulda found you."

I sat down across from Delcamino. "Okay, that's how you found me. Now tell me why."

Tommy D. looked everywhere but at me. He was struggling with himself, searching for the right words. "It's my kid, my son," he said, his booming voice oddly brittle.

"I didn't know you had kids."

"I don't. I mean, I don't, not no more."

I felt myself burn beneath my skin. "What the fuck, Tommy?"

He reached down beside him and put a faded green canvas backpack on the table. He unzipped it and took out a folded newspaper story. He unfolded it, smoothed it out, and laid it on the table in front of me with a kind of religious reverence. "He was murdered."

I was confused. "Who was?"

"My son, TJ. They murdered him. They put a beatin' on him, fuckin' tortured him. Broke all his fingers, broke his kneecaps. They burned him, too. They tied him up and burned him. Then them motherfuckas dumped him in a lot in Nesconset like a bag a garbage or something."

"Christ," I heard myself say. I started to cross myself and stopped.

Delcamino couldn't talk. He was crying, his chest heaving so that I could feel it through the table. He wiped his tears and snot on the sleeve of his jacket, leaving a smear of gray cement dust on his cheek.

And in that instant I was underwater, back down the hole I had just begun to crawl out of. All I saw in Delcamino's tears was my own rage and grief. It was all I could do not to smack him or cry myself. I sat there watching him, nausea welling up in me in a way it hadn't since the day we buried John Jr.

His tears stopped eventually and his heaving chest calmed, but then he started ranting.

"What the fuck kinda chance did a son a mine ever have with a piece a shit like me for a father?" he asked, not really wanting an answer. "What kinda life was a kid a mine gonna have?"

"Take it easy, Tommy."

"Take it easy! How the fuck can I take it easy? The cops won't even give me the time a day. I call the detectives and all they say is they're working the case and hang up on me. Look, Officer Mur—I mean, Mr. Murphy, I know I been a fuckup my whole life and that my kid was following right behind me, but that don't mean he was garbage. Don't he deserve some justice, too? Am I wrong? He was a fuckup like me. Sure he boosted some shit to pay for his drugs, but he was trying to get straight. He didn't do nothing so bad that he deserved what he got. He didn't deserve to die like that. Sometimes I can't sleep thinking about how afraid he musta been and how much he musta suffered alone like that. I swear there are nights I wake up hearin' him screamin' for me. I wasn't there to stand up for him when he was alive. I gotta stand up for him now. You can understand that, right?"

I nodded. "When did this happen, Tommy?"

"Last August," he said, tapping the newspaper article with his index finger. "It's all in here. See, that's him there in the picture."

"Handsome kid."

Delcamino smiled, then his lip turned down. "I mean, I been patient. I tried to let the detectives do their thing, you know? I know how this shit works. I know it ain't an easy job, but I gave 'em a list of TJ's asshole friends, the dickheads he used to run with. I got it all written down, what I gave 'em. I gave 'em copies of pictures, names, addresses, phone numbers." He patted the backpack. "I even did a little askin' around myself, got the names of the dealers he used to score from. Guys, you know, TJ mighta owed money to."

"And?"

"And nothing. I went back to some of the people I talked to and they said the detectives never even contacted them. I mean, for fuck's sake, Officer—"

"Gus. Call me Gus."

"Gus." He smiled, trying it on for size. I figured it felt like a small victory to him. It sure felt like one to me. It had been a long time since I made someone else smile.

"Why come to me?"

"Because you was always the rightest cop I ever met. You treated me like a person, like a human being."

"Look, Tommy, there's channels for this kind of thing, a chain of command, people to talk to."

"I done that. I talked to them till I'm blue in the face," he said. "I been up one side of that ladder and down the other. Either they don't listen or they don't give a fuck. Who am I, right? I'm a skel, a mutt, a piece a shit. And my kid wasn't no better. None of 'em said it, but they didn't have to. I may be stupid, but I ain't blind neither. Half of 'em thought, with TJ dead that was one less headache for them to deal with down the line."

I wanted to tell him he was wrong, but I didn't because he wasn't. Maybe he was a little harsh about it. Harsh was what he understood. I'd been on the other side of it. Any cop who tells you he doesn't judge some people as better than others is a liar. I did it. We all did. Like the badge and gun, judgments came with the territory. The trick was not treating people differently. The church teaches you that you're judged for your thoughts *and* deeds, but in the cathedral of the street, thoughts count for little. Deeds talk loudest.

I asked, "Have you tried hiring a PI?"

He reached into the backpack and came out with a fist-sized, rubber-banded roll of twenties. He put it on the table, right on top of the newspaper article. "That's three large there, give or take. It's all the money I got in the world."

"What's it for?"

"For you, Gus. I went to a few PIs. All they wanna do is suck you dry an hour at a time with no promises of finding nothing. I'd be drained in two, three weeks tops."

I could feel that burn beneath my skin again. "Who told you about my son?"

Delcamino tilted his head at me like a confused puppy. "Gus, I—"

"What, you think I'll help you because of what happened to John Jr.?"

He started talking, but I couldn't hear it. I shot up off the booth cushion, the fire now burning inside me and out. "Get outta here, Tommy D. Take your fucking money and get outta here!" I pounded the table, his coffee cup crashing to the floor, shattering. "I'm sorry about your kid, but don't you ever dare try to use my son to mess with me again. Understand? You want justice, well, fuck you! There isn't any. None. Not anywhere in this world. Now get outta here! Get outta here!"

When I calmed down, Tommy Delcamino was nowhere to be found. Felix, hand on my forearm, was standing next to me. He was peering up at me, his nearly black eyes filled with an odd cocktail of fear and admiration. Paolo, the dishwasher and busboy, was sweeping the broken shards of the coffee cup into a plastic dustpan. When I looked back at the table, I saw that the money and backpack were gone, but the newspaper article was still there.

I sat in the driver's seat, a howling wind buffeting the van as I waited on the 4:37 to pull into the station. We didn't get many calls for pickups at Ronkonkoma this early in the morning, but weather delays in the Midwest had caused someone to switch to a Southwest flight out of MacArthur later that day. The station was a cold and lonely place at that hour, and when a winter wind kicked up, blowing litter around in whirling eddies, hurling pebbles and grains of road sand into your windows, it felt like the end of the world. Maybe it was. I felt so fucking guilty about how I'd treated Tommy D. that I found myself hoping so.

I never used to be a guy who felt guilty much, mostly because I didn't think I had that much to feel guilty about. People live their lives somewhere on a scale of Have-to-dos and Want-to-dos and I was always the kind of guy who turned have-tos into want-tos. When it snowed and I shoveled my driveway, I'd shovel my neighbors' driveways, too. Not because I felt obliged to or because I thought I'd get some kind of payback, but because I wanted to. I'd had a happy nature once in spite of my miserable drunk of a dad and my shy, almost invisible mother.

Maybe it was because I never wanted for much. It was my experience that the real name of the devil was "wanting." I'd gotten those few things in life I did want: a loving family, a good job, a nice house. Simple things made me happy: watching a ball game, reading a book, sitting in the sun in my backyard. When you aren't ambitious, when you don't covet. When you keep your dreams simple and your grasp short, there's not much to lie about, no need for scheming or deception. Absent that stuff, what is there to feel guilty about? I don't know, until John Jr. died, I felt like I had my little piece of the world by the balls. I thought I understood the order in the universe. Turned out I understood nothing, let alone everything.

As I sat, waiting for Mr. Lembeck's train to show, I reread the newspaper clipping Tommy Delcamino had left behind. I didn't know why I was reading it again except to punish myself some more for acting like such an asshole. Whether he knew about my son or not was beside the point. If anyone on the planet should have understood Tommy D.'s frustration or had empathy for him, it should have been me. I had been exactly where he was now: lost, guilty, and grieving. I wondered if Tommy D. had other family—a wife, maybe, brothers and sisters. I wondered if they had done what we had done when we found out the hurt doesn't stop. That there is only you and your wife and your daughter. And somehow, blameless or not, you all wind up blaming each other and burning down everything you have because you have to do something with all the pain.

One thing was true, Tommy hadn't exaggerated about what they'd done to his kid. I could only imagine the mess those autopsy photos must have been. I wondered what it must have been like for Tommy D. to go identify his son. I'd been around the morgue enough to know the horror involved when a parent comes to identify a child. If there's anything that's wrong in the world by its very nature, it's that—a kid in the ground before his parents. For that reason alone, I should've at least heard Tommy D. out.

I knew the spot where they'd left his kid's body. It was only about five minutes north of the Ronkonkoma station. That area around Nesconset and Lake Grove was full of these little wooded lots choked with poison ivy, prickly vines, and shrubs in the summer. Mean with bare, twisted limbs and fallen branches come the cold. Places where the little neighborhood kids went to build forts or explore, and their older brothers and sisters went to drink or get high or study anatomy. As was often the case, a man walking his dog found the kid's body.

There was a banging on the van door window that had nothing to do with the wind. I looked up to see a man's angry face staring in at me. I looked beyond the face to see the train sitting in the station and noticed a few passengers fighting the wind and their exhaustion to get to their cars. I hopped out, opened the door for the rightfully angry Mr. Lembeck, and tossed his bags in the back of the van. There would be no tip for me at the end of this ride. That was okay. Mr. Lembeck couldn't punish me any more than I was already punishing myself.

Pulling up to the hotel, I noticed a car parked to the left of the main entrance. It was a car I didn't want to see. Its presence could only mean trouble in one form or another.

After unloading Mr. Lembeck's bags and apologizing once again, I thought about driving off. But Lembeck needed help with his bags. Slava Podalak, our crazy night bellman from Warsaw, was nowhere in sight, so I carried the bags to registration. When I got there, Rita, who sometimes worked the night desk, welcomed Mr. Lembeck. As he looked down, reaching for his credit card and ID, Rita tilted her head toward the Full Flaps Lounge, mouthing, *She's in there.*

The lounge was dark, almost lightless, but I was as familiar with her shape as my own. She was half-asleep, curled up on a row of old airline seats that were part of the bar's décor.

"What's up, Annie?" I asked my ex.

She unfurled herself and stretched her long, graceful body. I tried not to look at her dark figure, but couldn't help myself. For two plus decades, this woman had been the object of my love and desire. Since the day we got the call about John Jr., Annie and I had systematically taken each other apart. We'd ruined ourselves and our marriage, and we'd probably ruined ourselves for anybody else. I read once about this rare breed of wildcat, the Asian fishing cat, that were so ornery, so territorial, and such loners that they could only tolerate the presence of one of their own kind to mate. Even then, they often tried to kill each other after mating. That was us now, Annie and me. Every few months we'd find an excuse to get together to fight and then fuck our brains out. Then, afterward, we'd go back to our corners and wait for the bell to ring for the next round of war.

Why did we do it? I used to think it was our way of remembering our son and how he came to be in the first place. Or it was our way to numb the pain, sex as novocaine. That wasn't it. It was just another way to empty ourselves, a way to beat the remnants of love out of each other. Each time we walked away from those episodes, it felt like there was less of who we once had been. As I looked at her, I hoped that wasn't why she was here. I wasn't in the mood for any more punishment, self-inflicted or otherwise. Even in the dark, she could read my face.

"Don't worry, Gus," she said, reaching into her bag for a box of Newports. "I'm not here for that."

I didn't bother telling her she couldn't smoke in the hotel. She wouldn't've listened and to defy me would have only increased her pleasure in the act. She flicked the lighter and its flash framed Annie's lovely face. She looked older now. Near defeat, not defeated. Her hair was still that beautiful shade of rich dark brown. Her eyes still hazel. Her nose, perfect as if the work of a sculptor, but her skin was etched with deep ragged lines around her eyes and at the corners of her mouth. The flame, I thought, made them seem worse. The tip of her cigarette glowed there between us in the dark like an accusation. Then she stood and blew the smoke into my face. I didn't react.

She strolled out of the lounge into the light of the lobby. Annie's lean body cut through the air like an arrow. I followed at her heels, waiting for the hammer to drop. Slava had reappeared, but made himself scarce at the sight of my ex. He may not have known my story, yet he knew to avoid Annie and me. Rita and Mr. Lembeck were gone as well. Annie stopped, turned, and looked at me. Brushed her hand dismissively across the chest of my uniform jacket.

"Aren't you embarrassed by this job?"

"It's a job."

"God, I used to think you were so hot in your cop blues."

"I still get to wear a uniform," I said, poker-faced, pointing at my Paragon Hotel jacket.

"It's beneath you. Why do you do it?"

"You gave away the right to ask me those kinds of questions."

She shook her head. "You used to have pride."

"I used to have a lot of things I don't have anymore."

"What happened to you, Gus?"

"The same thing that happened to you. What are you doing here, Annie?"

She didn't answer immediately. We stood there, looking at each other, wondering what had become of us.

"It's Kristen."

She said our daughter's name as if it was answer enough. I guess it was. There had been a third casualty in the shitstorm that followed in the wake of my son's death. Kristen, always the most fragile of the Murphys, had lost more than any of us. She'd not only lost her brother, she'd lost her entire family. Worse, she'd been both complicit in and witness to the disintegration.

"What now?"

"She got pulled over again," Annie said with a shrug.

"Where?"

"If it wasn't so stupid it would be funny, Gus."

"That's not an answer."

"In front of the state office building on 347."

"You mean right in front of the Fourth Precinct!"

"See, I told you. It's almost funny."

"Not nearly, Annie. What was she doing this time?"

"Smoking weed. They also found an open bottle of vodka in the car."

"Fuck!"

"Don't worry, Gus. They're not charging her, but they're holding her until you get down there."

"Why didn't you just go get her?"

"Because I'm not a retired Suffolk County cop. I'm not the one with the connections. Anyway, he specifically asked for you to get her."

"He who?" I asked.

"Pete."

The name landed like a punch to the kidneys.

"Okay, I just have to let them know I'm leaving. Go ahead of me. I'll meet you over there."

"No, you won't. I've had it with her, Gus. I don't know what to say to her anymore. I've screamed at her until I'm blue in the face."

"How about not screaming?"

"How about fuck you?" She flipped me the bird and stormed out.

I didn't follow. Deep down I knew the reason she walked away had less to do with Kristen than with Pete.

(WEDNESDAY MORNING)

The new Fourth Precinct building was only a few years old. With its reflective blue glass, concrete-and-steel construction, it more resembled a bank or a suburban office building than a cop house. The inside was something else. Inside was inside and no matter how you dressed it up—and they had dressed it up—the same sort of business got done here as in the old house. The same scum, the same addicts and assholes, the same drunk drivers, the same murderers, thieves, and fools came through its doors. And the most recent fool was me.

For the majority of my career I'd been at the Second Precinct on Park Avenue in Huntington, so I didn't expect anybody except for Pete to know me here. Some of them might've heard my name or heard about me, but it was unlikely they could place me. Nothing like retiring from the police to validate the saying: Out of sight, out of mind. In that way, the department was like a sports team. Retired players weren't part of the team. They were gone. It didn't much matter why. Gone was gone was gone.

I was glad to be forgotten. One of the worst parts of the mourning process was dealing with people who were aware of your situation. Grieving was hard enough without having to manage other people's reactions. Half the time I wound up consoling *them*. Even when things didn't get to that point, it was always awkward. People don't know what to say or how to say it or whether to say anything at all. I hated it when they either pretended to not know or ignored it. It was like having a piece of spinach caught between your teeth. People would look at you funny, but just wouldn't tell you. I'd catch them staring at me out of the corners of their eyes. God, how I hated it. It was one of the reasons I liked my job at the Paragon. No one at the hotel knew my story. They knew I was divorced and that was that. Everyone who worked the night shift there seemed to me to be hiding out or running away. We all had stories not to tell.

Detective Peter Francis Xavier McCann came to collect what was left of me so that I could collect what was left of my daughter. Pete, a lean and handsome son of a bitch, was seven years my junior. I'd been one of his training officers when he came on the job. He'd been trans-ferred to the detective squad at the Fourth around the time I retired. He was a black-haired Irishman with oddly fair skin and the damned-est blue eyes. The bastard even had a cleft in his square chin, but it was his charm, not his chin, that was his deadliest weapon. He had the knack of making you feel you were the most important person in the world to him and the best friend he ever had. Problem was, believing you were Pete's best friend was like believing you were Napoleon in a psych ward full of people who swore *they* were the real Napoleon. And even so, even after what had gone on between us, I got a jolt at the sight of him.

There was awkwardness between us obliquely related to John Jr.'s death. Pete had been one of the pallbearers at the funeral. I think the only fully honest relationship Pete had ever had was with my kids, John Jr. in particular. Maybe because John had the gift of seeing right through people's bullshit. Pete's blarney and charm bounced off him like bullets off Superman. So Pete was forced to expose who he was underneath if he wanted to be that sage "uncle" to my kids. It would be no lie to say that John's death had been almost as hard on Pete as the rest of us. Almost. It was the way Pete chose to salve his wounds that was the issue.

"Come on back," Pete said, smiling, waving at me to follow him to his desk.

I followed him back and sat facing him. He offered me coffee. I nodded.

"Half-and-half, two Sweet'N Lows?" he asked, knowing the answer, and said he'd be right back.

I sipped my coffee. He sipped his. The only sounds around us came from the occasional ringing phones and the buzz of early-morning traffic on Route 347.

He said, "Good thing I happened to be here this morning early to clear up some shit."

"How's that, Pete?"

"PBA cards and courtesy shields don't work like they used to for DUI and DWI. If I wasn't around, the uniforms would have processed her for sure."

"Thanks." There wasn't much enthusiasm in my voice. He understood why.

"You still living out of that shitbox hotel by the airport?"

"Yep."

He made a sour face, shook his head without being conscious of it. That was okay. I was used to much harsher judgments, specifically my own.

"Where are Annie and Kristen living?"

"They're with Annie's brother and sister-in-law in East Setauket."

"East Setauket. Very nice. Somebody's done well for themselves," he said, his smile barely concealing his envy.

Unlike me, Pete was a man with ambition. He was a man who wanted everything and then some. It had taken me years of knowing him to figure out that he was most fond of things that belonged to other people, women in particular. When we'd all go out drinking after a shift, Pete would regale us with story after story about the women he was sleeping with, all of them well married: the Jets' running back's wife, the heart surgeon's wife, the CEO's wife. So I shouldn't've been surprised when I found out he had added Annie to the list.

I believed Annie when she said she had started sleeping with Pete out of grief over John Jr. When she said that she knew it would blow us apart. That she *meant* to blow us apart. That all she felt for me anymore was rage and sadness and that she had no will or desire to bear it. But when Pete tried to find cover for his betrayal in my son's death, I called bullshit on that. I knew him too well by then. In some ways, Annie was his ultimate prize, the cherry on top of the icing on the top of the cake. Once it was out in the open, though, their passion turned to dust. Annie, regardless of her intentions, was embarrassed by what she had done. For his part, Pete lost interest. Trophies, even the biggest, shiniest ones, lose their luster pretty quickly, especially when they come at the cost of friendship.

Still, it wasn't in me to hate Pete. Was I still furious with him? You bet. I was a lot of things, but hypocrite was not among them. I had listened as eagerly as the rest of the guys to Pete's tales of conquest. Listened to him detail how he had so many other men's wives in so many ways and I'd never once registered an ounce of protest or warning. I'd gotten what I deserved, but so too did Annie and Pete.

I let Pete's envious comment about East Setauket go.

He took note of my silence and said, "Why not sell your house in Commack? You guys aren't underwater, are you? Not with that house?"

"We can't bring ourselves to live there and we can't stand the thought of selling it. Besides, even if we wanted to sell it, its value isn't all the way back."

He seemed to understand.

I finally asked about my daughter. "How's Krissy?"

"You gotta get her some help, Gus. She's gonna do something soon that none of us can save her from."

"No shit! Don't you think we know that? We've tried everything with her. She just won't listen."

"Look, I know I'm not married and I don't have kids—"

"That you know of."

"That I know of," he repeated, smiling in spite of himself. "And you and Annie have your reasons for hating—"

"Just say your piece, Pete."

"Stop bailing her out. Stop letting your cop friends get her out of the shit she gets into. Let her fall down and scrape her knees. Parents aren't there to catch their kids when they're falling. Parents are there to help pick them up after they fall. If you don't let her suffer a little . . ."

He didn't finish his sentence. He didn't have to. The implication was clear enough. If we didn't do something soon, Krissy would self-destruct. Annie and I would have no living children. I hung my head because I knew he was right—I hated that he was—and because I knew I couldn't let Kristen suffer the consequences, not yet, anyway.

After Pete sent word down to bring Kristen from where they were holding her to his desk, it occurred to me to ask him about Tommy Delcamino's kid.

"Pete, you working the Delcamino homicide?"

He didn't seem to hear me. "What case?"

"You remember Tommy Delcamino," I said.

"That low-life piece of shit, sure. What about him?"

"They found his son tortured to death over in Nesconset last summer."

"Yeah, yeah, sure. Nope, not my case."

"Whose case is it?"

"Why you want to know?"

"Just curious," I said, and left it at that.

"That asshole Paxson and Lou Carey."

At first, he left it at that, but when he walked Kristen and me to the door, he grabbed me by the biceps and pulled me aside.

"Krissy," he said, "give your dad and me a second, okay?"

I gave her the keys to my car and told her to sit there and wait for me. She hesitated.

Pete prompted her. "Go ahead, honey. Your car's okay here. I'll make sure of it. You or your mom can come get it later."

Kristen, red-eyed and dejected, turned and walked away.

"What's up, Pete?" I asked when Kristen was out of earshot.

"Listen, Gus, I'm gonna give you some more advice you probably don't want to hear, but you need to listen to it. Stay away from the Delcamino case. Stay far, far away from it."

I could feel myself pull away from him, my face getting hard with anger. "You ever know me to run away from anything?"

He took a deep breath, then said, "Seems to me that since John died, all you've been doing is running away."

I wanted to grab him by the throat for saying that. If I had, I'm not sure I would have let go. He was right, in his way. But he was the last person I wanted to hear it from. I don't suppose it mattered now. I'm not sure what did anymore.

(WEDNESDAY MORNING)

For the first ten minutes of the ride east to her aunt and uncle's house, not a word passed between Krissy and me. For my part, I was busy turning Pete McCann's words over and over in my head. It was hard to know with Pete if he was being sincere or if he had something to gain by keeping me away from the Delcamino homicide. No matter how I spun it, I didn't get his play. The last two years had taken their toll; I didn't see anything clearly. But just because I couldn't figure Pete's angle didn't mean he didn't have one. Pete had so many angles they could've named a new branch of geometry after him. That was how he had collected all those women, all those friends and hangers-on. He understood human weaknesses about as well as anyone I ever met. He sure understood mine.

Out of the corner of my eye, I stared at my youngest. Krissy: beautiful and fragile. She'd had the good fortune of inheriting the best physical aspects of both her parents and the misfortune of inheriting my mother's reticent constitution. Kristen didn't have many friends, but had always been her big brother's favorite. John had doted on Kristen with an almost parental kind of love from the day she was born.

Whereas Annie and I had pretty much entered the final stages of our slow-motion self-immolations, Kristen still seemed in the thick of hers.

For a year after losing her big brother, best friend, and protector, she had withdrawn. She'd dropped out of college, broken up with her boyfriend, gained weight, and pretty much became a shut-in. Then, as if a switch had been thrown, she transformed into a person we didn't know. We were fooled at first, encouraged because she was finally getting out, reclaiming her life. Only the life she was reclaiming was someone else's, one that involved stupid risk taking. The drinking and the drugs—pot was the least of it—were bad enough, but then there were the men. All sorts of men, most of them the type of guy Krissy wouldn't have looked at twice. It was almost as if she couldn't bear destroying herself one bit at a time, so she took on a different personality to speed the process along.

"What's it gonna be next time, Krissy?"

She started. I'm not sure if it was what I said or the calm with which I said it, but it got her attention.

"I don't understand," she said in a little girl's voice, a voice I recognized from when she would lie to me as a kid. It had taken me only a few years of parenting to learn that kids have a lying voice.

"You understand, Krissy. You understand."

That was greeted by another few minutes of my daughter's tight-lipped silence.

"I'm sorry, Dad," she said as we drove past Smithtown toward St. James on 25A.

"For what part of it?"

"All of it, I guess."

"Guessing's not good enough."

"Then what is?"

"Stopping whatever it is you're doing to yourself."

"I'm not sure I know how," she said, turning to look out the window at a winter-bare and lonely nursery.

"You don't know how to, or you don't want to?"

"I don't even know, Dad. I don't know what to do with it." She turned away from the nursery to look at me. "Feels like the center of my life is gone. I mean, it's not even all about John anymore. I wish somebody could tell me what to do about that."

"Don't look at me, kid. Your mom and I haven't exactly set a great example, have we?"

She laughed. It was a sad laugh. Then she leaned over, resting her head on my shoulder like she used to do when she was little.

"Wanna know what's funny, kiddo?"

"What, Dad?"

"You get instruction booklets with everything in your life except the hardest parts: marriage, kids, and death. Your mom and me, we did pretty good for a while."

She didn't say anything to that, just kept resting her head on my shoulder. When we were passing the Stony Brook University campus, she lifted her head, craning her neck to try and see some of the buildings.

"You miss school?" I asked.

"Sometimes."

"Go back."

"I'm not sure I'm ready yet."

I felt a smile on my face. Kristen noticed it, too.

"What are you smiling at?" she said.

"Nothing."

She punched my arm. "What?"

"You said you weren't ready to go back *yet*."

"So?"

"Yet. There's hope in the word 'yet.'"

"Isn't there always hope, Dad?"

I was so happy to hear her ask, I just kept smiling. If I'd said anything, I would have been forced to use my lying voice, or worse, I would have had to tell the truth.

(WEDNESDAY AFTERNOON)

After last night's shift and this morning's drama with Krissy, I should have been exhausted. What I found instead was that I was oddly invigorated. For the first time in as long as I could remember, I was outside myself. My internal voice clicking off the tape loop of funeral dirges and self-pity in spite of the gloom that hung over Long Island like a shroud. The air was mean and raw, the sky a patchwork of ugly gray bruises. A thin layer of cold mist covered everything. A mist that seemed not so much to fall as to just be. Stepping out of my car, I was assaulted by a wind of pinpricks. A wind that smelled of the ocean. That briny odor was at odds with my distance from the ocean, at odds with December. I guess it was a perfect day to find myself standing before the wooded lot in which TJ Delcamino's body had been discovered.

The house to my right, a split ranch covered in white vinyl siding, had a nativity scene on the lawn. The figures were plaster, not cheap extruded plastic. And because all the figures had a weathered patina, I got the sense it had been in this family for many years. I could see places where the figures had been chipped and fractured over time. Some of the chips had been unskillfully repaired and coated with mismatching paint, while other scars were left to the mercy of the elements. The

Magi, Mary and Joseph, even the goats, the ass, and the sheep, seemed to huddle around the baby Jesus as much to shield him from the wind as to adore him. When I looked more closely at our infant savior, I saw he was impossibly large for a newborn and that someone had glued bright blue doll eyes onto his face. Eyes that followed my gaze. When I looked at him, he was looking back at me.

The house to the left of the lot was a pageant of bad taste. Santa, his sleigh, and his reindeer sat atop the roof of the cedar-shingled ranch. The Santa display was all mechanized. First, sleigh bells would sound as the reindeer legs moved to simulate landing. Rudolph's nose flashed red. Then as Santa stood up from his seat, a massive toy bag slung over his shoulder, his red pants would drop to expose his pale white flanks and a recording would play "Ho, ho, ho, Merry Christmas." The whole thing recycled every thirty seconds or so. I half expected the reindeer to poop plastic pellets. The house itself was covered in a grid of red, green, and white lights that would have given Times Square a run for its money. There was a huge blow-up snowman on the lawn, smoke coming out of his pipe. In front of the snowman were plastic figures of Alvin and the Chipmunks dressed as elves. A speaker hidden somewhere on the lawn played cover versions of the elfin rodents singing seasonal tunes and carols. "Little Drummer Boy" was just starting up when I got out of my car and now it was *ba-rump-ba-bump-ba*-ing to a close.

Fuckin' guineas and their Christmas crap. They have no fuckin' respect, those people. I heard my father's drunken refrain loud in my head as I waited for the Chipmunks' next selection. He particularly enjoyed saying stuff like that in front of my mom because some of her people were Italian and he knew it ate at her. And when he saw the hurt in her eyes, he'd say, "So you are alive in there after all. Christ knows, sometimes, I have my doubts." A real charmer, my old man.

About fifty feet wide and a hundred feet deep, the lot on Browns Road was vacant but not empty. It was full of misshapen, vine-strangled trees covered in scales of sickly ashen bark. Pine trees and maples, oaks and dwarf cherries, their limbs twisted and palsied, knotted and weak. The floor of this distorted little forest was carpeted in rotted mower clippings, pine straw, generations of leaf litter, and just plain litter. Newspapers turned back into mounds of gray pulp by the mist. Old car bumpers, their last remnants of chrome now just a few silvery flakes. Small piles of broken concrete blocks, jagged pieces of scrap wood, bent nails, and discarded wallboard. A dented refrigerator door. The frame of a bicycle. The rusted carcass of an abandoned oil tank, its vent pipe sticking up out of the leaves like the arm of a drowning man.

As I waded into the lot, the Chipmunks squealing "White Christmas," the smell of the ocean was quickly overwhelmed by the stench of fresh dog shit. There was also a heavy background odor of decay, of moldering vegetation, of dead animals—feral cats, squirrels, possums, raccoons, mice, bats, blue jays, and sparrows—and maybe some things I didn't want to think about. The ground was rocky and uneven beneath my feet. Thorns and vines grabbed at the bottoms of my jeans, snagged on my shoelaces. Still, it didn't seem like there was anything much about this lot that made it more special than the twenty other lots in the area. Like those other lots, it was the local dump, the convenient strainer at the bottom of the neighborhood's sink. The place where all the crap that nobody wanted or was too lazy to bring to the town dump got tossed. But why, I wondered, leave TJ Delcamino's body here? Why not any of those other area lots? The bigger question was the one I didn't want to think about. *Why did I give a shit?*

I made it to the back left corner of the lot. Above me, the noise of the gears from naughty Santa and his reindeer drowned out the Chipmunks. This was the spot where the newspaper said the kid's body was discovered. The lot was enclosed by the six-foot-tall stockade fencing from the surrounding properties, the two along its flanks and the house behind it. I stood there for a moment, scanning, imagining how different the lot would have been last August. This time of year, I could see through the vines and trees all the way to the street, but in summer, in the dark, that wouldn't've been the case. That time of year, I'm not sure I would have been able to see twenty feet ahead of me in any direction.

Although the paper was unclear about where the kid had been killed, it was fair to assume he'd been killed somewhere else. No matter how thick the vegetation in summer, the lot wasn't isolated enough to afford much privacy. None of the surrounding houses was more than fifty feet away from where I stood. And from Tommy D.'s description of what had been done to his boy, it was clear the kid's assailants had taken their time killing him. The torture and murder must have taken place somewhere else. In that way, the kid's body was like everything else dumped in the lot: used up, discarded, and left to rot.

Someone else might've wasted time wondering why. Not me. Not yet. Maybe not ever. As a cop, you know there are only a few reasons people murder. Sometimes the reasons even make sense, but mostly not. You take alcohol and drugs out of the murder equation and there'd be a lot fewer cases for homicide detectives to close. The greatest human accomplishment isn't landing a man on the moon or the Internet. It's impulse control. Early on, our ancestors understood we couldn't be trusted if left to our own devices. I mean, we created God to keep us in line, didn't we? You dampen impulse control with alcohol or drugs and you get blood. But as I stood on the spot where TJ Delcamino's body was found, I didn't think the kid's murder could be explained away by a lack of impulse control or a fit of sudden anger.

I stepped back out of the woods to the street. Behind me, Santa was mooning whoever cared to look. Alvin and the Chipmunks were crooning about roasting chestnuts. Before getting back in my car, I turned to look at the baby Jesus with his blue doll's eyes. He was still looking back.

(WEDNESDAY AFTERNOON)

D r. Rosen's office was in a medical building in Islandia, a few miles north of the Paragon Hotel on Vets Highway. I'd never taken the time to look at the exterior of his building before. What was the point? It was rectangular and had a main entrance. It had walls and windows. I didn't even know how many floors the building had. All I'd needed to know was how to get from the parking lot to room 207. Robots know only what they need to know. Now that I looked at the building, it kind of reminded me of the Fourth Precinct.

Dr. Rosen looked about as much like the stereotypical shrink as I looked like a steamed lobster. No gray beard. No glasses. No suit. No pipe or cigar. And he was a big man. Bigger than me. Bigger than Tommy Delcamino. Broader, too. Fifty, with slicked-back black hair, kindly brown eyes, and pitted skin, he moved gracefully for a man of his build. In spite of his imposing size, he wasn't very intimidating. It had been my experience that intimidation was a function of attitude, not size. The most intimidating guys I knew on either side of the law had been little men. Dr. Rosen was dressed in a brown corduroy blazer, a white sweater, and Levi's over brown half-boots, but I couldn't tell you what he'd worn last session or the session before that. Like I said, robots know only what they need to know.

We shook hands. We always shook hands. Then I sat in the black leather chair by the wall with the framed print that looked like a stained-glass church window. The real window was to my left. I didn't look out that window much. Maybe if there was something more fascinating to look at than the Long Island Expressway service road, the real window might have held greater appeal for me. Dr. Rosen pulled his office chair out from behind his desk, sat across from me, and leaned back, pad and pencil in hand.

"What's going on with you, John?" I liked that he called me by my proper name and not Gus, like everyone else.

Once a week for about a year, and always the same question. I'd come to look forward to it. Sometimes, like when I would sit at the train station waiting to pick up hotel guests, I'd think a lot about what I would say when he asked it next. On the ride over, I'd even prepared an answer for him. I meant to talk about what had gone on with Krissy. About seeing Annie. About seeing Pete McCann for the first time in months. But those weren't the words that came out of my mouth.

"Tommy Delcamino came to see me at the hotel yesterday."

"You haven't mentioned him before," Rosen said, his pencil scratching at his pad. "You're smiling. What's that about?"

Instead of answering, I shook my head and laughed.

Rosen tilted his head. "You're laughing, only you don't seem amused."

"Yeah, how do I seem?"

"You tell me."

"I don't know. Angry, I guess."

"At what?"

"I don't know . . . the world, myself."

"You've been angry at those things for two years. But what's different today?"

When I looked down, I saw my fists were clenched. He saw them, too.

"What's going on with you, John?" He looked at his pad. "You mentioned Tommy Delcamino. Is this about him?"

My jaw tightened.

"C'mon, John. Words. Talk to me."

"Tommy Delcamino's a guy I arrested for petty shit a few times when I was in uniform at the Second Precinct."

"Why had he sought you out?"

I didn't say anything, stared up at the ceiling. Rosen waited me out the way he always did.

"You know where I was this morning?" I said.

He shook his head.

"Kristen got herself jammed up again. She got pulled over in front of the state office building on 347. She was getting high and drinking vodka in her car. Annie was at the hotel waiting for me to tell me about it. And you know who came to the rescue?"

He shook his head again.

"Pete McCann. Pete fucking McCann. Can you believe it?"

Rosen took a deep breath. "John, do you like magic shows?"

I laughed. This time I meant it. "Not for nothing, Doc, but that's a weird question."

"Humor me."

"Magic shows?" I shrugged. "I guess I like them as much as the next guy, sure."

Rosen put his pad and pencil down on the carpet next to his chair and raised both his hands to about shoulder height. He wriggled the fingers of his right hand and kept at it. "Magic works by distraction. For instance, I can see you're staring intently at my right hand, and as long as you're staring so intently at it, I could be doing something with my left that you wouldn't notice. A good magician is skilled at distraction. The magician is saying, 'Hey, look over here. Here is what's interesting. Here is the magic.' But that's not where the magic is." He raised his left hand and waved it at me. "The magic is over here. And a really smart magician switches hands so that the audience won't catch on."

"Is there a message in there for me, Doc? Because if there is, I'm not getting it."

"Aren't you, though? There have been days when Kristen or Annie or Pete McCann were the magic, but not today. Today they're the wiggly fingers. Show me what's in your other hand, John."

I sat there in silence, my whole body clenching. Rosen sat across from me, leaning back in his chair. He had a way of looking at me without judgment, but with concern. I've got to say that I never felt like he was acting about that. This never seemed like a job to him. Maybe he was just a good magician. But whatever it was about that look, it worked. It always worked.

"Tommy Delcamino's son got murdered last August," I heard myself say in a strangled kind of voice. "They found his body in a wooded lot in Nesconset. He was tortured to death."

Rosen looked gut-punched when I told him about Delcamino's son, but he gathered himself. "And Tommy telling you this made you angry?"

"I don't know."

"Let's back up, then. Why did Tommy come to see you?"

"He said no one would help him. That the Suffolk PD wouldn't give him the time of day because of his record and because his son was mixed up in the same kinds of petty crap that he'd been mixed up with his whole life."

"But he thought you could help him?"

"I don't know what he thought," I said, that now-familiar heat rising beneath my skin. "He just said that I'd always treated him like a human being and that it never seemed to matter to me that he was a piece a shit. Fucking guy. You know what he did? He took out three thousand bucks in cash and begged me to help him."

"Do you know you're shouting?"

"Sorry, Doc."

"No need for that, John. Why were you shouting? Why are you so angry?"

"I don't know."

"C'mon. You know. You tell me you were a good cop. Be that good cop now."

I laughed a hollow laugh. "A good cop and look where that got me."

"Stop the magic act, John. Why are you so angry at Tommy?"

"All right, you wanna know?" I didn't need him to tell me I was shouting.

He nodded.

"I'll tell you why."

"Okay."

"I wasn't mad at Tommy D., not to begin with. I was jealous of him. I know that sounds fucked up, but there it is."

"Jealous?"

"I don't think I've been more jealous in my whole fucking life, Doc."

"Why?"

"Why? You wanna know why I'm jealous of a man whose son was beaten and tortured to death?"

He nodded again.

I waved at the window. I stood and walked to the window, showing Rosen my profile. "Because there are people out there with blood on their hands for his kid's murder. Because even if they never get caught, they're responsible. They have guilt. They have blame. And maybe someday Tommy D. can find them and make them pay. There are people to see about his kid's death. Who do I see about my son's death, Doc? Who? Who do you see when your kid drops dead playing pickup basketball? God? *Please!* There's nobody for me to see. No one to point my finger at. No one to blame. No one to hunt down. No justice. Who can I go see about that? Who, Doc? Who do I go see?"

"I don't know, John. I don't know who you see about the randomness of the universe. I wish I did, but I don't. But Tommy thought he knew who to see. He came to you."

I laughed that hollow laugh again. "Desperate people do stupid things."

"Sometimes."

I didn't speak. He waited me out.

"Do you know where I was a few hours ago? I went to the wooded lot in Nesconset where they found his kid's body. I stood right on the spot where they found him."

"Why did you do that?"

"I'm not sure. I honestly don't know."

"Are you going to help Tommy?"

"No . . . I don't know, Doc. I don't think so."

"We have to stop now, John."

"Okay, Doc," I said, but I couldn't make myself turn away from the window.

"John . . ."

"Why do you call me John, Doc? Everybody else calls me Gus."

"We'll talk about it next time if you like. Now it's time to go."

I turned finally, shook his hand, and headed for his office door. I left the office. A woman was seated in the waiting room. She held a magazine up close to her face as if to hide her identity. Funny, I thought, how she wouldn't have done that at a medical doctor's office. Then again, shrinks strip you down more naked than on the day you were born. Nobody wants to be seen like that. Nobody.

(THURSDAY)

t was my day off and I slept in late. I used to love days off, but now they'd become a burden, just more empty hours to fill; and all I'd had to fill them with was pain. After John's death, I'd just stay in my room, first at home, then at the hotel, endlessly cycling through the cable channels until I could sleep again. Sometimes I would read the books hotel guests would leave in the van or in their rooms. That was okay. I learned to love reading again, but a lot of the time the books made me ache worse. When I was in school I didn't realize that most fiction was about death and regret. About things people wished they had or hadn't said, done or hadn't done and how, for whatever reasons, saying or not saying, doing or not doing had buried them alive. I was already too familiar with that feeling to want to read much more about it. Lately I was sticking to nonfiction.

Then, when I started seeing Dr. Rosen, he suggested I get out of my room on my days off. It didn't much matter where I went or what I did, he said, as long as I got out. So for the last few months, I did that, got out. Sometimes I'd go to the movies. Long Island has plenty of movie theaters. Within fifteen minutes of the hotel, there were about forty movie screens. Problem was, they all showed the same ten movies, usually dumb superhero blockbusters. The other movies were like the found books: they made the ache worse. Eventually I settled on the Smith Haven Mall. Going to the mall made me a good Long Islander. Long Islanders believed that world peace would only be achieved through shopping, and not even the Dalai Lama himself worked as hard at world peace as the citizens of Nassau and Suffolk counties. My going to the mall seemed to please Dr. Rosen, though it took me a while to figure out why.

I'd go and zombie-walk. I'd walk and walk and walk. I didn't shop. I didn't even window-shop, not much, not really. At first, it just sort of felt like an incarnation of clicking through the channels, but when my eyes unclouded I came to understand Rosen's pleasure. Because in the mall, I was confronted by the sight of twenty-year-old men, men the same age as my son at the time of his death. That hurt more than any book or movie. I hadn't cried much since right after John Jr.'s death. That day, the day my eyes unclouded, I got back from the mall and cried so that I exhausted myself. I didn't go to therapy that week as a kind of *Fuck You!* to Rosen. Funny, my not showing up didn't seem to bother him. He was like that, seemingly unperturbed by my acting out.

That was the thing about Dr. Rosen, he didn't overreact. Christ, most of the time, he barely reacted at all. I guess that was good in the long run, his letting me learn things for myself. I was no Dr. Freud, but even a retired cop gets that learning for yourself, healing yourself, is the whole fucking point of therapy. There were times, though, I just wanted an answer, you know what I mean? Like yesterday, for example, all I wanted was an answer, any answer. I was just as clueless about whether I should help Tommy D. when I left Rosen's office as when I walked in. And neither Tommy Delcamino nor I could afford my long journey of self-discovery, not if he wanted my help. Not if I wanted to help him.

If there was anything I missed about the church, it was that: answers. Ready-made or custom-fit, the church was as full of answers as man was full of sin. Only problem was, I didn't buy it anymore. I lost my faith a long time before losing my son, and his death proved me right. There was one last someone of the church I loved and respected, someone to talk to. So I made a call and decided to skip my weekly trip to the mall.

Father Bill Kilkenny was the chaplain the union sent to comfort us after John's death. And if there was a God to thank for him, I would. More than family, more than our friends, it was Father Bill who kept us functioning during those first impossible days. He had been amazingly patient with us, but most especially with me. The last thing I wanted to hear from some strange priest was about God's infinite wisdom and his mysterious fucking ways. Father Bill seemed to sense that without being told. Before I could say a word about my own issues with the Almighty, he told me the story of his own lost faith and had exercised the wisdom not to share with me the details of how he'd reclaimed it. If, in fact, he had. Whether he had or hadn't was beside the point. He was who we needed when we needed him. In the end, isn't that what matters?

For nearly twelve months after John's death, during the time my family blew itself apart, when my wife and daughter moved into my brother-in-law's house, when I moved into the Paragon, during the period of Kristen's bent of self-destruction, Father Bill kept in touch with us and us with each other. Annie and Krissy would tell you the same, that Bill Kilkenny was the glue that held us together when the center would not hold. But the bond was strongest between Father Bill and me. Was it that we were men? Was it that we shared a loss of faith? I couldn't say then as I can't say now.

After a while though, the bond weakened. It was only natural, because seeing Father Bill gradually morphed from salve to sting. Being with him, hearing his voice on the phone, became a reminder of the trauma that had brought us together in the first place. To heal, I suppose, there needs to be forgetting. There's no healing if the scab is always pulled away. Seeing Father Bill did that, pulled the scab away. And beneath it, the blood was still moist and the pain still fresh. So as suddenly as he had come into my life, he was exiled. But somehow I knew there would be no bitterness in him about it. I was right, for when

I called to say I needed to discuss something important with him, his voice sparkled. I listened carefully to his tone for any hard edges, for signs of hurt, for resentment. There were none of those things. And picturing him there, the phone in his bony hand, a broad smile on his gaunt face, brought a sense of calm to me. It was good to think of Father Bill again without the pain and to let myself feel the gratitude, warmth, and kinship.

I hadn't given much thought to the address he'd given me in North Massapequa. I'd assumed it was a rectory or an apartment in a building owned by the new parish to which he'd been assigned. I heard that shortly after I closed my life to him, Father Bill had given up his post as a union chaplain. I didn't think that one had to do with the other. Just a matter of age, I thought. Though I never knew how old he was, he wasn't a young man—in his late sixties or maybe seventy. I knew he had served as a Marine chaplain in Vietnam, the place where he had first lost his faith. Funny how I felt I knew him, but how little I knew of the facts of his life.

When I pulled up to the address, I was surprised to see him standing beside a beige vinyl-sided ranch house. He was smoking a cigarette, staring off into the distance. Except in North Massapequa there wasn't anything to see in the distance besides the Sunrise Mall or an occasional tree. No, the distance he was staring into was inside his own head. I'd seen that vacant look on his face, seen that loose-limbed posture of his many times before, most often when he would grab a smoke. I asked him once where his head was at during one of those moments. He hadn't answered.

"Father Bill," I called to him as I approached.

He snuffed out his cigarette on the sole of his ugly black priest shoe and flicked it behind him. I extended my right hand to him, which he promptly slapped away.

"Here," he said, "give us a hug."

I was always surprised by how powerful a man he was given his thin frame and wiry build, never mind his age.

"Thanks for seeing me, Father Bill."

"It's just plain old Bill now. Found the Father title getting to be a bit cumbersome to carry about. A bit of an albatross, really." He pulled back, patting my cheeks with both his hands. "Let's have a look at you. Christ in heaven, it's good to see you, Gus Murphy."

Kilkenny was Bronx born and raised, his accent purely Kingsbridge, though he phrased and intoned his speech with a bit of a lilt. He used to say it put people at ease. *Like a lullaby,* he said. *Like a lullaby.*

"You've left the church?" I blurted out, unable to camouflage my surprise.

He laughed that devilish, whispering laugh of his. "Quite the opposite, lad. More like it left me."

"They fired you?"

He laughed again. "Nothing so dramatic, Gus. And before you say it, no, it hadn't a thing to do with the abuse of children. Isn't it a shame that is what comes first to mind, even to my mind?" He shook his gray head and crossed himself. "Come inside and we'll talk, you and me."

As I followed him, he stopped to pick up the cigarette butt he'd flicked away. It was a little thing, picking it up, but it said a lot about him.

The entrance to his basement apartment was around back of the ranch, down a few concrete steps, and through an unadorned, windowless door. It was a tidy little one-bedroom flat with a small living area, a galley kitchen, and a compact bathroom. It was neat but spare. The walls were white and nearly bare. Knowing Father Bill, I figured the few framed, sun-faded posters and prints on the walls came courtesy of previous renters. The nicest thing I could say about the furniture was that it was clean and functional, if somewhat institutional. Father Bill took note of me looking around as I tried to get comfortable on what passed for his couch. It was more like a bad church pew dressed up with thin, hard cushions.

"Gus," he said, handing me a glass of red wine, "I'm like a man who's been wrongly imprisoned for too long. A man who has dreamed of the luxury he would live in when finally set free. Ah, but then, when freedom came to him, he was still a prisoner. A man more at ease with the bland, even cruel things in this world."

It was our ritual: one glass of wine together and then talk.

"You were in the church, Father Bill, not Elmira, for chrissakes. *Sláinte*."

We clinked glasses. Had a few sips in silence. A silence he broke.

"All institutions share commonalities. Some more than others. I imagine you'll want me to explain myself about leaving the church before we get to why you've come for a visit."

I nodded.

"It's a brief tale to tell. What happened was that I finally rediscovered my faith after all these years, and when I did, I saw the folly of how the institution of the church operates. The church has become a separate thing from the faith so that you can barely find Jesus for the machinery. Once I had my faith restored, Gus, I found I had no need of the machinery to sustain me. Strange thing about finding my way back to God was that I had been a pretty damned good priest for all those years I'd been without him. But when I had the spirit back inside me, I seemed to have lost my skill or desire for the job. So I quit. It's that simple."

"It's never that simple, Bill."

He winked. "You doubt me?"

"Let's just say the next time we talk, I may want to hear the unabridged version."

He arched one wispy gray eyebrow. "Next time? Let's pray that less time passes between our next visit as between this and our last one. I mean, I'm getting to be an old fella and I can't afford these long pauses anymore. But Jesus, Gus, it's good to see you, man. You nearly resemble a human being."

I knew exactly what he meant. When we'd met, I was pretty much a ghost, as were Annie and Krissy. We were hollow things, walking around, breathing, but less than alive.

"I'm better, Fath—Bill. 'Almost' is the right word. I'm getting there."

He placed a hand on my shoulder. "That's the trick of it, pal. We're all always just getting there. And how are my girls?"

I shrugged. "Krissy still seems lost, but we had a good talk yesterday. Annie and me . . . we're divorced."

"I figured that was coming." He made a sad face. "Your boy's death hit her hardest. It always does the mother. No matter how close you and your boy were, there's no closeness like the one between mother and child. He was once part of her body, Gus. The death of a child to a mother can change her, make her bitterest of all. She'll come back to herself. I'll pray for it. I know there was once great love between you, a fierce passion. I saw it even in her raging at you. Is there no remnant of it left?"

"Of the rage, plenty. Of the love . . . not so much."

He laughed, sipped his wine. I noticed that I'd already finished mine.

"Here, let me take that for you," he said, fetching my empty glass. "Give the girls my love, will you?"

"Of course."

Bill poked his head out of the kitchen. "Now, why don't you tell me why you've come and sought me out?"

I told him about Tommy Delcamino's visit to the coffee shop at the Paragon. About how his son had been tortured to death. About my fury. About my going to visit the lot where the kid's body had been found. About Dr. Rosen and his wriggly fingers.

"And what is it you want from me, exactly?"

"Answers," I said, feeling myself blush at the stupidity of hearing the word come out of my mouth.

"Answers, is it? Wouldn't we all like some of those?"

"I guess."

"Perhaps if you shared the questions."

"Christ, Bill, you sound like my shrink."

"Clearly a gentleman and a scholar, your Dr. Rosen." He came out of the kitchen, a smile on his face, and sat across from me on a stiff-backed wooden chair. He patted my knee, focusing his faded gray eyes on mine. "Come on, what's going on with you?"

"I know I should just leave it be with Tommy Delcamino. It's not my business. His tragedy isn't mine."

"That's where you're wrong, Gus. None of our tragedies is ours alone to bear. We are all one family under Christ."

"This guy isn't my friend. I mean, for fuck's sake, I used to arrest this guy. He's a piece of shit, a low-life thieving—"

"He's your brother, Gus, as much as any man is. As much as I am. He may not deserve any more than anyone else, but he deserves no less. Don't we all deserve justice whether it comes in this life or the next?"

"But is it my job to help him find it?"

"So is that the question you want me to answer, is helping him your job?"

"Yes."

"No, I don't think it is your job to help this Delcamino fella." He stood, frowning, the deeply etched lines of his face suddenly grave. "What if he had come to you for help with anything else?"

"I'm not getting you, Bill."

He moved toward the kitchen. "I'm having another glass of wine. Would you like one?"

"No, thanks. But—"

"Wait a sec, will you?"

When Bill came back into the small living area, I noticed that he really was a prisoner of his old profession. His clothing was worn and frayed and ill-fitting. His pilled beige sweater and too-big brown polyester pants hung loosely on his scarecrow frame. And those shoes, those ugly black shoes, dull with age and wear. But he looked good. He sipped from his full glass.

"Where were we?" he asked as if he couldn't remember. He remembered, all right.

"Answers. You said that I knew the answer."

"To one question, you surely do. It's not your job to help this man, but you knew that even before you came. You knew it the second he asked for your help. To the question you really came here about, I'm not sure I can help you with that, Gus. I'm not sure anyone can."

"Forgive me, Bill, but I'm not sure I understand."

He took a gulp of wine, wiped his lips with a brush of his thumb, and put the glass down. "Some answers are meant to be found out and not revealed."

"Thanks, Yoda." I laughed a little, but he didn't.

"You'll only understand when you find what you're looking for."

I shook my head. I'd come here for answers and was now more confused than before.

"Jesus, Bill, you've been a big help."

"Would that be a wee bit of sarcasm I hear in your voice, boyo?" he asked, turning his implied lilt into a full B-movie priest brogue.

"Sorry."

"No need for that. There's no apologies between us, but I do think you owe this Tommy an apology, Gus. If anyone would understand his plight, I would think it would be your own self. Helping him may not be your duty, but a bit of respect and courtesy is due the man."

"If I thought I was going to get a priestly lecture, I'm not sure I would've come."

We both laughed at that.

"I guess I better be at it then," I said, getting up off the cushioned pew.

He put his glass down and embraced me again.

"I've missed your company, Gus, truly. Please let's talk again soon."

"It's a deal."

Now he offered *his* hand to me. When I took it, he said, "Come, I'll walk you out."

"I can find my way."

"You can't smoke my damned cigarette for me now, can you?"

We laughed again.

But when we got outside, Father Bill—I guess I would always think of him that way, collar or no collar—got that look on his face again.

"What's the face for?"

"I fear for you, Gus."

"I can take care of myself."

A sad smile replaced the grave look on his face. "I don't doubt it. I fear for you because I don't think you'll find what you are looking for."

"We'll see."

He nodded, blowing smoke out of the corner of his mouth.

When I turned back around at my car to wave goodbye, I saw Bill was as I had found him, staring off into the past.

(THURSDAY, EARLY EVENING)

Tommy D. hadn't told me the name of the place he worked, nor had he given me the address, but when I stopped at a local 7-Eleven for coffee, an oil truck driver told me Picture Perfect Paving and Masonry was the only such company in that part of Holtsville. He took a map out of the cab of his truck and showed me where I'd find it.

Right around where Union Avenue turns into Long Island Avenue is one of those ugly patches we Long Islanders like to pretend don't exist. A place where the dirty work gets done by brown-skinned men and the Tommy Delcaminos of the world. They did the dirty work so we could live with clean fingernails and enjoy pretty green lawns. Picture Perfect's yard was tucked in among the landscapers and home heating oil companies, and sat in the shadows of the Nicolls Road overpass. A quarter of a mile east of the Northville oil terminal and the PSEG power plant, it was also on the glide path to one of MacArthur's runways. And as I drove east down Union, an orange-bellied Southwest 737 roared overhead.

It was a little after four thirty when I pulled up to the yard, night falling all around me in the heartless way night falls at the edge of winter. There is danger in the darkness. Cops know it. Kids know it, too.

We work so hard to convince them it's silly to be afraid of the dark, but it isn't silly at all. Fear of the dark is a matter of survival. It's smart to be wary of the dark. We evolved as prey as much as predator. Prey knows there are eyes that can see you through the darkness. That there are claws and fangs and pointed beaks, bodies built to blanket themselves in blackness. Monsters do come out at night. I'd witnessed it for myself.

I parked along the fence and walked through the still-open gate. The yard was what I expected it to be. There were mounds of variously sized and colored pebbles. Stacks and stacks of red bricks and pavers, gray concrete blocks, Belgian blocks, big slabs of bluestone, hunks of granite, hills of sand and pea gravel. The largest pile was of black asphalt, and the air stank of it even in the cold. Parked to my left were a couple of Mack dump trucks, three Bobcats, a beat-up old front-end loader, its once bright yellow paint now faded and chipped. There were two small steamrollers parked side by side and three tar-stained asphalt boilers. All of the equipment was covered in a fine layer of dust.

At the back of the yard were three raggedy structures: two trailers propped up on concrete blocks and a steel equipment shed way off in one corner. I figured one of the trailers, the darkened one, was the office and the other, the one with the lights and TV shadows flickering on inside, was the one Tommy Delcamino lived in. Parked next to that trailer was a dinged and dented old Chevy Malibu, its rear bumper held on with duct tape and prayer. The tires were flat and the rear window was a sheet of cloudy plastic.

There wasn't much external light in the yard. Just one sulfur lamp perched high atop a pole behind the two trailers that bathed the area in a sickly yellow glow. With each step I took, darkness seemed to shrink the lighted patch of the yard until it was only a small triangular island in a night-black sea. The only noise came from the cars buzzing by along Nicolls Road. Then I heard something else. The tick-tick-ticking of a cooling car engine. I took a few more steps before it dawned on me that the ticking could not possibly be coming from the Malibu.

I stopped dead in my tracks. I don't know why another car being there should have bothered me, but it did, a lot. I mean, in spite of the darkness, it wasn't that late. The gate was still open. Then I realized that everything except the flickering shadows from inside the one trailer seemed so unnaturally still. It felt as if this little corner of the world itself was holding its breath. Two decades on the job had taught me to distrust stillness. Quiet, calm, they were different. They were products of nature or circumstance. Stillness was a matter of willful imposition. Something wasn't right. I squinted my eyes, searching for where the car with the cooling engine was parked and from where the trouble might come. I knelt down slowly as if to tie my shoe, but to actually retrieve the little Glock 26 I was carrying on my ankle.

Then, just as I thought I saw the silhouette of an SUV beyond the boundaries of the yellow light, over by the side of the equipment shed, the stillness erupted into a jumble of voices, flashes, and thunder.

"No, don't be shootin' him," a man screamed, his voice angry. "Don't!"

My head swung around from the silhouette of the SUV to where I thought the voice had come from, somewhere near the end of the darkened trailer. But that's not where the muzzle flashed. That came from my far right, near the Malibu. I went face first onto the ground, my gun still in my ankle holster. As I flattened myself in the dirt, a bullet whined as it passed over me. The sound of the shot echoed around the yard. I lifted my head just long enough to see a second flash, and before I could react, dirt kicked up into my face. Whoever was pulling the trigger hadn't missed me by much with his first two shots, and I wasn't going to stick around in that spot to give him a third. I had to get out of the light and find some cover.

I rolled onto my side, brought my knees up to my chest, and grabbed the gun out of its holster. I racked the slide, swung my gun hand over my head, aimed in the general direction of the Malibu, and squeezed the trigger, squeezed it again, and again. Figuring I'd bought myself a few seconds, I ran, keeping my body as bent over and close to the ground as I dared without losing my balance. Just as I reached the hazy border between the yellow light and the darkness, dirt kicked up at my shoes and something tore through my pant leg. My left calf was on fire and I felt my sock getting wet with blood. I hit the ground hard, the thump of it knocking the wind out of me, the Glock flying out of my hand. I palmed the ground madly, feeling for my gun, trying to catch my breath. It was no good. I heard a bang and dirt kicked up only about ten feet ahead of me. I had to move.

"Stop shooting, you dumbass motherfucka!"

There was that angry voice again, but the shooter was paying it no mind because as I forced myself up, the yard echoed with the sound of another shot. Rocks shattered over my shoulder and behind me. That helped me get a bearing on where I was and I didn't hesitate. I about-faced and ran as fast as I could manage, my left calf aching, my sock soggy with blood. When I felt gravel beneath the soles of my running shoes, felt the hill of gravel with my palms, I scrambled to put the pile of rocks between me and the shooter.

I sat with my back against the stones, trying to calm my breathing and to collect my thoughts. That odd stillness fell over the world again. The sound of the rush-hour traffic on Nicolls Road and the thumping of my heart were all I could hear. No footsteps. No shots. No shouting. Nothing. Then an engine turned over. Tires spun on dirt. Brakes screeched. An engine revved loudly and a dark-colored SUV—a Suburban, Escalade, or Navigator—flew by me, spitting gravel, kicking up a cloud of dust that made it impossible for me to see its tags or to make out anything of its occupants. When it was through the gate, its tires squealed and it was gone.

Tommy Delcamino wasn't in either trailer, the interiors of which had pretty much been turned inside out. I found him in the equipment shed. He was slumped forward, right arm tucked beneath him, legs splayed out before him. A big chunk of his head was missing, blood caking up on his hair around the edges of the wound. I'd seen bodies in worse shape than Tommy's. Bodies fished out of the sound after weeks in the water. Bodies stuffed into suitcases and left in hot apartments for

days. Bodies hacked up into pieces and thrown by the side of the Northern State Parkway. But none of them was any deader than Tommy.

Bloodied bits of his skull, brain, hair were splattered all over the
stacks of concrete sacks and vats of sealcoating on the shelves at his
back. After passing through Tommy, the bullet or bullets had ripped
through an eighty-pound bag of concrete mix. The gray powder had
leaked out onto the floor and formed a cone-shaped pile behind his
body. Staring at the powder, all I could think about was the grains of
sand in an hourglass. Tommy D.'s hour had come and gone. Whatever
torment he'd been suffering over the murder of his son was over. I didn't
bother checking for a pulse.

I retraced my steps, making sure not to touch anything, and
called 9-1-1.

There was no stillness, no calm, no quiet, not now, not in Picture Perfect's yard. As far as the SCPD was concerned, the whole area, from gate to back fence, from side to side, was a crime scene. The yard was lit up like a minor league baseball field. CSU guys combed the grounds, searching for bullets and shells, photographing and printing, while the ME looked after Tommy Delcamino's body. I was in the back of an ambulance, the open doors facing the yard. The EMT patching up my leg said the bullet hadn't done much damage, though he gave me a tetanus shot just to be safe. He said the bullet hadn't hit anything vital. I guess he didn't consider a thumb tip–sized chunk of lower leg vital. He wouldn't. It wasn't his fucking leg.

Out the back of the ambulance I was glad to see a familiar face coming my way. Al Roussis and I went back a long ways together, all the way to the academy. He'd gotten the bump to detective several years ago and was now a part of the Homicide squad. I'd already spoken to the uniforms, but now this was Al's case.

He poked his head into the ambulance and asked the EMT, "You almost done with this clown?"

"Pretty much."

"Will he live?"

"That he will. The bullet just grazed him."

Al rolled his too-big brown eyes. "That's too bad."

"Fuck you, Roussis," I said, staring at my blood-soaked sock there on the metal floor of the ambulance. I decided to go without it. My running shoe was also wet with my blood, but not so much that I couldn't wear it. I thanked the EMT and hopped down onto the street, Al Roussis lending a hand.

"Come on, Gus," he said, "let's you and me talk in my car."

Al was a bulldog, though he didn't look like one. He was slender and athletic. His downturned lips gave him an air of vague sadness, as if he were constantly disappointed at the state of the world. He was Greek through and through, and when we were in the Second Precinct together, the guys used to love to break his balls just to hear him curse at us in his dad's native tongue. We didn't understand a word he was saying, but we loved the music of it. Al had been at John Jr.'s funeral, so we didn't have to go through the awkward two-step bullshit of explanations and less-than-heartfelt condolences. Our friendship didn't mean he wasn't going to ask me hard questions.

"I'd ask you how you're doing, but Christ, Gus, what the fuck's going on with you that you're involved with a piece of shit like Tommy Delcamino?"

"Like I told those guys from the Sixth, I wasn't involved with him."

"Then what were you doing here? Looking for a quote on repaving your front steps?"

I gave him the same story I'd given the precinct detectives.

Al was shaking his head. "So what you're saying is Delcamino thought you would help him out because you lost your kid, too?"

"Who knows?" I said, getting into the passenger seat of Al's unmarked Ford Taurus. "I was so furious at him. I lost my mind when I kicked his ass out of the hotel coffee shop. I guess now we'll never know what he was thinking."

"I guess."

"So your story is you came here to apologize to him?"

"My story? Look, Al, we've known each other a lot of years. If I'm telling you that's why I'm here, that's why I'm here."

"Yeah, sorry, Gus. You know how it is with the job. Everybody lies to you about everything so that you don't even believe the mirror when you look into it." There was that sadness in his voice to match his expression. "Okay, so you came to apologize to him, but you weren't thinking of helping him?"

"Like I said, I was pretty rough on him, Al. Nobody deserves to get treated like that, especially by me. I understand the kind of pain he was suffering through. I owed him some respect for that."

"But you weren't going to help him?" Al asked again in a tone of voice that sounded more like a warning than a casual question.

"Not that it matters now, but what if I was going to help him?"

Al put his palms up. "Relax, Gus. I was just asking."

But that was bullshit. He wasn't just asking and I wasn't in the mood. I mean, I'd been shot. It wasn't lost on me that if the gunman had been a few feet luckier with his aim, I'd be just as dead as Tommy Delcamino.

"What's going on, Al? First Pete McCann warns me off this guy and now you. For chrissakes, the guy's been murdered and you're still sounding the warning alarm."

"Gus, you're way, way off base with that. I'm not warning you off anything and I don't give a fuck about Pete McCann. I'm just asking questions, doing my job. And I'm trying to do it the way a friend should do it with a friend. You know, I could really be busting your shoes here. You discharged your weapon at the scene of a homicide where the vic took two to the head. I could hold you on suspicion. I *should* hold you on suspicion, but I won't. So, come on, please just answer the questions."

"Sorry, Al, you're right. You're right."

"Can you think of any reason someone would want to kill Tommy Delcamino?"

I shrugged.

Roussis made a face. "I can't write down that you shrugged, Gus."

"Until two days ago, I didn't know him except to arrest the guy, and the last time I did that was what, five, six years ago? Then I had a ten-minute conversation with him and it's not like I got any intimate details of his life. But he did time. He was a street guy. There's a hundred reasons guys like him get killed."

Al liked that answer better. "Absolutely. So the only thing you guys talked about the other day was his kid?"

"Pretty much."

His pleasure with me was short-lived. "What's that supposed to mean, 'pretty much'?"

"Okay, yes, we only talked about his son's murder."

"What about it?"

"Mostly that he felt we—that the SCPD wasn't doing its job. He said he'd given a whole bunch of names and leads to the detectives handling his kid's case and that they blew him off. He said he'd gone over their heads, but that he got the same response from the brass as from Paxson and Carey."

"Which was what?" he asked.

"Which was basically go fuck yourself and don't bother us. That's why he came to me in the first place. He didn't know what else to do or who to go to."

"But why you?"

"I thought it was because he figured I would help him. You know, my son died, his was murdered. Like that. But he said it was because I always treated him with some respect, but who knows how the guy's mind worked?"

Al nodded. "How did you know that the kid's case belonged to Paxson and Carey?"

"Because I asked Pete McCann."

He turned to me, his face deadly serious. "See, Gus, this is where I get hung up. If you weren't going to help the guy, why ask Pete McCann about it? Why make inquiries?"

"It's a long story, Al, but I was in the Fourth and I had to talk to Pete anyway, so I asked. I was just curious."

"I got time, tell me the story."

I explained to him about Kristen getting pulled over and Pete McCann stepping in to keep her from getting arrested.

"I mean, Christ, Al, if Pete hadn't warned me off, I probably wouldn't even have given it a second thought."

"Okay," he said and scribbled some notes. When he looked up, he asked, "So the guys that shot at you, you think they were citizens?"

Citizens, that was current white-cop lingo for African-Americans. And in Suffolk County, that was almost all cops. For a while, "Canadians" was the code word. There were others. The code changed every now and then.

"I think at least one of them was black," I said. "I don't know about the shooter. He let his bullets do his talking. And before you ask, I didn't see either one of them. For all I know, there might've been more than two guys, but I can only be sure of two. And no, I didn't see the vehicle except that it was a big SUV."

He shook his head in mock disgust. "Didn't you used to be a cop? You're as useless as sharp corners on a bowling ball."

"Sorry, I was too busy getting shot, you prick."

Al laughed and patted my shoulder. "Okay, Gus, we're almost done here. Give me a minute to finish making some notes and . . ." His voice drifted off.

Something was eating at me. He had asked me all the right questions but one, so I asked him.

"What do you think they were looking for, Al?"

"Huh?" He didn't look up, but he heard me all right. His jaw clenched.

"The guys that killed Delcamino."

"What about them?"

"Before I found the body, I checked for him in both trailers. They were tossed and these guys were thorough. They dumped his cereal boxes, cut all the cushions, his mattress, pulled out every drawer, turned everything upside down. They must've been looking for something specific."

"Maybe."

"C'mon, Al, what the fuck's going on here? A few minutes ago you asked me why I thought Delcamino might've been killed. I mean—"

"Enough, Gus. Enough!"

"But—"

Al reached across me and pushed the Ford's passenger door open. "It's late. Go home. Get some rest. I've got what I need. I'll call you when forensics clears your weapon and you can come pick it up."

We shook hands and I slid off the seat. My leg had stiffened up and was killing me. I propped myself up, leaning one elbow on the open door and the other on the car roof. Al noticed.

"What'd the EMT tell you about the leg?"

"Gave me a starter dose of antibiotics and told me to get a full script from a doctor. Told me to stay off the leg for a while."

Al's expression went from his usual vague sadness to earnest.

"Don't listen to him, Gus. Stay on the leg long enough to walk away."

"What's that supposed—"

"We've been friends a long time, you and me. Walk away. Forget Tommy Delcamino."

I opened my mouth to say something else, but Al stretched out, grabbed the door handle, and yanked it shut.

I was feeling half-past dead when I pulled into the parking lot at the Paragon. My head was throbbing; worse than that, my leg was throbbing pretty bad. I'd been shot at before, a few times, but never shot. Don't let anyone tell you those are about the same thing. There's kind of an unreality to getting shot at. No unreality to getting a piece of your flesh torn off and burned away by a hot piece of metal. I'd been lucky. I knew that. Compared to most of the gunshot trauma I'd seen, my wound was nothing: a future scar, a story to tell the boys over beers at Commack Lanes. But it was also something more than that.

I sat in the front seat of my car and switched off the radio, tired of hearing the same sketchy reports of Tommy Delcamino's murder. Light travels faster than anything else in the universe. Bad news was a close second. I closed my eyes, rested my head, too beat to get out. At least part of my headache was frustration and maybe more than a little hurt. Al Roussis and I had been friends a long time. It was different than with Pete McCann. Like I said, Pete was always a guy with his own agenda, an ambitious man who wanted anything anyone else had. I'd always known that about him. So although I didn't understand his warning me off Delcamino, I just figured there had to be something in it for him. Brownie points with the brass? Who knows? But that wasn't Al Roussis, at least it wasn't who he used to be. Yet there he was, questioning my motives, warning me away from Delcamino.

I didn't get it. I mean, Christ, Tommy D. had just had his brains blown out the back of his head and his son was four months in the grave. So why warn me off a murdered man and a case that was as cold as tomorrow's forecast? I didn't know the answer and I wasn't going to work it out, not tonight. Things weren't what they seemed. They never are. Any cop will tell you that. Any schmuck with eyes in his head can tell you as much. The official story is just that, a story, a convenient narrative in which the facts played only a supporting role. The thing Al Roussis neglected to comprehend was that my getting shot made it personal. Bullets will do that, make it personal. Still, without Tommy Delcamino around to help me out, to tell me what those guys who shot him and me were looking for, I was at a dead end. Literally.

I'm not sure how long I stayed in the car. I think I must've dozed off for a little while. Then there was a rapping at my window and a fresh rush of adrenaline snapped me out of whatever daze I'd settled into. It was Slava, the night doorman, smiling his gapped and gold-toothed smile at me. After getting my heart out of my throat, I rolled down the window.

"I was worrying for you," Slava said in his broken English. "I see your car is pulling up here maybe forty minutes and you don't come."

"Thanks for caring." I pushed my door open. "Slava, what time is it?"

He lifted his wrist up to his smiling face. "Is eleven ten."

I don't even know why I asked him. The time was flashing right in front of me on the dashboard.

"Good. I'll be right in," I said.

The smile slid off his face. It was a warm face, but not a handsome one. One like a favorite ugly uncle's. He had a bulbous red nose that had been broken a few times, a big blunted jaw, and chapped, scarred lips.

"What is it, Slava?"

"For you in the lobby is waiting a strange little man."

"Strange?"

Slava waved one of his huge, meaty hands in front of his face. "He has . . . in English, how do you say this . . . ?" Then Slava rubbed his thick right index finger over his top lip. "Funny lip . . . like . . . animal, like rabbit."

"Harelip."

Slava clapped his hands together. "Yes, but also something else. You will see."

"Does he look like trouble?"

Slava went blank for a moment, trying to make sense of the idiom I had laughed at Felix for using about Tommy D. Then he smiled, shaking his hands. "No, no trouble. Is nervous little man. Scared, I think, not dangerous. No gun."

I wanted to ask Slava how he knew that about the gun, then decided against it. We all had our secrets at the Paragon and I didn't want to intrude on his.

I thanked him again and stepped out of my car. Slava's eyes got big at the sight of me. He pointed at my left leg. The dried blood on my jeans shone bright under the parking lot light and the blood on my running shoe was pretty obvious. So was the slit the EMT had cut from the hem up to the top of my calf.

"Dog bite," I said.

He snorted in disbelief, but didn't push. The clicking of the courtesy van's diesel engine interrupted our conversation.

"I must go now, Gus, to help Fredo. He has been picking up big party at airport."

"Go ahead, Slava. I'll be okay."

He gave me a long, unsure look, but hustled to meet the van. He moved very athletically for such a barrel-chested and bellied man.

By the time I limped over to the front entrance, Slava and Fredo were busy unloading the luggage onto a baggage cart. The five guests were lined up at the front desk, Rita tapping at the keyboard. All of them were too busy to pay me any mind.

Slava was right about the strange little man in the lobby. He was sitting on one of the threadbare sofas that faced the main entrance. Even at twenty feet I could see that he'd had surgery done on his lip, and that it hadn't been completely successful. But the botched surgery wasn't the little man's most prominent facial feature. Not nearly. He had a silver-dollar-sized muddy black birthmark on the right side of his face between his ear and cheek. He was a twitchy bastard, too, his head on a swivel. His arms were clutched against his body, hands clenched into fists. His arms and fists were shaking as if he was shivering in the cold. He must not have known what I looked like because his expression didn't change when I came through the doors.

"You looking for me," I said, standing over him.

"You Murphy?"

"I'm Gus Murphy."

"You was Suffolk PD once, right?"

I nodded. He stood up. He was about five-foot-six at most and couldn't have weighed more than a hundred thirty pounds.

"They call me Smudge," he said in a nasal voice, his nickname sounding like "Thmudge."

The birthmark made it easy to see why they'd call him that.

"What's this about, Smudge?"

He bent down and pulled something out from under the magazine-covered coffee table in front of the couch. When I saw what it was, I knew why he was there. It was the faded green canvas backpack Tommy Delcamino'd had with him when he came to see me on Tuesday morning.

Tears welled up in the little man's dirt-brown eyes. "I seen on the news about Tommy, but I can't believe it."

Now the tears flowed and he was sobbing, his little chest heaved. I looked over my shoulder and saw that the guests who'd come in on Fredo's van were taking notice.

"Come on with me, Smudge," I said, putting my hand on his shoulder and leading him to the coffee shop.

The coffee shop was closed for the night, but management kept the lights on until midnight in case the guests wanted a more private place than the lobby or the bar to chat or do work. We sat at the same booth Tommy Delcamino and I shared on Tuesday morning. It took him a few minutes to settle down, which was fine with me. I was just happy to get my weight off my leg.

"What's with the bag?" I asked, pointing at the backpack.

"Tommy asked me to bring this to you. He thought if I asked, you'd change your mind and help."

"Why would your asking make a difference?"

Smudge shrugged his little sloped shoulders. "Maybe because people feel sorry for me." He was crying again, quietly this time.

"I saw Tommy tonight after he was killed," I said. "I was there. I went to the yard to apologize to him for the way I talked to him the other day."

Smudge lifted his head and spoke in a choked, halting hush. "Tommy, he Googled you and saw what happened to your kid. That's the other thing."

"What?"

"He wanted me to tell you he swears he didn't know. He told me to tell you he swears on TJ's soul he didn't know."

"I believe you, Smudge. Did you guys talk about anything else when you went to see him?"

He shook his head.

"Why not?"

"I didn't ask Tommy no questions. He was my friend. Only friend I ever had in my whole stinking, fucking life. When we was inside together, he watched out for me. You know what woulda happened to a guy like me inside without Tommy watching out for me?"

I nodded.

"I been kicked around and pissed on my whole life. Tommy D. was the only person I ever met who didn't shit on me. He didn't give a fuck that I was a freak. Who liked me before Tommy? Nobody liked me, not even my family. Me less than anybody. So when Tommy says for me to do this thing, to bring this to you, to ask you to help him, I didn't ask why. He said you would know the right thing to do. That you were the rightest cop he knew."

I lifted the bag. "You know what's in here?"

"Nope. All I know is that Tommy wanted you should have it."

I looked across the table at the deformed little man and knew he was telling me the truth. He really didn't know what was inside the backpack and he didn't seem curious to know. His friend asked him to do a favor and he'd done it.

"Tommy didn't say anything else?"

"Just that if you needed help, to talk to Zee."

I didn't understand. "Zee?"

"Richie Zito. Tommy said you would—"

I waved for him to stop. "Yeah, I know Zee."

Smudge did what passed for a smile. We sat there in silence for a few more minutes. Me drifting off. Smudge grieving his friend.

"You can always call me here if you need me," I said as he stood to leave.

He just kind of nodded. As he walked away, I called after him.

"Smudge."

"What?"

"You said you and Tommy did a bid together. What were you in for?"

"Running a scam."

"What kind?"

"A charity thing. Like I said, people feel sorry for me."

"Did they give you money?"

"Some, not too much. It's easy for people to feel sorry for me. Who wouldn't, right? I wasn't so good at the money part. I guess I never felt like I was worth a lot."

"You got a real name, Smudge?"

"Yeah" was all he said.

He turned and walked away.

(FRIDAY, LATE MORNING)

Harrigan's Pub was a sad little bar in a run-down strip mall in Huntington Station, shouldered between a failed karate dojo and a taqueria. Even before the area's demographics had taken on a distinctly south-of-the-border flavor, Huntington Station had been the poor relation to Huntington Village and the moneyed enclaves of Cold Spring Harbor and Lloyd Neck. Those were places where a million bucks was chump change and the paid help had paid help. Huntington Station was where the action was in the Second Precinct. Gang-related violence had gotten worse since the population had shifted from working-class white to working-class Hispanic. No matter the immigrant group, they bring their joys and sorrows with them, their pleasures and their parasites. In Huntington Station, the gangs had followed from Mexico, El Salvador, Honduras, the Dominican Republic, and every other country from which the new arrivals had come.

Long Island had its share of dive bars, and Harrigan's was just another one of them. It was a classic losers' bar. The kind of place where even the young men were old. Where the *Daily Racing Form* passed for the news of the world and where the light of day was the common enemy. Cops weren't much favored either. Of course half the snitches and scumbags in the Second Precinct passed through Harrigan's doors during any given weekday. In other words, it was the kind of place Tommy Delcamino gravitated to.

When I pulled the door open, a shaft of light followed over my shoulders. That bought me a few steps of anonymity, if not much else. Maybe it's a refinement of their senses or instinct, but whatever it is, losers can smell cop on you. And no amount of OxiClean or cheap cologne washes it away or masks the scent. I worked with a guy, Bob Ward, who claimed that cops were born stinking of it. The losers turned their heads and looked, not so much out of curiosity as self-preservation. It was fair to say that most of the mutts in Harrigan's owed something to people on the street and they never knew if the next guy coming through the door was there to collect on their debts or to extract late fees. Late fees on the street were as much matters of skin and bone as dollars and cents. I sat down at the bar and ordered a Corona. When I did that, the losers exhaled and went back to waiting in the dark bar for the door to open again.

I waved the barman over. He was covered with so many tats that he looked like a '70s subway car. So much so that it was impossible to discern where one tattoo ended and another began. As far as I could tell, all the tats were gang- and motorcycle-related. Made sense. Harrigan's was owned by Richie "Zee" Zito, and Zee had once been the Long Island chapter leader of the Maniacs Motorcycle Club. Calling the Maniacs a club was like calling the Gestapo a club. They were thugs. Unlike his patrons, Zee generally liked cops. Why wouldn't he? His place was a great resource for the Suffolk PD. We knew all sorts of shit went on here, but as long as none of it got too out of hand, we kind of looked the other way. And Zee paid us back in kind. He wasn't averse to pointing us in the right direction when we needed a tip or a little help in finding a suspect.

"Four bucks," the barman said, slamming the bottle down in front of me.

I put a ten-spot up. "Zee around?"

The barman asked, "Who wants to know?"

"You're kidding me with that line, right? Tell him Gus Murphy wants a few minutes. It's about Tommy D."

That got his attention.

"Okay, wait here a minute," he said, leaving my ten on the bar. "I'll see what I can do."

He ducked under the service bar and walked down the hallway that led to the bathrooms and the office. I sipped at my beer and waited. When the bartender reappeared, he told me that the beer was on the house and that Zee was waiting for me in the office. I told him to keep the ten for himself and left the mostly full bottle on the bar.

The office door was open and I stuck my head inside.

"Come on in, Gus."

Zee's voice was all sandpaper and smoke, for which his leathery face was perfectly matched. The years of biking and hard living had caught up to him. He was maybe fifty-five, but looked older . . . nearly ancient. Zee had once been a good-looking man in a rough kind of way, but not anymore. He sat hunched over in his chair, stroking his untrimmed goatee with a single bent finger. What was left of his hair was pulled back in a messy gray mop that hung limp over the back of his beat-to-shit black leather vest. He wore a faded black and orange Harley shirt that must've fit him five years and twenty pounds ago. The rest of him was concealed by his desk.

The office stank of cigarette smoke, marijuana, and beer. Zee stuck out his arthritis-fucked right hand and I shook it. I didn't want to disrespect him by being too gentle with my grip, but I held back a little. Even so, I could see that put him in all kinds of pain. "Sit." He gestured at the chair across from his desk.

I sat.

"Gus Murphy," he said. "Been a few years."

"A few."

"Tough about your boy. Sorry."

"Thanks, Zee."

"You mind?" he asked, filling a small pipe's bowl full of pot. "It helps with the arthritis. Can you believe it, I got a script for this shit? When I was with the Maniacs, you guys used to send us away for bringing it into the state. And that shit wasn't half as good. This weed'll knock you on your ass and count you out." He shook his head as he fumbled with the lighter.

He was right about that. Even unlit, the scent of the bright green bud was intense. And when he finally managed to light up, the earthy sweet aroma filled up every corner of the little room. Zee took in a big lungful, held it, then blew it out, his breath lifting up the ragged edges of his floppy gray mustache. After a few seconds, he put the pipe down in an ashtray and stretched the fingers on both his hands.

"So, you're here about Tommy, huh? Fuck."

"I found his body."

"I heard that," he said.

I didn't bother asking how he knew. He was a guy who would know. He had a direct line to the street and the street to him. I guess that was part of the reason I was sitting there.

"Somebody blew most of his brain out the back of his head. Wasn't pretty."

"Usually isn't. You know, I don't think people would fuck with guns so much if they saw what bullets did to the human body."

"Christ, Zee, you should run for governor."

He laughed. "Not me, man. A month from now, I'll be out west somewheres living my life away from the crowds and the bullshit. I need me some dry warm weather for my old bones."

He saw the stunned look on my face.

"Yep, I'm outta here. Sold the place to the rice and beaners who own the food joint next door. Next year, this place'll be Jose's or Julio's or some other fucking wetback name."

I wasn't in the mood to debate race relations with a guy who was once the head honcho of a motorcycle gang that wasn't exactly known for their peace-and-love platform.

"What'll you live on?" I asked as if I cared.

"I made some scratch off the sale, not much, but some. I'll manage. I always have. But you came here about Tommy, not to hear about my IRA or 401(k), right?"

"Right. So how is it that you and Tommy were pals? He was a big guy, but he wasn't biker material, not by a long shot."

Zee grunted. "Nah, not Tommy. He was a lover, not a brawler. Though I seen what he could do to people if they crossed him. How we became friends?" He shrugged. "He used to come around the bar when I first bought the place and drink. I knew he was fencing shit in here, but so was everyone else. Tommy wasn't like all the other pricks. He would always give me a taste of what he made on a deal because he was using my place to do business. He didn't have to get told. He never tried to lie about it. He had respect, Tommy did. Then we just took to each other is all. I helped him out when I could. You mind if I ask you a question, Gus?"

"Fair's fair."

"How'd you know to come looking for me about Tommy?"

"He told me to."

Zee tilted his head at me and opened his mouth to ask a follow-up question.

I cut him off.

"Long story, Zee. Maybe some other time, okay?"

He nodded, then said, "So how can I help?"

I hadn't brought the green backpack with me. There was no need. I found in it what I thought I would. There was the roll of three thousand bucks cash he had offered to pay me. A black-and-white composition book like the ones I used in elementary school that was filled with notes, names, and addresses. There were photos, too. Some of the photos were pasted into the notebook. Tommy D. had been pretty thorough. I had to give him that. Many of the photos were of TJ Delcamino, whose face I recognized from the newspaper article Tommy had left behind at the coffee shop. The only other face I recognized in any of the photos was Tommy D. himself. There was a woman in many of them that I figured was TJ's mom. She was beautiful in a dark and sad kind of way.

The night before, looking over the photos before passing out, I'd marveled at the fact that even a low-level jerk-off like Tommy Delcamino had the same sort of silly family photographs as everyone else had. The ones you could get at the mall or the local photography studio. TJ as an infant looking cool in his Ninja Turtle Halloween onesie. Tommy smiling proudly yet looking uneasy dressed in a collared shirt, tie, and sports jacket, his arm over the darkly beautiful woman's shoulder, the three-year-old TJ in her lap. TJ in his Mets Little League uniform. TJ and that woman at a school graduation.

There were other shots, too, just like the ones Annie and I had of us and the kids: Christmas morning opening gifts in front of the tree. Confirmations. First communions. Proud grandmas and grandpas in front of their houses. Funny, seeing Tommy D.'s pictures brought Annie back to me in a way I hadn't felt about her since we'd begun to deconstruct. I remembered happy, funny Annie, loving Annie. The Annie who threw surprise parties and who waited up for me to come home after a bad shift. Annie who had swept me off my feet because I had never met another woman who was so much a mix of sexy and sweet. That was the Annie these photos brought back to me, not the angry, defeated Annie. But I'm sure that's not what Tommy D. had in mind when he stuffed them into the backpack.

I handed one of the photos of the dark-haired woman over to Zee.

"Is that Tommy D.'s wife, TJ's mom?"

He grunted again. "Marie, that twat. She was TJ's mom and Tommy's old lady but they never got hitched. She was something else to look at, man. That black hair, those black eyes, legs up to your chin, tits that wouldn't quit . . . But she was a whore and user. Had Tommy twisted around her pussy. Half the shit he got jammed up for was to feed her habit."

"You know where I can find her?"

"Sucking cock in purgatory."

"What?"

"Ding dong, the bitch is dead. OD-ed a few years ago." Zee lit up another bowlful. When he exhaled, he said, "That's one of the reasons Tommy was able to keep straight these last few years. He didn't have to support her appetite for drugs anymore. Good fucking riddance."

I left that discussion there. I felt bad for the crap Tommy had had to deal with, but for the moment I had other more important questions. Zee, on the other hand, wasn't quite as ready to move on as I was.

He waved the picture of Marie between two of his twisted fingers, offering it back to me.

"Where'd you get this?" he asked.

"Tommy gave it to me."

Zee didn't like that answer, but it was, strictly speaking, the truth. Besides, I didn't want to drift away from the reason I was there by bringing Smudge into the conversation. I was there to get information, not give it.

I took the photo out of his hand and said, "You got any idea who might've wanted to kill Tommy D.?"

Zee leaned forward. "C'mon, Gus. Tommy did time. Everybody makes enemies inside. I mean, I loved the guy, but he was a thief and not a very good one. I don't know anyone in particular who'd want to do him bad." He made a sweeping gesture with his balled left fist. "For all I know, it was one of those douchebags outside at the bar."

"I don't think so," I said aloud to myself.

But Zee heard it. "You don't think so what?"

"The guys who killed Tommy were looking for something specific. They ripped his trailer apart. You were close to Tommy, Zee. You have any idea what they could've been looking for?"

He shrugged again, looking pained. I couldn't tell if the pained look was about the arthritis or the loss of his friend.

"No idea, Gus. Sorry."

"How about TJ?"

"Same answer as with Tommy. TJ was a good kid. I was like an uncle to the kid, but he had both his folks' worst habits. He was a thief and a user. He was a better thief than his father, mostly cars and car parts, or so I'm told. And he was a bigger junkie than his whore mother. Heard that at the end his habit was getting pretty expensive. Coulda been anyone killed the kid."

"You think the murders are related?"

"I don't know," he said. "Could be . . . maybe. Your guess is as good as mine."

I stood up, offering him a fist bump instead of repeating the painful handshake. "Thanks for the time."

He didn't move. "You thinking about getting involved in this, Gus?"

"Christ, Zee, I don't know. It's not like I owed Tommy anything more than an apology. If the pricks who killed Tommy hadn't shot me, too, I'm not sure I would even be here talking to you."

I lifted up my pant leg and showed him the bandage.

He ignored that. "An apology. For what?"

I explained about how Tommy had come to me in the first place and how I'd treated him.

"Walk away, Gus. Leave it alone. Like you say, you don't owe Tommy nothing that you can give him now."

"You're the third person to tell me to walk away," I said.

"You sound disappointed."

"Could be, Zee. Could be."

"Why?"

Now it was my turn to shrug.

"One guy tells you something, fuck him. A second guy tells you the same thing, fuck him, too. A third guy . . . I don't know. Maybe it's just good advice. Nobody ever got hurt walking away." His eyes got a distant look in them not unlike Father Bill's. "I shoulda walked away a long time before I did. You're smart, you'll close that office door behind you, Gus, and forget you ever heard of Tommy Delcamino."

Now he gave me that fist bump.

"Thanks, Zee."

"Let me know if you decide to keep on going. I'll help you any way I can until I'm outta here."

I left the darkness of Harrigan's behind me, thinking I might just take Zee's advice. But when I answered my phone, I realized that walking away wasn't an option.

(FRIDAY, EARLY AFTERNOON)

Number 11 Pinetree Court in Commack had once been the happy center of my universe. The place where Annie had made a home for us. The place where Annie and I raised our kids. The place where we were going to grow old together. The place where we would watch our grandkids for John Jr. and Krissy when they wanted to get away for long weekends. We weren't the type of people who cared about fancy cars or expensive things. Our house was the one possession we took the most pride in. We had scrimped and saved for the down payment. We'd jumped through all kinds of hoops to get the mortgage. I'd even swallowed my pride and asked my dad to cosign. Something he lorded over me until the day he died. We'd worked on it until it was just how we wanted it. Then, in a single heartbeat, it turned into sawdust.

Nothing brought John's death back to me quite in the same way as seeing the old place. I could not separate my memories of him from the house. There wasn't a spot in the yard or inside the house itself that I could not see John. Even now, pulling up alongside the mailbox, I pictured John shooting free throw after free throw at the hoop in the driveway. The hoop was gone. I'd destroyed it in a drunken rage the night we'd buried John. But that didn't matter. I didn't believe in ghosts, though I did believe in hauntings. As much as we had loved the place, we couldn't bear to live there and we couldn't bear to sell it. The day would soon come when we would have to sell. The rent we were charging was a few hundred dollars short of the mortgage payment and we had lived in limbo for long enough.

Sue Sherman was standing in the driveway, waiting for me, her face twisted up into an expression that was one part panic, one part worry, and one part anger. I'd seen that look before, a hundred times. No one ever thinks they'll be a victim of a crime, so they are woefully unprepared for the aftermath. The sudden sense of insecurity. The intense, empty feeling of violation. The gnawing fear. The outrage. When she saw me getting out of my car, it all boiled over. Tears poured down her cheeks and she yelled something out at me that was utterly unintelligible, but completely understandable. I hugged her until she calmed down.

"I was out shopping and when I came home . . ." She was out of breath. "The cats were sitting on the front porch. I knew I didn't leave the door open. I figured they must have found a new way out of the house, but when I went to open the front door—"

"It was already open." I finished the sentence for her. "Did you go inside?"

"No. I called my husband, who told me to call you."

"Did you call 9-1-1?"

"I guess I should have but I didn't know what to do because I haven't been in the house."

"It's okay, Sue," I said, patting her shoulder. "You did the right thing. Are the cats okay? Where are they?"

She pointed at her car in the driveway. Two little brown Siamese faces stared out at us.

"Get in your car and drive down the block. Then call 9-1-1. I'm going to take a quick look around. Whoever was inside is gone now," I said, although I had no way of being certain if that was true or not. Sue seemed uncertain, but I told her to go on, that I would be all right.

When she backed out of the driveway, I reached down toward my ankle. I was halfway bent over before I remembered that the Crime Scene Unit had my little Glock and that I hadn't taken my old service weapon with me. I didn't go directly into the house. For one thing, I couldn't be sure Sue had been accurate about not having left the door open or a window open a crack so that the cats might've gotten out. People forget all sorts of things. Second, if it really was a crime scene, I didn't want to taint it. But the real reason was that I didn't want to go in. I don't think I ever wanted to go into that house again. So I found a fallen twig and used it to unlatch the gate to the white vinyl fence I'd put up a few years ago.

The right side of the house looked fine. Nothing was disturbed, but as soon as I got around back and saw that the sliding doors had been smashed through, I knew Sue hadn't forgotten about leaving the front door or a window open. Our old backyard was bordered by a Polish cemetery run by a Catholic parish in Greenpoint, Brooklyn. There was a small woods between the cemetery and our back fence, but that was easy enough to navigate and the fence easy enough to climb. As long as someone kept his head down, the side fencing would prevent him from being spotted by a neighbor.

I climbed the short flight of wooden steps up to the sliding doors and looked inside. The hallway leading into the kitchen and living room was a total mess. The closets had been emptied, their contents dumped onto the white linoleum floor. I stepped back down onto the winter-dormant grass and peeked through every window. All the rooms had been trashed. John Jr.'s bedroom, too—a room the Shermans agreed never to use or to enter. It was the same as it had been the night before in Tommy's trailer. This made it very personal now, even more so than getting shot.

It was too big a coincidence to believe that my old house getting tossed had nothing to do with what had gone on the previous evening. I wasn't a big fan of coincidence. I believed in it about as much as the Virgin Birth. Someone was looking for something, something they thought Tommy Delcamino once had. Something they thought he might have given me. Unless I was blind or just plain stupid, the green backpack wasn't it. There wasn't anything in the backpack worth risking prison for. Certainly not a bunch of old photos or a roll of twenty-dollar bills.

When I heard the sirens, I went back around to the front of the house and waited. But I was through waiting to make up my mind. I was in now, with both feet.

(FRIDAY NIGHT)

It had already been a long tough shift by the time I took my first break. The Full Flaps Lounge was jam-packed and rocking the '80s. The crowd was younger than usual. Much younger. I guess that was due to the fact that it was Christmas office party season. For whatever reason, people seemed to be coming through the door already half-lit. Some were so shitfaced we'd been forced to escort them out before they'd even properly warmed their barstools. A few of them were belligerent about it, but none enough to rate an ass-kicking.

Younger crowds were trouble because it screwed with the club's usual vibe. Having younger, unmarried women around meant the older men paid less attention to the women who'd come to get their attention. It meant that the younger men hit on the older women to see if what they'd heard about cougars was true. Everyone got a little more sensitive. Tempers got shorter. Competition got fiercer. Insults got nastier. And nights like these were worse because the bar was three deep, the dance floor so densely packed that there was no hope of keeping potential warring parties at arm's length. On more than a few occasions, we'd had to separate guys who were getting chesty with each other and just a shove away from a first punch. It was all very schoolyard, but I'd seen schoolyard bullshit turn into murder and that wasn't going to happen on my watch.

It was on nights like these that I wished I was out driving the van. But when I stopped to think about it, I realized I was in a pretty bad frame of mind to begin with. This afternoon, on my way back to the Paragon, I stopped at a walk-in clinic on Portion Road in Ronkonkoma. I'd had them check the dressing on my leg and write me a script for antibiotics. I'd made up a story for the doctor about how I'd taken out that chunk of my calf with a piece of hot metal in my garage. You mention a gunshot wound to a doctor and, by law, he or she must contact the cops. I wasn't up for explaining myself, thank you very much.

Between Tommy Delcamino's murder and the break-in at 11 Pinetree, I'd spent way too much time over the last twenty-four hours with my old colleagues at the SCPD. The detectives from the Fourth Precinct who responded to the break-in didn't connect that crime to Tommy D.'s murder. Why would they? Two different crimes. Two different precincts. Two different detective squads. But I knew better. Although I lived at the Paragon, my official address was 11 Pinetree Court, and anyone who didn't know about the fallout from my son's death would assume my family still lived there. I guess I was also more than a little annoyed at the fact that I'd moved myself into a different room at the hotel. It was a matter of precaution. I figured that it wouldn't take too long for the guys who had killed Tommy and tossed my old house to track me down to my room at the Paragon. For now, only Felix and I knew I'd moved.

Just before midnight, I walked out the entrance of the Full Flaps Lounge. I needed some fresh air, cold as it might be. As soon as I stepped into the brisk night air, I got a face full of cigarette smoke. Off to my right was a group of ten men and women huddled together, smoking, keeping warm, and chatting. The word was that many of the hookups happened out here and not inside the club. I didn't doubt it. It was often so loud inside the club that it was impossible to hear your own internal voice, let alone ask for someone's number. A few of the regulars said hello to me, patting me on the shoulder as I passed. Thankfully, none of them whacked on the arm where I'd gotten the tetanus shot. Damned thing hurt almost as much as the leg wound. I nodded and kept moving.

I stopped at the corner of the building, leaning back against the rough concrete wall. I hoped the quiet would ease the ringing in my ears and help stop "Rock Lobster" from going round and round in my brain. I let the cool night air wash over me. It was warm inside the Full Flaps when it was half-empty. On nights like this, it was downright tropical.

A woman's voice came out of the darkness. "Are you all right?"

"I don't even know what all right means anymore." The words came out of me like yesterday's weather, nasty and raw.

"This was a mistake. I'm sorry," she said. "I'll leave you alone."

The sound of her heels clicking against the pavement echoed in the quiet of midnight. I called after her. Limped after her. Clutched her gently by her right biceps when I finally caught up to her.

"No, no, please. I didn't mean to be so rude. There's no excuse for that. I'm the one who's sorry."

I took my hand away from her arm. Her face was familiar to me. She wasn't a regular at the club, but she was there often enough so that we'd nod hello to each other when I'd stamped her hand for reentry. She was in her midthirties, on the short side, and maybe a little heavier than she wanted to be. Maybe not. I think I assumed as much because she always seemed self-conscious in the club. She wasn't the type who initiated conversations, but would sit at the bar nursing her drinks or stand at the edges of the dance floor waiting. I'd seen her leave with men on occasion, but she'd be back alone the next time. I seemed to know a lot about her, a lot more than I would have believed. Not her name, though.

"What are you smiling at?" she asked, the look on her face unsure.

It was a pretty face, but it was her eyes that I took most notice of. They were light blue and had that cracked-ice-crystal quality to them.

They also had a paradoxical warmth about them so that they almost seemed to glow.

"I was smiling at you, I guess. You have beautiful—"

"Eyes," she finished my sentence. "Thank you."

"I take it I'm not the first person to tell you that."

She shook her head, smiling shyly, hinting at the straight white teeth behind her pink lips. "Not even the first tonight. But I'm glad you think so."

I thought she might've been blushing a little, but it was hard to tell in the harsh parking lot light.

"I'm okay, by the way," I said. "Just hurt my leg a little, is all."

"What?"

"That's how this started, remember? You asked me—"

She laughed a kind of goofy laugh. "Right. Right. I saw you were limping in the club earlier and then when I saw you leaning against the wall, I was just wondering."

"That's a helluva a laugh you've got there."

"I know. My ex says it's one of the reasons he asked for a divorce. He couldn't take it anymore."

"I like it. I might even like your name if I knew it."

Now she definitely was blushing. "Casey. People call me Casey."

"But that's not your name?"

"Not nearly," she said, ducking her head and wrapping her arms around the shoulders of her red leather jacket. "God, it's cold out here."

"It is, but you're not changing subjects that easy."

We both laughed at that. But she scrunched her lips closed and shook her head no at me like a little girl.

"So, you're not gonna tell me your name, huh?"

"Not tonight," she said.

I offered her my right hand. "Well, I'm Gus Murphy."

Her hand fit comfortably in mine. It was warm and soft, but not too soft. It was a hand that worked for a living.

Casey looked me directly in the eyes. "I know who you are."

"Do you?"

"People talk."

She was lovely. Her hair was coal black and parted on the left. It was long, too, and fell over her shoulders as it pleased. She had an angular jawline and a willful chin. And when she wasn't being shy, her smile was bright and alive. Her lips weren't overly pouty or thick, but they had great curves to them.

"What do you know about me, Casey whose name isn't Casey?"

"You were a cop and . . ."

There it was, that look. She knew about John. I wasn't in the mood for the usual awkwardness nor was I in the mood to be unkind. Being here with her had changed my frame of mind.

"It's okay," I said, touching her cheek. Somehow I knew it would be okay for me to do that. "It's not good to pretend."

When she didn't apologize, I swear I almost kissed her. I found the thought of kissing her suddenly a pleasant idea, but I kept it as just that, a pleasant thought.

"I've wanted to talk to you for a long time, Gus, but I could never work up the nerve before tonight. It never seemed like you would want to talk. This isn't coming out right. It's not that I thought you wouldn't want to talk to me. What I'm saying is that you always seemed like you were closed."

"I *was* closed," I said, realizing my hand was still pressed to her cheek. I took it away, but not quickly. "What did you want to talk about?"

"The truth?"

"It's usually a good place to start."

"Dinner," she said.

I was confused. "What about dinner?"

She laughed that goofy laugh again and I was even more confused. "What?"

"I've wanted you to ask me that question for months."

"*What about dinner?*" I repeated it in my head and aloud, trying to understand. Then, "Oh, now I understand."

"You're smiling, Gus."

"Am I? I don't smile much anymore."

"You should. It suits you. You're very handsome when you smile."

"Thanks."

She turned her palms up. "Well?"

"Well what?"

Casey smiled. "What about dinner?"

"We better stop this or it's going to turn into a version of 'Who's on first?'"

"What?"

"No, he's on second."

"Who is?"

"Never mind." I laughed, shaking my head at her. "Would you like to go to dinner sometime?"

"Very much."

"Listen, Casey . . . I'm not sure I'll be very good company."

"Nothing is sure."

I thought of my son and said, "You're right about that. Nothing is."

"What's your number?"

I pointed at the hotel. "Call the hotel and ask for me." Then I stopped being mysterious and gave her my cell number. "My schedule is kind of screwy, but—"

"You already trying to back out on me?" She wagged a finger.

I shook my head. "Scout's honor. C'mon, I'll walk you back to the club."

"No," she said, smiling. "I don't think so. I've got what I came for."

"Your car, then."

Casey threw a thumb over her shoulder at the old blue Honda Civic behind her. "You already have." She put her hands on my shoulders, got on her toes, and kissed me softly on my cheek. "I'll call in a couple of days."

Stunned, I watched her get into her car and drive off. As her taillights turned into small red specks and then disappeared, I thought of all the questions I should have asked her, of all the warnings about me I should have given her. But it was too late now. As I turned to limp back to the club, I noticed that neither my leg nor arm hurt quite as much as they had only fifteen minutes before. Then, about four strides short of where I would've made the turn around the corner to the Full Flaps, something else came out of the darkness at me. Something cold and hard and far more deadly than Casey's voice. I stopped in my tracks. The feel of gunmetal against your neck will do that to you—stop you from moving. Stop the world from turning.

Before I could react, two massive, powerful hands clutched my elbows and squeezed my arms together behind me. Another hand, the free hand of the man pressing the gun to my neck, reached under my jacket and removed my old service weapon from the holster on my right hip. Suddenly, I was being moved along toward the space between a parked cargo van and a black Escalade, my feet barely touching the ground beneath them. I was a dead man. I smiled at the absurdity of it, for there had been so many times during the last two years I wouldn't have cared. That I would have relished an end to all the pain and constant grief. It was different now. Was it as simple as having met a woman other than Annie whose lips I found I wanted to kiss? Was it that Tommy Delcamino's murder had given me a sense of purpose beyond mourning my loss? I couldn't say. All I knew was that I desperately wanted to see the sun rise again.

didn't know about the guy pressing the gun to my neck. I didn't have to. The thing in his hand had bullets and went bang. I wouldn't hear the bang . . . or would I? I would find out soon enough. I knew all I needed to know about the other guy, the one squeezing the life out of my arms. He was country strong. I wasn't exactly a small man and he was pushing me along to a spot between a black Escalade and a van as if I were made out of papier-mâché. I didn't have a whole lot of options besides stalling and begging. I was willing to stall. I figured if I stalled long enough, my guys from the club would come looking for me. If that didn't work, I guessed I was fucked. I could envision myself begging for Krissy's life. For Annie's, too, in spite of everything. But not for my own life, no. The last two years had left me with precious little pride and I planned to hold on to whatever small bits of it remained in me even if it meant taking it to the grave.

As we approached the back bumper of the Escalade, I said as calmly as I could manage, "You guys know I'm Suffolk PD, right? You kill a cop and you're gonna do the hardest kinda time there is to do and it will be for the rest of your lives. And that's only if my friends don't pay someone to stick a shiv in your neck. Maybe you should think about that before you do something you can't undo."

"Shut your damn mouth, chump," whispered the man holding the gun to my neck. "Shut it and keep your white cracker ass movin'." Although he spoke in a whisper, there was a familiar quality to his voice. I was too preoccupied to place it.

I had sweat-soaked through my shirt by the time we came to a stop between the van and the Caddy. Then the gun was off my neck. My arms were free, but I knew the man who'd pushed me here was close behind me. I could hear him breathing. Feel him there. My arm and leg were aching badly, my heart pumping blood as hard as it could. There was just enough ambient light for me to see an African-American man standing in front of me. He was twenty-five, if that, with a face like a cliff wall and about as welcoming. He was much smaller than me, but the Beretta he had pointed at my chest more than made up for that. Still, if I was going to make a move, it had to be soon. My arms were free and the guy with the gun was standing a little closer to me than he should have been. He seemed to have read my mind.

He shook his head at me in disappointment. "Nah, man, don't even be thinkin' 'bout that. Don't be stupid, now." He looked past me, over my shoulder, and said, "Okay, Antwone, pat his ass down and make sure he only had the one piece on him."

Before I could blink, the strong man behind me was patting me down.

"He clean." Antwone's voice was deep as a moonless night. "What-chu wan' me to do with him, Jamal?"

I looked over my shoulder, slowly, to take a peek at Antwone. I wanted to see the man who had handled me with such ease. He was massive. I wasn't sure how he'd even fit into such a tight space. One thing was for sure, if I wanted to run, there was no room for me to get past him.

Jamal shook his head at Antwone. Then the dome light popped on in the Escalade. Jamal stepped back, opening the rear passenger door with his free hand. Antwone put his hand on my shoulder to discourage me from getting any bright ideas.

An elegant-looking black man in his late twenties—head shaved, a gold, diamond-encrusted hoop earring thick as a wedding band dangling from his left ear—stepped out of the Escalade and came very close to me. Jamal closed the door behind him. The man staring at me with cruel brown eyes cool enough to lower the temperature stood about six feet tall. He was lean and moved like a big cat. He wore a camel-colored coat over a few thousand bucks' worth of pinstriped navy wool. His shirt was white, the collar open, but stiffly ironed so that it dared not move without permission. There was a tasteful gold rope chain—thick, but not clownish—around his neck. He was handsome in a hard way. A fair amount of scar tissue had built up his brow and around the corners of his eyes. His nose was flatter than it should have been and didn't look like there was much cartilage beneath its rich black skin. I didn't pay any mind to the fancy clothes and the elegance. His presence alone was more intimidating than the Beretta in Jamal's hand.

"Give me and the gentleman here a minute to get acquainted, yo."

His tone was pleasant enough, but I gave that about as much weight as the rest of his artifice. His eyes told me everything about him I needed to know.

Jamal didn't like it. "But you—"

"Nah, Jamal, ain't no thing. We cool. Ain't that right, Gus?" he said more than asked, patting my left arm, then grabbing my forearm. His grasp was nearly as powerful as Antwone's.

"As cool as the weather," I said.

"See, Jamal, I tol' you Mr. Murphy here was a smart man. He know which way is up and it's for damn sure he know which way is down."

I nodded that I did.

He let go of my arm. "Now, Jamal, you and Antwone go over there and let us be. The grown-ups got to talk."

Jamal backed up and walked around the front of the Escalade, along the driver's side, and wound up behind Antwone. I turned to see them back away several feet, but not far enough for me to make a run for it or to feel secure. I turned back to the big cat.

"You know my name. And you are . . . ?"

"Nah, that ain't the way this gonna play, yo."

"How about you telling me what *this* is. Then we can worry about how it'll play."

He laughed. It had nothing to do with good humor. "You think I'm fuckin' around witch y'all? You wan' me bring my boys back over here?"

I shrugged. "If you wanted to hurt me, I'd already be hurt."

"Or worse."

"Or worse."

He laughed again, which I found as comforting as a glass splinter. His eyes softened a little. "Y'all got some cojones on you, man. I give you that." The softness vanished. "But your balls ain't at issue, yo. Y'all got something that belongs to me."

Oddly, the minute he said that, it hit me. I knew where I'd heard Jamal's voice before. He'd been screaming at someone, presumably Antwone, not to shoot me. They'd killed Tommy.

"Motherfucker," I said to myself. Apparently not.

My elegant friend heard it, too, and with lightning-fast movements, he stuck a Sig into the fleshy part of my neck. "What the fuck you call me?"

"I didn't call you anything," I said, my voice choked by the muzzle of his gun.

"Then what?"

"I realized your boys killed Tommy Delcamino."

There was a second of confusion in his eyes. "Nah, my boys ain't killed nobody. That dumbass man was dead already."

"Bullshit!"

He shoved the gun into my flesh so hard it lifted up my head. "Man, ain't nobody talk to me like that. You hungry to die?"

In spite of the pressure, I managed to say, "Not anymore."

That confused him again and he eased back a little.

"Look, I recognize Jamal's voice. Your boys were there at that paving yard."

My elegant friend smiled an expensive smile at me. "I never said they wasn't. I said they ain't killed nobody."

"They ransacked my old house. Went into a place they shouldn't have gone into and fucked it up. A sacred place to me and my family."

He shook his head at me. "Weren't my boys. I got no business at your house, man."

I wasn't sure I believed him, but I didn't think I should argue the point. "Maybe not, but they shot me in the leg when they were at the paving yard."

The smile ran away from his face. My guess was Jamal and Antwone hadn't mentioned that to him. "Don't change nothin'. You got something that belong to me. Now we gonna do this easy or hard?"

And in that moment it came to me that Tommy's murder was just the second act to his son's murder.

"By 'hard,' you mean the way you tortured TJ Delcamino to death?" I guessed I was talking a little too loudly to suit my friend holding the gun to my throat.

"Yo, you raise your voice to me again, I won't be givin' y'all a choice 'bout easy or hard. My boys'll be all over your ass."

"What do you need them for? You look like you could handle yourself just fine. What'd you fight as, super middleweight?"

I'd appealed to his vanity. "Uh-huh. Put on a pound or two since them days. But you ain't worth gettin' my hands all fucked up for." Then he leaned in closer to me so that I could feel the warmth of his breath on my cheek. "And trus' me when I tell you, y'all don't ever want me dealin' with you direct." And when he pulled his head back, his eyes were as cold and blank and devoid of humanity as any eyes I'd ever looked into, and that was saying something.

"You know I'm Suffolk PD?"

He smiled again, but with only half his face. It never reached his eyes. "That s'posed to scare me?" He laughed. "I know all 'bout you. I found you here, ain't I? Nah, Gus Murphy, cops don't scare me none. You ain't even on the job no more anyways."

"You mind telling me what of yours I'm supposed to have?"

He shook his shaved head and made a clucking sound with his tongue. "Man, don't be playin' it that way. I don't want to hurt you. I got sympathy for y'all. Be a shame for your ex and your girl to have to grieve you so soon afta losin' your boy that way."

I lost it and let go a short chopping right hand that landed flush on the left side of his face. But he didn't shoot me. He took it. Shook it off. Nodded his head. Smiled. Lowered the Sig. Then something like a baseball bat hit me flush in the liver. I thought my guts had exploded. I'd never felt physical pain like that before. I was down on my hands and knees, nauseous. I could barely hold myself up for how his punch reverberated through me.

"Like I say, you got some balls on you, Gus. Some balls. Too bad y'all gonna make this tough on yourself. Jamal! Antwone!"

But there was no answer. No sound of footsteps. Nothing. I managed to swing my head around and look behind me, but nothing was moving and the only thing disturbing the silence was the muted voice of Billy Idol singing "Dancing with Myself" coming from the Full Flaps Lounge. When I stared up, I saw my friend was scanning the darkness, wondering from which corner of the night his trouble would come. He was swinging the Sig slowly from side to side . . . ready.

In the meantime, using the Escalade's running board and door handle, I pulled myself up to my feet. I was pretty wobbly. My friend ignored me, understanding that I wasn't the real threat. Then there were footsteps from behind him, coming upon him so quickly even he couldn't react. His eyes got big with something that looked like fear and he dropped his Sig to the ground. He froze. Only the puffs of steamy breath coming from his mouth and nostrils hinted that he wasn't made of onyx.

"You are putting hands on top of your head and getting on your knees, mister. You will do so now, please."

It was Slava. And when the guy got on his knees, I saw that Slava was holding what looked to be Jamal's Beretta to the back of my elegant friend's head. Slava was sixty if a day, more burly than big. He had thin wisps of gray hair atop his ugly head and his eyes were a weary shade of faded blue. But I guessed I was going to have to reconfigure my assessment of him as a kindly old uncle.

"Are you okay, Gus? This man is hurting you?"

"I'm okay," I lied, unsure of how Slava might react. I didn't want to risk him pulling the trigger. "Where are his pals?"

Slava's laugh was a series of snorts and gasps. "They are resting on sidewalk." His Ws sounded like Vs so that "sidewalk" was "sidevalk."

I picked up my elegant pal's Sig. I was curious about how Slava had managed to convince Jamal and Antwone to rest on the sidewalk, but that would have to wait. I pointed the Sig at my friend, who'd remained silent and unmoving on his knees through the whole process.

"On your feet," I said.

He stood. I frisked him and removed his wallet. Embossed black alligator, it was, like the rest of his clothing and accessories, top shelf. I rubbed my fingers over the embossed initials KS.

"KS, huh?" I flipped the wallet open and looked at his driver's license. "Kareem Shivers," I said. He was thirty-two and his photo was anything but elegant. Looked more like a booking photo. I removed his license from his wallet and stuffed the wallet back in his pocket. I turned to Slava. "Could you give Mr. Shivers and me a minute? Maybe keep an eye on his friends."

Slava was gone.

"What are we gonna do now, Mr. Shivers?"

He was smiling again. "Do whatchu got to do."

"You're a pretty confident man."

He didn't answer, just kept smiling.

I said, "I'm not real fond of getting shot, being threatened, or having guns stuck in my throat."

"I ain't much for people possessin' what ain't theirs to possess, specially when it be mine. You feel me?"

"Like I told you before, whatever it is of yours you think I got, I don't. Or if I do, I don't know it."

He shook his head at me again. "Nah, man. Your lips are movin', but I ain't heard nothing."

"Nothing but the truth. You know, Kareem, seems to me that you're in no position to dismiss me."

"Jus' 'cause you holdin' a gun in your hand don't mean shit. Any advantage is temporary. No matter how big an edge you got, it last only so long. Usually not as long as people thinkin'."

"You're quite a philosopher."

"Boxin' teach a man anything, it teach him about havin' the edge and when to use it."

I had a decision to make. I could hold Shivers, Jamal, and Antwone and let the cops sort through whatever it was that was going on, which would probably only muddy the waters more than they already were and further convince Kareem Shivers I had whatever he was looking for. My other option was to buy myself some goodwill and credit, maybe even a little help.

I said, "Okay, you're right. A man has to know when to use his edge. He also has to know how to use it."

He nodded. "True that."

"So here's the deal. You tell me your boys didn't kill Tommy and that they didn't wreck my old house. For some reason, I believe you. I'm telling you I don't have whatever it is you're looking for. That's the truth. Believing it . . . well, that's your burden, not mine. You keep away from my family and tell your boys not to go shooting their guns off in the dark and we won't have a problem with each other."

I unlocked the clip from the Sig and let it fall to ground. I kicked the clip away, listening to it skim along the pavement beneath the row of parked cars. I popped out the chambered round and watched it tumble away in a wide arc from the pistol. I handed the Sig to Shivers.

"Collect Jamal and Antwone and get out of here."

He held out his left hand. "My license."

"Nope. Not part of the deal and it's non-negotiable. I give you my word I'll get it back to you."

Kareem studied my face, screwed up his lips, and shrugged. "That the way it got to be, that the way it got to be." He put his left hand back down by his side.

"Slava!" I called out, keeping an eye on Shivers.

"What is happened, Gus?"

"When I step out from between the cars, you can let those two assholes go."

There was a very loud silence. Then, "I am not liking this."

"It's okay, Slava. It's okay."

Relieved of the weight of the pistol, I found myself rubbing my abdomen where Kareem Shivers had laid into me.

He was smiling again, only this time with his whole face, eyes too. "Hurt bad, don't it?"

"Hurt doesn't quite say it. Why'd a man who can hit like you stop fighting?"

"I stopped boxin'. Ain't never stopped fightin'."

"I'll get your license back to you," I said, backing out of the spot between the van and the Escalade.

"I know you will." He was still smiling, but not with his eyes.

When I turned and walked to where Slava was, I noticed Antwone and Jamal were seated on the curb that ran around the entire perimeter of the Paragon. Antwone was rubbing the back of his big head with his massive left hand. The hand was shiny and wet with blood. His blood. Jamal was glassy-eyed.

"Up!" Slava shouted at them, nudging them to their feet with the toe of his bulky black doorman shoes. "Up!"

Antwone was up first and turned to stare at Slava with a look of anger and a kind of awe. I suppose he was still wondering how a fat old white man took him. I was wondering pretty much the same thing. With his right hand, Antwone lifted up Jamal, who was wobbly and unsteady on his feet. They walked slowly over to the Escalade. Slava and I stood next to each other and watched.

When the Caddy was gone, Slava pulled my gun out of his waistband and handed it to me. He smiled that smile of his. "What is this trouble about, Gus?"

I thought about it for a second before I answered. "About something I don't have—not yet, anyway."

19

(SATURDAY, EARLY MORNING)

Slava was eagerly devouring his four eggs, corned beef hash, sausages, bacon, toast, and home-fried potatoes while I sipped at my coffee, waiting for him to slow down or finish. I figured it would have been rude to discuss what had happened at midnight in the parking lot at the Paragon before he'd gotten some food in him. He had, after all, saved me from a beating. Might even have saved my life. At the end of his shift, I came down from my room and took him to the airport diner. He seemed reluctant to accept my invitation, but I made it pretty clear to him that no wasn't an option. He also knew I would want to hear about how he'd managed to get the drop on three armed men, one the size of Mount Rushmore.

"I have seen the two black men in lobby of hotel," Slava said without prompting, his mouth full of eggs. "They are looking around all the time to see if they are being watched. This gets my attention, how they are acting and how they have on them weapons." He patted his side to indicate where a shoulder holster would hang beneath a jacket or coat. "When they get into elevator, I see they go up to the floor where is your room. Ten minutes later, they are coming down looking angry. So I am keeping my eye on them out the door."

"You saw the big man pushing me along and the other one holding the Beretta to my neck."

He nodded, shoveling more food into his mouth.

"But that doesn't explain how you—"

Slava didn't let me finish my sentence. "They thought they were safe, that no one is seeing them. When men are thinking they are having no threat, they are sloppy. They were not paying to me any attention. Was easy for me to coming behind them. The big man, him I am clubbing first."

"Clubbing with what?"

Slava swallowed his mouthful of food, washed it down with coffee. He then swung his right arm down by his side, raised it back up, and laid it flat on the table. When he took his hand away, a well-worn leather-covered sap sat on the table where his palm had been. Saps were old school, but effective. I picked it up to feel its heft, slapping it against my palm, then placed it back on the table.

"I can make for you one if you wish," he said, making it disappear beneath his big mitt of a hand.

"No wonder Antwone's head was bloodied."

"He will live. I am not hitting him so hard to kill him. He will have headaches for many days." Slava took a forkful of food, chewed a little, said, "The other one, the one with Beretta, him I am putting in sleeper hold. You were policeman. You are knowing it, yes?"

I nodded that I did. A sleeper hold was a polite euphemism for choking someone into unconsciousness. They used to teach cops how to do it with their forearms or nightsticks, but it was risky because there wasn't much room for error between sleep and suffocation.

"But what if things had gone sideways?" I asked.

"What is meaning 'sideways'?"

"Wrong, what if things had gone wrong?"

He gasped and snorted that laugh of his. He leaned forward, placing his arms beneath the table. I felt a hard tap on my knee.

"Look down and take it, Gus. Put in lap and look."

And there in my lap was a semiautomatic pistol, but one I didn't recognize. It resembled a Walther, but it was bigger, heavier.

Slava said, "Is Makarov. Russian gun."

"Russian, huh?" I smiled. "I heard you were from Poland."

"No, France." He laughed at his own joke.

"Figures. You know ex-cops, we're always getting our European countries mixed up."

Slava stopped smiling and stopped eating. "Gus, I am liking you. I know I am having to explain about last night, but please to leave it there. It would not be good to be curious about Slava," he referred to himself in the third person. "That is the word, 'curious'?"

"Curious, yeah."

"That would be bad, to be curious about Slava."

"For you or me?"

He turned stony-faced. "For both, I am thinking."

"I get the message, Slava."

He went back to finishing his meal.

A few minutes later I said, "But maybe someday you'll tell me your story."

His happy eating expression went mournful and grave. "No, Gus. I am never telling you this. I am shamed in my soul. Please you are not asking me this again. Promise to me this."

I reached across the table with my right hand. "I promise."

He took my hand and, feeling the incredible strength in his grasp, I understood how he had been able to do what he had done earlier in the parking lot. Yet there was more than power in his grip. I can't explain it except to say I somehow knew that his right hand had done more than wield a sap or pistol. Until our palms and fingers meshed, I wouldn't have believed it possible to transmit sadness and regret through touch. I believed it now.

As we left the diner, he clapped me on the shoulder, squeezed the back of my neck, and whispered, "If you are ever needing my help, I give it."

"Thanks, Slava, but what if—"

"No, Gus. No what if. I am having in me too much shame to worry about what if."

I offered him a ride back to the Paragon to pick up his car, but he refused. He said he preferred to walk, that he had things to think about. I didn't doubt it.

20

(SATURDAY, EARLY AFTERNOON)

After breakfast with Slava, I'd gotten a few hours' sleep before the ache in my leg and the throbbing in my arm roused me. My new room was much like my old room, as it was like almost every other room at the hotel. The Paragon wasn't the kind of place with bridal or presidential suites. It wasn't the kind of place with suites at all. There were some larger rooms on the top floor that the original owners had built to be their club floor. I caught myself shaking my head in the mirror, thinking about a club floor at the Paragon. No one came here to be pampered or to have free wine at five or complimentary continental breakfast in the morning. People came here to leave.

I caught something else in the mirror, too. The room might have looked the same as my old one, but I didn't. I looked tired, but also alive. There was light in my eyes. I hadn't been able to say that for a very long time. Maybe that had something to do with meeting Casey. Maybe not. It was very odd, I thought, that I should feel this way in the wake of Tommy D.'s murder and getting a chunk of my calf shot off. I didn't question it. All I had done for two years was ask questions that had gone as unanswered as an old woman's prayers. The universe was nothing so much as deaf and unjudging. I'd learned to take some comfort in that. What else was left to me? Moral judgments were a man-made albatross, so I didn't beat myself up for feeling even a little bit alive again in the midst of spilled blood.

I put in a call to Al Roussis to see how the investigation into Tommy's murder was going and to see if the forensics and/or ballistics backed up Kareem Shivers' claim that his boys had nothing to do with Tommy's murder. After last night, I also wanted my gun back. Given how easily Jamal and Antwone had handled me, I felt pretty naked with just my old service weapon to carry. And I wouldn't have Slava around to watch my back, not off premises. I got Al's voice mail and asked him to call me back.

When I hung up the phone, I found myself staring at the green canvas backpack that Smudge had brought me the night Tommy was killed. If the last few days had convinced me of anything, it was that Tommy Delcamino's murder was somehow connected to his son's murder. It all seemed to be set in motion by the visit Tommy had paid me last Tuesday. I figured Al Roussis would make the connection between the father/son murders soon enough. In the meantime, I thought that I'd see what I could find out about the kid's death. If I stuck my nose into an active investigation, I'd get shut down in seconds flat. I'd stashed the bankroll in my drawer for safekeeping and had already looked at all the photos, but I'd taken only a quick look through the black-and-white composition book. Nothing of what I'd scanned had stuck. I got the notebook out and plopped back down on the bed. Before I could flip the cover open, there was a knock at my door.

I didn't answer. Instead, I put the notebook down and reached over to the nightstand to retrieve the one gun left to me. The last five days had made me think caution first. I held my breath. There was that knock again. This time the rapping lasted a while longer. Again, I didn't answer. It persisted, growing louder, and more insistent.

"Who's there?" I asked.

The only answer was more knocking. I wasn't going to be able to wait out the person on the other side of the door. It was stupid of me, I know, because if the person on the other side of the door meant me harm, all they had to do was shoot through the door, but I moved to the door as quietly as I could manage. In one quick motion, I flung the door back and raised my weapon. Then I lowered it.

Annie was standing there, the heat coming off her in waves. Her hair was freshly cut and styled the way I liked it, razor straight and parted down the middle, some of it falling across her left cheek. The air smelled of her perfume, the musky, patchouli-based one. The one that when blended with her own scent made me hard. I knew why she had come. That she was wearing the belted, tan leather coat I'd given her for her birthday three years ago over red patent leather stilettos cleared up any doubts I might have had about her intentions.

She gave me a feral smile and came toward me, closing the door behind her. She pushed herself against me, the smell of the perfume even stronger now and mixing with the scent of the leather. I was dizzy. She took the gun out of my hand, placed it on the rug, and again pressed her body into mine. I pulled her head back by the hair and kissed her hard on the mouth. She let out a sigh, her body clenching. I could feel her muscles contract beneath the butter-soft leather.

For reasons I can't explain, I asked, "What are you doing here?"

Annie pushed back, using her hands against my chest, untied the belt of the duster, undid the buttons, and slid out of the coat, letting it fall to the floor around her heels. The only thing she'd been wearing beneath the leather was that perfume. She dropped to her knees, sliding my boxers down to the floor with her.

"Do you still want to know what I'm doing here?"

When I didn't answer, she put me in her mouth.

An hour later, we lay on opposite sides of the bed, the air, the sheets, the room reeking of us. Silent, we were staring through the shade-drawn darkness, looking for answers that had eluded us for the last two years, answers we would never find. Not in bed. Not anywhere. I waited for Annie to speak first because, as was the pattern since John's death, she was the one who had initiated the encounter. Sex between us now was about everything else except sex. This time it had been different, though. Since we had separated, the sex between us had been urgent, ferocious, angry—a mixture of punishment and pain, revenge and grief. And it usually began with a fight. A fight over issues real or imagined, over something or nothing. It was a fight that gave us an excuse to scratch an itch.

Today there had been no fight to start with and there were real moments between us, moments of tenderness. The kind of tenderness that hadn't been part of our intimacy for years, even before John's death. We kissed. And the kissing wasn't all the fevered, hair-pulling, tongue-jabbing kissing that usually followed our screaming at one another and preceded our tearing at each other's clothes. She had let me hold her. Had wanted to be held. Had let me trace my fingers lightly over her hip, along her thigh, and slide them inside her. She had held on tightly to my wrist as I helped her to climax. Annie had done things to me she hadn't done since we'd dated, and they seemed to excite her as much now as then. But that was all gone. There was only that darkness between us, and silence, and only the air clung to what had passed between us.

"What was that about?" I said, no longer willing to wait for her to cut through the dark.

"That was about goodbye."

"Goodbye?"

"Goodbye."

She let that land there for a minute before continuing.

"I wanted to have a last time, something to look back at and say that was that, enough. I wanted it to be special and I wanted to enjoy it. I even wanted you to enjoy it. I wanted you to enjoy it so that you'll miss it."

"Mission accomplished, Annie. But what just happened between us . . . that wasn't us," I said, sitting up and kicking my legs over the side of the bed. "That wasn't us, not since we got married. Maybe not even then. Maybe that was us when we dated. The things we just did, those were amazing things, but it was like living a greatest hits album. I loved you once like I never thought I was capable of loving a woman and I was really happy being married to you, but it was never about the sex."

"What was the gun for, Gus?" she asked. "And why the change of room?"

I was hoping she would have forgotten about the gun and hadn't noticed the room switch. "There's been some trouble lately."

"Is that what the bandage on your leg is about?"

I nodded, then said, "And the house—"

"The house? Eleven Pinetree?"

"Yeah, it was broken into and ransacked pretty bad."

I stood, flicking on the bedside lamp. My ex, shielding her eyes with her hand. I have to say, she did look amazing there, her breasts still beautiful and firm, her body taut and slender, her hair now wild yet glimmering. But the look on her face drew a sharp contrast to her body. She wore an angry, fearful expression. Fearful of asking me the question about John's room. More fearful of the answer.

"Yeah, they wrecked that, too," I said, bowing my head. "I asked Sue Sherman, the tenant, to clean it up as best she could and—"

Annie was out of bed now, furiously gathering up her coat and shoes.

"The tenant! How could you leave it to a stranger to touch John's things? Why didn't you do it yourself, Gus? How could you—"

"I couldn't, Annie. I just couldn't."

She ran at me and slapped me across the face. "You're a fucking coward, John Murphy. How could you?" Tears streamed down her cheeks. "How could you let a stranger touch his things?"

"I'm sorry." It was a feeble thing to say, true as it was.

She threw on her coat, belted it up, and ran out of the room in bare feet, her fingers hooked through the straps of her stilettos. I'm not sure that she'd meant what she'd said before about this encounter of ours really being a gesture of goodbye. It was hard to know with Annie. But I was pretty certain it was goodbye now that I had told her about John's room. And if this was goodbye, I would miss the feel of her, the taste of her, and most of all the scent of the smoke we made when we burned together.

(SUNDAY LUNCH)

The Old Main Pub was a bar restaurant in a strip mall located just west of where Route 111 met Main Street in Smithtown. The strip mall was prototypic Suffolk County—a big chain gym, flanked on either side by a liquor store, a sandwich shop, a pet supply store, a pizzeria, a bank, and half a dozen small businesses of one sort or another. You drive east or west down Main Street a mile or two and you'd come across another mall just like it. Although I'd lived almost my entire life within a twenty-mile radius of the place, I never got the need for so many damn strip centers. The differences between them were like the variations in a deck of cards: the cards were the same, only the shuffle was different.

I'd known Lou Carey since I'd gotten on the job. A pleasant, button-down guy, he was an okay cop who figured the best way to get ahead was by keeping his head down, and to paint by the numbers and stay inside the lines when he did. His wardrobe was strictly Kmart and so too were his dreams, though he wasn't altogether unambitious. He'd made detective. Most don't. He had wanted the bump not because he had a passion for doing the right thing, but because he preferred the schedule and liked that it was a safer way to put in the rest of his thirty years than by doing traffic stops and responding to domestics. Nothing wrong with that. Not everyone wants to be Don Quixote. There's a need for Sancho Panza, too. Someone has to shine the shoes and do the paperwork.

Everything was cool until we went inside and I saw Milt Paxson at the table.

"What's he doing here, Lou?"

"He caught the case. It's his baby, not mine."

I knew Paxson, too, mostly by reputation. I was glad for that because on the few occasions we'd crossed paths, I'd walked away regretting I hadn't laid him out. There was something dislikable about the guy, something that got under my skin, under everybody's skin. Unlike Lou, Paxson was the kind of dipshit who wanted the job for all the wrong reasons—the badge, the gun, and the power. He was the type of chesty moron that usually washed out of the academy, but he had connections with juice. His Uncle Joe was a captain and his first cousin was a big wheel in county politics. I suppose the brass thought Lou's by-the-book nature and calm demeanor would temper Paxson's bullying tendencies. Yeah, like that ever worked.

"He's my partner, Gus, for better or worse," Lou continued, hearing the disappointment in my voice. "I couldn't go behind his back."

I should have figured Lou would color inside the lines even when it came to doing things off the clock. My bad. Paxson was a nasty package: hatchet-faced and high-strung. He was already stuffing his mouth with the fried bread and cheese spread for which the Old Main was famous. He was studying the menu, too, no doubt looking for the most expensive thing on it. When I'd called Lou to ask for the meeting after Annie had stormed out, I'd promised that the meal would be on me. He'd clearly passed that message on to Paxson.

The dining room was pretty empty for a football Sunday in December, but both the Jets and Giants were out of it and people were probably out doing Christmas shopping.

"Give it a rest, Milt," I said. "Leave a little room for lunch."

"Well, if you'd showed on time, I wouldn't have to shove this shit down my gut. Fucking fried bread and cheese spread. Wisconsin fucking health food."

"Yo, Milt, language." Lou wagged a finger. "This is a family place. Ease up on the F-bombs."

"Yeah, well, I told you that if this yoyo was paying we shoulda switched to Pace's and had us a real meal. Get a good steak there, not this second-rate pub crap."

Lou shook his head. "Relax, Milt. I like it here. Good solid food. Good value. I take the family here sometimes."

The waitress came over and took our drink orders. Lou and I ordered Heinekens. Paxson ordered a fancy bourbon. And like the dick that he was, he ordered it with Coke, which kind of defeated the point of ordering fine bourbon. But that wasn't the point for him. The point was to stick it to me. Not knowing any better, the waitress asked Paxson if he was sure he wanted to mix a single-barrel bourbon with Coke. He didn't like being questioned, not one little bit.

"Listen, honey, you worry about how big your ass looks in those tight pants and let me worry about what I drink."

A different waitress brought us our drinks. No surprise there. Before she could leave, Paxson ordered another drink and demanded to order his meal as well. Lou and I ordered burgers. Milt ordered shrimp cocktail to start and the lobster and steak combo. I bit my lip and proposed a thank-you toast. We clinked glasses, Paxson reluctantly. Lou and I sipped our beers. Not Milt. And when the waitress brought his second round and his shrimp cocktail, the schmuck ordered a third drink.

Lou had had enough and asked the waitress to hold on for a second. Then he turned to his partner.

"See this man here"—Lou pointed at me—"he's a brother. Stop abusing his generosity, Milt. Stop it now. We're doing him a courtesy by being here. Be courteous."

Paxson liked Lou's lecture about as much as being questioned by the waitress, but he relented.

"Whatever, Lou. Never mind the bourbon," he said. "Just bring me the Coke."

But it was a half hour later, after Paxson had put a big dent in his lobster tail and steak, that he turned to me.

"Thanks for the meal, Murphy. That was big of you, but fuck you. This ain't gonna get you anywhere. We're not talking to you about the TJ Delcamino case, dead fucking skel piece a shit that he is, or any other case, brother officer bullshit notwithstanding."

"Impressive," I said.

Paxson was puzzled. "What is?"

"That you know a four-syllable word and actually seem to know what it means."

"Well, fuck you, Murphy."

"You're repeating yourself, asshole."

"Like I said, this is my case. I caught it and I'm not talking about it with you. My business is my business. How I run my investigation is my affair." He turned away and took another forkful of steak. "And don't even try to pull that dead-kid card with me, you—"

He didn't finish the word because I was busy slamming his face into his plate. Then I held him down. He was flailing his arms, kicking his legs, trying anything to get me to let go. Lou Carey clamped a bear hug on me and pulled me away from the table.

"You motherfucker!" Paxson screamed, his face red and dripping with steak juice and drawn butter. "You almost broke my fucking nose."

"If your partner didn't stop me, I would've broken your neck, you worthless little piece of—"

"Enough!" Lou said. "Enough."

Paxson reached under his jacket for his cuffs. "I'm placing you under arrest for assaulting an—"

Lou Carey let go of me and stepped between Paxson and me. "You're not arresting anyone for anything," he said. "I won't back you on this, partner or not. Far as I can tell, you deserved what you got. Worse, maybe."

"But we're partners, Lou." Paxson sounded hurt.

"Lord help me, we are, but it doesn't mean you're not an asshole most of the time. Now get in the men's room and wash yourself off."

Paxson turned to go and then turned back. "This ain't over between us, Murphy, not by a long fucking shot."

When I opened my mouth to answer, Lou Carey shook his head no at me. "Don't."

I didn't. I settled the bill and walked outside with Lou.

"Half of the time I'd like to do that to him myself," he confessed. "The guy just doesn't know when to give it a rest. He shouldn't have said that thing about your son, Gus. I'm sorry about that. But listen, I've always liked you and we've always gotten along—"

"But . . ."

"But I'm gonna give you some advice. Your name's coming up a lot where it shouldn't. You were at the homicide scene of the kid's dad and your old house got broken into the other day, too. Not good, Gus. Not good. Walk away from this case. Walk away from the father's case. Leave it alone. Don't make trouble for yourself when you've had so much heartache."

"I'm off the job, Lou. How much harder can the universe punish me than it already has?"

"It's not the universe I'd worry about."

"Fair enough, Lou. All I want to know is why you guys didn't follow up on the leads that Tommy Delcamino gave you? And please don't bother telling me he didn't know what he was talking about. I looked at his notes. They were as thorough as any good detective's. Look, I know who Tommy Delcamino was. I arrested him plenty of times. And it's likely his kid was no better. But none of that means they don't deserve some justice."

"You're sounding a little naïve there, Gus. The kid was a junkie and a mutt. He was involved with all sorts of the wrong kind of people and it came back to bite him in the ass the same way it caught up to his father. Neither one of 'em may have deserved the deaths they got, but either one or both of them was gonna get dead before their time. Leave it there, please, for your own sake."

"Maybe I am sounding naïve."

"There are no answers to get from me. I'm sorry, but you'll have to get them somewheres else."

"I think I might just do that."

"That would be a stupid thing to do, Gus."

"You're not threatening me, are you, Lou?"

Carey looked as if I had just gut-punched him the way Kareem Shivers had hit me two nights earlier. "Come on, you know me better than that."

"I thought I did," I said, shaking his hand. "Thanks for meeting me, at least."

When I was almost to my car, he called after me, "Watch your back, Gus. Your front and sides, too."

As I pulled out of the lot, I took Lou's advice to heart and paid close attention to what was in my rearview mirror. At the moment, all that I saw was parked cars and gray skies.

Milt Paxson hadn't meant to do me a favor, but he had. His stupid remark about playing the dead-kid card and Annie's slapping me across the face were reminders to do something I hadn't done for a few weeks. There was someone I needed to go see. Someone who resided only a few minutes from the Old Main Pub. So I turned left off Route 111 onto Cross Street and right onto Mount Pleasant. Less than a hundred yards on Mount Pleasant, I made another right, this one beneath the stone and mortar archway of St. Patrick's Cemetery.

The original plan was to bury John Jr. at Calvary Cemetery in Queens, but I couldn't bring myself to do it, to bury him there in the city so far away from home and from me. At least that's what I told my wife when she accused me of losing it. It was the truth, as far as it went. The real truth, the deeper truth was something I was ashamed of and something I held so close that I could not share it, not even with Annie. It was a thing that haunted me so that I could barely bear to remember it.

When John was a little boy, maybe four years old, and the two of us were going to visit my grandparents in Brooklyn, he looked out the window as we were exiting the LIE for the Brooklyn-Queens Expressway. And there, stretching out below him, was Calvary Cemetery—acre after seemingly endless acre of green grass and granite.

"What's that place, Daddy?" he asked, pointing to his right, an innocent, confused look on his face.

I didn't know what to say. It's one thing to tell yourself you'll never lie to your kids before you have kids. It's a different matter after you have them. Then those things you told yourself get tested. They get tested hard.

"Do you know what dying is, John?"

"You mean like when Tigger went sleepies?"

Tigger had been Annie's cat since she was twelve and he was part of the package when we got married. By the time John Jr. was three, Tigger was ancient and suffering so bad he had to be put down.

"Yeah, kiddo, just like that."

"But what's that place, Daddy? The place with all the tall rocks?"

"When people go sleepies like Tigger did, they go to places like that to be together" was the only thing I could think to say.

"But Tigger's in the backyard near us and Mommy and where we can show Krissy when she gets bigger like me. That's where I wanna be when I go sleepies, Daddy. I wanna go in the backyard near you and Mommy and Krissy."

"Don't ever talk like that, John!" I heard myself scream at my son.

He didn't cry, but I could tell he wanted to. He had already learned some of the wrong lessons about manhood by then. Lessons learned at my side. I'm sure that moment was lost to my son by the following week, but it was never lost to me. And when he died, it came back to me so hard that I threatened the life of anyone who dared mention burying my boy at Calvary. So with Father Bill's help, some strings got pulled, and although St. Pat's wasn't our parish, a plot was secured for John Jr.

Annie was furious because there would not be plots for the rest of us when we passed, but there was no changing my mind. Looking back now, I realize that might have been the first fissure in what would eventually collapse our marriage. Who knows, really? Maybe there were already plenty of cracks and fractures. After John's death, I don't think there was enough glue and plaster in the world to keep us together.

It was busy today. Sundays usually were, even on raw December Sundays. I think it was the coming of Christmas and the New Year. Memories are everywhere, cued by songs or smells, the sights of holiday decorations. I left my car on the path and walked over to his grave. That was one of the things I liked about St. Pat's, its intimacy. There were too many mega cemeteries like Calvary, places so expansive, with so many burials going on at once that they felt more like factories than graveyards. Rows and rows of hearses and processions lined up to wait their turn to head into the cemetery. Lined up like fidgety customers at the deli counter at the supermarket. Where was the dignity in that? Here, I could just leave my car where it was and not worry about holding up the line.

My son was buried in the far corner near where the black wrought-iron railing gave way to the cyclone fencing. There was a house close by, a tall white vinyl fence blocking the view of the graves. Sometimes when I visited John during the week, I heard kids playing behind the white fence. I liked that. I liked the sounds of life going on. I wished John could hear them, too. I wished it real hard. I knew it was a waste of time, that all wishing was. That John was beyond the reach of joy and of kids at play, but also beyond the reach of pain, callousness, cruelty, and indifference. I took less comfort in that than I should have. If he had only gotten to be old enough to live a little, to know not only the joys in life, but its weight and the tolls it takes on a man, then I might have been more at ease with his passing. When you're twenty, you only think you know everything there is to know. You only think you've felt everything there is to feel. You haven't, though. You really haven't.

He would never experience the Knicks or the Rangers winning a championship. He'd never see a Jets quarterback hoisting the Lombardi Trophy. At least he'd seen the Yankees win another World Series. That's what I was thinking about when the caretaker came to stand by me. Over the last two years, we had formed a kinship of strangers, the caretaker and me. It was something akin to the one I had formed with Aziza, the counter girl at Dunkin' Donuts. But I didn't even know the caretaker's name. I'd never asked for it. He'd never offered it. He would just come stand by me. Sometimes he would say a word or two. Sometimes not. Our relationship was more about small gestures: a nod, a wave, a furrowed brow, a pat on the shoulder. Like that. He would always cross himself. Today was no different.

After a minute he said, "Your wife was by to see your boy yesterday late."

I smiled a sad smile and shook my head. She had come to see John after leaving me at the hotel. She had come to apologize to him for his things being disturbed and for his father's cowardice. But it wasn't cowardice. It was love.

"Those flowers," he said, pointing at the base of his headstone, "she left them."

I nodded.

He nodded.

"I'll leave you two be." He patted my shoulder. It barely registered.

Before he got too far away, I said, "If I don't see you before then, Merry Christmas."

"And to you, Merry Christmas."

There had been a time not too long ago I might not have been able to hear those words without feeling gutted and resenting the person who'd spoken them. Now there was only the twinge of guilt. Guilt for feeling that a merry Christmas was even a possibility without my boy walking the earth. It was only a twinge. I guess the time had passed when I felt I had no right to happiness. That I had failed and needed to suffer continuously for the remainder of my life. It's a sad truth that I had turned my grief into a selfish thing. I had made John's death into a platform for my own purgatory. I became judge and jury and revisited all my sins, meting out punishment without mercy. But I suppose grief is, by its very nature, a selfish thing, perhaps the most selfish thing there is. John was certainly beyond its reach. It was the one feeling I was glad he would never have to fully experience.

As I drove away, turning left onto Route 347, I thought about Tommy Delcamino. I wondered who would bury him. I had his three grand in my drawer back at the Paragon. Maybe I knew how I would put that money to work. Then the radio went off, Bluetooth kicking in, and a number came up I didn't recognize. By the time the conversation was over, I knew I'd have to find another use for Tommy's bankroll.

23

(MONDAY, MID-MORNING)

Marsden Brothers was on Larkfield Road in East Northport. I knew it well because for the last ten years of my time in the Second Precinct, it was in my patrol sector. I'd driven by the tired old aluminum-sided building several times a shift without giving it much thought. Cops don't get many calls to respond to funeral homes. At least I didn't. And when I walked through the doors and onto the somber patterned carpeting, it was the first time I'd ever seen the inside of the place. What did it matter, first time or thousandth? The thing is, my knees went weak. That's why I was glad Father Bill had agreed to come with me to the viewing. We both knew walking into a place like this would be a tough test of my resolve. In any case, Bill propped me up until I could force some string back into my legs and spine.

I think maybe Annie was right. I was a coward. Over the last two years I'd missed several funerals of family and friends. At first I didn't bother making excuses, hoping that the grieving family would understand my reluctance to be present. Then as time passed, I would make excuses about work or illness or whatever I could think of at the moment. Eventually I stopped making excuses and sent flowers instead. I'm sure there were people out there really upset with me, but talk about impotent bullets. What could their disappointment do to me that life hadn't already?

It was a viewing only insomuch as you could view Tommy's coffin. The lid was closed. I expected it would be. With half of his head missing when I found him, I figured it would be a lids-down affair. And it wasn't much of an affair at that. Besides Bill and me, there was Smudge, Richie Zito, Al Roussis, and his partner, Dan Hellman, a guy I only knew a little bit. I'd asked Bill along because I wasn't sure I could manage this without a shoulder to lean on.

There was a shabby priest on hand as well who looked more interested in staying awake than in giving his blessings to the dead or solace to the living. It had been Zee on the phone to me the day before as I was pulling out of St. Pat's. He said he had made arrangements to bury Tommy, that as his friend it was the right thing to do. Who was I to argue the point? Male bonding is an irrational thing. It was impossible to know exactly why Richie felt close to Tommy or why he felt obliged. For Tommy's sake, I was glad he had someone to look after him in death.

I made the rounds, shaking hands and making introductions. Al and his partner hung back, but it was hard to hide in a big room with so few people in attendance. Al knew Bill and, like me, couldn't help calling him Father Bill. That was how everyone connected to the Suffolk County Police Department knew him and thought of him. One of Bill's strength was intuiting when to be present and when to fade. One look at Al Roussis and something told Bill it was time to fade, to make small talk with the shabby priest or take a trip to the men's room. Dan Hellman did not possess Father Bill's intuition and had to be told to disappear.

Al said, "Dan, give us a minute."

Hellman, good-looking in a bland sort of way, made a face, but did as was suggested to him.

"I thought you said you weren't involved with this mutt, Gus. Now you show up here."

"Until Zee called me yesterday afternoon, I had no idea about this. I mean, Christ, Al, I found the poor schmuck. I think maybe his coming to me in the first place got him killed."

I knew I shouldn't have said that even as the words were leaving my mouth, but the past two years had left me less guarded about what to say and when to say it. I'd never liked hiding or lying, though the job sometimes imposed the need to do those things on you.

His eyes got big. "What makes you say that?"

"Just a feeling," I lied, shrugging my shoulders. "Look, he comes to me on Tuesday and he's dead on Thursday. Maybe I'm just doing the math, but I was bad at math."

"Just a feeling, huh?" He was shaking his head, disbelieving. "So, you have any feelings about why coming to you might've gotten him killed?"

"His kid."

"What about his kid?"

"My guess is that the dad's murder is connected to the kid's murder," I said.

"Believe it or not, Gus, even my rocket scientist partner figured that one out."

"I didn't say it was the most brilliant idea since sliced bread. You asked me if I had a feeling and I answered the question."

"You're right. Sorry. I guess the question I should have asked is, do you have a sense of how the father/son murders are connected?"

I lied again. "No."

I wasn't even sure why I lied. I wasn't usually a reflexive liar. I wasn't even usually a liar. It would have been easy enough for me to tell Al about Kareem Shivers. About this thing he claimed Tommy Delcamino had, the thing he'd thought I had, and probably suspected I still had. The thing that, if I was to believe Shivers, someone else apparently thought I had, too. I don't know. Maybe I didn't like having my integrity questioned. Or maybe I felt some sense of obligation. If I'd only heard Tommy out . . . If I'd only been kinder . . . If I hadn't kicked his ass out of the Paragon . . . If. If. If. Or maybe it was that my life had been so valueless for the last two years that I wanted to hang on to something. I'd explore that with Doc Rosen when we met again after the holidays. For now I had to deal with it myself.

"So you don't think your old house getting tossed is connected to this?" he said as if he'd thrown a live grenade into my lap.

I tossed it back at him. "Word gets around fast. I seem to be a popular subject of discussion around the squad room water cooler these days. Things musta changed a lot since I put in my papers."

"How so?"

"Come on, Al. We're talking two homicides here, four months apart, and a break-in. Different precincts, different squads, and everybody seems interested in my business. When I was on the job, there were times the right hand didn't know what the left was doing. Shit, there were times the index finger didn't know what the thumb was doing. What, is the department issuing daily updates on me or what?"

He ignored that. "Whatever."

I took that as my cue to walk away, but I didn't get too far.

"Listen, Gus, you wanna fuck around with Lou Carey and that asshole Paxson, be my guest, but don't get in my way."

"Fair enough, Al. Just a few things, since you didn't return my call."

"What?"

"The ballistics. What killed Tommy?"

Roussis thought about that for a second. He didn't owe it to me to tell me anything, but under the tough-guy shit he was pulling today, he really was a good guy.

"A .357 Magnum, hollow point." Al threw his chin at the closed coffin. "You saw what it did to him."

"I did. And the other bullets, the ones fired at me?" I asked.

"Nine mil. Standard stuff."

"Good thing. If my leg had gotten hit by the ammo that killed Tommy, I wouldn't be standing up so well. How about my—"

"You'll get a call on your weapon. Not my responsibility."

I shook Al's hand. He shook it back, but didn't let it go.

"What?"

"I know you're holding back, Gus. Don't. Come clean and walk away. In any case, walk away."

"That a threat, Al?"

"That's good advice from an old friend, is what it is. Walk away."

He let go of my hand and I walked away, but only as far as the other side of the room.

"This was good of you to do, Zee," I said to Richie. He was painful to look at, hunched up and gnarled as he was. His eyes were red, but not from tears.

"He didn't have many friends in this fucking life, Tommy. I know what that feels like."

"What about the Maniacs?"

"That was different. Sure, I had some friends with the Maniacs . . . that was different," he repeated himself. "I used to think the Maniacs was family, you know, but it was business. A different-looking kinda business from the outside, but it was business. Fuck them guys."

I wasn't going to argue with him, and besides, he didn't seem interested in talking anymore. I nodded for Smudge to meet me out in the hallway.

When he did, I noticed his eyes were red, too, and not from medical marijuana. I'd spoken to this guy only once and for not more than ten minutes, but I knew he had really loved Tommy Delcamino. I think he was probably the only person in that room who was there out of love and not from some sense of obligation or guilt. I was glad Tommy had one true mourner. Everyone deserves at least that.

In his own way, Smudge was as hard to look at as Zee, maybe harder. To look at him was to know his history. To know he'd been bullied and picked on and rejected his whole life. When I looked at him, I just knew that I was right to have given up on God. No perfect being could ever hang the burden on Smudge that had been hung on him. No one would swoop in to rescue him. Love wouldn't find its way to him. He was born fucked, would live fucked, and would die the same way.

"Thanks for being here," he said in his nasally lisp.

"Sure. I'm glad to be here."

He smiled what passed for his smile.

"Listen, Smudge, do you know if Tommy was hiding something valuable? Do you know what it was?"

"Nah. Nuh-uh." He shook his little head furiously.

I didn't believe him.

"You sure?"

Now he was nodding his head as fast as he had shaken it before.

"Okay. I'm glad Tommy had a real friend like you."

This time when Smudge smiled, it was broader. He didn't care about his malformed mouth or the giant birthmark or anything. Then he dissolved into tears.

I patted his shoulders and walked back into the viewing room. I pulled Father Bill over into one corner.

"How would you like to play cop for a day, Fa—Bill?"

Kilkenny lit up like he'd just won the lotto. "Ya bet, Gus."

"That little ugly guy I was just talking to."

Bill's face saddened just at the mention of Smudge. "What about the poor man?"

"I think he knows more than he's saying, but I don't know what it is that he's not saying."

"And what is it, Gus, you propose I do about that?"

I smiled at him. "C'mon, Bill, no one has to school you on talking to the bereaved. And trust me, that man has lost the only friend he's ever had in this world. Talk to him."

Bill understood what I was saying beneath the words. *If you could deal with my grief, Bill. If you could get me to talk to you after John died, you can deal with anyone.*

He nodded. "I'll call you when I need you to come fetch me."

After we spoke, I went and did the thing I most feared to do in coming here. I put my knees to the kneeler before the coffin. I wouldn't cross myself. I wouldn't do that for anyone, not ever again. I apologized to Tommy in my own head, but I wouldn't mouth the words. I knew it was a waste of time. That Tommy was beyond the reach of my apology and that there was no God to hear my silent thoughts. But some things are worth doing just because there's value in the things themselves. And when I stood up, the shabby priest made some noises to the others about saying some prayers. I didn't bother sticking around. I had a place to go, a place I never wanted to go to. It was a day for that.

24

(MONDAY NOON)

drove up Larkfield Road and turned right onto Bellerose Avenue. As
I got close to Vets Park, it came back to me, all the worst of it. My
heart felt like it was clawing its way out of my chest. My hands were
wet on the wheel and the pulse in my head was hammering. I was blind
for the tears as I pulled into the narrow parking lot in front of the basketball courts. The sun burned alone in the sky against a wall of cloud-
less blue, its rays sharp as a serrated edge. But the sun was a liar, for
although it hurt my eyes to stare into its featureless face, it gave me no
warmth, no comfort. The parking lot was empty. There was no comfort
in that, either. The courts were deserted, the half-moon backboards and
nets swaying in the nasty December wind.

I could not get out of my car. I told myself I wanted to. I *did* want
to, but I was inert, my hands glued to the steering wheel. If there were
only some kids around, if only there were a hoops game, if only there
were some sign of life, it might have been easier. Instead there was only
the wind. I'd come to hate the wind. I'd been to John's grave many
times. At first, all I did was cry at St. Pat's. When I ran out of tears,
there came the months of silent rage. Then came the long talks with his

headstone. The ones I thought I would never have. I felt so foolish that first time, looking around to make sure no one was close enough to hear me or see my lips moving. Then I stopped caring. Why not? I'd stopped caring about everything else. Then came days like yesterday. Silent days, standing with the caretaker.

But this wasn't his grave. This wasn't the church. This wasn't the funeral home or the hospital. Those were all places where his body had been. Places where all that was left of John was bone and flesh in the shape of my son, but wasn't my son. By the time he got to the hospital, he was somewhere else. Somewhere in the wind. His memories, his sense of humor, his love and anger, his smarts and his fuckups gone. Just like that—gone. What was left of him lived now only as pieces of the people who had known him. And when we were dead and in the wind, he would be forgotten. That was still the hardest part to take, that he would be forgotten so soon.

Don't tell me about photos and videos, about how we live on in those things. It's a lie. Go get out one of your parents' photo albums, one with their parents and grandparents in it. Look, really look carefully at all the faces of the dead. Sure, you may recognize your great-grandparents, but you might not. Even if you do, what of their relatives, what of their friends? What of the faces unrecognized? That is our future, our shared destiny: all born to be forgotten.

Then I was out of my car, walking up the short concrete steps to the courts. I leaned my head against the metal fencing, trying not to look at the red, green, and white painted courts. All the years of play had worn the paint down to blacktop from baseline to foul line. Dillon Donovan, John's best friend, had told me how it happened and explained just where it happened, too.

John had come down with a rebound and was taking the ball back, dribbling out to the three-point line when he went down. We thought he slipped or something. Maybe that his knee gave way, you know, but he wasn't moving or nothing. When I went over to see what was up with that, he wasn't breathing, Mr. Murphy. I swear. I checked. He was already gone, I think. It was on the second court, you know, the one we always played on, the one closest to Larkfield.

I'd never come to see where it happened, not because it was where he died, but because it was the last place he was alive. Until I knelt in front of Tommy's coffin, I hadn't been sure I could handle it. I didn't think I'd ever be able to. I stared out at the court through the fence. He'd died just a few feet away from where I stood on the other side of that fence. I looked out at where he had taken his last breath. I shook my head. I didn't walk out onto the court. I didn't say anything. I was numb. I turned and stared up into the sun, using my hand as visor. I turned away and let the cold wind wash over me. And then I forgave it for carrying my son away from me forever.

I sat in my car for a few minutes, trying to find what was left of me. I'd done some difficult things in my life, but being here, at these courts, was nearly as hard as watching a group of faceless, nameless strangers lower my son into the ground. When I was fully aware again, my cell phone was in my hand and I could hear muted ringing in my ear. I'd called someone. I wasn't sure who, exactly. Then there was a voice.

"Dad . . . Dad . . . are you there? Mom, I think Dad butt-dialed me."

"No, Krissy, sorry," I said, maybe too loudly.

"Are you okay? You sound weird, Dad."

"I'm fine. I'm fine." I said it twice to convince myself. "I just wanted to hear the sound of your voice."

"Are you sure you're fine? You sound spacey. Is everything all right?"

"No, but I'm better now."

"Where are you? Mom and I can come get you."

"No, Krissy, definitely not. I'm good. Please leave your mom out of this. She's not real pleased with me just now."

"Yeah, I heard. That's fucked up, Dad, about John's room. Mom spoke to Mrs. Sherman. We're going to go over there later and, I don't know, fix his things up."

"Krissy."

"What?"

"I love you. I love you very much."

There was silence from her end of the phone, but it was very loud, full of grief and heartache. The three of us had become experts on such silences.

"Listen, kiddo, I'm not gonna lecture you about anything or tell you what to do with your life, but please stop and think the next time you mean to do something like you did last week. We have all lost so much already. It's just got to stop sometime."

The silence dragged on, and then, "Okay, Dad, maybe you're right."

"I love you, Krissy."

"You, too, Dad."

I hung up after that. What else was there to say?

The Northport Manor on Larkfield Road was a second-rate catering hall, its façade recently redone in a Long Island version of Tuscan design. Which is to say that a Tuscan would have thought it looked like an ugly building from Long Island. Still, it was an improvement over its previous incarnation, which had been kind of a concrete and stucco bomb shelter. Like Marsden Brothers, I'd driven past the Manor every shift for the last ten years I was on the job, but unlike the funeral home, I'd been inside the Northport Manor many, many times. Our old house on Pinetree was no more than a five- or ten-minute drive away.

The huge parking lot behind the place was nearly as empty as the lot by the basketball courts had been. Nearly. There was a black Cadillac CTS Coupe parked in one of the four reserved spots and a white BMW 650i convertible parked right beside it. The Caddy belonged to Freddy Guccione, the Manor's owner. The Beemer belonged to Meri Klein, the banquet manager. Freddy and Meri were married, just not to each other, and they'd been having an affair for years. Cops get to know the business owners in their patrol sectors, and the owners sometimes share more than they should. Half the cops I'd worked with, men and women alike, were fucking around, so I wasn't judging Freddy and Meri.

They were happy. That counted for a lot in this world. If I hadn't been completely convinced of that before John's death, I was now.

There were a few other cars in the lot as well: a drab Camry, a Ford Focus, a brown Honda CR-V, and a ridiculous lime-green Plymouth Neon with a custom paint job covered in several coats of clear-coat lacquer. The old Neon was tricked out with elaborate rims, low-profile tires, ground effects, and a rear spoiler. I had a pretty good sense of who the funky Neon belonged to. The man I had come here to see: Ralph O'Connell.

O'Connell's was the first name listed in the notebook that Tommy Delcamino had left behind. According to Tommy, O'Connell and TJ had been best friends and had run together for a long time. A lot of that running had involved "some stupid shit" like drugs and stolen car parts, but Tommy also mentioned that O'Connell was "a good kid who didn't mean no harm." Tommy didn't think Ralph had anything to do with TJ's murder, but thought he might have some idea of who did.

I walked into the Manor through the back entrance as I had countless times before, both as a cop and as a father bringing his kids to confirmation parties, bar mitzvahs, sweet sixteens, and sports awards dinners. I was glad to see Freddy had redone the interior as well, and more successfully than the outside of the place. Meri noticed me right away and excused herself from a young couple she'd been pitching about a wedding. As she approached, the light of recognition went on in her eyes. Her handsome, overly made-up face crinkled into a beaming smile. Then it happened. She remembered there was something she knew about me, something bad. Remembering what it was took the crinkled joy right out of her. The arms she had been extending to hug me out of happiness became a hug of pity and remorse. I accepted her embrace. What else could I do? And there was genuine warmth in her touch.

When she pushed away, she said, "I heard about John Jr., may he rest in peace. I'm so sorry, Gus."

"Thanks, Meri."

"Are you okay? How's your family coping?"

I didn't answer. I didn't really have to.

She shook her head. "I'm such an idiot. In college I majored in stupid questions. I got all As."

"Don't beat yourself up over it. I know you meant well."

She sagged, relieved I'd let her off her own hook. "You here to see Freddy? He didn't mention you coming—"

"No, sorry. I'm here to see your maintenance guy, Ralph O'Connell."

Meri made a face like she'd just bitten into a frozen steak. "Ralphy! What do you want with him?"

"Just to talk."

Her expression told me she didn't quite believe me, but she said, "Suit yourself, Gus. He's in the Venice Room, setting up the dance floor for an office Christmas party we got booked for later. When you're done with Ralphy, please stop in to say hello to Freddy. He'll be mad if you don't at least say hello."

I winked at her, hugged her, and left her to deal with the young couple.

The walls of the Venice Room were covered in cartoonish murals of canals, gondolas, bridges, and weathered old buildings. An oversized crystal chandelier hung from the domed ceiling. Fake columns and ornate moldings were also part of the décor, but the intended effect was ruined because all the lighting was turned way up. A muffled bang got my attention. Over to one side of the large room, a guy in blue coveralls was dropping big wooden squares off a cart onto the carpeting. I walked up behind him and he half turned to take a look at me. His unwashed coveralls stank of a week's worth of sweat and the room smelled of last night's rubbery prime rib and over-roasted potatoes.

"You Ralphy O'Connell?" I asked, though I knew it was him. Even if Meri hadn't told me so, I would have recognized his doughy face from the photo next to his name in Tommy's notebook. He was in several of the other photos, too, that Tommy had stuffed into the backpack. I had to give Tommy D. props for compiling this notebook like he had. It was really unusual, especially for someone who wasn't very bright. Whether it was love or guilt that drove him to do it was beside the point. What mattered now was that he had.

O'Connell turned back and continued his work. "You a cop? Took you long enough to come talk to me. TJ's dad—" Ralph stopped talking and crossed himself.

"What about Tommy D.?"

"He's dead."

"I know that, kid," I said, even though he wasn't a kid, not really. "I'm not here about Tommy. I'm here about your friend, about TJ."

That got his attention. He stopped what he was doing, stood straight up, and looked me in the eye. *His* eyes were full of regret. I was good at spotting it.

"What about TJ?"

"C'mon, kid, let's you and me get a cup of coffee across the street."

He didn't argue, just brushed his palms on the thighs of his coveralls, and started walking.

(MONDAY AFTERNOON)

Frank and Joey, the guys from the Larkport Deli across the street from the Manor, were glad to see me, their happiness not dampened by my portable dark cloud. If they didn't know about my son, I wasn't going to tell them. It was a great relief to share a greeting unlike the one I'd had with Meri, a greeting unfreighted with funeral wreaths and dirges. We spent a few minutes busting each other's chops the way we used to when I'd stop in for coffee on a rainy night. Ralphy had just taken his coffee and found a quiet two-top in the back.

"That your green Neon parked behind the Manor?" I asked as I sat across from him.

He nodded and kind of grunted, unsure what to make of me. Even so, he couldn't hide his proud smile at the mention of his car.

"That paint job alone must've cost you some major bucks."

"Fuckin' A— Sorry, man."

"I've heard the word before, kid. And just so we're straight, I'm not a cop, not anymore. Used to be. So anything you say to me stays with me."

I sipped my coffee, let its familiar taste bring back pleasant memories. I wanted to give Ralph a chance to absorb what I'd said. Give him a second to try it on for size and readjust his expectations. His time was up.

"So tell me about your car."

"I did most of the work on her myself. Well, me and TJ." Then Ralphy looked around to make sure no one else was listening and lowered his voice anyway. "TJ kinda helped me get some of the parts, if you know what I mean. He was something with cars."

"You and TJ were tight?"

"Real tight. TJ and me, we went back to, like, third grade together." He laughed quietly, a sad smile on his crooked mouth. "Man, we got into all sorts a shit together, me and TJ."

"That's what I hear."

"It wasn't like that. I know TJ's dad thought our crew was a bunch of assholes, but we were just friends out doing some stupid shit, is all. What group of guys don't get into some stupid shit, like, when they're young? My dad, he says that the only thing that separates the good guys from the bad is getting caught."

Spoken like the yoyo who always got caught, I thought. I was pretty tired of hearing this self-serving crap. I'd listened to it the whole time I was in uniform, though like all bullshit, there was a little bit of truth behind the stink. Everybody speeds, yet only a tiny percentage of speeders gets ticketed. So, are the unlucky schmoes who get caught the only bad guys? I just kept quiet, hoping Ralph would fill the empty space with chatter. I sipped my coffee and listened. He obliged.

"Sure, I mean, we got in trouble for some stuff. We sold a little weed and shit, sold some fake X at clubs. Mostly we boosted cars or stripped 'em down for parts." He shrugged and made a face. "No biggie. We never hurt nobody."

I had neither the time nor inclination to explain to him how wrong he was, not that he would have understood if I had.

"Listen, Ralph, I'm not here about any petty shit. Before he got killed himself, Tommy Delcamino came to me and asked me to help him find out who'd killed his son. Can you think of anybody who might've wanted to do TJ any harm?"

The expression on his meaty face changed, churning from smug innocence to something that looked like fear. Beads of liquid formed on his upper lip, and that wasn't the only part of him that was sweating. I got a powerful whiff of him and immediately stuck my nose into my coffee cup.

"Don't hold back on me now, Ralph."

"Come on, man. That was over, like, a year ago." He stood up. "Thanks for the coffee and all, but I gotta get back to—"

I gave him my best fish-eyed cop stare. "Sit the fuck back down, Ralphy. Right now!"

He puffed out his chest. "Yeah, or what?"

I stood up and leaned across the table so my face was very close to his. "Or I'll kick your chubby bee-hind up and down Larkfield Road. Then I'll drag you across the street and have Freddy fire your ass. That work for you?"

He sat back down. I hesitated for a second before I did, too.

"Talk to me, Ralphy."

"TJ got me mixed up in a drug deal that went to shit."

"A drug deal. That's a start. Give me the details."

"Black Molly," he whispered. "It's like Ecstasy on steroids."

"I know what Molly is, Ralph. I was a street cop for twenty years."

"Okay, okay. Man, you don't have to bust my balls. So TJ comes to me and says we can kill it and that he can get a hold of a shitload of this stuff if we can scrape a few thousand bucks together."

"Ralphy, no offense, but—"

"I had some bread saved up, like ten grand I was gonna use on the Neon."

"You gave it to him just like that?"

"Just like that," he said. "We was best friends. TJ never done me wrong the whole time we were buds."

"And where did a guy like TJ get his stake?"

Ralph looked everywhere but at me. I could see he was about to lie.

"Don't start lying to me now, Ralphy. I'm not looking to hurt you here."

"Car parts."

"See, that wasn't so hard. So you gave him your money and he had his money and what happened?"

"We fucked up, I guess. All of a sudden we had like a shitload of product and we didn't know what to do with it all. I mean, we used to sell maybe a hundred bogus pills in a good month. Now we had thousands of the real thing and we had no idea how to get rid of them all, you know? And we was scared, too. We could do some real serious time inside if we got caught with that much stuff."

There's an old adage I learned my first week in the academy: If criminals had half a brain, the cops would be in trouble. TJ and Ralph O'Connell were exhibits A and B. They had thought about only half of the equation, about getting cheap product, without considering how they would sell it. All they saw were dollar signs at the end of the road, not the road itself. Was it any wonder that losers stayed losers?

"What did you guys do?"

Clenching his lips together, he made that reluctant little-boy face again.

"Don't make me pull teeth, Ralph."

His fleshy cheeks turned bright red and he was sweating again. "We tried to give it back."

I didn't want to laugh, but couldn't help it. When I stifled myself, I said, "There's no do-overs in drug dealing. No money-back guarantees, but I guess you found that out, huh?"

He hung his head and nodded. "We didn't try to give it back, not exactly. We tried to sell it back."

"I figured. Who were you dealing with?"

He shrugged. "I don't know, some little nigger from Wyandanch that TJ knew."

"Watch your mouth, asshole."

He was perplexed. "What's up with that?"

"This is the twenty-first century in Suffolk County, Ralphy, not Selma in sixty-four."

"Who the fuck is Selma?"

"Never mind. This dealer you guys tried to sell it back to have a name?"

"Little nig—"

"Mouth!"

"Little black gangsta called Lazy Eye."

"Where'd this go down?"

"Some house in Wyandanch somewheres. I don't know. TJ drove."

I finished my coffee. "What happened?"

"Nothing good, man."

"Meaning?"

"Lazy Eye offered us four grand back, take it or leave it."

I winced involuntarily. "Ooh, twenty cents on the dollar. That's not much of an offer."

But O'Connell's face brightened. "TJ told the little—told Lazy Eye to go fuck himself. That we wanted our stake back. Lazy Eye laughed at him and that's when things got all crazy and shit. TJ pulled out a nine mil and—"

"TJ was carrying?"

"That night he was. I'd never seen him carrying before. He always said that his dad taught him that guns were trouble."

"So."

"So when TJ pulls the nine, we hear this *cha-ching cha-ching* behind us. We turn around and there's these two other brothers standing there. One of 'em, the big one, he's holdin' a pump-action shotgun at us and the other one's got a nine on us. I nearly shit myself. Lazy Eye swiped the nine mil outta TJ's hand and cracked him across the face with it. Split his lip open and his cheek was bleeding like a bastard."

I didn't exactly get a chill when he mentioned the men holding the guns on them, but I did get a feeling in my gut.

"And what happened to you?"

He turned red again. "Little fuckin' nigger kicked me in the nuts, but I fucked him for that. I puked all over his rug."

"Listen, Ralph, you say nigger again and I'll do more than kick you in the nuts. Understand?"

He nodded.

"You're lucky to be alive," I said.

"Don't you think I know that?"

"The two brothers holding the guns on you, they have names?"

He shrugged. "Who the fuck knows? I was interested in their guns, not dating them."

"Describe them to me."

"One was skinny and chill. The other one was big all over. Why you so interested in them anyways?"

"Let me worry about why, okay? How big was the big man?"

"Taller than you. Huge." Ralph held his hands about a foot apart. "Had the biggest head I ever seen and that shotgun looked tiny in his hands. The other guy just looked mean."

I guess I was smiling.

Ralphy didn't like that. "What's so funny?"

"Sorry. So what happened after that? After you puked and TJ went down?"

"They threw us a beatin', kicked the ever-lovin' crap out of us. Broke my ribs. It was two months till I could breathe right again. Took a whole mess a stitches to close the cuts on TJ's face."

"So you were out twenty grand and the drugs."

"I told you we fucked up."

"I'd say so. This was about a year ago."

The coffee seemed to turn bitter in his mouth. "Yeah, almost exactly a year."

"And how were things between you and TJ after that?"

"Not so good. I only saw him once after that. He called me a few times when he was high, swearin' he'd get me my money back, sayin' we should get together and shit, but it never happened. I guess he felt bad about how it went down and gone to shit and how we got the crap beat outta us. I mean, I cared about losing all the money—who wouldn't, right? And I didn't like the beatin' I took, but it wasn't all his fault. We were buds forever, you know? And the whole thing kinda woke me up. That's when I got a straight job. Workin' across the street . . . it's not much, but it's something. Freddy and Meri, they're all right."

I understood that. Boy, did I ever. I was glad to hear that the shit-head had some ability to reflect on his life and make a change.

"You say you only saw him once again. When was that?"

Ralph actually got teary-eyed and had to gather himself before he could speak. "The week he was killed, maybe a day or two before. He showed up at my folks' place, outside my bedroom window at, like, three in the morning. It was really weird."

"How so?"

"He was really high and he looked like he'd taken another beatin'. He had a black eye and his bottom lip was all swollen and shit."

"Did he want something, to borrow money or to hide out or any-thing?"

Ralph shook his head and smiled a goofy smile. "No. That's the thing. He brought *me* money. Twelve thousand bucks. He said it was to pay back the money he lost me on the drug deal, plus interest."

"Where'd he get twelve thousand bucks?"

"He wouldn't tell me. All he would say is that he'd hit a fuckin' jack-pot and made the score of a lifetime. He said that the twelve grand was just the beginning, that the two of us would be flush for a long time."

"Did he explain any—"

He shook his head. "Nope. I'm just telling you how it was."

"What about his face?"

"He said it was no big thing, just part of the price he had to pay for the score."

I didn't like it. "That's all he said?"

"Man, I was still half-asleep and I was happy to get my money back. I didn't know that was the last time I was going to see him. If—" He choked up again.

"Okay, okay. Take a minute."

After he collected himself, he stood again and said, "I really got to get back to work."

"One last thing and then we're good, Ralphy."

"What?"

"Did you tell any of this to the cops?"

If derisive laughter had a defining sound, Ralph O'Connell was making it.

"Cops! What cops? Nobody ever talked to me about this or nothing else. I know you think I'm stupid, but I'm not that dumb. I know TJ's dad musta given my name to the SCPD, but nobody came knockin'. And I sure as shit wasn't going to them. *Hey, fellas, you wanna hear about our fucked-up drug deal?* I mean, come on."

"If they had knocked, would you have told them what you just told me?"

He shrugged. "Some of it, yeah. I wouldn'ta told them about the drug deal or nothin' like that, but I woulda told them something."

That much I believed.

I stood up, too, and offered him my hand. "Okay, Ralph, thanks. I appreciate you talking to me this way."

He shook my hand and said, "I hope you find the fuckers who hurt TJ that way. He was the best friend I ever had and I'm never gonna have a friend like him again. I know he was a fuckup, but nobody deserves to die like that."

I handed him a card from the Paragon, one with my cell number written on the back, and told him to call me if he could remember anything else that might help or if he wanted to talk. He just kind of nodded and left. I followed a few minutes later.

I considered going back through the Manor and stopping in for a word with Freddy, but decided I wasn't up for it. I did have to go collect Father Bill at some point before heading in for that night's shift. I'd also had enough sadness, enough looking back and behind me for one day. As I walked around the Manor, I looked up to see where the sun was. It was lower in the sky, having taken its false promises toward New York City and points west.

(TUESDAY, LATE MORNING)

Driving the Paragon courtesy van was, at least at the beginning, suicide prevention. Yesterday had proven as much to me. When I first started driving the van, I would have never been able to bear going to a viewing or to see the spot where John's lurking heart defect had taken him away from us. Back then, the job of driving the drab and faceless guests to and from the hotel was a way to hold the walls back from closing in on me. Even so, there were times it almost didn't, times when the walls nearly touched. Times when I'd been the sad cliché of the drunken ex-cop sitting for hours at the edge of his hotel bed, alternating between the bottle and the barrel of his gun. Like I'd told Pete McCann when he'd tried to warn me off, running wasn't in my nature. That didn't mean running didn't tempt me. Sometimes, temptation is the only thing a man has to hold on to.

It wasn't that I thought pulling the trigger would take me to a better place. I didn't believe in better places or those horseshit Mitch Albom books where you have reunions in heaven with the blissful dead. Where you are magically forgiven for your sins, your guilt stripped away so you don't have to feel shitty for the harm you've done. A few well-meaning friends had given those books to Annie and me, saying they would bring us comfort. Well, no. My faith in God, heaven, and rainbow-coated unicorns named Sparkles had vanished a long time before my son's death. You don't really understand the insidious nature of faith until you lose it. And once I saw faith for what it was, I never wanted it back.

That's what Bill and I had argued about when I picked him up outside Smudge's dingy little house in the North Bay Shore. Bay Shore was like a lot of towns south of the LIE on the island. Between Montauk Highway and the water, it was quite beautiful, with some kickass mansions to rival the ones on the more famous Gold Coast. Places that had thriving little downtown areas with restaurants and shops. But wander a little farther north, up past Sunrise Highway toward Brentwood, and Bay Shore's resemblance to West Egg or East quickly dissolved. Not unlike Huntington Station, whole swaths of Bay Shore had fallen prey to drugs and gangs. Smudge lived on a side street off Fifth Avenue in a tiny shitbox of a house that looked like it had been a drug den or a grow house. Half the windows were covered with plywood and the other half were coated with a filthy yellow film. I was glad that I picked Bill up in front and didn't have to go inside.

Outsiders don't get Long Island; most New Yorkers don't understand it. They can't see past the beaches and the sound, the Hamptons and the Gold Coast, the country clubs and the marinas. But most of the island isn't about Gatsby. A current of poverty and violence roils beneath the surface here, too. A lot of senseless blood gets spilled. What off-islanders see is the 24-karat gilding along the edges where the money flows, not the fool's gold in the middle where the rats race as hard as in the city and where the stray dogs lie in wait.

Bill sighed when he got into my car. "Poor man."

"No kidding. I bet you he can count the happy days in his life on one hand."

"You were right about him, Gus. He's lost the only true friend he's ever had in Mr. Delcamino."

"You guys talked?"

"Some in the cab on the way over from the wake."

"Some?"

"For the most part we prayed together."

I blew air through mostly closed lips and shook my head at him. "So, Bill, you got him to drink the Kool-Aid, huh?"

"Nothing of the sort. He's a devout Catholic. Went to mass before coming to the viewing earlier. Goes every day."

Now I was really shaking my head in disgust.

Bill said, "Care to put that into words for me, Gus?"

"Christ, Kilkenny, you sound like my shrink. He's always saying stuff like that."

"Obviously a sage fellow, but I'm interested for my own sake. What's all the head shaking and sound effects for?"

"Did you take a good look at Smudge, Bill? Your lot are so fond of saying things like 'Jesus is love.' Well, where's the love in Smudge's life? God sure hung the 'Kick me' sign on him. The guy's probably never had an ounce of love or a woman's affection in his entire life."

"We all have crosses to bear, Gus. You know that better than most. And the man's had God's love and his faith to sustain him."

"It wasn't God's love or his faith that sustained him in prison, Bill. That was Tommy Delcamino."

"God's love comes in many forms."

"Like in the form of petty thieves."

"Sometimes, yes."

"And who sustained TJ Delcamino while he was being tortured to death and his father while someone was putting a .357 hollow point through his head?"

"When we first met, I understood your bitterness, Gus. And I certainly understood your loss of faith, but surely you are a different man now," Bill said, his voice rich with yearning.

"I lost my faith a long time before John died. You know that."

"But for you to look at a fella like Smudge and know he still has faith—"

We were at a red light and I raised my hand like I was on traffic duty. "Bill, I've missed these little talks of ours, but did you find out anything from Smudge that will help me find who killed Tommy or his son?"

Bill flushed a little. "Sorry, Gus, I suppose I was getting a bit carried away there."

"No apologies necessary."

"He was raised by his maternal grandparents. Never finished high school and has been in and out of trouble of one sort or another his whole life."

"That's all well and good, Bill, but—"

"Patience, Gus, I'm getting there. I believe him. I don't think he knows anything more than what he's told you. I could be wrong, mind you. He is wary even of me."

"Do you think he's afraid?"

"For a man like him, fear is second nature. It hurts to say so, but I think he lives in fear and it has always been so. Whether he is more afraid of something specifically now, I can't begin to say. He has faith, but very little else. Does that help you at all?"

"In a general way, yeah, it does. I may have to circle back to him and have a heart-to-heart about his pal Tommy, but for now I have other fish to fry."

"Do you mind if I were to see him again? He does seem so alone in the world. Priests, even broken-down old ex-priests, understand loneliness better than most."

"Sure."

But that was yesterday and I'd moved on from Smudge and my lack of faith to Kareem Shivers. Unlike Bill's chat with Smudge, mine with Ralph O'Connell had opened up some doors for me. He might not have realized it, but Ralph had finally given me something to work with. Actually, he'd given me a lot. Now it was time to see what I could do with it.

Exit 50 on the LIE puts you onto Bagatelle Road, a thoroughfare of two divergent natures. Just off the LIE, you're in the prosperous bedroom community of Melville. Melville is a new-money town of large houses—most tasteful and lovely, some not so much—three-car garages, cobbled driveways, swimming pools, cabanas, manicured lawns, and fancy gardens. People still worked for their money here, but not at McDonald's. No, they were more apt to own the McDonald's. Go a few miles south along Bagatelle and you're in the heart of Wyandanch. Wyandanch, where TJ and Ralphy's drug deal had gone wrong, was a poor, largely African-American enclave and the busiest area the SCPD dealt with. While it wasn't nearly as dangerous or crime-ridden as East New York in Brooklyn, it was about as rough and dangerous as Suffolk County got. So it was no wonder to me that many of the folks who made it out of Wyandanch, whether they were doctors or lawyers, ballplayers or boxers, hip-hop performers or professors, moved only a couple of miles north up Bagatelle. It was a way to stay close and yet be a million miles away all at once. Kareem Shivers had bought into that notion, too.

I'd done a little checking up on Mr. Shivers after dropping Bill off in Massapequa. I hadn't been able to shake the feeling I'd gotten when Ralphy was describing the two men who had provided the gun and muscle for Lazy Eye. They sounded an awful lot like Jamal and Antwone to me. So I put in a call to Detective Alvaro Peña. You want to know anything about drugs and/or gangs in Suffolk County, Peña is the man. Drugs and gangs often went hand in hand, and Alvaro had served on just about every drug and gang task force the SCPD had formed over the last fifteen years. Problem was that as much as I wanted to talk to Alvaro, that's how much he didn't want to talk with me.

"What'd you do, Gus, fuck the chief of detective's wife or something?"

"What kinda shit are you talking now, Alvaro?"

"No shit, Gus. You are bad medicine, bro. You're more radioactive than Fukushima."

"And how did this word come down? They send out a memo about me?"

"Come on, man. You know how it works. Word comes down how word comes down. You're off limits. You don't know who first whispered in whose ear, but the word gets spread and it's been spread about you. I'm hangin' up now."

"You owe me, Al, and I've never cashed in that marker. I'm cashing it in now. Without me, your girl's in Riker's instead of Rutgers."

"I know, Papi. I know. I owe you big-time for what you did. What you need?"

"Kareem Shivers."

There was a short but very loud silence on his end of the phone. Then, "What about him?"

"Everything about him."

"You got a week? That's one bad puppy there."

"No offense, Al, but I didn't need you to tell me that. I've met the man."

"No shit? And you're still breathing?" His voice was full of surprise. "His street handle is K-Shivs. He was a Golden Gloves champ, turned pro, but he got head-butted bad in, like, his fifth professional fight by some Russian guy. Word is the butt was intentional because the Russian was losing bad early before they went to the scorecards. Cracked Shivers' skull and forced him outta that game and into another."

"Drugs?"

"Bingo, Gus. Now you almost sound like a cop."

"Fuck you. So . . ."

"First he was just muscle for the Danch Boyz. They're like an off-shoot of the Crips. But it didn't take him too long to go from being the muscle to being the man. My guess is you can figure out how he managed that. Word is that he gets a taste of every packet of heroin and coke that gets sold in the county. You seen the latest stats on heroin deaths in Suffolk? It's bad and getting worse, Papi. But the fucker is Teflon. Smart and brutal, but only when he has to be. He knows too much blood is bad for the cash register."

"But you guys haven't been able to lay a glove on him?"

"Bad pun, Gus. No, we haven't been able to touch him. And get this shit, the bastard even has a carry permit."

"Yeah, I know. I found out the hard way."

"You a cat or something, 'cause you must have a lot of lives. What's your business with this guy?"

"I'm not sure yet." It was only half a lie.

"Be careful with him. He's not only brutal and smart, he's lucky . . . too lucky."

I opened my mouth to ask the next logical question, but shut it. I knew exactly what he meant. Besides, had I asked, he wouldn't have answered the question.

"Okay, Al, thanks. That should do me. We're square."

But he didn't let me go that quickly.

"Gus, I'm not joking around here about Shivers. Remember that Russian who head-butted him?"

"Yeah."

"About a year after the fight, they found his body in a plastic garbage bag in front of a Russian Orthodox church in Sea Cliff. His skull was caved in, all of his teeth had been pulled out, and every bone in his body was broken. Worse than broken, they were all crushed. The Nassau County ME said they had tied off each part of the guy's body and they had broken him apart one piece at a time. Said the Russian was a long time in dying before his skull got hammered. Don't cross Shivers, Gus. Just don't."

"Strictly Marquess of Queensberry for me and K-Shivs, Al. I promise."

I didn't need Alvaro to tell me that Kareem Shivers was a nasty piece of work, but until we spoke I had no idea of just how nasty. Nor were the details of how Shivers had disposed of the Russian boxer lost on me. Although TJ Delcamino's murder wasn't an exact duplicate of the Russian boxer's, there were a few inescapable similarities: the brutality, the broken bones, the body in the plastic bag. I tried putting all that out of my head as my tires *tha-dump tha-dump*ed down the streets of Melville.

Except for a giant concrete and brushed aluminum monstrosity across the street from Shivers' address, the houses on the block were an eclectic grouping of attractive homes that had been built just before the era of the faux Victorian McMansion. Many, if not all, had been expanded well beyond their original footprints, but skillfully so. There were no lean-tos or mismatched sheds, no vinyl siding or fake stone façades to be seen. Shivers' house was a big brick Colonial with a lawn and garden that had been landscaped to within an inch of its life. Nothing about the place screamed for attention, but I'd run across men like Shivers before. They were territorial and they had a need to mark their turf as their own. Some were just more subtle about it than others.

I parked at the edge of the driveway, took a deep breath, and closed my car door behind me. There was a steel-gray Mercedes 500 S coupe parked in his semicircular driveway, and when I saw the vanity plate—K-SHIVS—I smiled in spite of myself. But the subtle marking of territory didn't stop there. For as I made my way up to the house along the flagstone path that followed the arc of the driveway, I noticed that each stone had etched into it what looked like a skull and crossbones. On closer inspection, I saw that wasn't it at all. The skull was actually a dangling boxing glove and the crossbones were a pair of crossed pistols. The name "Shivers" was written in a beautiful cursive beneath the crossed pistols. At least the black Escalade from Friday night was nowhere to be seen. That gave me some encouragement that I might be able to chat with Shivers without having to go through Antwone and Jamal. I got the sense that they weren't the forgive-and-forget types and might want a little payback for how a fat old white man had embarrassed them in front of their boss.

As I neared the double front doors, I saw that the boxing glove and pistols motif was repeated in the brushed nickel door knockers. Even before I reached the threshold, I heard the fevered pacing of dog paws and nails against a hard surface behind the doors. I was less and less thrilled at the prospect of returning Kareem Shivers' driver's license. During drug raids, I'd had the misfortune of coming across some badass dogs. Dogs who'd been trained to be killing machines. Dogs who'd had their vocal cords cut so that they could come up on you silently. I was in no mood to find out if K-Shivs had one on the premises. Whether I was in the mood for it or not, I was about to find out. I rang the doorbell and took a step back.

(TUESDAY, LATE MORNING)

The young woman standing barefoot in the empty doorway couldn't have been much older than Krissy. Striking to look at, she still had some girlishness about her. I don't know how to explain it, exactly. Maybe it was something in her mischievous smile or the careless, loose-jointed posture of her curvy body. It could have been the fire in her green eyes or the lingering fresh-cut lemon scent of her shampoo. Her hair was a long cascade of water-darkened reddish curls that flowed over her shoulders and framed her triangular face. Her skin was the shade of medium dark coffee lightened with a few drops of cream, yet her face was dotted here and there with freckles. She wasn't wearing very much: a short black T cut to expose her flat abdomen and black silken panties that went most of the way toward rendering my imagination useless.

The dog at her calf, a happy-faced and excited chocolate Lab, was no man-eater. The pup, still months away from growing into her legs and paws, ran to me, jumping on my leg, yelping, wagging her tail a mile a minute, begging to be petted. I knelt down and obliged, rubbing her belly, scratching under her chin. Then the woman in the doorway called the pooch back in with a whistle and a snap of her fingers.

The pup hesitated for a second, then gave in and left me to wipe fur off my hands.

"Missy ain't learned to be choosy with her affections jus' yet," she said.

I stood. "Have you learned?"

Her face hardened, the girlishness vanishing. "Whatchu want, yo? I ain't got time for this shit, Detective."

Detective! Maybe I did smell like a cop. I didn't do anything to disabuse her of her mistake.

"Is Mr. Shivers at home?"

"K-Shivs ain't here, yo," she said, bobbing her head slightly as she spoke, gesturing with her hands. They were fine hands with beautifully manicured piano fingers. There was a diamond-encrusted ring on her left hand. The featured stone, cut in a star shape, was enormous.

"Nice ring. You engaged?"

She smiled, staring down at the ring with love and pride. Then she remembered I was there.

"He ain't home," she said.

I turned and pointed at the Mercedes.

"That says different."

She laughed at me, but she hadn't mastered the art of the sarcastic laugh just yet. That came with time and experience she lacked. "Shit, you thinkin' K-Shivs only have one ride? That's *my* ride, fool."

I was right, then. Shivers really was marking off what he perceived as his property. But regardless of the accuracy of my insights, I wasn't big on some twenty-year-old calling me a fool.

"You're sure Mr. Shivers isn't at home?" I asked, my voice steely as I could manage.

"You deaf or somethin'?"

"No, and I don't appreciate your bad manners. I know your mama didn't raise you to talk to people that way. To call your elders fools. I've been nothing but courteous to you."

She glared at me, the fire in her eyes no longer so innocent. "Don't you talk about my moms."

"Even if I'm saying something good about her? What's your name?" I asked in my best cop voice.

"I don't have to—"

"What's your name," I repeated, my voice even more stern.

"Katy. Katy Smalls. Why?"

"There, that wasn't so hard was it? I have a daughter your age, Katy, and—"

She wasn't interested. "What's this about, anyways?"

"Drugs and murder."

She blanched a bit, then got control of herself. Next, she leaned in close to me, the lemon scent of her shampoo much stronger now. "Y'all best get gone, Detective, if you know what's good for you."

I stepped back. "Yeah, why's that? Kareem gonna get Jamal and Antwone to kick my ass?"

She curled her finger at me to come even closer. When I did, she put her lips close to my ear, her breath warm and moist. She whispered, "If you don't leave and leave me be, Kareem and his boys will be the least of your worries."

Her voice was soft but it had teeth, sharp ones. I couldn't help but wonder if her threats did.

"Okay, Kareem's not home, but do me a favor."

She was wary, but curious, too. "Depends."

I handed her Shivers' driver's license. "Give that back to him for me, will you? Tell him to give me a call."

Her hard, ghetto girl persona seemed to vanish in a sea of confusion that brought back the girlishness to her face and posture. She seemed not to know what to say, so I saved her the trouble.

"Thanks. It was nice to meet you, Katy. Please give that to Kareem."

She nodded. I waved and turned. I waited for the door to slam shut behind me, but it didn't. I turned back to see Katy still standing in the doorway, her eyes watching my retreat. She seemed a very lonely figure there in the big empty doorway. Then, finally, as I reached my car, she closed the door. She was a very exotic-looking young woman. She wasn't wearing very much and she smelled great, but I just kind of felt sorry for her. I wasn't even sure why. What I was sure of, though, was that I wasn't the only person interested in Kareem Shivers. I knew that because as I drove down his street, I passed an older, unmarked Crown Vic about as inconspicuous as a lump of coal in a basket full of eggs.

(TUESDAY AFTERNOON)

When I got back to Bagatelle, I turned right and drove those few miles south into Wyandanch to find Lamar English's address. Unlike the listing in Tommy's notebook for Ralph O'Connell, which had come complete with notes and a photograph, the listing for English was nothing more than a name and address. And if I hadn't spoken to Ralph, Lamar English would have been an afterthought. A name in a notebook full of names. A name I probably would have passed over. I'm not even sure where Tommy D. had gotten English's name and address. I suppose he might have culled it from his late son's cell phone. With Tommy dead, might-haves and guesses were the best I was going to do. And frankly, I was guessing now. Was it purely coincidence that Lamar English's initials matched Lazy Eye's? Maybe. Probably. But of all the listings in Tommy's notebook, the only address in Wyandanch was this one.

Long Island is divided up into townships within the counties, and when you neared the end of Bagatelle you crossed from Huntington Township into Babylon. Babylon indeed. Even as you crossed the invisible line marking the transition from Melville to Half Hollow Hills to Wheatley Heights to Wyandanch, from whiter to blacker, and from

more money to less, even the name of the street changed. Bagatelle
Road became Conklin Avenue. Long Island was like that, a place of
demarcations: some subtle and gradual, some obvious and ugly.

Wyandanch is black and poor and the system is set up to keep it
that way. When you're a cop, you're not supposed to think about things
like that. Not supposed to have opinions about what makes drugs, violence, and poverty possible, about what causes them to flourish and
persist. You're just a triage nurse with a badge and a gun, treating the
victims and passing them along. But I wasn't a cop anymore, and when
I was, I had opinions. I wasn't blind or deaf or dumb then. I wasn't now.
The point is that the system is set up to maintain the status quo. And a
big part of that system is about those lines of demarcation.

Whenever I tell people there's something like one hundred thirty
distinct school districts on Long Island, they stare at me like I'm the
dolphin boy at the Coney Island Freak Show. But I've got no fins or
flippers and the facts are the facts. The reason we have so many school
districts in a relatively confined area is a simple one: de facto segrega-
tion. And the formula to perpetuate it is equally simple: The more
exclusive the address, the smaller the district, the higher the property
taxes, the less likely lower-income families can afford to live in the area.
Sometimes life really is as simple as A then B then C. You don't need
white hoods and burning crosses when you've got high property taxes.
It's one of the great unspoken truths of Long Island that, in many ways,
the 1950s are still alive and well here. If Ike ran for King of Long
Island, he'd win in a landslide.

From the air or on Google Earth, Wyandanch would look like any
working-class suburb, a place of small single-family houses with tiny
lawns on crooked blocks and boulevards—some numbered, some
named after the revered dead, others for forest animals and trees. And
as you came closer to earth, you might hear the amens coming from the
storefront hallelujah churches. You might even think it was like any
other working-class suburb. Only, people lived on the street, not looking down at it, and the streets of Wyandanch could be mean ones.

Lamar English lived on Jefferson. His yard littered with car parts. Stacks of old batteries, worn tires, bent axles, and shock absorbers. The concrete driveway stained with dark splotches of engine fluids. There were matching grooves in the concrete where steel ramps were placed so that someone, presumably Lamar, could access the undersides of cars. It didn't take a genius to figure out that Lamar and TJ shared an interest in cars, but it was a leap from there to conclude that their business extended beyond stolen car parts to drugs. I'd have to have a look at the man before taking that leap.

As I got out of my car, a little boy, no more than five or six, walked right up to the edge of his yard to have a look at me. His house was next door to English's. He was a handsome kid, very dark-skinned, and had already developed eyes wary of white faces.

"You lookin' for Lamar, mista?"

"How'd you know that?" I said, smiling at the kid.

"I'm smart."

"I bet you are. What's your name?"

He didn't answer the question. "Lamar ain't home."

"You know where he's at?"

The kid shook his head.

"You know when he'll get back?"

More head shaking.

"Did you see him leave?"

He stopped moving his head, but he didn't speak, either. He was thinking about it. In other words, he had seen Lamar leave. He just wasn't sure he should tell me. Over the kid's left shoulder, the front window shade was pulled back to one side.

"Does Lamar like to work on cars?"

That made the kid smile. "He shows me stuff sometimes."

The shade moved again.

"You like Lamar?"

Lots of nodding.

The front door opened. I needed to find out if my guess about Lamar was right or if I was wasting my time.

"That funny eye of his, doesn't it scare you? It scares me."

He smiled, shaking his head proudly. "No. That don't bother me."

"Whatchu want with my boy, mister? Whatchu botherin' my boy for?"

The woman coming toward me was pretty, a little heavy, and wasn't much more than a teenager herself. Her son had her face, her eyes, too, and I could also see where he'd gotten his wariness from.

"Sorry, ma'am, I wasn't bothering your son. We were just discussing Lamar, your next-door neighbor," I said in a voice that was calm and steady. "Isn't that right, little man?"

The boy nodded, but it still didn't sit well with his mom. She grabbed him by the arm and shouted at him, "Isaac, how many times I tol' you, don't be talkin' to people you don't know. Now get on in the house. Right now, boy."

Isaac did as he was told, but before he did, he turned back to me and waved. I winked at him.

"That man, he ain't none of our business," Isaac's mom said, her pretty face full of worry. "You wanna talk to him, you talk to him your own self. Leave me and my boy out of it."

I tilted my head at Lamar's house and asked, "You ever hear anyone refer to him as Lazy Eye?"

"Mister, I don't know nothing and I don't wanna know nothing about that man. You understand me?"

"Better than you think I do."

She turned and fairly ran back inside. I didn't bother calling after her. I sat on Lamar's steps for another hour, but he didn't show. Just as I went to twist my ignition key to leave, my cell phone buzzed. When I realized who it was, I couldn't stop smiling.

I pulled into her driveway as she asked me to. Casey lived in a nice little saltbox on St. James Parkway in Nesconset. The house was only a few blocks away from the wooded lot where TJ Delcamino's body had been discovered. I tried not to think about the murdered Delcaminos as I drove to pick her up. Murder doesn't usually make for light and airy first-date chitchat. Then again, maybe it did. How the hell would I know? I hadn't been on a first date, or any other kind of date, in over two decades. The other subject I tried not to think about was Annie. While she wasn't the only woman I'd ever been with, she was the only woman I'd been with for a very long time. And while Saturday's encounter with her had ended badly, very badly, it was hard not to think about the intensity and comfort of it. But if this was a new start, I had to keep those subjects out of the conversation even if it was impossible to keep them out of my mind.

Our plans were a little hazy. I would come over and we'd figure out what to eat after I got there. One thing that had improved in Suffolk County over the last decade or so was the quality and number of restaurants. When I was growing up here, the choices were, to say the least, limited. A big night out to eat for us when I was a kid was the Ground

Round or really mediocre Chinese food. Even the pizza sucked pretty bad and it's hard to make bad pizza in New York. I'd stopped at the big wine store on Main Street in Smithtown and picked up a good bottle of Cabernet. Well, I didn't know if it was actually good. I wouldn't know that until I tasted it. I might not even know then. I wasn't much of a wine drinker. What I knew was that the salesman said it was good and that it was expensive. Experience had taught me that those two things weren't always synonymous. I'd also done a goofy thing that I regretted doing the second I did it: I stopped at the florist in Lake Grove and bought her a half-dozen mixed roses. It was too much, I thought, but I was never a man to take things back. I didn't suffer buyer's remorse because I didn't usually buy things on impulse. But that was who I used to be. And while I didn't know who I was now or would be, I knew I was no longer that man. More important, I knew what real remorse was. I could teach a class in it.

I was sitting there in the front seat of my car, arguing with myself about whether or not to bring the roses with me when someone rapped on the driver's side window. I jumped out of my skin. When I got back in it, I saw Casey standing at the side of the car. I rolled the window down.

"You stay out here any longer, I'm going to charge you rent."

"Sorry."

She leaned into me and kissed me gently on the lips. "Stop saying sorry to me, Gus. I was only teasing."

My heart was pounding pretty good after that kiss and I almost said sorry again. All I did was smile up at her. And when I got out of the car, the wine and flowers came with me.

As we walked the short distance to her front door, I noticed that Casey was dressed in a way that I wouldn't have expected her to be dressed. The quality of food around the area may have taken a great leap forward, but generally it was casual dress. There wasn't a thing casual about the simple but incredibly flattering black dress she wore. It did this kind of magical thing in that it both hung slightly loose off her yet seemed to cling to every curve on her body. It was cut low enough to reveal some cleavage, but not in a sort of crass come-and-get-it way. And the hem was cut high enough to reveal the muscular beauty and pleasing taper of her legs, yet not so high that it was an invitation. Her sheer black stockings had a thick seam in them that ran down the back of the leg and into the black stilettos on her feet. I liked that she wanted me to look at her and like what I saw. I did, very much. I liked it that she liked how she looked, too.

When we got inside I knew that I'd been duped, but gladly so. The house smelled of cooking, of a clash of great, mouth-watering scents. Of sweet frying butter and olive oil. Of roasted garlic, rosemary, oregano, torn basil leaves. Of balsamic vinegar, raw red onion, and arugula. But playing the deeper notes beneath all the other incredible aromas was the intense smell and heat of baking chocolate. Casey had cooked for me, for us. She saw the look on my face.

"When I thought about dinner and about us going out . . . for me, I'd waited for it for so many months, I wanted it to be only about the two of us talking."

"Is that what you usually wear to talk?"

She blushed a little, but not too much.

I handed her the flowers. "Here, these are for you. This," I said, waving the wine bottle, "is for us. And if my nose is working okay— veal, right?—it's the right color."

"Thank you, Gus. And your nose is still working very well."

Dinner was pretty great—pounded veal, lightly breaded and sau- téed, topped with arugula, shaved red onions, and chopped tomatoes with a balsamic reduction over a bed of spinach. And the salesman at the wine shop hadn't lied to me after all. The red was great and went per- fectly with dinner. It also went well with the chocolate cake. What doesn't go well with chocolate cake? But the best part of the meal didn't involve eating or drinking. It was the conversation. For two years I'd been as good as frozen. I'd forgotten the simple joy in getting to know someone. It was an incredible relief to hear about someone else's life. About their tragedies and small victories.

I was right about Casey's hands. She worked for a living as an occupational therapist, treating kids at a center for the physically and learning disabled. *There's a lot of teaching by showing and by doing. You'd be amazed at how many times a day I do things we take for granted, like tying sneaker laces or buttoning a shirt. You can't imagine how much satisfaction there is for the kids in accomplishing those things.* I didn't have to imagine. I could see it in her face. She didn't have any kids herself. *My husband couldn't have kids, and when you do what I do for a living . . .* She never finished that sentence, but she didn't really have to. She'd loved her husband, a contractor, but, like Annie and me, they'd gotten married young. *After fifteen years together, neither one of us could figure out why we should stay married anymore.* Eventually we got around to talking about me. About Annie, Krissy, and John Jr. After I'd finished talking about John, she stood up from her seat and came over to me. She placed her right index finger across my lips and took me by the hand. I let her take me.

Now the damp skin of her back was pressed against the warm, damp hair on my chest. We were breathing heavily, my heart pounding against Casey's skin so that it seemed to reverberate through her flesh and bone and back into my arms. The room was silent of noise but loud with unspoken questions. *Was I any good? Did you like it? Was I what you'd dreamed I would be? Was I better than your wife? Your husband? Should I have been gentler? Rougher?* Like that. I don't suppose it ever changes regardless of age or experience. First times are always so fucking weighty, so fraught with judgment and anticipation.

Like I said, it was over twenty years since I'd been with somebody else, and in that there was a kind of anxious joy. In not knowing her body. There was a surprise at every turn. At the mildness of her taste. Her scent. In the soft gasping sounds she made and the rippling muscle contractions of her body in orgasm. But the sex was the easy part, the natural part. What happened in the aftermath between us was the highwire part of the evening. Finally, when her body settled down, her breathing almost normal, she spun herself around in my arms to face me. She stared at me, hesitated, then kissed me.

"I like the way I taste on you," she whispered, her voice husky and a bit drowsy.

I curled my hand around a hank of her. She had another small aftershock. "I like the way you taste on me, too."

We kissed again and fell into a more comfortable silence, Casey closing her eyes and nestling her head in the crook of my upper arm and chest. With no apparent prompting, she was laughing that goofy laugh of hers.

I was confused. "What?"

"I was just so afraid of you for so long."

"That's funny?"

"I guess I'm just laughing at myself," she said. "If I had only had the nerve, we could have—"

It was my turn to put my finger across her lips. "No, Casey. If you had approached me even two weeks ago . . . I'm just happy we met when we did."

"You believe in fate?"

"Just the opposite. I believe in chance."

I kissed her again, hard on the mouth, pulling at her hair and rolling on top of her. Neither one of us was laughing or talking.

This time when we were done, we were done. We were like two spent fighters hanging on to each other in the middle of the ring, praying for the final bell. I stroked her hair. She twirled her fingers through my chest hair. Some of the unspoken questions had been answered. Some not. But at least enough to satisfy the both of us and to let us fall easily into sleep.

(WEDNESDAY MORNING)

Casey was gone by the time I opened my eyes. I realized that she hadn't asked me about the bandage on my left calf. I was thankful for that. Nor had we gotten around to the subject of her real name. I hoped we'd have plenty of opportunities to get to that. The truth was I was glad she was already gone, because I woke thinking of Annie, though not out of some sense of misplaced loyalty or guilt. It was about moving on. My old man wasn't generally full of wisdom. Mostly he was full of misery and Jameson, but this one thing he said to me about not looking back has always stayed with me.

He'd driven me to his old Brooklyn neighborhood on a Sunday afternoon. I don't know why. I don't know why he did half the shit he did. Maybe he thought it would be a bonding experience. More likely he was just lonely and I was the best he could do for an audience on short notice. My old man always liked an audience. Anyway, as he drove around he would tell me stories of things he and his friends had done on this street here and that one there. He drove by his old school-yard and told me about the stickball games he'd played and the fights he'd had there. After the schoolyard, we drove a few blocks and parked. My old man didn't say a word, just stared across the street at a beat-up row house for what felt like an hour. When I finally got up the nerve to ask him whose house that was, he turned to me with a look on his face I'd never seen before or since. He was on the verge of tears, I think.

"Once you leave a place, don't look back. Move on. Once something is gone, John Augustus, it's gone forever." He cupped my cheeks in his hands as he said the words. It was the only tender moment we ever shared. "Once you step ahead, keep going, 'cause there's no going back. Even the people you thought you knew . . . they change, too."

He never told me who lived in that row house. The next time I asked him, a few weeks later, he smacked me. I didn't ask again. I'd like to think it was his first love's house, or better still, the house of the girl that had gotten away. I even gave her a name: Colleen. I liked to think of her as a redheaded beauty because it helped me explain away some of the bitterness and cruelty he showed to my mom. I don't imagine it really mattered who lived in that house because I've never forgotten that moment, nor what he said. It's not like that sentiment hadn't been expressed a million times before or since. There was nothing very original about my old man. It was just that look in his eyes that I'll never get out of my head.

So yeah, I woke up thinking about what last night with Casey meant for Annie and me, for whatever was left of Annie and me. I laughed to myself because I realized that my dad had said those things to me about not looking back when that's exactly what he was doing. That had never occurred to me before. I wondered if it ever dawned on him. By the time I'd showered and borrowed Casey's toothbrush and got dressed, I wasn't thinking of my dad or Annie. I was thinking of Casey. I left her a note, asking if we might try for a real dinner out sooner rather than later and promising to call. I was thinking about something else as well as I closed her front door behind me. I was thinking of my proximity to where TJ Delcamino's body had been found.

Just like I did the first time I visited the scene, I parked by the wooded lot on Browns Road. As I drove up, I noticed that the plug had been pulled on the naughty Santa display on the roof of the house to my left. Oh, Santa and the reindeer were still up there, but unlit and unmoving. Long Islanders can be a fairly tolerant bunch as long as you don't screw up their food orders or take too long making their lattes. Oh yeah, there's one other thing that makes us mental: property values. A mother lioness protecting her cubs has nothing on a Long Islander whose property value is threatened. Apparently, the neighbors had had enough of Santa mooning the passersby. At least Alvin and the Chipmunks were still at it, crooning away. *You can keep the singing rodents, but Santa's gotta go!* When I looked to my right, the baby Jesus was staring at me from his mat of plaster straw, his blue doll eyes unblinking. I turned away, deciding I'd have a talk with the owner of the rude Santa house.

As I made my way over to the front door, it occurred to me that Christmas was fast approaching and that I hadn't done any shopping. That first year after John died was the worst. Beginning the week of Thanksgiving—and what the fuck was I supposed to be thankful for, exactly—stretching through New Year's was pure hell. There were reminders of John everywhere and in everything. And with the reminders came the reminders of our loss. From moment to moment, we relived his death over and over and over. Even the ads for Black Friday did us in. *Remember that year Johnny had his heart set on that one Transformer and you got up at four and . . .* There wasn't a sight, a sound, a smell, a taste, anything, that wasn't an assault on my heart. Nothing that didn't bring him back to me and rip my guts out anew. Annie and I were well into our descent into oblivion by then, but the three of us were still living together in the house in Commack that year. And I think it was our Christmas there that finally drove us out. I made a mental note to call Krissy again when I was done, maybe take her for dinner.

Close up, under the façade of bad taste, the Chipmunk ranch house was actually not a bad place at all. The cedar shingles that covered it weren't chipped or split and had turned that lovely shade on the color spectrum between silver and faded brown. The driveway had been recently repaved and the lot was almost completely free of fallen leaves. No mean feat for a house next to a wooded lot and in an area full of big old oaks and maples. The storm door was new and the front entrance featured a shining red door and tasteful stained-glass side panels. It was hard to tell much about the rest of the place given the vast array of lights and decorations that covered the house and yard.

A balding man with a wisp or two of gray hair on his head opened the front door but not the glass storm door. He was in his seventies if a day and seemed about as happy to see me as a sad-faced oncologist. I knew the look. No need for words. *I don't want any. Go away!* That's when I shouted to him, "I used to be a Suffolk County cop." I threw my thumb at the lot that his property bordered. "I need to talk to you about the body they found there in August."

Did I think that approach would work? I wasn't sure. I thought it might, but what else was I going to say? I didn't want to lie to the guy. I mean, if he gave me the chance, I could prove I'd been on the job. If I got caught in a lie, he'd shut me down.

He smiled and opened the storm door. "A cop? Sure, come on in."

I guess he hadn't heard me completely through the storm door, but as he was welcoming me, I wasn't going to correct his mistake until I was in his house.

When he closed the doors behind me, he said, "So, you're on the job?"

"Used to be. Twenty years, mostly in the Second Precinct. Now I'm working private."

"Twenty years, huh? Maybe you know my grandson. My son's boy. He's on the job in Suffolk, too."

"Maybe. What's his—"

"Pauly Martino. He works in the Marine Bureau."

"Sorry, Mr. Martino. I've been off the SCPD for a few years now and never had much to do with the Marine Bureau."

He shrugged his old shoulders. "I figured I'd ask."

"Sure. My name is Gus Murphy." I offered him my hand.

Shaking it, and holding his other hand up to his ear, he said, "My hearing ain't so great anymore. Gus, is it?"

I nodded.

"You wanted to talk to me about the lot next door?"

"About the body they found in the lot last August."

Now he was nodding. "Yeah, sure, sure. C'mon into the kitchen. Sit."

I was thinking of my old man again, about how he would never have shown a stranger the courtesy that Mr. Martino was showing me. I followed Mr. Martino into the kitchen. We passed through a nice living room with a beautifully decorated tree. The whole house was well kept and clean as could be. But the kitchen really looked lived in, comfortable, a bit dated. Very 1970s. A lot of Harvest Gold appliances. I sat at the breakfast nook by the bay window. Had it been a sunny morning instead of a blustery gray one, it would have been a great spot to greet the day. Mr. Martino stood over by the coffee maker.

"Want some?" He wiggled the pot at me.

"That would be great. Milk and if you got a Sweet'N Low—"

He pointed at the crystal sugar caddy on the table and the little cow-shaped milk dispenser. Over the first cup, we got the small talk out of the way. He showed me photos of his grandson in uniform, of his great-grandkids. Told me that he did all the Christmas decorations because it reminded him of his days growing up in the Bronx and of his own kids.

"They thought that silly Santa thing on the roof was just the best thing ever, and the grandkids, they loved it even better. That's what all this stuff is for, to make the kids happy. For all the years we lived here, nobody ever said nothing about that Santa, but now people are all so sensitive. You know what I mean, all politically correct?"

I told him that I did.

"I got a registered letter in my mailbox the other day from the town telling me that the neighbors were complaining and that the seasonal display on my roof was in violation of some town ordinance or something like that. They told me to shut it off or take it down or I was gonna get fined or something. I was gonna fight it, but what for? No one got a sense a humor no more. And since the wife died last year . . ."

No need for him to finish that sentence, certainly not for me.

"I bet it was that jerk next door that started the trouble," he said, unwilling to let it go. "That *strunz* on the other side of the lot. Family's lived there since October and the prick won't even wave to me."

That gave me the opening I was looking for. "So they didn't live there when the kid's body was found in August?"

"Nah, the Cohens, great neighbors, they moved to Florida soon as they sold the place. Nice Jewish family, never bitched once about the decorations the whole time they lived there. The wife, Leah, she used to bring us over latkes at Hanukkah. Nice people, but everyone's moving away. Who can afford to live on the island anymore? The property taxes could choke a horse."

Mr. Martino didn't know it, but his rant had just saved me a visit. No need to talk to the neighbors with the doll-eyed baby Jesus if they hadn't lived there when TJ's body was discovered. I brought the subject of the body back up again. Unfortunately, Mr. Martino was more eloquent on the subject of property taxes.

"There wasn't anything to see," he said, pouring me more coffee. "By the time I got out there, the police had everything all blocked off. If there was something to see, I didn't see it. I musta been back in the house and asleep by the time they removed the body."

To be polite, I stayed a few more minutes, sipping at the unwanted second cup of coffee. I thanked him for his time and hospitality and asked him again if he was sure there weren't any details he might've forgotten about that August night. He shook his head no, but as I was leaving, he told me to hold on a second.

"You know, Gus, there was one thing that didn't make no sense to me. The next day I read in the paper that the guy they found dead in the woods was a nobody. I don't mean to speak bad of the dead or nothing, but—"

I put my hands up as a gesture of understanding. "I get it, Mr. Martino. Go ahead."

"He was a small-time car thief, right? So it made me scratch my head."

"What did?"

"That night, the night they found the kid, I figured whoever he was had to be pretty big or connected, because why else would the chief show up?"

That got my attention. "The chief? The chief of detectives?"

"Nah." Martino made a face. "The chief! The big chief. The big Irishman. What the hell is his name? My grandson is always talking about him."

"Jimmy Regan?"

Martino smiled. "That's the one. The big Irishman," he repeated.

"The chief of the department showed up?" I said as much to myself as to Martino. "How did you know it was him?"

"Are you kidding me? All the guys in uniform looked like they were gonna kneel and kiss his ring. And that red hair . . . you can't miss it. My grandson tells me the guy's a legend."

"He is."

"Besides, I overheard the blond girl who's now our local COPE officer whispering to her buddy. They were as surprised as I was to see the guy."

I tried not to react. I'm not sure I hid it very well. I thanked Martino again and got out of there. I knew Jimmy Regan well enough, though not so well to call him a friend. Mr. Martino had spoken the truth, though. Jimmy Regan was a cop's cop: fearless, loyal, dogged, street smart, and just plain smart. I never had much use for the brass. They were usually the ambitious men and women who tended to pick their spots and polish their own apples. Not Regan. His rep was well-earned. I knew guys who had come up with him. To a man they said Regan was the best cop they ever saw. Always the first guy through the door. Never asked anyone to do anything he wouldn't do himself. I had a sergeant who used to tell Regan stories like he was talking about Babe Ruth. Yet, odd as it was for the chief of the department to show up at some petty thief's murder scene, it wasn't out of the realm of possibility. He might have just dropped in unexpectedly to observe his troops handle the situation. But what Jimmy Regan was or was not doing at the murder scene was beside the point. What mattered was who killed TJ Delcamino, and that's what I was thinking when I turned the corner to talk to the folks whose back fence bordered the wooded lot.

(WEDNESDAY AFTERNOON)

I found the local COPE—Community Oriented Police Enforcement—officer parked in the lot of the Lake Grove Village Hall on Hawkins Avenue. Wedged between Nesconset and Centereach, Lake Grove had no lake and no grove, but it did have the Smith Haven Mall, the largest indoor mall in the county. That counted for a lot around here. Kind of like having the biggest cathedral, only better.

The COPE officer was yakking on her phone as I approached her unit and she adopted her best cop face—hard and falsely neutral. Beneath all your expressions as a cop, there's a requisite air of implied threat. I'd seen a lot of *Don't Fuck with Me* expressions in my time, most of them on the faces of other cops. It made sense. Your expression, the way you carried yourself, they were your first lines of defense. Having a Glock on your hip and a vest under your shirt doesn't make you invulnerable. Most of the time you're either outnumbered or outgunned. Sometimes both. Someone gets it in his head to fuck with you, he's going to fuck with you no matter what.

She sat low in the driver's seat, her head not reaching much above the wheel. She had wiry blond hair pulled back tight in a ragged ponytail and her skin was that weird shade of orange/brown that screamed tanning salon. As I came closer to her car, she stepped out and gave me more attitude. She was taller than Casey, about five seven, and not petite. Her neck was thicker than I expected and her upper torso was severely V-shaped. That was obvious in spite of her vest. *A gym rat*, I thought. I don't know. You're a cop long enough and you get a sense of these things, of who people are beneath the things they show you.

Everything about her body language told me not to come any closer, so I put my hands up and I smiled.

"I come in peace," I said.

She laughed at that and then took a careful look at me, squinted her eyes. "You look familiar. You on the job?"

"Retired. I was in the Second for most of the career."

"Then you must know Pete."

"McCann. Yeah, I know Pete."

She got that look on her face. She wouldn't have been the first woman in the bag to fall for Pete. I thought about warning her that she'd only have a shot with him if she was with someone else. The charms of being willing and available were lost on Pete. You also needed to be taken. I decided not to go there.

"What's your name?" she asked.

"Gus Murphy."

She got another look on her face, but this one wasn't about Pete McCann. "I heard about your son. Sorry. That was a few years ago, right?"

"Two. Thanks."

Her face changed again. She seemed almost in physical pain. "Does it get any easier, losing your kid, I mean?"

"Easier, yeah, but never better. You got kids?"

"A little boy, Drew."

I smiled. "I know what you're thinking, but you can't really protect him the way you think you can. Just let him live his life as happy as he can."

I didn't even know where those words came from. They just seemed to force their way out of my mouth.

She was smiling again, shaking my hand. "Corinne Durney. What can I do for you, Murphy?" Apparently, word hadn't drifted down as far as COPE about me being off limits.

Closer to her now, after her iron handshake, I felt pretty sure I was right about her. Durney definitely worked out. You could see by the way she held herself when she was relaxed that she was proud of her body, but not in a coy way.

"You lift?"

She lit up like the Christmas tree in Mr. Martino's living room. "Not as much as I used to. Used to compete when I was younger. So how can I help you?"

"I'm doing a little fishing around on my own these days and I was talking to Mr. Martino on Browns Road."

She laughed. "Guy with the Santa on the roof, right?"

"That's him."

"Nice man, too bad his grandson's a prick," Durney volunteered without prompting. "A real hothead, Pauly is. They threw him on the Marine Bureau to keep him away from people. So why were you talking to the old man?"

"We were talking about the body found in the woods next to his house last August. I heard you were there."

Her face hardened. "Why you interested?"

"Officially? I can't say."

"Unofficially?"

"Unofficially, I'm working for a party who's interested in purchasing the lot and is looking for any way to drive down the price."

That lie came out of my mouth a little too easily to suit me, but come out it did and it seemed to work well enough.

"Okay," she said, "I was there that night. It was only about a month before I got assigned to COPE."

"How you like it?"

She shrugged. "It's all right. Boring sometimes, but boring ain't so bad, right?"

"Right."

"Neighborhood guy walking his mutt called it in. By the time I got to the scene, the place was already crawling with other cops."

"You see the vic?"

Durney made a sick face, shaking her head as if to rid herself of the memory. "Wish I hadn't. Kid was in bad shape. Bloody. Burnt-up. Bones sticking through the skin. He didn't go easy."

"Anything unusual about the scene?"

"Other than it was in Nesconset? Not the kind of thing we generally run into in the Fourth."

"I heard Chief Regan made an appearance," I said as innocently as I could manage.

"I guess that was pretty unusual. He got there about a minute after me and I was on scene pretty quick. But like I said, the scene was already turning into a zoo."

"Anybody figure out why he was there?"

I could tell there was something she wanted to say, but she didn't know me well enough to trust me, so I gave her a push.

"C'mon, Durney. It's all off the record here."

"The first detectives on the scene, they were pretty shocked that Chief Regan showed up. I overheard them talking."

"About what?"

She shrugged again, but I couldn't tell if she meant it. I don't think she liked the excited tone in my voice or where these questions were going. I could see her retreating. She even took a step back.

"I don't know," she said, pulling her unit's door open. "Look, I gotta get back out on patrol. Again, sorry about your son. Merry Christmas." She got sat behind the wheel and slammed the door shut. "It's okay to wish you Merry Christmas, right?"

"Sure, Durney. Merry Christmas to you and yours. And don't worry about talking to me. Your name will never come up." I handed her a Paragon hotel card with my cell number on the back. "You wanna talk again, let me know who those first detectives on the scene were, give me a call."

She took the card. "Or not."

"Or not."

She put the window back up and the car in reverse. The car rolled back a foot, stopped. She rolled her window down. "And not for nothing, Murphy, that bullshit about a buyer wanting to drive the price down . . . you gotta do better than that. That lot is designated green space. It can't be built on. You want me to be straight with you, you should be straight with me."

"Fair enough," I said. "Here's some straight advice for you. Stay away from Pete McCann. Far away. He'll fuck up your life and throw you away. Don't let him do that to you."

She didn't say anything to that, but you could see she was thinking about it. I was glad for that much at least.

After checking back in at the walk-in clinic to have my calf wound dressing replaced, I drove down to Massapequa to have coffee with Bill Kilkenny. I hadn't seen the poor man in a year, and now I was making myself as hard to be rid of as his own shadow. I don't suppose he minded. I could have handled it over the phone, but the thing about Bill was I liked being around him when we had our chats. And the words weren't always the most important aspect of our conversations. Not *his* words, at least. It was often his facial expression or his body language that had the most impact on me. Sometimes, just the way he arched his eyebrows were his way of screaming at me, *Pay attention to this part, Gus. Pay attention carefully.*

The diner was on Sunrise Highway and Bill was already seated at the booth when I walked in. He was chatting up the waitress, asking her about her kids and her ailing husband. That was Bill. My bet was he was pals with everyone who worked in the place, front of the house and back. Probably half the regulars, too. It was his nature to listen, to give support, to comfort. Although he was fond of prescribing big doses of Jesus and the church, even when he didn't quite have faith in them himself, he wasn't ever pushy about it. And he'd never tried it with me. When we first met, he'd understood my needs better than I did.

"Well, honey, God bless," he was saying to the waitress, patting her forearm as I approached. "I'll be by to visit your husband tomorrow. Ah, here's my friend now. He's a coffee man. Half-and-half, too."

"Any pal of Father Bill's is a friend of mine," she said, gesturing at the cushion across from the ex-priest. "I'll be right back."

I slid in. "Guess I'm not the only one who can't get used to you without your former title."

He smiled a sly smile.

The waitress dropped off my coffee and creamers. I plinked the pink packets of sweetener with my index finger, ripped off their tops, and poured white powder into the black coffee. When I added the half-and-half and looked back up, Bill was staring at me.

"What?"

"Something's changed in you, Gus. To the good, I think."

Was I that easy to read?

"I met someone."

"I knew it. Good on you. Tell me about her."

"Maybe some other time, Bill, if that's okay?"

"Of course. Of course. What is it you'd like to talk about?"

I took a swallow of coffee. "Are you still close to Jimmy Regan?"

"We were quite close. Less so since I've shed the collar and before he took over the department. Why do you ask?"

"Because his name came up today."

Bill put his hand to his face, rubbing the slight stubble on his cheek. "How so, if you don't mind me asking?"

"Sure you can ask. I was speaking to the people who live near where Tommy Delcamino's son's body was discovered. It appears that Jimmy Regan showed up at the kid's crime scene and not so long after it was called in."

"I take it that his being there was somehow extraordinary."

"It's not unheard of. You know, when a cop gets shot or something like that. Or sometimes, if there's good publicity to be had for the department, the chief will show. But not usually for the murder of a low-rent car thief and drug user. His showing up for that, yeah, Bill, that's unusual. Especially when it happens in a precinct where that kind of thing doesn't often happen. You don't want to call attention to yourself and the department. You just want to make it go away as fast as you can."

"I can see that, but you know Regan," Bill said, shaking his head. "If there's a chief who would show, it would be him. He's not a man to shy away from bad press if he thought his cops needed him to be there. The man's never shied away from a tough spot in his life."

"I know. Maybe there was a good reason for him to be there." I shrugged. "I admit that. I mean, what I'm hearing is secondhand memories from people who were recounting events from August."

"There you go, then."

I shook my head. "If that's all there was, we wouldn't be having this conversation."

Bill said, "There's more?"

"Maybe."

He was confused. "Maybe?"

"From the first time I mentioned Tommy Delcamino or his kid's case to anyone on the SCPD, I've been treated like a leper."

"Surely you're exaggerating."

"No, Bill, I wish I was. I've been warned off and threatened by a whole bunch of detectives, including friends. I had a friend tell me straight out that I was poison and that word had filtered down from on high not to speak to me. You've been around the department longer than I have. You know how that works."

"I do indeed. Did this friend of yours mention Jimmy Regan by name? Did any of these men?"

"They wouldn't. And I'm not saying it was him, but it was somebody. This stuff doesn't come out of thin air."

Bill didn't speak right away. He rubbed at his stubble a bit more as he considered what I'd said.

"It's bad math, Gus. You've got two over here and you're adding it to two over there and coming up with four, but it sounds like five to me. I know Jimmy Regan too well to believe he would do anything to thwart someone trying to do the right thing. Now, I'm not saying Jimmy's a saint. By no means is the man a saint, but he was born to do right and has always tried to do right."

I felt silly now. Speaking to Bill about this had seemed like a good idea, but even as I was saying the words, I knew I'd made a mistake. How often in life do things sound like good ideas in your own head, then when you utter them aloud . . . This was one of those times.

"I know that, Bill. I've met the man, too. I know his rep."

Father Bill reached across the table and patted my forearm much as he had patted the waitress's. "No harm in discussing it. Like I said, Jimmy's no saint. What man is? But when it comes to the job itself, I think he'd sooner eat his gun than do anything to disgrace the shield. No, Gus, I think you're looking for demons where there are none to be found."

"Maybe so, Bill. Maybe so."

"Besides, what possible interest could Jimmy Regan have with Tommy or his boy? Jimmy has been off the street for many years."

"I suppose I was hoping you could explain that to me?"

Bill and I had a laugh at that. We had a second cup of coffee—I would have no trouble staying awake for my shift tonight—and then I offered to drive him home. He thanked me, but said he'd prefer to walk. That walking helped him think. Before I left, though, he squeezed my hand hard and grabbed my arm with his left hand.

"You must tell me about this woman soon."

"Casey," I said.

"Casey, is it?" He smiled so broadly it made my cheeks ache. "You must tell me about fair Casey."

"I think I need to get to know her a little myself first."

He nodded. "And, Gus . . . welcome back to the living."

I thought about saying something and decided not to. He let go of my hand and arm.

I sat in the front seat of my car, watching Bill through the diner window. He was chatting once again with the waitress. But really I was thinking of that last question he had asked me. It's funny how you can have a million thoughts and ideas of your own and a simple question can clarify everything. Was there a connection between the Delcaminos and Jimmy Regan? And if there was, what could it be? But I reminded myself not to go off on tangents, that even if I could establish a connection between Chief Regan and the Delcaminos, so what? So what if the chief had shown up at the wooded lot on that August night? I heard Doc Rosen's voice in my head. I had to stop looking at the wriggling fingers and turn my focus back down on the street. Because it was down on the street where the violence and dark magic was done. I had to stop staring at Jimmy Regan and take a closer look at Kareem Shivers. There was also another name in Tommy's black-and-white composition book that needed my attention. And I didn't need any help from Alvaro Peña or anyone else on the job to tell me about the man who bore the name Frankie Tacos.

Since I'd gotten involved with this mess, it seemed I was destined to tour Suffolk County's warts and wormholes. And by wormholes I didn't mean portals for time travel but places where human worms burrowed in to hide themselves from the light. Rusty's Salvage Yard on Long Island Avenue in Deer Park was just such a garden spot. Shouldered in among other salvage yards, concrete yards, body shops, and trucking companies, Rusty's wasn't any uglier or filthier than the other businesses along that stretch of road that flanked the Ronkonkoma line of the Long Island Rail Road. I pulled into the cracked concrete lot and right up to the shack that served as the front office. Behind the shack, rising up three stories into the sky, were metal storage racks crammed with wheels and windshields, car hoods and trunk lids, headlamps and taillights.

For some reason I couldn't put my finger on, I knew Rusty's. Then, after I parked and made my way through the front door of the office, I remembered. And when I remembered, I got pretty fucking steamed. In the wake of the 9/11 attacks, Rusty's owner had been indicted for selling off scrap metal from Ground Zero, scrap metal that still contained human remains. There were some hefty fines levied, but no one went to jail for it because almost all the scrap was recovered. That and the fact that the owner, a real piece of shit, disappeared. The cops found his body in a concrete-filled oil drum on the side of the Belt Parkway. It was a well-known secret that many of the salvage yards in the New York metro area were actually owned by one Mob family or the other.

The guy at the counter looked the part. He weighed four hundred pounds if an ounce, the skin of his jowls hanging off his jawbone like sheets of flesh-colored wax. His face was covered in salt-and-pepper stubble and something that he probably thought looked like a mustache. The fat man was dressed in a blue and gray flannel shirt the size of a tent. It didn't look or smell like it had ever been washed. I guess he was afraid of shrinking it for fear of not being able to get another one that size.

"Frankie around?" I asked.

The fat man didn't look up from the newspaper he was reading, using his index finger to follow along. His lips moved as he read, silently sounding out the big words. Even from across the counter, I caught whiffs of his breath. Yesterday's coffee and thirty years of cigarettes, it smelled worse than his shirt.

Finally, he said, "Huh?"

"Frankie, is he around?"

He lit up a cigarette, blew out some smoke. "Which one?"

Progress.

"Frankie Tacos."

He looked up at me, his eyes barely visible in the folds of his Shar-Pei-like face. "Who's asking?"

"See anyone else standing here? I'm asking."

He ignored that.

"What kinda parts you looking for? We got every kinda Honda, Toyota part you could want."

"Good for you. I'm not looking for parts. I'm looking for Frankie Tacos."

"Huh?"

We were back to that again. Sometimes it really sucked not having a badge anymore. Flashing tin tended to cut through the bullshit. But I wasn't a cop and I didn't want to pretend to be one. I'd pulled it off with Mr. Martino only because he was old and didn't hear me too well through the storm door. As thick as the fat man was, I didn't think it would work with him. So I did the next best thing to cut through the bullshit. I took a twenty out of my wallet and put it on top of the paper in front of him.

I said, "Maybe that'll help your hearing."

"Frankie Tacos . . . yeah, I think I heard that name somewhere before."

I put up another twenty. "The first one was for your hearing. This one's for your memory, but that's all the help you're getting from me, Jabba."

"Joba was my favorite Yankee, but they fucked him all up with them stupid rules and yanking him in and outta the pen. Ruined his arm. I woulda gone to Detroit, too, even if it was to freakin' Detroit. What a fucking shithole, Detroit."

I didn't have time to point out the irony of a guy like him sitting in a junkyard, calling Detroit names. Nor was I willing to explain that I was talking about Jabba the Hut, not Joba Chamberlain, the former Yankees pitcher.

"Frankie Tacos," I repeated, reaching for the twenties.

Jabba's hand moved quicker than I expected and he snatched up the bills. After he did, he took the cigarette out of his mouth and pointed over his shoulder with it.

"Come around the counter, go t'rew this door here, and you'll find him in the engine shack. That's the red steel building. He got his own office in there."

"Thanks."

Frankie Tacos was right where the fat man said he would be, at a desk in a small office inside the red steel building. The building was full of car engines in all states of dissection and disrepair. When I knocked at the open office door, the man at the desk looked up at me and I immediately recognized him as Frankie Tacos. His colorful moniker had nothing to do with Mexican food, but with his family name: Tacaspina. His father was Frankie "Spins" Tacaspina Sr., the man who had been running the carting business in Smithtown and Brookhaven for the Piazza family. The carting business, like the salvage business, had long been run by the Mob.

"Yeah," he said looking up at me, "what can I do for you?"

I put a photograph of TJ Delcamino on his desk. He didn't flinch. The son of Frankie Spins wouldn't.

"Suffolk PD or DA's office?" he asked, a smirk on his face. "You're no Fed, that much I know."

"How?"

"You ain't wearing a tie and you don't look like you got a metal rod permanently stuck up your ass."

We both laughed.

"Suffolk, retired," I said, a smile still on my face. "Name's Gus Murphy. You recognize the kid in the photograph?"

"You know I do, but that's all I'm saying without some explanation."

So I explained.

"Look, Murphy, I don't know who sent you my way, but I had zero to do with TJ's killing. I liked the kid. Liked him a lot. He didn't try to be a hard guy, you know what I mean?"

I nodded that I did.

"So who sent you to look at me?"

"His father," I said.

"The kid's father, Tommy D.?"

I nodded some more.

"But the old man's dead. How'd he send you my way?"

I'd left Tommy D.'s murder out of the explanation. That he knew about it wasn't exactly a revelation, but it told me some things about Frankie Tacos.

"So, you know about Tommy Delcamino's murder?"

He laughed a little too loudly. "C'mon, Murphy. It ain't exactly a state secret."

"But you knew who Tommy was, that he was TJ's dad?"

Frankie Tacos' expression was shifting. Like with all real hard men, like Shivers, he could smile with half his face. I wasn't sure I had hit nerve, but I knew that I was annoying him.

"Again, no state secret. Tommy D. wasn't unknown to me, but now neither are you," he said, the half-smile on his face turning predatory. "Between you and me, Murphy, the father was a bum, but the kid had some skills. I hear that there wasn't a vehicle made by man the kid couldn't handle. Too bad the kid couldn't handle his drugs the same way."

"You hear?"

His smile turned from predatory to cruel. "Yeah, you hear things. Cops, even retired ones, they hear things. No crime in that."

"None," I agreed. "When was the last time you saw the kid?"

Frankie scratched his cheek and gave it some thought. "I don't know . . . maybe a week before he was killed. Sometime last August or something like that." He shrugged. "He was in a bad way, you know?"

"Drugs?"

"Yeah, but not how you think. He looked like he needed some, and soon. His nose was running, had the chills, needed to get healthy and soon."

"Besides that, did he look all right?"

Frankie was confused. "What the fuck does that even mean? I told you, he—"

"Did he look like he'd taken a beating? Did he have a black eye or anything like that?"

Frankie was shaking his head. "Nah, nothing like that. Why?"

"Just curious," I said. I suppose he could have been lying about it, but it didn't feel that way to me. "Can I ask you why he came to you?"

That stopped the conversation in its tracks.

"I thought you said you weren't a cop, Murphy, but you're asking a whole lotta cop questions. And why are you even here? I mean, the old man is dead. The kid is dead. What's in it for you?"

"I'm not a cop. Not anymore. And you're right, both of them are dead. Still, I got my reasons for wanting to know what happened to them. They might be dumb reasons, but they're mine. No matter what they are, you don't have to worry. I'm not wearing a wire," I said peeling off my leather jacket, slipping my sweater off over my head, and laying them down on the floor. "I'm not trying to entrap you or get evidence. I'm just trying to find out what happened. If you wanna come check me more carefully, come on."

Only a stupid man, one destined for prison or an early grave, would have taken my word for it and Frankie was not a stupid man. He came around the desk and patted me down, made me drop my pants, and gave me an examination that my urologist would have envied. He threw my jacket outside the office.

"Okay," I said, slipping my sweater back over my head and zipping up my pants, "now that you've had a close look, can you tell me why TJ came to see you?"

"The kid came to me with an air bag to pedal," he said as casually as if he was telling me what he'd had for breakfast. "One stinking air bag." He shook his head, a sad expression on his face.

"Did you take it?"

"Nah. I just gave him two hundred bucks for his troubles and sent him on his way with the air bag."

"Why'd you give him the bread?"

"I liked the kid and we'd done some good business together."

"Yeah," I said, "I bet. Like around ten thousand bucks' worth of business last Christmas?"

That wiped all the friendly pretense away. Frankie's smiles, the half and full ones, vanished. The sad expression, too. All that was left was the hardness. "Look, Murphy, I told you, I didn't have anything to do with the kid's murder and I didn't even know his old man, so back the fuck off. We're done talking."

I didn't back off. "Okay, you didn't do it. Can you think of anyone you like for it?"

"Go talk to the kid's shithead friends. That bunch of morons must have some ideas."

"I didn't ask about his friends."

"Even if I had an idea, I wouldn't share it with you. I'm no rat. I don't like rats. Rats are why my dad's spending the rest of his life in some shithole prison in some buttfuck state in the middle of nowhere."

"Yeah, and I thought it was because he bashed in Wally Malone's head with a shovel for daring to open up a carting business in Medford."

Frankie almost smiled at that. Almost. "You missed your calling, Murphy. You shoulda been a comedian or a freakin' diplomat. You really know how to make friends and influence people."

"I'm not trying to make friends. I'm trying to get some answers and justice for the kid."

"Justice ain't gonna do the kid no good where he's at."

"Maybe not, but maybe that doesn't matter to me."

"We got lotsa spare things here: rims, tires, fenders. You name the part, we got it or we can get it. Justice, answers . . . none of that shit around here."

"None to share, not even for a kid you liked?"

"None. Not much of it anywhere around that I can see. I'm in the salvage business, not the salvation business. Don't go confusing the two. You want salvation, go the fuck to church."

I thought Father Bill might've said something similar, if not exactly in the same way. I guess I was smiling at the thought. Frankie didn't much care for that. When I looked up, he was smiling his predatory smile back at me. He was also pressing a buzzer on his desk. I went and collected my jacket. When I was done putting it on, I heard footsteps echoing through the big steel building. Some of the footsteps were human, some not. When I turned to look back at Frankie Tacos, I noticed he was pointing a gun at me, a .357 Magnum like the one that had killed Tommy Delcamino.

"Stick around. I want you to meet some friends of mine." It wasn't a suggestion. "Come on back in here."

I stepped back inside the office. About ten seconds after I did so, Frankie and I had company. The guy holding the two pit bulls outside the office entrance was a real zipperhead with slicked-back black hair and a build like Hercules. He was a juicer with a lupine face, but I was more focused on the two dogs—one brindle-coated, the other a pure gray—straining at their leashes and eyeing me with nasty intent.

My old service Glock was in my jacket pocket and I thought about going for it. Frankie must have read my mind.

"If you came in here carrying, that was a pretty ballsy thing to do," he said, mock admiration in his voice. "But my gun's bigger than yours and mine is in my hand. And you're trespassing."

"This guy giving you a hard time, boss?" Hercules asked.

"You know, Nardo, as a matter of fact, he is."

Nardo's wolflike smile unnerved me as much as the growling dogs. "Should I feed him to the pups?"

Frankie's face got serious. "Nah, Nardo. This guy is a pest, like a flea on a dog. But he does look like a guy who keeps in shape. He must be a runner. You a runner, Murphy?"

"Not really."

"Well, that's all about to change for you. Now get the fuck outta here and don't let me catch you here again. Trust me when I tell you I got more friends on the job than you do. Now get lost."

With that, Frankie sat down in his chair and picked up his phone. He was done with me and had already moved on. It was time for me to do the same. I turned and walked out of the office, but Nardo and the dogs stayed in place. When I was almost out of the building, I turned back to see Nardo and the dogs coming my way. When I got outside, I closed the door behind me.

Normally, I would've liked my chances. It wasn't all that far from the entrance of the engine building to the door of the front office shack, fifty yards or so, about the width of a football field. Too bad for me, this wasn't normally. My leg wound was healing all right, but it wasn't totally healed and I hadn't tested the calf by running. And there was the fact that the run, as short as it was, wouldn't be a straight one. There were lots of narrow lanes between car chaises, axles, fenders, radiators, bumpers, and brake rotors. Loose parts like nuts and bolts and hoses littered the paths, and the base of the paths themselves was a mixture of crumbled concrete and packed dirt. No, this wasn't going to be fun at all. At least if the dogs got to me, I'd already had a tetanus shot. I ran.

I'd made it about halfway when I heard Nardo scream, "Blood! Blood!"

I picked up the pace, forcing myself not to look behind me as I ran. My legs, especially my left one, felt like wet rope—thick, heavy, hard to flex. It seemed like minutes passed between the sounds of my footfalls. Each of my breaths was isolated, disconnected from the one coming and the one prior. Yet even as I foundered, I was amazed at the speed with which my mind burned through scenarios. As I negotiated the last twenty yards, through tiny valleys of junked cars and their parts, I looked for where I might escape the dogs if they got too close. I calculated how much speed it would cost me to stop pumping my arms and to grab the Glock out of my jacket pocket. I weighed the speed lost against the advantage of having the gun in hand. I heard their paws thumping behind me. Louder. Louder still. I looked back. Mistake. Big mistake. Because looking back slowed me down and because I saw only one of the dogs. I could feel the panic trying to impose itself on whatever calm and clear thought I was struggling to maintain. I shoved it back down.

I felt a sharp tug on my left pant leg and just about lost it. I jumped into a pile of discarded tires. The impact took some of the wind out of me and I no longer felt that tug on my pant leg. The brindle-coated pit bull came skidding past me, its nails failing to grab on the concrete. He slammed into rows of more neatly stacked tires, which toppled over on him. He yelped in pain as he struggled to get out from under. I was only about ten yards from the office door and if I had any clue where the gray dog was, I might've risked it. But I didn't know where he was, so I took the Glock out of my pocket, racked a bullet into the chamber, and fired two shots into a car door that was propped up against a wire bin. Those shots were plenty loud and they echoed around the yard. I meant them as a warning to Nardo that I would kill the dogs or him if I had to. He got the message.

"No. No!" he screamed, emerging through one of the narrow paths of parts. "Don't shoot 'em. They're only doin' what they're supposed to do. Don't shoot 'em! I'll get 'em. I'll get 'em."

Jabba heard the shots, too, and came hulking out of the office to see what all the commotion was about. He moved as deliberately as a man of his size would, each step seeming to take seconds of motor planning and a lot of energy. I got tired just watching him. I shouted to him to warn him about the dogs, but it was no good. Too late. The gray pit bull came out of nowhere and lunged at him. Jabba was bleating in panic, his forearm in the dog's jaws. The dog was tearing at him with its full weight, violently yanking its head from side to side.

"Stay on your feet," I yelled, running to help him. "Stay upright."

But Nardo was already there, commanding the gray pit bull to release Jabba's arm. The fat man's shirt was soaked through with blood, and when he saw it, he fainted. He went down with a sickening thud as his head smacked against the broken concrete. Nardo was beside himself, screaming at the top of his lungs, not at the dog, but at Jabba.

"Stay the fuck in the office, you fat piece of shit! You know you ain't supposed to come back here."

I didn't waste any more time. I ran. I don't think I breathed again until I was driving down Deer Park Avenue, heading toward the LIE.

(THURSDAY, LATE AFTERNOON)

Two things happened after my audition as the mechanical rabbit at
the dog track: I went into the hotel manager's office at the Paragon
and asked for my two-week vacation to begin immediately, and I
called Al Roussis to ask for a meeting later that afternoon. The symme-
try seemed perverse yet perfect, as we'd be getting together at roughly
the same time Tommy Delcamino had been murdered the week before.
Neither Kurt Bonacker, the hotel manager, nor Al Roussis was very
pleased with my request, but both relented. Bonacker agreed but only if
I could arrange for my shifts to be covered. That was easy enough.
Between Fredo, who had a new baby on the way and was always looking for extra shifts, and our relief driver, it took me all of twenty minutes to make the arrangements. Covering my shifts at the Full Flaps
was no sweat at all. There was an endless supply of retired cops looking
to pick up two hundred bucks off the books for a night of checking IDs
and checking out divorced women. Al Roussis, though unhappy, agreed
without preconditions, which made me suspicious as hell. What made
me even more suspicious was where he chose to meet.

Brady Park in Smithtown was across the street from Millers Pond,
on the corner of Maple Avenue and Wildwood Lane. I knew it well,

had played basketball there as a kid and softball as part of a few different leagues. John Jr. had played some of his Little League games there, too. It didn't hold any special significance to me, not like Vets Park, so I figured it must have held a special place in Al's cosmology. His car was already in the empty L-shaped parking lot when I got there. He was parked nose out by the bench next to the main basketball court. In true cop tradition, I pulled up next to him, nose in, so we could talk through our rolled-down driver's side windows. But when I rolled down my window, Al said, "Come on. Let's walk. I feel like stretching my legs."

I wasn't going to argue with him. He didn't say much and he had a kind of sad, wistful look on his face as we strolled through the parking lot, turning left at the corner of the L, heading toward the Little League baseball field that abutted Maple Avenue. It was a day and a place to be wistful and sad, I guess. There's something particularly sad about empty places, and empty parks were especially sad. For me, anyway. Al, too, from the look of him. The sky was a steel gray, covered in a solid sheet of clouds. The air was moist and raw and smelled of composting, rotting leaves from the woods that surrounded the park on the south and west sides. At the boundary fence we could hear the plaintive honking of the geese and ducks from Millers Pond. The geese and ducks too sick or too old to make the flight south. The geese and ducks abandoned by the kids with their bags of Goldfish crackers and white bread, the kids who had gone back to school or grown beyond their fascination.

I was about to break the silence when Al said, "Do you think they know they're doomed?"

"They?"

"The geese. Do you think they know this is it for them? You know, that they won't see another spring?"

"I never thought about it, Al. I knew you were Greek, but I didn't know you were a philosopher, too."

He ignored that. "You know, where you're standing is where they found her."

"Found who?"

"She was under a pile of leaves, her tights ripped off and wrapped around her throat and stuff had been rammed in her—" He couldn't finish his sentence.

"Who?"

"Alison St. Jean."

He didn't need to say another word. Alison St. Jean was a thirteen-year-old girl who had lived about two blocks away from Brady Park. On Halloween night 1987, she went out trick-or-treating with a group of friends, but she never came back. I couldn't remember all of the details, but it turned out that a group of sixteen-year-old girls, two of whom lived on her block, had taken her bag of candy. When Alison, a willful girl by all accounts, said she would rat the older girls out, they murdered her and tried to make it look as if a man had sexually assaulted her. It was one of "those" cases, the kind that make the national news because the victim was white and pretty and young. Because there was a sexual element involved. Because the police got it wrong and then got it right. Because, because, because . . .

The thing was, neither Al Roussis nor I was on the job then and neither of us had any connection to the case. And it wasn't like it was a case that haunted the SCPD. In spite of some early missteps, they got it right in the end. Justice was served as much as justice could be served in such a stupid and violent act. But I guess that when you were a homicide detective these were the types of cases that you couldn't get out of your head, no matter if they involved you or not.

"Nightmare for the parents," I said.

"Must have been. They still live there, you know?" He pointed back toward the entrance to the park. "And the girls, the girls who murdered her, their families still live there, too."

"I didn't know."

"It's crazy. Why do you think they killed her?"

I said, "You're the homicide detective. I guess they panicked."

"But the things they did."

"We're all still animals, Al. Animals with big brains. Doesn't make us smart."

He thought about that for a few seconds. Al was a man you could see think. "Does it still hurt you, Gus, what happened to John? I even find myself thinking about him sometimes."

"Hurts like a motherfucker all the time, but you learn to live with it. I mean, I'm learning to live with it."

"I'm sorry. I'm really sorry."

"Is that why you came, because you feel bad about my son? Alvaro Peña as much as told me I was cancer and that word had come down from on high not to touch me with someone else's ten-foot pole."

He shrugged. "We're friends and you were a good cop."

I wasn't going to argue the point. He was here. I changed subjects. "Any progress on Delcamino?"

"None. We got plenty of evidence, ballistics, but it doesn't point anywhere at anyone. By the way, you can go collect your weapon. It's been checked out and cleared."

"Thanks."

"So, Gus, now you wanna tell me why you wanted to meet?" He sounded more like his old self, more like a detective.

"Speaking of ballistics . . ."

That got his attention. "Yeah."

"You said the gun that killed Delcamino was a .357 Magnum, correct?"

"Uh-huh."

"Well, I was having a little powwow with Frankie Tacaspina Jr. this morning and—"

"And what were you doing talking to Frankie Tacos? Are you nuts?"

"Am I nuts? I think maybe I am. And you don't wanna know what I was doing talking to him."

"Okay, I'll take your word for it. So what happened during this meeting that you want to tell me about?"

"Frankie Tacos knew TJ Delcamino. The kid was a car thief and used to do business with Frankie."

Roussis shook his head at me. "Not my case, Gus. The father's murder is my worry. Besides, I'm sure that even those two clowns, Carey and Paxson, know about the connection between Tacos and the kid."

"But do you think they know that Frankie Tacos keeps a .357 Magnum in his desk drawer at Rusty's Salvage Yard?"

Al squinted his eyes in interest. "How do you know he does?"

"He showed it to me this morning," I said, smiling.

"Showed it to you?"

"In a manner of speaking, yeah. He showed it to me."

Al flexed his fingers against the cold as he thought about it, huge puffs of steam coming out of his nostrils and mouth.

"You want to press charges, Gus?"

I shook my head. "I'm nuts, not suicidal. At least not anymore. I survived one run-in with the guy and I don't wanna press my luck. Anyway, it would only be my word against his, and you know how that would go."

"Then it's going to be tough to get a warrant to look at the piece."

"You were always a pretty creative guy, Al. Put that noodle of yours to work."

He extended his right hand to me. "I appreciate the tip, Gus. How's the leg wound?"

"Healing," I said, shaking his hand.

I told him that I had to get going, that I was meeting Krissy for dinner. He said he was staying put and that he needed time alone to think.

"Why'd you pick to meet here?" I asked before he got into his car.

He answered only with a smile. I knew there was a message in his smile for me somewhere. What it was, I hadn't a clue. And my cell phone didn't give me much time to think about it.

"Yeah," I said, picking up. "Gus Murphy."

"Man, why you got to be botherin' my girl for?"

It was Kareem Shivers. Although the question seemed almost whiny, there was nothing whiny about the tone of his voice. It was easy for me to picture his face, his dead-eyed stare.

"All I did was return your license, like I said I would."

"Nah, man, you could have just put it in my mailbox. No need for you to bring up murder and shit. That wasn't right."

"Hey, K-Shivs, I don't need to be lectured about right and wrong from you."

But if I thought that was going to get a rise out of him, I was mistaken.

"There's right and then there's street right, Gus Murphy. Now we enemies, you and me."

"I'll keep my eyes open for Jamal and Antwone."

"Only stupid fighters keep coming at you with the same approach, specially after they lost the first bout that way. That's not my style."

"I heard you were good."

"Undefeated," he said, the pride in his voice unmistakable.

"Short career, though. Heard about the cracked skull. Do me a favor, don't dump my body by a Russian Orthodox church. I was born Catholic."

He laughed like a shark would laugh if sharks laughed. "Like I say before, you got some balls on you, Gus. But I ain't gonna come at you like that. You look out for Jamal and Antwone all you want. That jus' make it easy for me."

I pretended to ignore that. "Any luck finding what you were look-ing for?"

But he didn't answer. He was already gone.

(THURSDAY, EARLY EVENING)

Krissy had picked a new Chinese restaurant in Stony Brook. She looked healthier than she had only last week on the morning Pete McCann kicked her out of the Fourth Precinct lockup. She looked better than she had in months. Her face had some color in it and her eyes lacked the bloodshot red that had become so much a part of them since John's death. She even looked as if she had taken off a pound or two. She seemed more like my daughter again. I laughed to myself, recalling how many times during our kids' childhoods that Annie and I joked about how the alien pod people had come and replaced our sweet, beautiful, well-behaved girl and boy with evil duplicates. I suppose all parents go through some version of that. But the explanation of Krissy's transformation had nothing to do with pod people. Her reasons were grounded in the most human of experiences.

We sat on opposite sides of the table, looking everywhere except at each other. We listened and watched as the nearby diners struggled to comprehend the waitress's broken English. That distracted us for only so long. Then we finally had to speak.

"Where'd you find this place?" I asked, hoping to avoid the

minefield that had been our common ground over the last two years. I
didn't doubt that we'd end up there sooner or later. We always did.

"The newspaper."

"You ever eat here before?"

"Once."

"With Mom?"

She nodded, keeping her eyes on the menu. Great. It had taken all
of thirty seconds for our conversation to degenerate from a two-word
answer to one word to a nod of her head. She'd skipped right past
grunts and sign language.

"C'mon, kiddo, give me a break here."

She understood without me having to explain, but chose to avoid
the minefield for now. "Their hot and sour soup is great. You wanna
just let me order?"

"Sure."

Well, that was progress. When the waitress came over, Krissy rattled off an order that I only half caught. I ordered a beer and waited to
be surprised. Krissy ordered a Diet Coke.

"You don't have to pretend around me," I said. "You want a beer,
have a beer."

"I'm not drinking anymore, Dad, not for the time being. I don't like
how I get when I drink." She smiled a beaming smile at me. "I'm back
at the gym."

I was glad and told her so, but I knew better than to strike up the
band. She'd had too many shifts in behavior in the last few years for me
to celebrate. She'd made similar pronouncements several times only to
make immediate U-turns and stumble into her uncle's house completely
stoned or blotto. Then I'd get the call from Annie or, like the other
night, Annie would just show up at work.

When the waitress brought our drinks, Krissy raised her glass and
said, "To John."

"To John," I repeated, his name sticking in my throat.

We clinked bottle to glass and drank in silence.

"I'm trying to reregister for the spring term at Stony Brook," she said, an anxious half-smile on her mouth.

My smile was a full one.

Was this, I wondered, what it was like coming out of a coma? Is that what Krissy, Annie, and I were doing? Were we coming around at last? Had enough time elapsed? Had we all finished acting out? Had we finally proved to ourselves and one another that no amount of pain or grief or self-flagellation or magical thinking or deals with God or guilt or fury would restore to us who we had lost? Was it okay to live again? Or was this another false start? A new rug to be pulled out from under us? I hoped not. I hoped it was real, but I knew hope was the meanest feeling humans were capable of. Nothing tortured you the way hope could. Nothing.

Krissy was right. The food was great. And though I didn't dare say it aloud, I thought about bringing Casey here. The soup alone would have been worth it. I watched my daughter watching me enjoy the meal. She was so pleased to have been right. To have seen pride in my eyes for her again. She got a kick out of teaching me how to properly eat soup dumplings—dumplings with hot soup in them, not them in the hot soup. It seemed like a lifetime ago we laughed together over anything at all. I didn't care that it was over my lack of skill with soup dumplings.

Then, when there was no food left, Krissy did the inevitable: she opened the gate to the minefield.

"Dad?"

I looked up and saw Krissy was no longer smiling.

"What's up, kiddo? What's wrong?"

"What's going on with you and Mom?"

"Why?"

"Dad, we can't keep answering each other with questions."

"Why not?" I said, keeping a poker face.

She looked exasperated, but when I laughed at her, she laughed with me.

"It's complicated with me and your mom. Maybe it always was

and I was too happy to realize it. I think we will always love each other in a way, but John's dying . . . it took the soul out of us."

"That's not what I meant, Dad."

"Tell me what you meant and I will give you as honest an answer as I can."

Krissy didn't answer immediately. Instead, she asked the waitress for the bill and when it came, she insisted on paying it. I didn't fight her, but I left the tip.

"Okay, kiddo, stalling time is over."

"Mom is seeing someone."

The residual flavor of the food turned bitter in my mouth. I forced myself to smile, but it was no good. Krissy picked up on it. What Annie had done with Pete McCann was one thing. I hated it, but I understood it. Sleeping with him was like stepping on the third rail, a move guaranteed to be fatal to our marriage. But even after what had gone on between us this past weekend, the bitterness and the goodbyes, this was different somehow. This hurt because I guess I didn't really believe Annie's goodbyes or believe that she would want to be with someone else. It was idiotic to think that, I know. The crazy aspect of my reaction was that it felt like disloyalty. Disloyalty not to me. Disloyalty to John. How nuts is that? And since I'd just slept with Casey, the height of hypocrisy. Still, I was tired of beating myself up for the way I felt, so I let myself feel it.

"We're divorced. Your mom has a right to be happy. Does he make her happy?"

"But you guys . . . I know that you two . . . you know what I mean."

I knew.

"It's complicated, Krissy. After John died, it was a way to grieve and to let go," I said, reaching across the table and taking her hand. "It was all about pushing and pulling. We all went a little crazy there for a while. But your mom and me . . . it's over, kiddo."

Intellectually, she accepted it, but kids, no matter how old, never want their parents to split apart and stay apart. I told myself that no matter how tempted I was to let her know about Casey, I didn't want to add to her burden. And the truth was, I wanted Casey to be only mine for a little while, to see if there was anything really there. If Casey and I developed into a couple, then I would risk exposing her to my family. As far as I was concerned, those fireworks could wait.

"So who is he?"

"His name is Rob something. He and Mom used to date in high school and he found her on Facebook."

I'd heard about Rob. Seen pictures of him in old photo albums. When they were younger, Rob had been on the wrong side of the love equation. He was the one who'd fallen more deeply. Never fun to be the one who's more in love when things go south. I tried remembering his face, tried picturing how he might look now. But it didn't matter what he looked like or even who he was. He wasn't me and that was going to take some getting used to.

"Your mother is on Facebook?" I said to camouflage my feelings.

"Aren't you even a little bit jealous?"

"Sure I am, but that doesn't change anything."

"What about you?"

"What about me?"

"Are you moving on?"

I let go of her hand and tousled her hair. "I sure hope so. Yeah, kiddo, I think so. I'd like to think that John would be happy for all of us."

I could see her wheels churning, wondering if she should ask me to be more specific. Thankfully, she left it there.

"Come on, Dad, walk me out. I've got to get to the gym."

Outside, a light mist was falling and it lent a softening blur to all the lights.

"Are you coming to Grandma's for Christmas Eve?" she asked after I kissed her on the forehead.

"I haven't thought about it. I haven't shopped—"

"Please, Dad, for me."

"But your mom will bring Rob and—"

"Just bring whoever you're seeing," she said, a smile flashing across her face. "And don't even lie to me."

"We'll see."

"Dad!"

"'We'll see' is the best I can do."

I watched her get into her car and drive away into the blur of head-lights on Stony Brook Road. I was feeling a lot of things as I turned for my car, but mostly relief that Krissy seemed to be reclaiming her life. I wasn't ready to proclaim it a done deal. I'd have to see where we all stood after the holidays. All in all, I was feeling okay. And one added benefit to where Krissy had taken me to dinner was the restaurant's proximity to the Smith Haven Mall. If I was ever going to do Christmas shopping, this was it.

was still feeling pretty good when I headed out of Macy's, shopping bags in hand. That lasted until I got to where I'd parked. There, leaning against the rear bumper of my car, was a man in his late twenties. He was dressed in a green flannel shirt, down vest, Levi's, and work boots, but he had cop written all over him. Maybe it was the military haircut or the uniformlike way his clothing hung on his six-foot, hundred-eighty-pound frame. He had a belligerent smirk on his face, one that hinted at underlying violence. The belligerence was especially evident in the eyes. They were the angry eyes of a man always spoiling for a fight. I knew the type.

"Pretty girl, your daughter. Those all for her?" he said, tilting his head at the bags in my hands, his voice full of implied threat. "Be a shame if some stranger came around bothering her about shit she had nothing to do with. Like if someone approached her after leaving the Chinese restaurant or even followed her home. She woulda been pretty easy to follow. Maybe next time."

I fought the instinct to drop my bags and kick the shit out of this guy because I sensed that was exactly what he wanted. Maybe I'd give in to him, just not yet, not until I got what I wanted first.

"A real shame," I said, picking up on his threat, "because then you'd have to deal with me."

But even as I spoke, I was distracted. The closer I looked at this guy, the more familiar he seemed.

He laughed a sneering, unpleasant laugh. "Tough guy, huh?"

"Depends."

"On what, tough guy?"

"On what a guy who's on the job is doing leaning against my car and talking shit." My voice was less than neutral, but not threatening.

"I know all about you, Murphy. You got a big rep, but you just seem like a bag of leaves to me. Weak and sorry because grieving's taken the heart and balls out of you."

This guy was really pushing me hard, but I wasn't that easily goaded.

"You talk a good line of shit, junior," I said with all the condescension I could muster. Then I raised my right hand and flapped my fingers against my thumb. "And you talk a lot."

That got his attention and he came at me. He didn't charge me. He wasn't quite at the point of losing his mind or throwing a punch, but he was getting there. He stepped up real close to me. He was well built, for sure, though I was bigger. The size difference was magnified by his proximity to me. Then it clicked. I knew who he was. I'd seen his photo at his grandfather's house. I felt an involuntary smile spreading across my face. He saw it. He didn't like it, but it sure as shit unnerved him.

"What the fuck you smiling at?" he growled, trying hard to get his feet back under him.

"I know all about you, too, Pauly. You really are the hothead everyone says you are, Martino. How's the Marine Bureau these days? The blue-fish behaving themselves? Giving out speeding tickets to the porgies?"

That did it to him. I could have sworn the stiffness went out of his spine there for a second. I'm sure I must've imagined it, but I knew I had him now.

"You stay away from my grandfather," he shouted at me, his distorted face turning a bright red. "He don't have nothing to do with what happened to that mutt Delcamino. And neither should you, ass-hole. Take this as a warning from a brother to a brother, stay outta this. You think you know what's what, Murphy, but you got no idea. The shit's deep and you're about to be up to your nipples in it."

"Okay, Pauly, you know all about it. Enlighten me."

He poked me in the chest. "You're playing with fire here. People are gonna fuck you up if you don't back off and get back to driving your van and living in that flea-bag hotel."

"People. What people?"

"Powerful people," he said, then seemed to regret saying it.

"What people? Jimmy Regan?"

He didn't react, at least not the way I hoped he would. He just kind of made a face at me like I was crazy or something.

"Just stay away from my granddad and leave it alone."

I wasn't ready to stop pushing him, not yet.

"What people? People like you?" I laughed at him and he knew it was at him. I shook my hands in mock fear. "Gee, I'm shaking in my shoes."

That did it. He was girding himself to throw the punch I think he'd wanted to throw from the second I walked up to my car. It wouldn't've taken much for me to push him over the edge, but even an idiot would know that Martino had been put up to this and I was no idiot. Someone was yanking his chain. Someone who knew Martino had a bad temper and a short fuse. Maybe the person behind this fig-ured that I'd catch a beating or that any damage Martino might do to me would be enough to make me reconsider what I was doing. Of course Pauly Martino would lose his job in the process, but puppet masters don't worry about the damage to their marionettes. Martino probably wasn't worried about it, either. Then again, he wasn't thinking straight. Hotheads seldom do until it's too late.

I nodded over my shoulder at the light pole right behind me. He noticed and hesitated.

"What?"

"There's a CCTV camera up there aimed at this section of the parking lot," I said. "Whatever happens between us will be digital, and digital is forever."

"So what?" He looked right past me directly at the camera.

"You know what, or at least you should know what. You throw that punch at me and you're done. You'd be suspended and off the job like that." I snapped my fingers. "You'd be lucky not to do time for assault. I'd be bruised, but you'd be fucked."

Some of the air went out of him, though he immediately tried to pump his rage back up. He failed. Maybe I had gotten through to him and he realized that he'd come this close to ruining his police career and possibly his life. I wasn't satisfied to leave it there.

"I don't know who put you up to this, but whoever it was didn't give a shit about you or your granddad, Martino."

"Shut up! Just shut up. Nobody put me up to this." He was angry at me, sure, but there was doubt in his eyes where rage had been only seconds ago.

I pulled a Paragon card out of my wallet and stuffed it in his vest pocket. "Remember, Martino, whoever put you onto me was willing to let you blow yourself up just so you could throw me a beating. You feel like sharing, call me at that number."

"I already told you, nobody put me up to this," he repeated, only louder and less convincing. He turned to walk away, then stopped and looked back. "Remember what I said. Leave my family alone and stay outta this shit, Murphy. I'm telling you for your own good." He yanked the Paragon card out of his pocket, looked at it, and shoved it back into his pocket.

As I drove back to the hotel, something occurred to me that made me pull to the side of the road. I understood how Martino found my car at the mall. He'd followed me from the Chinese restaurant. But how had he known I was at the restaurant in the first place?

(THURSDAY NIGHT)

When I got back on the road, I worked out a way to move ahead. I would need someone's help. Who? I'd worry about that later. But until I got to the hotel, I had to keep calm. So I did something I very rarely did anymore: I listened to the news. Since the day John died, I'd pretty much given up on current events. I mean, you hear things, but I never sought out information. Never watched or listened to the news. Never read the newspaper past the sports pages. Never went to the business center computers in the lobby to scan the home page for updates. At first it was that I didn't think I could bear to hear about anyone else's tragedy for fear of breaking down all over again in sympathy. That wasn't it. Not for a second. It was that I wasn't interested in anyone else's tragedy. *Fuck them*, I thought. *Fuck them. My pain wins.*

And what I heard on the news did nothing to convince me that I'd missed a thing. Death and tragedy were still everywhere and they came in all shapes and sizes. I was about to shut the radio off when a story caught my ear. It was about a candlelight vigil being held for a Smithtown girl, a high school junior who had OD-d on heroin. I shook my head, thinking about what her parents must've been going through.

What surprised me, though, was my anger. How it was still there. How fresh it was. Who was I angry at? At the girl for being so stupid to throw her life away. At her parents for letting her. At the universe for robbing me of my son. I was even jealous of the girl's parents in the same way I think I'd been jealous of Tommy Delcamino. There were answers for them to get. There was a cause for them to march about. There was a place for their hurt and grief and anger.

What really got my attention was the sound bite of the police official discussing the rash of overdoses in Suffolk County and what his department was doing about it. That man was Jimmy Regan. You could hear the emotion in his voice, the commitment and determination. Maybe a little bit too much Jameson as well, but hell, he was entitled. I'd always heard drink was a bit of an issue for him and that's what I assumed Father Bill had been referring to when he said that Regan was no saint. Jimmy Regan wasn't hiding from the spotlight, wasn't waiting for the ugliness to pass. No, instead he was out in front of it, giving a voice and face to the department. Here he was again: first through the door. Still . . .

I parked right out front of the Paragon, just past the main entrance. The lighting was brightest here and would afford me the best chance of finding what I was looking for. I popped the trunk, removed the shopping bags of gifts, retrieved an old blanket, and took out the big Maglite flashlight I kept in there for emergencies. When I first got on the job, a Maglite was as effective a weapon as a nightstick. You put somebody down with one of those, they didn't stand up and ask for another. For the moment, though, I wanted to use the big flash for the purpose for which it was originally manufactured.

I stretched the blanket on the ground by the rear driver's side tire, lay down on the blanket, and aimed the flash directly into the wheel well. Nothing. I repeated this three more times at the other three tires, but failed to find what I was sure I would find. I got the tire ramps out of the trunk and drove the front wheels onto them, so I might comfortably get under the car to look. Nothing. By the time I'd driven off the ramps and put them and the blanket back in the trunk, Slava had taken notice.

"What for you are looking, Gus?" he said to me, a kind of wary yet knowing expression on his ugly face.

"Nothing," I lied, disgusted. "Forget it."

"Get back blanket. Open car door. Give to me flashlight."

I figured, *What the hell*, and did as he asked. He'd surprised me once and saved my ass. Maybe he had a few other surprises in his bag of tricks. He laid the blanket on the ground near the rear passenger door and got on his knees. Two minutes later, a film of sweat covering his forehead, he stood up. There was a self-satisfied, gap-toothed smile on his face. The flashlight was in his left hand and in his right was a black plastic box about the size of a pack of cigarettes.

"For this, Gus, is what you are looking? Tracking device. Under front passenger seat. No one is ever looking there."

"No one but you. How did you—"

But all Slava did was shake his head no. *Don't ask.*

"Okay," I said, "I won't. Secrets, right?"

He handed me the black box, a veil of sadness falling across his face. "And shame."

"How would you like to make a few hundred extra bucks?"

His face lit up, then the wariness returned to his expression. "How I am making this money?"

I asked, "You have a car?"

He nodded. "Like me. Not so pretty but is working good. What you want Slava to do?"

"To follow my car around tomorrow to see—"

"If someone is following you, no?"

"Exactly." I laughed. "My guess is that I don't need to teach you how to follow me without being spotted."

He was shaking his head again, smiling. "I teach you, maybe." He winked.

"Yeah, I figured. You seem to know a lot about this stuff."

He shrugged. "Some things, yes. Too much things I am knowing." There was that sadness again.

We exchanged cell phone numbers.

"I'll call you when I'm—"

He shook his head. "No call to Slava. Act same like always. Do as you do."

"Okay. One more thing."

"Yes, Gus?"

After memorizing the brand and model number of the tracking device, I handed it back to him. "Put this under the seat where you found it."

Slava laughed that snorting gasping laugh of his and touched a thick finger to his temple. "Smart man. Smart."

I didn't know how smart I was, but I was a quick learner.

(FRIDAY MORNING)

At eleven the next morning, I found myself on a barstool at Harrigan's, sitting across from Richie Zito. We were alone. Zee told me that we'd have about a half hour of privacy, that the losers didn't begin drifting in until around eleven thirty. He brewed up a pot of coffee. Watching him manage it was pretty painful. Everybody's got their fears about how they're going to die. I certainly had mine. One thing I was thankful for was that John's death had been instantaneous, or so we were told. There were no long years of suffering and waiting. The suffering and the waiting, the dying by the inch like Zee was doing, that was the thing that freaked most people out.

He poured me a mug and put it up on the bar. Hand as gnarled and shaky as it was, he managed to do it without spilling. He was less sure-handed with the milk. I wiped the drops of milk away with a few bar naps.

"Sugar?" His voice was raspy and his breath already smelled of pot. "Sweet'N Low?"

He shook his head.

"Then sugar it is."

Zee tossed a few packets onto the bar top. "Not that I ain't thrilled to see you, Gus, but what are you doing here?"

Excellent question. I was there because I didn't know where else to turn. Sure, I had Slava in place, watching my back, but I needed to talk to someone, to say the things in my head aloud to try and make sense of it. To make sense of it, I needed to speak to someone who knew the landscape, who had done his swimming in murky water. Yeah, I trusted Zee about as far as I could throw him, but if you want to learn about bottom-feeders you don't speak to the angels. I knew he was familiar with most of the players or would at least have heard of the ones he didn't know. And one thing I knew as a cop from the Second was that Zee's information was almost always credible. There was also the fact that he seemed to have really cared for Tommy D., and since he'd paid to bury the man, I guessed he'd be as motivated as me to find out what the hell was going on.

"That was a good thing you did, burying Tommy D. that way," I said, sipping the coffee.

He made a face. "It was selfish. When you're alone in the world like Tommy and me was, you hope someone will do you the kindness of putting you in the ground proper. I guess I'm hoping there will be someone to do me the kindness. But that's not why you're here, Gus. Long way to come to tell me something you could say over the phone."

"No, you're right. I needed to talk to you, face-to-face. Needed to hear myself say it out loud, you know?"

"Talk about what?" He leaned in, putting his elbows on the bar. "You find something out?"

"Some stuff, yeah, but I can't make it hang together in a way that gives anyone a motive for torturing TJ to death or for killing Tommy D."

"And you're hoping, what? That I can supply the glue?"

I nodded.

He looked at his watch. "We got about twenty minutes."

I gave it to him. I told him about my confrontations with Kareem

Shivers and Frankie Tacos. About my conversation with Ralphy O'Connell.

"So you see what I got?" I said. "I'm pretty sure TJ raised money for this drug deal that went sideways by doing business with Frankie Tacaspina Jr. The drug deal is with this guy in Wyandanch they call Lazy Eye, whose real name is Lamar English. And I'm almost certain the guys who did the shakedown on TJ and Ralph O'Connell for the drugs and money work for Kareem Shivers. And it wasn't even me who really even pieced this together. It was Tommy D. All I did was what the detectives who caught TJ's case didn't or wouldn't do."

"Fucking cops!" He snorted. "No offense, Gus."

"In this case, you're right."

"Sorry, man, I got no glue for you. For one thing, between Kareem Shivers and Frankie Tacos, you got two top candidates for the baddest badass in Suffolk. And with me a week or two from getting the fuck out of Dodge, I don't want to cross either one of them guys. For another, yeah, you make it all sound connected, but you got no real proof, and even if you did, I don't see the motive here, not for two murders."

I sipped some more coffee, thinking that I much preferred fake sugar to the real thing. "But here's the thing, Zee, I think I know where I can find the motive."

If how far his sleepy lids rose was any indication of his interest, that last thing I'd said about finding a motive had gotten his attention like nothing else I'd mentioned. Unfortunately, the first loser of the day chose that moment to stroll into the bar.

"Get the fuck outta here!" Zee shouted at him, coming around the bar. "We ain't open yet for another ten minutes."

The guy pointed at me. "But he's—"

"He's none of your fucking business, asshole. You want to drink in this place again, you'll get out of here." Zee grabbed the loser's coat and pushed him toward the door.

"Okay, okay, I'm going."

"And tell any of the other assholes out there that if they try and come in here—"

"I got the point. Okay."

Zee stood there, scowling. Making sure the loser was stationed in front of the door.

"Sorry about that, Gus," Zee said, flexing his hands, slowly walking back around the bar.

"You were moving pretty good there. Latched onto that guy's coat like a vise."

He snorted. "I can summon it up when I have to." He poured himself a shot of Jack Daniel's and gunned it down. "Want one?"

I shook my head.

"Gus, you were saying something about motive when that clown came in."

"It's like this. TJ shows up at Rusty's Salvage Yard a week before he's murdered with a stolen air bag that Frankie Tacos wants no part of. The kid's desperate for money, needing a fix, so Tacos gives him a few hundred bucks and sends TJ on his way."

Zee was skeptical. "You believe Tacaspina? The guy's a world-class scumbag and, if you believe the rumors, he made his bones before he got laid."

"You know, I do believe him. He didn't have to tell me any of that. He could have just had the dogs chew my ass off and send me on my way. He really seemed to have liked TJ and he certainly had respect for his skills with cars."

Zee nodded. "Okay, so let's say Tacaspina's telling the truth. So what? Where's the motive? He killed the kid because . . . why?"

"No. I don't think he killed TJ or Tommy D. So here's TJ a week before his murder. He's totally strung out and desperate, without two nickels to rub together. Four or five days later, he shows up at Ralphy O'Connell's. He's not strung out, but just the opposite. He's high as a kite and he's flush, but his face is swollen and he'd sporting a black eye like he's taken a beating. He gives twelve grand cash to his pal to make amends for the drug deal, with a little something extra on top, promising there's much more to come. See what I mean? The motive is in that time frame somewhere. All I have to find out is how TJ got that money and who he got it from and—"

"Bingo."

"Yeah, great." I shrugged. "Sounds nice, but where did that money come from and whose was it to begin with? Who beat the kid up? How the hell am I supposed to find that out? If only the cops had looked at these guys or cared even a little bit."

Zee made another face and turned his palms up to the ceiling as best he could. "That's the second time you brought up the cops, Gus."

"Come on. I know the detectives that caught these cases."

"Like I said, you brought 'em up, not me."

"Yeah, but where would homicide detectives get their hands on big money? There's money in vice and narcotics, not homicide."

He was shaking his head at me, with a sneer on his face.

"What?"

"Stop thinking like a cop, Gus," he said, holding the coffeepot handle with both hands as he refilled my cup. "Forget the detectives. Just because you were in uniform, it don't mean detectives aren't pawns. They take fucking orders, too. Look over their heads."

I guess I must've made a face.

Zee smiled a crooked smile at me. "You winced there," he said. "I hit a nerve or something?"

"I have taken a look at the brass."

"You come up with a name?"

"It's ridiculous."

"What's ridiculous?"

"Jimmy Regan." The name spilled out of my mouth.

"Saint Superman Regan, huh? Wait, let me kneel and cross myself. Fuck him!"

"Wait a second, Zee, I—"

"You guys crack me up. You get all weak-kneed at the mention of that prick's name, but there's shit you don't know about him."

"Like what?"

"No, sir. No way. Like I said before, I'm this close to being out of Dodge. And just like I don't need any shit from Tacaspina and Shivers, I don't need any cop trouble neither on my way out the door."

"I thought you were Tommy's friend. I thought you liked his kid. So you'll bury Tommy, but you won't help me—"

Zee's face twisted up and turned red. He slammed his tree knot of a right fist down onto the bar.

"Get the fuck outta here, Gus, and send my paying customers in. Don't bother coming back in here again until the spics run this place. Fuck you and fuck Jimmy Regan, that hypocritical piece of crap. Go get ahold of his service record from the mid-'90s. Then you can go pray at his fucking altar. Until then, get outta here!"

I stood up and left. When I passed the loser on my way out, I told him it was okay to go in. He looked hurt about how Zee had treated him, but he went in just the same.

(FRIDAY AFTERNOON)

I didn't know what to make of the things Zee hinted at before he sent me packing. You couldn't just dismiss what he had to say because snitches were more than sponges. They did more than just hear things. They traded information to get information. So if he said what he said about Jimmy Regan, there had to be at least something there, though maybe something less than what he'd been told. But I knew beyond Zee, I knew that no one had forced Jimmy Regan's name from between my lips. In spite of Bill Kilkenny's assurances and Chief Regan's stand on the heroin flooding into Suffolk County, I had doubts of my own. As much as I didn't like hearing what Zee had implied and as much as I couldn't bring myself to believe that a person or persons inside the SCPD might be implicated in two murders, there was no getting around the fact that someone inside the department was determined not to have TJ Delcamino's murder looked at too carefully. It was one thing to warn me off. It was something else for Lou Carey and Milt Paxson not to do their jobs. Milt Paxson, okay, he was an incompetent schmuck. Not Lou Carey. Problem was that all I had for evidence was a lot of smoke and supposition. Which is to say I had nothing.

At least now I knew where to go and who to talk to. I wondered if I would get any answers from him. I doubted it, but I had to try. So before I sat down in my car, I fished my cell out of my pocket and made to punch in Father Bill's number. Before I could tap in even one digit, the phone buzzed in my hand. I recognized the number: the Paragon Hotel.

"Gus Murphy."

"Gus, it is Felix."

"Hey, Felix. You miss me already? I saw you an hour ago."

"You are not so funny, Gus," he said. "Remember you promised we would go for a Filipino meal together soon."

"I remember. Is that why you called?"

"No. A man called for you."

"Did he leave a name?"

"He did not, but he said that you would know him. That you met in the Macy's parking lot."

Pauly Martino.

"Did he leave a message?"

"A kind of a message."

"What does that even mean, Felix?"

"It is very brief, two words, I think, but I am not certain I heard him clearly. He sounded quite agitated when we spoke."

"Yeah, that guy's always agitated. What's the message?"

"It makes no sense. The message is PacSun."

"PacSun? Like the store in the mall?"

"Yes, exactly, Gus. PacSun. It makes no sense."

"Could he have said Paxson?"

"Yes, that is what he said, PacSun."

"Okay," I said, "thanks."

"Gus, this makes sense to you?"

"All the sense in the world, Felix. All the sense in the world."

I didn't have time to deal with it at the moment, not that I was sure how I would deal with Milt Paxson when I found the time. And Pauly Martino's admission that it was Paxson who put him onto me raised more questions than it answered. *One thing at a time,* I thought. *One thing at a time.* First I had to go talk with Bill.

As he was the first time I'd come to his basement apartment in Massapequa, Bill was at the side of the house, smoking a cigarette and looking off into the distance. He didn't notice my car, not at first, and I sat there watching him, wondering if what he'd done in Vietnam ever really left him. I didn't doubt him for a second when he said he had gotten his faith back, finally. I wondered just how powerful his faith was as a hedge against the blackness. Or was it a topical salve, something to apply to the wound to bring relief, to bring a little bit of light into the void? Was there ever an escape from your past? I knew I was wondering about these things in terms of Bill, though my pain and grief were as much in question as Bill's nightmare experiences in Vietnam. All those silly analogies about unscrambling eggs and unringing bells crossed my mind. And I thought, did I really want to forget? If all the grief and pain could vanish, but it meant truly forgetting, would I make that bargain?

Of course, there are no such bargains to be made. No one to make them with. Not for me. Bill, I supposed, believed such things could happen. The Holy Trinity as dealmaker. I also supposed he felt he deserved his pain. That somehow, through some sin of his own or through the one he was born with, he had earned it. He finished his cigarette, and as he snuffed it out, his eyes refocused on the present. That's when he noticed my car and waved me in.

He poured us glasses of red wine without bothering to ask.

"I knew you'd be back to talk," he said, lifting his glass. *"Sláinte."*

"Sláinte."

We clinked and drank.

"So far today my calories have all been of the liquid variety. Coffee and wine."

"Is that complaint I hear in your voice? Would you like something to eat? I don't have much in the way of food. I can scramble you up some eggs?"

I laughed.

"That's me, Gus, a short-order comedian. You ever hear the one about the strip of bacon, the sausage, and the omelet that walked into the bar?"

"Sorry, Bill. When I was out in the car I was thinking about undoing the past."

"I see, unscrambling the eggs, you mean?" he said with a sad smile.

"When you were out there smoking, were you remembering 'Nam?"

"Christ help me, I was. Forty plus years and eight thousand miles away, yet it's never far from me."

"If you could unsee what you saw, unhear what you heard—"

"Would I? What man wouldn't? Surely, Gus, each of us has moments in our lives we would undo?"

"How about Jimmy Regan?"

He laughed, but not because he thought it was funny. "I believe I just gave you an answer to that. What man wouldn't?"

"It's an answer, but it's pretty vague."

"How did I know you wouldn't be satisfied with our last talk?"

I shrugged. "Bill, I don't want to believe Regan has any connection to all this violence, but I keep coming back around to him."

"You're wrong about this, Gus. I feel sure of it."

"The other day when we spoke," I said, taking a gulp of the wine, "you said Regan was no saint."

"Nor are the two men in this room."

I ignored that since his statement was true on its face. "When you said that about him, I thought you were talking about his drinking. Everyone in the department knows he used to have a problem with that and that he's gotten it under control. But that's not what you were talking about, was it, Bill?"

He finished the whole of his wine in a single swallow. He walked over to the sink of the tiny kitchen, poured himself some more, and gestured at me with the bottle.

"Sure, why not?" I walked over by him, letting him fill a third of the glass before I waved him to stop. I looked down, once again taking note of Bill's ugly black shoes, the shoes he wore when he still wore the collar.

"Jesus, Bill, why don't you buy yourself a pair of running shoes or cross-trainers?"

He patted my jacket pocket where I had my gun stashed. "And why don't you stop carrying that damned thing around with you?" He didn't wait for an answer. "Because we are who we are. We all find comfort in odd things."

"Comfort can be a kind of prison of its own."

"There are any number of prisons, Gus. Some of our making and to our taste. Some not."

"Fair enough," I said, raising my glass to him, "but you haven't answered my question about Regan."

"You're wrong about Jimmy, because I know the man."

"Bill, you know a lot of things. I'll give you that. You're maybe the most intuitive person about human feelings I've ever met. Believe me, that's saying something. You saved me, probably from killing myself. You helped save what was left of my family—"

"I sense a 'but' coming down the road here shortly."

I obliged him. "But there's something life and being on the job has taught me."

"Care to share it with a broken-down ex-priest?"

"It's impossible to really know somebody else."

"And why is that, Gus?"

"Because we don't even know ourselves. Sure, from day to day, inside the confines of our lives, we're pretty good at predicting how we'll react. But that's not knowing yourself."

He had no snappy comeback, no handy scripture quotation. Instead he sat down and sipped his wine. I knew he was thinking about it, that he had thought about this very subject many times before.

"There's truth in what you say. To deny it would make me a liar or a fool. I know with some certainty that I'm not much for lying, but I don't suppose I will find out if I'm a fool until I've drawn my last breath." Bill let a smile light up his gaunt face. "My, we've gone a bit far afield, haven't we, though?"

I nodded.

"I'm sorry, Gus, but the things you want to know about Jimmy Regan . . . I cannot help you there."

"Can't or won't?"

"Both, I suppose."

I thought I understood. "Did you hear his confession?"

"For a few years there, I was his confessor, but I won't rely solely on the sanctity of confession to deflect your questions. Jimmy and I are friends, much as I'd like to think you and I are friends. My friendship with Jimmy was forged like ours, Gus, in the midst of very personal crisis. And it is neither my place as a priest nor as a friend to share the details or the nature of that crisis. Though I will say to you that it was many years ago and I can't see how it would have any bearing on what's going on here."

"Okay, Bill. I understand and I owe you far too much to press you on this. But can you answer me one question and then I'll leave it be between us?"

"If I can."

"This crisis, whatever it was, did it happen in the mid-1990s?"

He didn't have to answer in words. The look on his face was answer enough.

(FRIDAY, LATE AFTERNOON)

Dusk was taking a sharp turn toward night as I swung left off the Southern State onto the northbound Sagtikos/Sunken Meadow Parkway. With schools out and people getting an early jump on holiday travel, traffic was sparse on both sides of the road. I was more than a little preoccupied by any number of things when I saw the flashing lights in my rearview mirror. I immediately looked at my speedometer. I was doing seventy, fifteen over the Sag speed limit, though by Long Island standards I was crawling.

I wasn't really worried about getting a ticket. Cops, even retired ones, can usually escape that fate. No, the problem was that the Sag, like the Southern State and Northern State Parkways and unlike the Long Island Expressway, was patrolled by state troopers, not the SCPD. It was that territorial thing. State troopers weren't particularly fond of local cops and resented the hell out of our contracts, so they took a strange delight in any opportunity to bust our balls, and traffic stops were perfect opportunities for just that.

There was a brief moment when I thought that maybe the lights weren't for me. A very brief moment. When the unmarked Crown Vic zoomed up behind me, I knew it was game on. I pulled onto the shoulder, my tires kicking up a cloud of dust. I saw the Crown Vic emerge out of the dust as it pulled to a stop directly behind me. I flicked on my interior lights and rolled down my window. I retrieved my license, registration, and union card. I put the documentation in my left hand and stuck my hands on the steering wheel and watched out my sideview mirror, waiting for the trooper's inevitable approach. But the second the trooper shut off his Crown Vic's in-grille-mounted red-and-blue flashing lights, I got the sense that something was wrong. I just didn't know how wrong.

With those flashing lights off, we would be less conspicuous to passing cars. That was if passing cars would even notice us in the dying light. But it was only when the door of the Crown Vic opened and the man behind the wheel stepped out that I knew I might be in more serious trouble than just a little ball busting. The guy who got out of the unmarked Ford wasn't in uniform. He wasn't dressed in state trooper grays, nor did he have on a beige felt trooper hat. That didn't mean anything by itself. The troopers had plainclothes personnel, too, but I had never seen one doing a traffic stop. And then there was the fact that he already had his weapon fully drawn. That wasn't exactly doing it by the book. Look, traffic stops can be dangerous and there are times you have to have the attitude *proper procedure be damned*. The thing was, I couldn't see how this was one of those times. I'd been speeding, sure, but there was nothing about my car or the way I'd been driving to call particular attention to myself or to mark me as dangerous. I was being set up.

Then I realized I had my old service weapon in the pocket of my leather jacket. Not in a holster as it should have been. *Fuck!* Easy enough to shoot me and claim I'd been reaching for it, but it was too late for me to ditch it or to yank my jacket off and throw it in the backseat. Any sudden movement I might make would only give the guy an excuse to fire. Easy enough to call it all a tragic accident. So easy I could hear the guy's testimony in my head. *He jerked his right hand while I was approaching his vehicle, and when next I saw his hand, he had a weapon in it. What choice did I have?* I had to keep absolutely still and wait for Slava to pull up. That was, if he was still behind me.

"Get out of the car," the cop said, voice on edge, his gun no more than a foot or two from my head.

I kept my eyes straight ahead, making sure not to turn too rapidly. "No."

He hadn't expected that. "No?" his voice cracked.

"No." I nodded at my left hand, lifted it slowly, offering him my license, reg, and union card. "You'll see, I used to be on the job in Suffolk."

He slapped the stuff out of my hand and onto the floor of the front seat.

"Get the fuck out of the car!"

"No," I repeated, putting my left hand back on the steering wheel with my right. "You're not a trooper, are you? I'm guessing you're Suffolk County. Regan send you?"

Bang! I didn't see it coming, but I felt it. He hit me so hard in the temple with the butt of his Glock that I fell sideways onto the center console. My left ear was ringing like crazy and pain shot through my head and neck. I was stunned. There was a second there that I might have been completely out of it. While I was woozy, I thought I felt him reach into the car and reach into my jacket. I don't know. I was so disoriented for a time that I thought I might've imagined it. When my lids flickered open, the vision in my left eye was blurred. Then I felt a hand around my jacket collar, yanking me upright.

"I'm not gonna ask you again, asshole. Get the fuck outta the car!"

I was rubber-legged, blood from where he'd hit me leaking into my eyes, stinging, but I did as I was told, making sure my hands stayed as far away from my jacket pockets as possible. If this prick was going to shoot me, he was going to have to summon up the nerve to do it on his own. I wasn't going to help him.

"There's a Glock in my right jacket pocket," I said, standing on unsteady legs. "I'm still licensed to carry. You can check my—"

"Shut the fuck up and assume the position."

Before I could react, he slammed my head against the roof of my car, almost daring me to make a move. Instead, I kept as calm as I could manage, placing my arms wide and my hands flat against the roof. I moved my legs back at an angle away from the car. As he used his foot to kick my legs further apart, another car pulled up onto the shoulder.

"Fuck!" I heard the cop whisper to himself.

I had mixed feelings about it. Sure, I was happy that this guy wouldn't be able to execute me in cold blood, if that's what he meant to do. But if it was Slava, and he had that Russian pistol on him, I realized things could get really ugly in a hurry. I didn't turn my head fully around to look. Instead I took a peek under my right arm. It was Slava getting out of a ratty-looking old Honda Civic.

"Mr. Police, Mr. Police," he was screaming, clutching at his chest. "I am having heart attack. I am not so good breathing. You are helping me, please. You are helping. I have calling already 9-1-1 and told them where am I, but you are helping."

The cop was confused and he hesitated. If other cops were on the way, he couldn't very well just shoot me in front of a potential witness. Or he would have to shoot us both. It was one thing if he'd been ordered to get rid of me, but shooting a civilian . . . that was something else entirely. Then Slava, as if to make the cop hesitate even longer, dropped to his knees and then collapsed completely to the ground.

"Help me! Help, Mr. Police. Help!" he screamed again.

"Aren't you gonna help that man?" I said.

"No one asked you."

Sirens wailed in the distance and were coming our way, but the cop was undeterred. He reached into my jacket pocket and removed my gun. He stuffed it in his pocket. Next he shut off my car and took the keys out of the ignition. He then handcuffed my hands through the steering wheel. That left me in a very awkward position, but it was better than being dead. With the sirens almost upon us, the cop finally went over to tend to Slava.

Half a minute later the area was lit up like the Rockefeller Center skating rink at Christmas, but I didn't feel much like celebrating. Especially after the ambulance showed and one of the uniformed cops who responded to the scene finished frisking me.

"Look at this!" the uniform said, holding five small white paper packets in his palm. Each packet had a stamp of a crudely rendered dinosaur on it. Beneath the image of the dinosaur was the word "Raptor" in red ink.

The cop who pulled me over and who had since turned the care of Slava over to the EMTs clapped his hands together. "Yeah, Raptor, that's the same heroin that's been on the street, killing all these kids. We'll have to add possession charges to reckless driving, assaulting an officer, and resisting arrest. Good work," he told the uniform.

When the uniform went to his unit, the guy who pulled me over came very close to me and whispered in my ear, "You were warned, Murphy. You should've listened. Now it's time to start praying."

I didn't bother saying anything to him, nor did I pray. Since John's death, I had learned a lesson about wasting my time.

(FRIDAY NIGHT/SATURDAY MORNING)

I wasn't sure of the time, but I was sure of the place: a holding cell in the Third Precinct. Beyond that, there wasn't much I could be sure of, but I could make some pretty educated guesses. I was probably fucked, big-time. You didn't have to be a genius or a jurist to imagine the narrative an ADA would spin at trial. *The sudden and tragic loss of his beloved son knocked Mr. Murphy off his bearings. His entire life and family were blown apart. Who among us can't empathize with his plight? And for two years he tried in vain to hold it together, taking a menial job at a low-rent hotel, but just recently he had begun acting oddly, even irrationally, associating with known criminals, making wild accusations against one of the most respected police officials in our county and against the department itself. And so on and so on . . .*

Well, that was if things ever got as far as a trial. I didn't doubt there'd be a bargain on the table and a deal to make, one keeping my time inside to a minimum, but one that would ruin me nonetheless. No time inside was minimal enough for a cop, retired or not. Oh, everyone would be sympathetic as hell. *Poor, poor Gus, he just went off the deep end. Do you think he meant to use the heroin to do himself in?* Sympathy, as the last two years had schooled me, has serious limitations.

Something else I was sure of was that I had the mother of all headaches. That cop who pulled me over, whoever he was, had a heavy hand. At least the cut wasn't too bad, and when the EMT who arrived to take care of Slava's fake heart attack patched me up, I let him know that I'd recently had a tetanus shot. But just at the moment, tetanus and lockjaw were about the last things on my mind. There was a part of me, though, that took perverse satisfaction in all of this. I must have mightily pissed somebody off, that or I was getting close. Close to what, I wasn't sure. Because as far as the Delcamino murders were concerned, I had smoke but no mirrors, nothing to hold on to.

One thing was clear to me. Even if Milt Paxson had been responsible for sending Pauly Martino at me, he wasn't responsible for this. He didn't have that kind of juice. It was one thing to instigate a fistfight in a mall parking lot. Assault, false arrest, planting evidence, that was in a whole other league altogether. No one was going to risk his career and meaningful jail time by doing Milt Paxson that kind of favor. Nope, all this had me looking straight up at Jimmy Regan all over again. Or, if I was wrong about Regan and somebody was playing me, maybe that was exactly where they wanted me to look and who they wanted me to look at.

There was a thin string of hope I was clinging to. Although I'd been put through the pantomime of an arrest, had my rights recited to me, I hadn't been booked. Hadn't been printed. Hadn't had my photo taken. So I wasn't in the system. Not officially. Not yet. I hadn't even been interviewed. And it was because of those anomalies in procedure that I hadn't made a single phone call. Don't think I wasn't tempted to call Tammy Wang, a reporter I knew who worked the local crime beat for *Newsday*. I was so furious I wanted to scream it from the mountaintop, but this was Suffolk County. No mountains. No mountaintops. Just a few steep hills in Farmingville. Even if we had mountains, who would've listened?

There were other people I thought about calling. Annie? I didn't want to give her the satisfaction and I didn't want to upset Krissy.

Father Bill? He was too close to Jimmy Regan. Casey? Not exactly the follow-up phone call you want to make after a first date. Dr. Rosen? He was away. Pete McCann? Al Roussis? If I was radioactive before this, no cop would want to get within five miles of me now.

That's when it struck me again like it had the night before this whole mess began. The night before Tommy Delcamino showed up at the Paragon. It struck me that my world had grown so small. I once had so many friends I couldn't count them all, once measured my wealth not in terms of money but in terms of friends and goodwill. But now my world would fit inside the bottom half of a bathroom Dixie cup and I had been foolish with my wealth. Grief and pain cut me off, had let me shed my friends as a careless bird loses his feathers, one here, two there, failing to grow them back, losing so many he can no longer fly. Now when I thought about who my friends were, the list was tiny, made up more of acquaintances than friends, really. And not far down the list, just after Slava, Felix, and Fredo, was Aziza, the Pakistani girl from Dunkin' Donuts. These were people I barely knew who barely knew me. People who knew me only in terms of how much cream I liked in my coffee. Some of them didn't know that much.

At some point, I simply surrendered to the pain in my head and the weariness. So I had no idea what time it was when the cell door swung open. This was it. I was off to get fingerprinted and to pose for my close-up. To get interviewed, finally. Or maybe they'd just skip past all that and haul me over to the courthouse in Central Islip to room D11 for arraignment. I was pulled up into a sitting position. The air smelled strongly of coffee. Funny that the aroma of coffee should be so present because of how I'd been thinking of Aziza and of coffee before drifting off to sleep.

"Gus, come on," a voice from three rooms away called to me. Then my face got slapped, not so gently. "Come on, get up."

I opened my eyes and a blurry face appeared in front of me. It had the outlines of a familiar face and I waited for its mouth to move again, to speak again.

"Come on, Gus, you're getting kicked, free and clear. Drink some of this."

The blurry face with the now more familiar voice put a paper coffee cup in my hand and squeezed my stiff, cold fingers around it to make sure I had hold of it. The coffee was hot and how I liked it. It tasted like salvation. After a few swallows, my vision cleared and I recognized the voice and the face to which it belonged.

"Pete?"

"Come on." He yanked me to my feet. "You're getting released. Don't give anybody a chance to rethink this. You can't afford it."

We walked, him propping me up on our journey through the precinct out onto Fifth Avenue. Morning was about an hour away from breaking and it wouldn't break with a smile. December on Long Island could be a fickle month and this one had been fairly miserable on several accounts. They hadn't predicted snow, but it was here, about three inches of it blanketing the ground in the parking lot, the wind whipping it into our faces like pieces of crudely cut glass. If I wasn't fully awake before we got outside, I was now.

"My wallet and things," I said, gasping for breath against the wind, turning to head back into the precinct.

"I've got them," Pete said. "They're on the front seat. Everything but your gun. You're not getting that back so fast."

I thought about arguing with him about that, but I needed to get out of the weather.

"But where's my car?"

He pointed over my shoulder. "It's right there, for chrissakes. After we talk, I'll drive you back here to get it."

I was too tired and cold to fight about it and got in.

(SATURDAY MORNING)

I thought we'd end up in a diner, but Pete McCann wasn't about diners. Pete was all about wanting and getting, so at something like five thirty on a snowy Saturday morning the week before Christmas, we ended up at Malo, an after-hours club in an industrial park in Hauppauge. The doorman, a Polynesian guy as big as a backyard shed and whose eyes were about as feeling as a headstone, didn't even look twice at Pete and didn't ask for the cover. He sneered at me, shaking his head. I would have sneered at me, too. I hadn't had a chance to clean up or to look at myself in the mirror before Pete hauled me out of the holding cell. I didn't doubt that I looked a mess, the bloody bandage on my head adding to my visual charm. And I'm sure I didn't exactly smell great. Jail cells have a certain stink, a kind of sickening mash-up of pine-scented disinfectant and human decay that sinks deep into your pores and coats your skin. Sometime soon, I'd be spending a long time in a hot shower with several little bars of hotel soap.

Pete guided me over to a red vinyl banquette, but it wasn't like there was much competition for any of the seats in the place. Besides us, there were eight people in the club, and that was counting the guy at the door, the bored-looking barely dressed blond woman behind the bar, and the equally unenthusiastic and completely undressed black chick dancing on a makeshift stage in the center of the room. Though the music to which she was performing was some disposable piece of electro-thump trash, she was as evocative as an assembly-line robot, going through the motions as if doing it in her sleep. I'd been there. I knew all about that, about robotics. The other people in Malo were three too-loud, too-drunk guys, and two well-dressed white men in their midthirties. Real ruler-of-the-universe types who probably got hard-ons dreaming of subprime mortgages and Warren Buffett. One of Three Stooges was apparently on the verge of marriage.

I'd been to places like this with Pete before. Before, when we were pals. Before he became a detective. Before he fucked my wife and then kicked her to the curb. Before John died. That's just how my life, however I moved forward, was going to be divided from now on. This was the perfect venue for Pete, the ultimate hunting ground, because these places attracted people with money, people who liked bending the rules, people who had things like bored trophy wives looking to warm their feet in someone else's bed.

The blonde came out from behind the bar to take our order. She was wearing tight gold lamé hot pants, a really sheer black halter, and black stilettos. I wondered why she bothered. In a way, she was more naked than the dancer. Her expression was certainly less veiled. This wasn't the life she wanted, but it was the one she had and it was eating her alive. She was pretty and had probably been a knockout once.

"Pete," she said, nodding at him as if he were another piece of the furniture. "Glenlivet neat, right?"

"Can't sneak one past you, can I, Mags?"

She turned to me. Her face brightened. "And you, sir?"

"Irish coffee. Just the Irish and the coffee, okay?"

"Sure, anything for a friend of Pete's." She spoke it as if a death sentence.

"Then don't bother," I said, sounding cruel and especially nasty. "He's no friend of mine."

But if I thought my tone would put her off, I was wrong. She smiled. It was a really gorgeous smile. One I bet she had forgotten all about.

"In that case, it's on the house. He's no friend of mine, either." She turned and walked away, the lower cheeks of her heart-shaped ass flexing as she retreated to the bar.

"You make fans everywhere you go, huh, Pete?"

"Mags was my favorite mistake," he said, looking genuinely regretful. "Used to be on TV on soaps. Some minor roles, but never made it past there. Married a personal injury lawyer from Kings Point."

"This is a long way from Kings Point."

"Yeah, about as far as you can get. When she took the plunge, I guess she didn't realize her husband went through wives like wet naps at a rib restaurant. First hint shoulda been the prenup he made her sign."

"I'm sure you fucked her before the divorce."

"Years before," he said without an ounce of guile or guilt. "Christ, she was wicked in bed. Wicked good."

And just as he said those words, Mags brought our drinks. I reached for my wallet, but she shook her head at me. "No, I meant it. Drinks are on the house. Nice to see that Pete knows some people who have some manners and don't assume I'm community property."

"Community property." Pete laughed. "See what happens when you marry a lawyer. Stick to serving drinks and showing off your tits, Mags."

She turned and left.

"You really are an asshole, aren't you, Pete?"

His face went blank. I guess the time had come for us to talk about what we had really come here to talk about.

"Gus, I need you to listen to me and know that I'm not fucking around."

"Just say what you gotta say, Pete."

He smiled that disarming smile of his. "You know what a warning shot across the bow means, don't ya?"

I took a swallow of my drink, the smell of Jameson whiskey cutting through the coffee like a straight razor. It was a scent I knew too well. It smelled like my father, like my childhood.

"Let me finish my drink if we're gonna do this in riddles."

"Okay, Gus, you want it like that? Fine. Cut the crap and go back to doing what you were doing two weeks ago. Go back to mourning John, driving that stinking courtesy van, and making something out of what's left of your life. But leave the Delcaminos in your past. Forget about them. Pretend they were two anonymous people who got killed in a fucking avalanche in Switzerland or in a tsunami in Indonesia or some other fucking place. Do what you gotta do to get them out of your head, but do it and do it today. Do it now."

"Or else what, Pete?"

"Or else there won't be some poor Russian schmuck having a heart attack to save your ass. You know how close you came to going away last night?"

I nodded, drinking my drink.

"That can happen to you anytime. Worse can happen."

"You know, Pete, last night in the holding cell I had lots of time to think."

"That's trouble waiting to happen. What were you thinking about?"

"All sorts of things. Like about how small my life's gotten and how I don't have many friends anymore. But I was also thinking about how desperation makes people do some stupid shit."

"Oh, yeah, how's that?"

"I want you to tell the man pulling on your little marionette strings something for me."

"Gus!"

"No, Pete, hear me out and then I will consider myself duly warned and threatened."

He shook his head at me, but didn't speak.

"I don't know exactly why TJ Delcamino or his father were killed, but I pretty much know when the thing happened that led to their murders. I wasn't sure before yesterday, but I am now. Something happened four or five days before the kid was killed that led to the bloodshed. He found something out or stole something or stumbled into something that made him a lot of money fast and got him killed for the bother. And when I narrow that window down, when I find out what that thing was, it won't be me who'll be going away."

Something flickered across Pete's face. It was a barely perceptible change in his expression, something a person who didn't know him the way I knew him would have missed. Then he stood up, took what was left of his drink, and threw it in my face.

"You're a fucking fool with a death wish, Gus Murphy."

"Maybe so."

"I'm trying to help you out here."

"The only person you ever tried to help was yourself, and it usually involved helping yourself to things that didn't belong to you. Well, Pete, this is my fucking life and you can't have any more of it. And if there's not much time left to me, that's my choice, not your boss's. So go fuck yourself and fuck him, too."

He stormed out.

When I turned around to look, everyone else in the place except the dancer was staring at me in silence. The dancer continued to go through the motions, her taut, flexible body shining with sweat and glitter. Now she was the lone robot in Malo. I was done going through the motions.

The old Mercedes didn't exactly cut through the snow like it was on rails, but I was just happy for the lift back to my car. After Pete threw the drink in my face and left me at Malo, I'd called five different car services and local taxis to pick me up, but they all told me the same thing: Go fuck yourself and have a nice day. Those weren't the words they used, not even close, but they meant the same thing. Three of the places had their cars off the road because of the snow and the other two were so busy that they couldn't promise a car would get to me for three hours minimum.

When I came out of the bathroom after washing the single malt out of my hair, Mags came over to me and offered me a lift if I could wait an hour until she got off. Not that I had much choice, but I would have waited if it was sunny and seventy outside. I wanted to talk to her. Anyone who had been burned by Pete the way she had interested me. Anyone who had the sand to talk to him the way she did interested me. And I was a man who had eyes in his head. While I waited for her to dress in more functional clothing and to clean up after her shift, I helped the big man at the door break up a fight among the Three Stooges and throw them out into the snow. It felt good not to be on the receiving end for once.

"Thanks, bruddah," the big guy said, his hand swallowing mine. "I'm Malo."

"This is your place?"

He shook his head at me. He kind of reminded me of those statues on Easter Island. His head was almost large enough to be one.

"Silent partners, huh?"

He smiled. It was good to see he could smile, though his eyes didn't quite warm up. "You could say that."

Like Rusty's Salvage, Malo's was owned by people who didn't want the world to know they owned it. That used to mean the Mob. Not anymore. It might've been owned by the Bloods or the Crips, by K-Shivs or some celebrity who thought it would be cool to be the king. In any case, Malo wasn't going to discuss it with me.

"You're a long way from home, Malo."

"Long, long way." He left it at that, then added, "You know Pete?"

"We were on the job together. Used to be close."

"Kinda like being close to a snake, no?"

"Not kind of. He come in here a lot?"

Malo nodded that head of his, but I could see he wanted to wrap up our chat. "You come back anytime," he said before walking away to talk to the dancer, who had mercifully stopped going through the motions.

Fifteen minutes later I was outside warming up Mags' car, cleaning the snow off the Mercedes coupe. It was the least I could do. Like its owner, the car was still a fine piece of work, but fraying at the edges, showing little dings and dents and battle scars.

"It was my ex's parting gift to me," she said of the car as we pulled out of the lot. "A kind of a pat on the head for being a good girl and going away quietly. And I was such a chump that I was happy about it. I should've sold it. Taken the money and run. You have any idea how much these things cost to get serviced?" She didn't wait for an answer.

"And the parts . . . Christ! But I didn't know. Stan used to take care of all of that. Some parting gift."

I let her talk. As pretty as she was, I found bitterness, justified or not, really unattractive. I found it particularly unattractive in me, though it was what I had subsisted on for months at a time. She caught on.

"Sorry. Can we start over?"

"Sure."

She took her right hand off the steering wheel but kept her eyes on the road. She offered me her hand. "I'm Magdalena. Everyone calls me Mags."

"Gus Murphy." I took her hand. "Would it be okay if I called you Magdalena?"

"I would love that. Gus, is that really your name?

"John Augustus Murphy." I laughed. "Don't ask and please, don't call me John or Augustus."

"Deal," she said, taking back her hand and putting it on the wheel.

It got silent in the car.

"You smell great," I said just to say something and because it was true.

"Not for much longer. Stan, my ex, he had my perfume blended up specially for me in Grasse, France. Some of the ingredients are horrible things, but it does smell like spring. That's what it smells like to me, like new sweet flowers and honey, like grass and sage when you rub the leaves together in your hands. But there isn't much left. And when that's gone, that's that. I can't afford anything that doesn't come off the shelf." Then she caught the bitterness leaking into her voice. "Did Pete tell you about us?"

"He did, but you don't have to tell me about you and Pete, Magdalena. There's nothing you could say about the kind of man he is that I don't already know."

The car fell quiet again so that the only sound was the *thwap-thwap-thwap*ing of the wiper blades, but this time she broke the silence.

"Why so sad, Gus?"

I didn't know what to say, so I said, "What?"

"You're sad."

"And you're smart."

"Not smart. Far from smart. But when you do what I do, when you've been with the men I've been with . . ." She didn't finish the sentence. She didn't have to.

"Maybe we can talk about it some other time," I said, then pointed to the Third Precinct. "This is where I get off."

She turned the Mercedes into the lot. As we sat in her car, waiting for my car to warm up, she said, "Is there going to be some other time?"

"Sure."

But she had heard that answer many times before and didn't exactly brighten at hearing it from my lips.

"We don't know each other, Magdalena, but I keep my promises. Don't judge me because I used to be close to Pete."

"Okay."

"Can I ask you about Pete, but not about you and Pete?"

She shrugged. "Why not? But I thought you didn't want to talk about Pete."

"Not about him. About . . . you know what? Forget it. I'm glad I met you and I don't want to spoil it. Pete's spoiled enough things in my life."

Her face lit up and I was caught completely off guard when she leaned into me and kissed me hard on the mouth, opening my lips with hers and sliding her tongue on top of mine. At the same time, her left hand was on my thigh. I can't say that I didn't kiss her back or that I yanked her hand off me. But when the kiss hit a natural valley, I moved my head back and slipped my fingers into her hand.

"Didn't you like that?"

"Very much."

"But . . ."

"But I think there's something the both of us need and maybe even want more than being together."

She pulled back, looking confused, but not hurt. "What's that?"

"A friend."

She seemed to relax and let her head fall against my shoulder. "I could sure use one of those, but does that mean never?"

I said, "It means let's see what comes."

"The future's never been very kind to me, Gus."

"Or the past to me. That leaves us with now, I guess. And I could really use a friend in my life. Besides, look at me. I'm a mess."

"A handsome mess, but you look like you could use some fixing up." She touched the bandage on my head. "Does it hurt?"

I felt a big smile on my face. "Not just now, no. I could really use a shower and some sleep."

"Nice shower and bed in my condo."

"Magdalena!"

"Can't blame a girl for trying."

We exchanged cell phone numbers. She waited around until most of the snow had melted off the glass. Then I watched her pull onto Fifth Avenue and disappear behind a swirling curtain of white flakes.

46

(SATURDAY MORNING)

Felix's eyes got big at the sight of me as I trudged through the doors of the Paragon. The lobby was busier than I'd ever seen it. In spite of the line at the registration desk being twenty deep, Felix waved me over to talk to him.

"What has happened to you, Gus?" he asked, typing a guest's info into his computer. The guest, a skeleton with a suntan and a Delray Beach golf hat on his gray head, was impatiently clacking his tongue against ill-fitting dentures.

"Long story. What's the line about?"

"Canceled flights. We are nearly fully booked."

"Kurt Bonacker will be happy."

"Yes, I believe he is in his office popping the Champagne corks."

"Felix, you made a joke."

He smiled in spite of himself.

"Is this going to take much longer?" Mr. Delray Beach whined.

The smile disappeared from Felix's face. "Just one more moment, sir."

"Okay," I said, "I'll let you get back to your work."

"Wait, Gus. One more thing. It is the reason why I called you over."

"What is it?"

"Slava is waiting for you in your room. He needed a place to sleep. I was not sure if that would be okay with you, but you did not answer your cell phone and we did not have a spare room for—"

"No problem, Felix. It's fine. Thanks."

Slava, looking as disheveled as I felt, as I must have looked, was sitting on the edge of the bed, holding my son's framed photo in his hand. It was the shot of John Jr. at thirteen, spinning a basketball on the tip of his index finger, a proud smile a mile wide across his face. It was my favorite picture of him. Even though he had grown into a really handsome young man and an accomplished ballplayer, it was John at this age that I held on to. John with braces on his teeth and a bit of acne on his slightly pudgy face. This was my son on the verge of all of his firsts, on the verge of growing into his manhood. A thing he never got to finish. I wondered if any of us ever finished.

Slava held the photo up to me. "Is your boy?"

I nodded. "John Jr."

Slava put the frame back on the nightstand. "He is dead, no?"

Those words took the breath out of me because in two years I don't think anyone else ever had the courage to say them to me. They had said words that meant the same thing—gone, passed away, perished, left us, no longer with us, a thousand different euphemisms—but I can't recall someone just saying the word "dead." I didn't know whether to cry or to kiss that ugly Polack for his bluntness. I did neither.

"Two years." I pointed at my chest. "He had a heart defect that never showed up in tests. One day he was playing basketball . . ."

"He is where it hurts in you."

"He is where it hurts."

"It never will leave you, this hurt," Slava said, touching a big beefy hand to his own chest. "Never it is leaving, but it is good to be remembering."

Slava was full of surprises, a gorilla with the instincts of a cop and the soul of a poet.

"I remember."

He changed subjects. "What is happening to you after the police are taking you away?"

"Nothing," I said. "They threw me in a cell overnight and then had an old friend of mine read me the riot act."

A puzzled look spread across his face. "What is riot act?"

"He warned me to drop it or worse was going to happen to me than what happened last night."

The confusion vanished. "Are you dropping it?"

"Fuck no."

Slava clapped his hands together and pulled two airline bottles of vodka out of his jacket pocket.

We drank them down.

"And what happened to you?" I asked.

"Also nothing. They tell cop I am having panic attack, not heart attack. Then I go away."

"You might've saved my life there, Slava. I owe you for that."

"What is expression in English? Someday maybe you are returning the favor for me."

"Okay."

He stood and offered me his hand. When he took mine in his, there was nothing casual about it. It was nothing like shaking hands the way I had earlier with Malo or Magdalena. This was a blood oath. And when Slava stared into my eyes, I knew this was a pact not to be treated lightly.

"What we are doing now, Gus?"

"Nothing today. With this weather, I think we're okay for a while. Go home and clean up. Get some rest. It's what I'm planning to do."

He didn't argue with me. "I am going."

"Are you on tomorrow night, Slava?"

He nodded.

"Can you come in early if you have to?"

He smiled that gap-toothed smile of his.

"Okay, we'll talk."

When he left, I clicked the privacy lock behind him. The shower was singing a siren's song to me, but there was a call I had to make first. A call I should have made days ago.

Casey didn't answer her phone the first few times I tried her. Frustrated, I finally gave into the siren's song of a long hot shower and sleep.

I dreamed of my son, but not how I had dreamed of him so many times in the past. There was no guilt involved, no anger. Not on my part, anyway. John wasn't angry, I don't think. Mostly, he seemed frustrated at me in the way a teacher might be angry with a favorite student who just wasn't getting the obvious lesson. We were in Brady Park, where I'd been with Al Roussis only a few days before. John was standing beneath the backboard support on the main basketball court, pointing to where Al and I had stood in the far corner of the park. At first John's pointing was just that, pointing. Then, as I failed to understand what he was pointing at or why, his gesturing became more animated, more insistent. The gestures spoke for John, *Come on, Dad. Come on. The answer is there. Right there!*

I know I asked him what I was missing, but when he opened his mouth to answer, his words were drowned out by the deafening honking of geese. Suddenly, in the sky above us, a thousand geese, ten thousand, a million. So many they blotted out the sun. Then one dropped out of the sky. Then another and another until it was raining dead geese. After the rain stopped and they were gone, the sun shone again. The corpses of the geese that only seconds before had littered every inch of the park were gone, too, but for one. It lay beneath a pile of leaves, neck snapped. When I looked up, John was walking away toward the far corner of the park. I called after him. Ran after him. Couldn't catch up. Then a buzzing sound filled up the empty spaces in my dream. I was no longer dreaming. I was awake, grabbing my cell phone off the nightstand.

It was Casey. I asked her to hold on for just a second as I tried to orient myself. I saw that it was still snowing, but without the ferocity of the morning. I drew the shades and sat back down on the bed. I clicked on the TV and muted the sound.

When I got back on the phone, Casey said, "I see you worked your way down the list of things to do and finally got around to me."

"I guess I deserved that."

"Look, Gus, one of the reasons I'm divorced is I got tired of being a second thought," she said, a mixture of anger and hurt in her voice. "No one lives to be someone else's next best option."

"I'm sorry. I know I should have called sooner, but I got caught up in some stuff that . . . it's hard to explain."

"Try."

"I'm not sure I can and I'm not sure you want to hear."

She wasn't buying it. "Don't treat me like that, like you know better for me. I'm a big girl. I'm all grown up. I tie my own shoes and cut my own meat and everything. I'll let you know if I want to hear."

I didn't answer immediately because I was drifting, thinking about how we scar each other. About how Annie and I had scarred each other. About Magdalena's obvious scars. No one comes out the other end of any collision unscathed or, at the minimum, unchanged.

"I spent last night in a jail cell."

There was silence on the other end of the line. I'd shocked her. I suppose that's what I meant to do.

"Why? I mean, what did you do?" she asked, her voice thinner, unsure.

"I got pulled over on the Sagtikos and the cops planted five packets of heroin on me."

"Oh, my God!"

"See what I mean, Casey? It's complicated."

"Can't you go to the . . ."

"To the police? Is that what you were going to say? Can't go to the police when they're the ones trying to screw with you. There's something I'm doing that they don't like and they're willing to go a long way to stop me. Until last night, I wasn't sure how far."

"Gus, I . . . I don't know how I'm supposed to react."

"There is no how, no playbook about this stuff. I like you. Tuesday night was great. Being with you was amazing, but I may not be who you thought I was. And that's okay. I didn't come into this with expectations. You did. That nice, quiet guy with the empty heart you saw at the club on the weekends, he's a guy you created in my image. Now you're dealing with who I am. And if I'm a disappointment, I'm sorry because I like you and because you can really cook."

She laughed, but not hard enough.

"Casey, let me make this easy for the both of us, okay?"

"Okay."

"Let me finish this thing I have to do and then, if you feel like you want to try this again, we can. Besides, you're better off keeping your distance from me until this thing blows over. Then, if you feel like you're not up for it, we'll always have that one night."

There was a palpable sense of relief from her end of the phone. That was answer enough, but she said, "I'm sorry, Gus."

"Don't be."

She blurted out, "It's Jocasta."

"What is?"

"My name."

"It's different."

"No one wants to be that different when they're growing up," she said.

"Your secret's safe with me, Casey."

And that was that. I didn't fool myself that there would be a future for us, but I wasn't sad about it. I'd learned an unexpected lesson. Not only wasn't I who Casey thought I was. I wasn't who I thought I was.

I flipped around the channels for a while, settling on the local cable news channel to see how bad the storm had been and to give myself a chance to absorb the events of the day. Even more than Pete McCann's warning, more than Casey's disappointment and relief, it was the dream I couldn't shake. There was a message in there I was leaving for myself as Al Roussis had left for me when we met in the park. Unfortunately, I wasn't any closer to figuring it out now than I had been a few minutes ago or a few days ago.

The storm had pretty much blown itself out after dumping six inches on the island. What was left was only the very tail end of it. The unfortunately chipper weatherman, pointing at a front over the Rockies, said that we might very well be in for a white Christmas. I wasn't in the mood for his happy smile and predictions of snow, so I turned my attention away from the screen until I heard the teaser for the next segment. *Next up on News Channel 12, the Feds raid a salvage yard in Deer Park. Stay tuned to see what they came up with.* When I looked back at the screen, there was video footage showing the front entrance to Rusty's Salvage, and from the video, they switched to an old booking photo of Frankie Tacaspina Jr.

I didn't bother waiting to watch the report.

"Roussis," he said picking up the phone.

"How'd you manage it?"

"Manage what?" he said, a smile in his voice.

"Cut the shit, Al."

"I have a friend in the government who owed me a big favor."

"Did you get it?"

"The .357? Yeah, it was in his desk. He claims it's not his, but belongs to some Nardo character who works there. May take a day or two for us to get it from the Feds to do the prints and ballistics to see if it matches the weapon that killed Tommy Delcamino. On the positive side, my friend says it looks like it's been fired recently."

"So," I said, "your Fed buddy come up with anything else worthwhile besides the revolver?"

"Nothing they can tie to Frankie Tacos, no. Sure, yeah, there was some hot merchandise on the premises, but not more than might be there innocently. And as far as your pal Tacaspina is concerned, he's claiming he just rents space from the owners of Rusty's. He even had rent receipts to prove it."

"You believe him?"

"Of course not, but what I believe doesn't mean a whole lot."

"The Feds holding him?"

"He made bail in thirty seconds. The gun better prove out or he'll walk. It would help if we had a motive for him to kill the father. You have a motive for him killing the father?"

"One that I can tie directly to Frankie Tacos and not a hundred other people? No. But I'm close on having a motive on at least the kid's murder."

"It's not my case."

"So you keep saying, Al, but what if the murders are connected?"

"It isn't something I can work with. Give me something to work with."

I changed the subject. "When you agreed to meet me the other day, why did you pick Brady Park?"

"You used to be a good cop, Gus, what happened to you?"

"Dumb question."

"Sorry, that's not what I meant."

"For chrissakes, Al, what did you mean?"

He didn't answer the question. "As soon as we get the ballistics back, I'll call you."

I began to tell him about spending the previous night at the Third Precinct and about Pete McCann's threats, then I realized that I really didn't know who I should trust. For all I knew, Al Roussis was as much a part of this as Pete McCann.

"Yeah, Al, do that. Call me when you get the results."

After I hung up, I paced the floor of my room. I thought about calling Slava and going over my idea about how to deal with Milt Paxson. I considered calling Magdalena and tossing our proposed trial period as friends right out the window, but I couldn't get the dream of John and the geese out of my head. It had to be something about the case Al Roussis had talked about when we were in the park, the Alison St. Jean case. That had to be it. I was on my way out the door to head to the business center to do some research when the hotel phone rang. It was Felix.

"What's up?"

"There are two men waiting for you in the coffee shop. One says he's a friend. Bill is his name."

"Thin man, dressed badly, ugly shoes. Smells like cigarettes."

Felix laughed. "Yes, that is him."

"And the other man?"

"He did not offer his name."

"What's he look like?"

"He is very tall. Older than you. His hair is red with gray—"

"Okay, Felix. Thanks."

"Do you know this other man?"

"I do," I said before hanging up the phone.

Then I mouthed the name: Jimmy Regan.

(SATURDAY EVENING)

As fate or luck or karma or whatever the fuck you'd call it would have it, Father Bill and Jimmy Regan were seated and waiting for me at the same booth and wingtip table that Tommy Delcamino had sat at and waited. Only this time the coffee shop was buzzing with activity because of the unexpected flood of guests. Both of them had cups of coffee in front of them that only Bill showed any interest in. Regan just stared at his with a kind of disdain, a drinker's disdain. I recognized the look from seeing it on my father's face more times than I could count. It was as if drinking wasn't worth the effort if there wasn't going to be a bit of a burn down your throat or in your belly at the end of it.

"Bill." I nodded. "Chief Regan."

Jimmy Regan stood up, extending his right hand. Although he was no taller than me and had me by at least fifteen years in age, he projected this larger-than-life image that somehow made me feel much smaller and in awe. It was amazing how he did it and how he did it even now in spite of my being so suspicious of him. Was it his big avuncular smile that seemed to say, *Come on, son, give us a hug. You're safe as long as you're with your Uncle Jimmy.* Or was it the fire in what was left of his red hair or the sparkle of mischief in his green eyes? He was a paradox, half Finn McCool, half leprechaun. But unlike Bill Kilkenny, Jimmy Regan didn't try to affect a lilt or inject old-country phrasing into his speech.

"Murphy," he said as if I was still on the job. "I hear from Bill you've got some questions. I've got some answers. Let's trade."

"Sounds like a plan." I tried not to sound intimidated, but I wasn't sure how successful I was. "But first let's get out of here. Follow me." I didn't make it optional. "Bring your coffees if you'd like. I'll be able to add something to them to freshen them up."

Regan took his. Bill, too, though he eyed me with great suspicion. When Bill made to put some money on the table, I told him to forget it, that I would see to it and make sure the waitress got a nice tip. He seemed relieved, but no less suspicious.

The bar was closed to the guests as it was being transformed into the Full Flaps Lounge. The club wouldn't be open for an hour yet. With the weather the way it was, I doubted they were going to get many of the usual crowd, most of whom came from other parts of the island. Yet with the hotel so full of guests unfamiliar with the area and without cars, they'd probably do all right regardless. For now the bar area itself was quiet and the only activity in the room was the DJ setting up his sound equipment and portable lights by the dance floor. I gestured at the barstools and, to counteract Jimmy Regan's aura, I got behind the bar. I stood over him and Bill as I pulled a bottle of Jameson eighteen-year-old Limited Reserve from the very top shelf.

"This is as good as it gets, gentlemen. A hundred twenty bucks a bottle in stores."

"Seems a shame to spoil it with coffee," Regan said.

I poured him two neat fingers' worth in a rocks glass. Bill pointed at his coffee and held his thumb and index finger slightly apart.

"Just a touch, Gus."

I obliged. I left the bottle on the bar within easy reach of Jimmy Regan's left hand. I took a Corona out of the fridge.

"Up yours!" Regan said with a laugh as we clinked bottle to glass to coffee cup.

Regan took his in a swallow. "That goes down smooth. May I?" He took hold of the bottle.

"Of course."

Regan poured himself two fingers again, but was careful not to take it all in a gulp.

"So, Murphy, are you back on your feet yet?"

I knew what he meant. He hadn't come to John's funeral, but had sent lovely flowers. It was he who suggested to the union head that Bill Kilkenny be the priest to help us through John's death. I owed him something for that.

"Not sure I will ever be fully back, but I can say my footing is better, Chief."

He raised his glass. "To your boy."

We all drank to that. He poured himself another without bothering to ask this time. Bill glared at me, but kept his silence.

"What questions do you have for me, Murphy?" he asked, sipping at his third glass of Irish.

"I heard you showed up at the murder scene of TJ Delcamino last August. Not for nothing, Chief, but TJ Delcamino wasn't exactly a high-profile criminal or local personality. Why show up there at all?"

"Truth?"

"Saves a lot of trouble, don't you think?"

"I got an anonymous tip on my cell that there'd be a body in that lot in Nesconset," he said. "I called it in, but someone, I think a neighbor walking a dog, had already put in the call. I went to the scene because I was close by, a Turkish restaurant in Setauket, and I was curious about why I'd received the call." He put up his palms like a traffic cop. "Before you ask, the call was traced back to a prepaid cell. So I've got no idea who it was who called me or why. And no, I didn't recognize the voice."

"So before that night in August, there was no connection between you and the dead kid?"

"Like you say, Murphy, this Delcamino kid, he wasn't exactly a high-profile criminal. I was probably off the streets before he was out of diapers."

"And his father, Tommy Delcamino, you didn't know him, either."

"I wasn't in the Second long enough to cross paths with him, no." The chief had finished his third whiskey and was conscious of it. He slid the bottle away from himself, but not completely out of arm's reach. He may once have had his drinking under control, but it was pretty clear those days were over. He had the jones bad.

Bill was still glaring at me, but even if he hadn't been, I wouldn't have poured Regan another. If he wanted to get wasted, I wasn't going to keep pouring. From that first drink on, it was his doing. That's what I told myself, anyway.

"Chief, can you tell me why I've been warned by everyone from Pete McCann to Lou Carey to Milt Paxson to Alvaro Peña to Al Roussis to Pauly Martino to keep my nose out of the Delcamino cases?"

He made a face when I mentioned Martino and poured himself another drink. "Who in Christ's name is—sorry, Bill—who the fuck is Pauly Martino?"

"A hothead from the Marine Bureau. And look, Chief, let's not pretend that word didn't come down from on high. Even before I got involved with this, the father, Tommy Delcamino, went to Carey and Paxson with solid leads and names and they ignored him."

Regan's face twisted into a red knot. "Let's not pretend! Just who in the hell do you think you're talking to, Murphy? Do you know who I am?"

"I know who you are, Chief Regan. I know."

Regan realized he was losing it and took a few deep breaths. "Sorry, Murphy, that was uncalled for." He held up his glass, jiggled it at me, and smiled. "Yes, I suppose you know exactly who I am." He finished the drink just the same and motioned for me to put the bottle back on the shelf. "This is where you're living these days? In this ratty hotel?"

"And working," I said, wondering where he was going with this.

"Working?"

"I drive the courtesy van at night and I am what passes for a house detective around here. I also work security for this club on Friday and Saturday nights. It's not much of a life, but it's the one I've got."

Then he showed his hand. "Why not come back to the job and do what it is you're good at? Be among your own. We could find a place for you in any bureau you like. You could come work for me."

Bill's glare changed to shock.

"Thanks, Chief. It's tempting. Maybe after we clear this stuff up I can come in and we can discuss it."

"My door's always open to you. Just before, you mentioned that this Delcamino guy, the father of the vic, had gone to Carey and Paxson with names, solid leads, you said."

"I did."

"You know they're solid how?"

"Because I checked them out."

"Did you? I thought you were a courtesy van driver and did hotel security," he said, a jolly smile on his face. But I could see him staring up at the bottle of Jameson I had since placed back on the very top shelf.

"Just did what I used to do in uniform. I asked a few questions, is all."

"And the names the father gave you, who are they?"

"A kid named Ralph O'Connell who grew up with TJ Delcamino. A drug dealer who goes by the handle Lazy Eye, but whose real name is Lamar English. Lives over in Wyandanch. The other two you will have heard of: Frankie Tacaspina Jr. and Kareem Shivers."

Jimmy Regan clapped his hands together and laughed. "Well, Frankie Tacos has new worries of his own, the thieving prick. He's worse than his father. But this Kareem Shivers, sorry, don't know him."

"Ex-boxer, gang enforcer, now moves drugs all over the island. Also goes by the name K-Shivs. Lives over in Melville."

Regan shrugged. "I got nothing, but I will personally pass the names on to Lou Carey and his *new* partner and make sure they follow up. You have my hand on that." He offered it to me and I shook it for a second time. "About the word from on high . . . It sounds like you're right about that, like someone's put out the word to shut you out," he said, placing his hand on his heart, "but it wasn't me. My honor on that. And I will make sure a different word comes down tomorrow. From Monday morning on, I guarantee you that no one will be chasing you off or threatening you."

"Thanks. I would really appreciate that." I noticed his mention of Lou Carey's new partner, but didn't ask about it. If he wanted to explain further, he would. I also thought about bringing up my night in the Third Precinct, but decided to play a waiting game.

"Murphy, do you think I could have one for the road? Doesn't have to be fine stuff."

I pulled the expensive Jameson back down from its lofty perch and poured him a healthy one for the road. I held the bottle up to Bill.

"Red wine, I think, Gus," Bill said, pushing his empty coffee cup aside.

I poured him a glass of a Chianti.

After Chief Regan had taken a few sips of that drink for the road, he said, "And I've heard about that little incident involving you and some of my detectives last evening. I've taken steps to discipline those involved. That Milt Paxson has been a thorn in my ass since the day he made detective, the chesty bastard. I've been looking for a way to take him down a few pegs and he's given it to me. Well, maybe he and his pal who pulled you over will enjoy their time back in uniform."

"You know they planted—"

Regan raised his right hand. "I know. It was only talcum powder."

"So that was Paxson's doing?"

"Like I said, Murphy, the man's been a pain in my ass for years. He has a strong distaste for you. But please, let's keep this in-house. Let me take care of it without raising a public stink. I know you've got every right to scream bloody murder about it, but do this for me and the department. All this heroin flowing into the high schools . . . it makes us look bad and the last thing we need is to air this laundry in the media. I'm glad to take it in the face for the team for now, but if the press gets a whiff of this . . ."

"I can do that, Chief."

While we finished our drinks in silence, the DJ tested his lighting effects. First he turned the room lights off. He turned a bright narrow spotlight on a mirrored ball that hung from a tall pole next to his turntables. As the ball spun round, a whirl of stars appeared on the walls of the club, on the fixtures, and on our faces. The DJ put various filters in front of the spotlight, changing the color of the whirling stars from red to orange to green to blue to yellow. Then, as I turned to put the bottle of Irish back in its spot, the room went black again and the DJ turned on his strobe. In the bar mirror I noticed Bill raising his glass to his lips. Each part of his movement was broken up into singular frames. His glass and arm were here, then there, then here again. It was Regan I was focused on, though. And in the flashes of light, his expression morphed from a nasty drunken scowl to fury, his green eyes seeming to glow with rage. *His eyes,* I thought, *there's something about his eyes.* But before I could figure out what that something was, the strobe shut off and the lights came up.

"Are we good now, Murphy?" Regan asked, slamming his glass upside down on the bar.

"We always were, Chief. Thanks again."

"Oh, Christ, Kilkenny," Regan said, skipping the apologies to Bill, "I need to get something to eat." He then pointed at the hallway that led to the club exit. "Can we get out that way?"

"Sure, go ahead. It leaves you on the south side of the building."

Regan went straight for the exit, but Father Bill lagged behind. A look of pure consternation on his gaunt, pale face.

"We'll talk, the two of us," he said to me.

I nodded.

"For fuck's sake, Kilkenny," Regan shouted from the hallway, "are you coming to get some dinner with me or walking home to that shithole basement apartment of yours? Massapequa, Jesus!"

Bill turned and left. I hadn't been certain of anything until now, but one thing this little visit made crystal clear. Jimmy Regan was involved in this mess. I didn't know how and I didn't know how deep: up to his ankles or up to his eyeballs. I would have staked my life on it. The thing was, I was afraid that's what it would come to.

liked the lobby late at night or very early in the morning. It was a place I had spent a lot of time in over the last year. Between runs to the station and the airport, it was usually where I sat reading those left-behind and forgotten novels. I didn't usually go back up to my room. I didn't like doing that. When I was at work, I was at work. Besides, my room could get awfully claustrophobic. My room, that's where and when John would come back to me. The space of the lobby let me breathe easier. And I could talk to Slava or whoever was working the night registration desk. But reading a guest's forgotten novel wasn't why I was in the lobby at that hour.

When Jimmy Regan and Bill showed up, I'd been on my way down to the business center to do some nosing around about the Alison St. Jean case. I had tried to get a turn at one of our two computers several times during the evening, but with the hotel full and everyone shuffling to make new travel plans, there was actually a line out the door of the business center for several hours. So I spent some time in the club, lending a hand. The crowd was bigger than I expected it would be and, because so many of the people at the club had rooms at the hotel for the night, they drank way more than the regulars dared. The bar got a hundred dollars' worth of my money, too. That just about covered the cost of Bill's Chianti, my beer, and Jimmy Regan's thirst for fine Irish whiskey. Another twenty went for their bill and tip to the coffee shop.

Part of me hoped Casey would show up and that I'd be able to explain more fully why I hadn't been attentive enough. Part of me wished she would have showed so that I might talk her into my bed. Both of those parts of me were disappointed, probably for the better. There was no denying a woman like Casey would be well rid of me whether the sex was good between us or not. I was damaged goods, a dented can. Like I'd said to her, I was who I was, not who she had wanted me to be.

Afterward, when the crowd thinned out, I went up to my room, watched *SportsCenter* and slept for a few hours. Then, sometime around three, I made myself coffee with the one-cup machine in my room—coffee creamer, yuck!—and wandered back down to the lobby. The business center was finally empty, though it did look as if a bomb had hit it. At least one of the computers was still in working order. If I wasn't such a low-tech kind of guy, I might have downloaded the app for how to do this on my smartphone.

I got several pages of hits even before I finished typing Alison St. Jean's name into the search engine. As I wasn't sure what I was looking for, I went through the first couple of hits very carefully. Mostly they were newspaper stories recounting the very early stages of the investigation when it was believed Alison had been the victim of a sexual predator. Then, after the autopsy had been performed and the motive for Alison's death became murkier, the reporting got less feverish. The area residents who consented to be quoted expressed an odd sense of relief. At least the killer, whoever he was, wasn't a sexual predator. That was something to hang on to, wasn't it? When the pins get knocked out from under you, you look for anything to hang on to. Anything. Things didn't get really ugly until the deeper truth of what happened to Alison St. Jean came to light, when it was discovered that it was a group of neighborhood girls who had done this terrible thing and that two of her killers had babysat Alison. Yet as chilling and horrifying as it was, none of it rang any bells for me in terms of the Delcamino homicides.

Halfway down the page, though, I found a site that bore a newspaper headline, and that headline rang the bells loudly and rattled my memory, all right. The headline read: "Hero Cop Speaks for Murdered Girl." That hero cop's name was James Regan. And when I clicked on the site, the full article appeared. There, side by side, were grainy black-and-white photos of Alison St. Jean and a very much younger Jimmy Regan in uniform. Although the events happened over twenty-five years ago, just seeing the headline and those photos brought most of it back for me.

The story goes that Regan, whose wife had recently given birth to a baby girl, and another uniform from the Fourth had worked off the clock for two weeks straight, talking to hundreds of people who lived in the vicinity of Brady Park and Millers Pond. Then they finally found an older gentleman who remembered seeing a girl who fit Alison's description with a pack of older girls heading toward the park. Not only did he recall seeing a girl who resembled Alison with those girls, but he also remembered some of the costumes those older girls were wearing. It was easy police work from there, tracking down the girls who had worn those particular costumes. Once one of them talked, they were all finished. On the next page of hits was a piece detailing the promotion to detective of hero cop Jimmy Regan. The piece also mentioned the promotion of Neil Furlong to detective. Buried deep in the body of the story were a few lines about how Furlong had been a help to Regan in his quest to bring Alison St. Jean's killer or killers to justice.

Neil Furlong. Neil Furlong. I repeated the name to myself over and over again. He had been a detective in the Second before I got on the job. I didn't know him more than to nod at, and he'd been transferred out of the Second before I'd done my first year. He wasn't exactly a friendly guy—pretty sour-faced and bitter, was my recollection—but there was something else about him that I should have remembered. I didn't have to strain very hard because the Internet made refreshing one's memory pretty damned easy. When I typed his name into Google, I got several hits. Not nearly as many as I had for Alison St. Jean, but enough for my purposes.

In 1994, Neil Furlong had been caught in an Internal Affairs Bureau sting involving a joint narcotics/vice task force that had been set up to explore the long-rumored linkage between prostitution and drug distribution in Nassau and Suffolk counties. It didn't take long for a few of the detectives involved to fall prey to the obvious temptations of that line of work. And it took even less time for IAB to jump on the accusations made against the task force detectives. Furlong escaped criminal prosecution, but he hadn't escaped with much else. He lost his job and his pension.

When I walked out of the business center, I noticed there was a stir of activity in the lobby and that the sun had risen, if only barely. I smelled that the coffee shop was open and made my way there. I wanted to get some food in me and a few more hours of sleep behind me before I went digging into the past.

51

(SUNDAY, EARLY AFTERNOON)

he roads were mostly clear as I drove north to the LIE, then east toward Mastic, but the tracking device that had been planted under my front passenger seat wasn't coming along for the ride. I'd thrown it in a sewer. The only place it would lead anyone was to a water treatment plant. I didn't want any company with me where I was going. I made sure to check my mirrors frequently to be certain I was by my lonesome. Saturday's storm and today's clear skies helped me with that. There were many fewer cars on the road, and if anyone was tailing me, it was by drone.

As I approached the LIE, I turned my eyes right to look at Dr. Rosen's building. It seemed like an eternity since I'd sat in his office, though it had only been twelve days. For two years, my world had been a sad and painful play reprised at irregular intervals by a close-knit troupe of actors whose only purpose it seemed was to deepen the wounds we shared. Murder had changed all that, shaking me from my grief-stricken sleepwalk. I owed Tommy Delcamino for that, and it was a bill I meant to pay.

I got off at William Floyd Parkway south. If I had gone north instead, I would have passed by the Brookhaven National Laboratory and miles of wildlife-laden forest as I headed toward Shoreham-Wading River. But no, I was headed due south, deep into the heart of Long Island's great contradiction: the areas of Mastic, Mastic Beach, and Shirley. So close to the south shore with lots of beachfront property and wetlands, so near Smith Point Park, yet still within a two-hour train ride of Manhattan, they should have been prime, thriving communities, maybe even a poorer man's Hamptons. They weren't, though. Don't get me wrong, there were some beautiful houses down here and things had improved, but this area had always had a weird vibe and a somewhat dangerous rep. The rep wasn't completely undeserved. Ask any cop who'd ever served in the Seventh Precinct.

But I wasn't interested in any cop just at the moment. I was interested in Neil Furlong. Furlong lived on Neptune Avenue in Mastic, a short rock toss away from the Poospatuck Indian Reservation. Don't be fooled by the enchanting Indian name. There were times the Poospatuck was seventy acres of hell surrounded on two sides by the Forge River and Poospatuck Creek. This smallest of New York State's reservations was the realm of the Unkechaug Tribe. It was home to about three hundred people, double-wide trailers, cheap cigarette shops, and the same problems that plagued reservations everywhere: alcohol, drugs, crime, and hopelessness.

Furlong's house was small and shabby. Someone had tried to vinyl-side the place, but seemed to have given up three quarters of the way through the job so that the east-facing flank of the house was covered only in foiled squares of rigid insulation and sun-bleached tar paper. Several of the vinyl strips on the rest of the place were either bulging or missing altogether. The cyclone fencing around the perimeter of the lot was more rust and memory than metal, and there were two cars up on concrete blocks in the driveway. The only thing missing seemed to be a nasty, drooling Rottweiler on a chain. The six inches of snow that had fallen yesterday were undisturbed on Furlong's lot except for a lone set of raccoon prints. The blanket of white powder covered a multitude of sins, but it would have taken a blizzard to disguise them all. If not for the steady stream of steam pouring out a dryer vent on the west side of the house, I might have thought no one was home.

I walked carefully up to the sagging wooden porch, not knowing what hazards might be hiding beneath the snow. I was smart to have been cautious. There were piles of uncollected newspapers and sales circulars lurking, the soles of my shoes slipping here and there on the plastic bags in which they were wrapped. Good thing I didn't turn an ankle. When I got up to the porch, I noticed a wooden wheelchair ramp at the left end of the porch, screened by a tangle of overgrown hedges that hadn't seen trimming since Obama and hope had been synonymous.

The doorbell didn't work and the glass pane was missing from the top of the storm door. So I stuck my hand through the storm door and rapped my knuckles against the steel-clad front door. It didn't take long until I heard a woman's voice come from the other side of the door.

"Who is there?" She had a clear, strong voice that was very Haitian.

"My name's Gus Murphy. I'm here to speak to Mr. Furlong, if I could."

That was met with momentary silence. Then, *"Ne quittez pas!* Please wait."

I heard footsteps, some muffled voices.

She was back. "What is this about, that you wish to speak to Mr. Neil—Mr. Furlong?"

"Jimmy Regan."

I might just as well have said "Open Sesame," for after a second or two, the door pulled back.

The woman who greeted me was very heavy and very dark-skinned with a lovely kind face. She was dressed in blue nurse's scrubs. She told me her name was Fernand and that she was Mr. Furlong's home health care aide. When she walked me into what passed for the living room, she didn't have to explain any further. Furlong was in a wheelchair, one that he had been in a long time. You could just tell. And you could tell he was a broken man. I'm not referring to the fact that he was missing his right leg or that he had plastic tubing that led from his nostrils, over his ears, behind his shoulder to a small metal tank attached to his chair. It was the look of his unshaven face, the stained white T-shirt, and the empty, faded nature of his eyes. He noticed me noticing.

"Yep, Gus, I hit the daily double: diabetes and emphysema. Just a race to see which one kills me first." He winked. "My money's on cancer." He laughed, but after a few seconds, he gasped for air and coughed.

Fernand walked quickly over to him and turned up the flow of oxygen. She stroked his back to calm him.

"Now, Mr. Neil, you must not excite yourself so," she scolded, then turn her scowl to me.

I saluted her. "Message received."

"*Bon.* Good. I will leave you men to your talking. Would you like some coffee?"

"No, thank you."

She left the room, her smile back on her face. When she did, I sat down on a beat-up old wing chair next to Furlong's wheelchair. In the few photos I had seen of Furlong, he'd looked like a pretty sturdy guy, though not as big as Jimmy Regan. Regan looked a lot better for wear, but those were old photos and their lives had gone very separate ways.

"You a reporter?" he said when Fernand was out of earshot.

I shook my head. "Was on the job until three years ago. Mostly in the Second."

"You one of Jimmy's boys?"

He may have been sick, but not too sick to notice the confusion on my face.

"Every few years, Jimmy sends one of his ass-lickers around. Sometimes they say they're reporters. Sometimes lawyers or PIs, but I'm still sharp. My mind ain't half as in shitshape as my body."

"Why would he do that, send people to play head games with you?"

"To see if I'll talk."

"Talk about what?"

"About what I know."

"Know about what?"

"See," he said, stopping to collect his breath, "I might be inclined to tell you if every one of these conversations didn't start out exactly the same way. So you better start dancing a little faster or you can get the fuck outta here and tell that sanctimonious hypocritical prick that his old pal still has his mouth clamped shut."

After I finished telling Furlong the whole story of how I came to be sitting in his living room on the Sunday morning before Christmas, I said, "Was that dancing fast enough?"

"Yeah, Murphy, that was fast enough and I got a story to tell, but I don't see how it's gonna help you any."

"Let's hear it and we'll see."

"First thing to tell is that it was me who found the old guy on the St. Jean case, not Jimmy, but it was Jimmy who combed the girls that killed her out of the statements we got. He got all the press, all the recognition, not me."

"But you got the bump and the commendation, just like he did."

"Yeah, back then Jimmy was good that way. He told the brass that it was the both of us who worked the case. That it was both of us down the line, so that if he got the bump, I had to get it, too. But you see, he was already maneuvering, negotiating. I shoulda gotten the bump on my own merit, not because Jimmy Regan negotiated it for me. See what I mean? He made it so that I would owe him. He was good at that stuff. That's Jimmy. He could see the angles in anything. He could see how to use it to climb the ladder. Me, I wasn't interested in that and I didn't have the blarney in me like him."

I'd heard a lot of sour grapes in my life and this one-legged, barely breathing man had a lot to be bitter about, so I wasn't buying Furlong's story like it was gospel. I challenged him on it.

"So you're saying that Jimmy Regan's rep as a cop's cop is bullshit."

"No, Murphy, you're missing the point. Jimmy was a great cop. I'll never say different. All that stuff about him being the first through the door, it's true. But Jimmy always had an eye out for how to turn things to his advantage, is all I'm saying."

That rang true, but I needed more than this to make headway.

"Okay, Furlong, I get it. Jimmy stole some of your thunder and he had ambition, but you did get the bump."

"Boy, there's some stuff you don't know about the great St. Jimmy, isn't there?"

"That's why I'm here. And before you go into it, I know he has a drinking problem."

Furlong laughed again, but made certain to not lose it the way he had before. "A drinking problem! That's like saying a fish kind of likes water, as if he could take it or leave it." His face rearranged itself into an all-out sneer. "Hell, when we were on that task force together . . ." He paused purposely to see my reaction. He must've gotten the reaction he was looking for. "That's right, Gus, Jimmy and me were on that task force together, but I bet you didn't see his name mentioned anywhere in them reports you were reading, huh?"

"No."

"Yeah, well, we were on that task force, partnered up together, too." The sneer on his face vanished, replaced by something that was wistful and happily so. "We stepped in shit, the two of us. There were all the girls you could handle and drugs and drug money up the wazoo. And did I mention there were girls? Christ, now I can't even get fat old Fernand to give me a second look. Ain't I a catch?"

I ignored his riff of self-pity. "You're telling me that Jimmy Regan took drug money."

"No, not St. Jimmy. I'm not saying he wasn't tempted, but he didn't take it. He wouldn't. No, it was me. I took the money," he said without any hesitation. "But it wasn't like Jimmy was bathing in holy fucking water, either. He was hooked up with one of the girls pretty steep."

"With a pro?"

The sneer returned to his face as he nodded. "Jimmy was drinking heavy in those days. You can say what you want about him, but he had an eye for beauty, did Jimmy Regan. He fell hard for her. Hard with a big H. That wasn't just about humping neither, that relationship. It was about true love, at least for him. I think Jimmy was drinking so much because he was actually thinking about leaving Kathleen and his girls for her."

I repeated, "Was she a pro?"

"She was kind of the boss, the madam of a massage parlor in Wyandanch. Fucking gorgeous black chick with white features, kinda like Halle Berry's younger, almost-as-good-looking sister. She ran the girls, but we knew she was connected to the drug trade. It was her who tried buying us off, and she didn't make that kind of cash from having ten girls hooking and kicking up to her."

"Okay, Furlong, I get that you resent Regan stealing your thunder on the St. Jean case. But I don't see what the thing is with the task force. Guys hook up. They do stupid things when it comes to women, really stupid things, but it was you who took the money. It was you who pissed on the shield by warning people about raids, putting other cops in danger."

He laughed again, but cruelly. "I'm not making excuses for what I did and I've paid for it plenty, but I wasn't the only one who got jammed up. Jimmy got caught, too, not for taking money. His woman, a convicted felon, mind you, got pulled over by Highway Patrol in our car with a loaded gun under her seat, Jimmy's gun. And there was a few grams of coke on her, too. Maybe it wasn't as bad as what I did, but you don't just walk away from that with your ass intact and become chief of the department."

"Fuck."

"That's right, Gus. You seem like a smart man and a good cop. I think you can see where this is going."

"He gave you up, didn't he?"

Furlong nodded, tears streaming down his face. I let him cry and gave him a few minutes until he was ready to start talking again.

"He rolled on me. I deserved it. Like you said, I pissed on the shield, but Jimmy got away clean and look at him now. That ain't right. I'm going to die soon and—"

"So why keep quiet for all these years?"

"Because part of the deal he made was to keep me out of jail. The DA confirmed it for me. She said that Jimmy insisted that jail time for me was a deal breaker. Imagine that, even in the middle of getting jammed up, that cocksucker found a way to come out looking like he was throwing himself on the sword for me. And I've kept it quiet because he's been giving me money all these years. When you're in the position I'm in, you take the money and shut your mouth."

"Why tell me?"

"Because I needed to tell someone before I died. Someone else had to know. But here's the thing," he said, "I don't see how this helps you. I got jammed up in late '93, early '94. Jimmy cut off his relationship with his woman after she got arrested. He went to the honor farm to dry out. When he got off the farm, he was assigned to the Fourth Precinct detective squad and then Homicide. As far as I know, he's never strayed since. See, by the time he got off the farm, Kathleen, that's his wife, had their third girl. His girls mean everything to Jimmy. He could be a tough motherfucker and a backstabbing son of a bitch, but he doted on his girls. They are his pride and joy. I think the idea that he once risked losing them has kept him in line all these years."

I was curious. "How do you know so much about him?"

"He used to come see me a few times a year. We'd talk. Jimmy has his failings, but he has guilt, too. Haunts the ever-living shit out of him, what he did to me. I used to take some comfort in that, but not anymore. Death is too close for that."

"You said he *used* to come visit. Not anymore? How long has it been?"

"A year. Maybe a year and a half, but the money's still coming in."

"Would it surprise you to know he's drinking again?"

He shrugged. "Once a drunk . . . Still, what happened between us was twenty years ago. None of it has anything to do with your homicides."

"What if someone was blackmailing him with this?" I said.

"Jimmy would quietly resign and the cops would deny it. Too many people have too much to lose to let themselves get all that egg on their faces. If those records even exist anymore, I bet they are sealed as sealed can be."

"I guess you're right, Furlong," I admitted, but reluctantly.

We said a few more things to each other about the weather and the raccoons, about his proximity to the rez and about getting his siding fixed up. I stuck my head into the laundry room and said so long to Fernand. But on my way out, I went back in the living room.

"What was the girlfriend's name?"

Furlong looked confused.

"The woman Jimmy was mixed up with back then in '94?"

"Ilana. Ilana Little or something like that." He shrugged and made a face. "I just called her Ilana. She was some piece of ass."

Outside, the sun was brilliant and the glare off the snow hurt my eyes. I thought about taking a ride over to the rez and picking up some cigarettes for Bill. Then I thought better of it, not because I was a crusader against smoking. At Bill's age, he wasn't going to quit unless it was his idea. No, I didn't buy him cigarettes because I had to figure out how to talk to Bill now that I knew some of Jimmy Regan's secrets. Furlong was right. I couldn't see how Jimmy's secrets, as dirty as they might be, had anything to do with the Delcamino murders. Still, given the way he had acted last night, the way he had sought me out to plead his innocence, the way he had gotten four drinks down his belly in such short order, let me know Jimmy Regan was involved somehow. I couldn't help but remember something Furlong has said. Jimmy has guilt.

52

(MONDAY MORNING)

I'd spent the remainder of my Sunday back at the Paragon, watching football games. I'd also spent a lot of time thinking things through. When Slava came in for his shift, we worked through a plan to give Milt Paxson a little payback for his putting Martino onto me. I wasn't going to let his bullshit pass, but that wasn't really the point. I didn't believe Jimmy Regan for a second about how Paxson, an inept putz with a nasty streak, was the mastermind behind arranging my Friday night adventures. And say what you will about Pete McCann, he had even less respect for Paxson than I did. There was no way Pete would have taken part in any plan that Paxson cooked up. That's how I knew Jimmy Regan was full of shit. While I didn't believe Regan, I found it interesting that he was willing to let Paxson take the fall and that Paxson was willing to take it. That said to me that Paxson might know something, maybe something useful. Or not. But with Slava's help, I meant to find out. There had to be a connection between Jimmy Regan and the Delcaminos. There *had* to be. I was hoping that Paxson could supply the link.

If there was any truth to what Regan had promised me on Saturday during his visit with Bill, I would no longer be persona non grata with the SCPD and I'd get cooperation when I asked for it. So the first thing I did after showering was to put Regan's word to the test by calling Alvaro Peña.

"Peña."

"It's me, Alvaro, Mr. Radioactive."

"Not anymore, *jefe*. I don't know how you did it, but it seems like the Pope's given you special dispensation or something like that. Word filtered down from on high yesterday that if you wanted your lily-white Irish ass to get kissed, I was to pucker up my sweet Dominican lips and do my duty."

"I never much cared for ass kissers, Alvaro."

"Good thing, because I would have put in my fucking papers. So what else can I do for you?"

"Ilana Little, that name mean anything to you?"

"Should it?" he asked, the sound of his fingers tapping at a keyboard came through the phone.

"Not necessarily."

"How do you spell that?"

"Not sure," I said. "I-l-a-n-a, I guess, and Little the way you spell 'little.'"

"Sorry, my man. Nada. Any reason she should be in the system?"

"Convicted felon, so I'm told. She also ran a massage parlor in Wyandanch in the '90s. Do me a solid and keep checking. Ask around. She was right in the middle of some trouble with a drug/vice task force in '94. Try different spellings, okay? My source is good."

"No problemo. I can do that. And, *jefe* . . ."

"Yeah?"

"Put in a good word with the Pope for me."

"Next time I see him, Alvaro, I'll make sure to kiss the ring once extra for you."

"Can't ask for more than that."

"You ever hear of a dealer, a guy goes by the name of Lazy Eye or Lamar English?"

There was a sudden chill in the air and a frosty silence from Alvaro's end of the phone. All of his happy cooperative chatter came to an abrupt stop.

"Uh-uh. No way, Gus," Peña said at last, his voice all business. "We can't be going there and you can't be going anywhere near him."

I tried to keep the mood light. "Why not? I thought word came down about how I was reborn a good guy, one you could talk to."

"If I tell you why I can't discuss this with you, my man, it will defeat the purpose of me not discussing it with you. You understand me now?"

"I believe I do," I said. "Consider it off the table."

"Done. Anything else?"

"No, Alvaro, thanks. That should do me."

We wished each other a good day, but I could tell I'd walked into a minefield. A minefield I wasn't supposed to step into or even know existed. I'd gotten good at spotting the signs. After John died, there were mines everywhere and you couldn't breathe without setting one off. There wasn't a safe subject or a word or facial expression or sigh that didn't explode in all our faces. So I knew.

There were only two reasons Alvaro could have reacted the way he did. Either Lazy Eye was the target of an investigation, or he was working for the department. I still wasn't sure that got me any closer to making sense of the jumble of facts, but it didn't get me any further away. That was something. I was feeling pretty good about that until the phone rang in my hand.

"It's not the gun," a familiar voice blurted out before I could say hello. It was Roussis.

"What?"

"The gun we seized from Frankie Tacos' desk."

"Yeah."

"It's the same type of gun that killed Tommy Delcamino, but it's not *the* gun. Bullets don't match."

"Shit!"

"You can say that again."

"Shit. So," I asked, "are you back to square one?"

"Pretty much."

"Listen, Al, I think we need to talk in person again."

"Oh yeah, why's that? You gonna send me on another wild-goose chase, tell me maybe that it was Jimmy fucking Hoffa."

"Funny you should use that term 'goose chase.'"

"What's so funny? Because I'm not laughing."

"Meet me for lunch."

"Where?"

"You pick," I said. "It's on me."

"You know that Mexican place in the shopping center in Hauppauge near the diner and the library?"

"Mazatlan?"

"One o'clock?"

"One."

I didn't know what was going to come of what I was about to do, but I figured it was about time to shake things up a little and to see what happened.

53

(MONDAY AFTERNOON)

For a slim, athletic guy, Al Roussis could eat. He had a burrito the size of a football topped by a layer of melted cheese, sour cream, guacamole, and chipotle salsa with sides of black beans and rice. I got nauseous just listening to him order. I had a chicken salad that I didn't finish because I was too busy watching him inhale his food. I think I began the conversation just to distract myself.

"The other day," I said, "when we met in Brady Park."

He stopped chewing long enough to say, "What about it?"

"You talked to me about the Alison St. Jean murder case."

His shoulders slumped, his expression sad. "Terrible."

"Very, but I wanted you to know I got your message."

He tilted his head at me as if he didn't understand the words I was saying. "Message?"

"Yeah, the message."

"What message?"

Christ, he was going to play dumb, I thought. I understood that he had to protect himself, that if Jimmy Regan could trace anything back to him, he would be screwed. But it was just the two of us alone at a table in an empty Mexican restaurant in Hauppauge. I think the closest English speakers were four stores over in the Four Sisters burger joint.

"Come on, Al. There's no one here to hide from. No need to play dumb. I'm not gonna tell Regan."

"I don't know what the fuck you're talking about, Gus. I met you over there because I was at the Fourth interviewing somebody on another case, and I talked about the case because it haunts me."

"So you didn't meet me there and talk about the St. Jean case to drop hints about Jimmy Regan and Neil Furlong?"

"Neil who?"

"You're kidding, right?"

He shook his head, stood up. "You want more soda? I'm getting some."

"No, thanks."

As Al Roussis walked over to the soda machine, I thought I was losing my mind. He had to have meant for me to look into the St. Jean case. He had to.

"So what's this crap about Chief Regan?" he asked, settling back down in his seat. "What's Jimmy Regan and this Neil what's his name got to do with Alison St. Jean?"

"Furlong. Neil Furlong."

"Sorry, Gus, never heard of him."

"It was Jimmy Regan and this Furlong guy who broke the St. Jean case when they were in uniform. That helped them get the bump to detective. You're telling me you didn't know any of this?"

"That's what I'm telling you."

"Then why would the Alison St. Jean case haunt you?"

"Because of my little cousin Apollonia." He laughed. "I guess she's not so little anymore."

"What about her?"

"My Uncle Christos used to live around the corner from the St. Jeans. Apollonia went trick-or-treating with Alison that night, but went home early because she got a little sick from eating too much candy. That's why it haunts me. It could have been her that wound up strangled in the park with her tights wrapped around her throat and things shoved into her. She was my favorite cousin. She married some Jewish guy and moved to California. They have two kids and a big house in the valley. Wherever that is. I didn't even know about Jimmy Regan and this Furlong guy."

Now I was laughing. In spite of the hardest lesson I'd ever had to learn, I sometimes fell into my old ways of thinking. I should have known the universe didn't work according to the way we assumed it did. That it operated without regard to human plans and visions. It operated without regard to consequence. It just did what it did, coldly, without reason except whatever reason was built into neutrinos. If the universe had a sense of humor, it would have been laughing at me as I was laughing at my own ridiculousness.

"What are you laughing at?" Roussis wanted to know.

"Forget it."

"Thanks for lunch, but is this mysterious message you got that I never meant to deliver why you wanted to see me?"

"Yeah, and something else that might help you not have to go all the way back to square one with Tommy Delcamino's murder."

That got his attention. "I'm listening."

"I think I have some idea of who those guys were who took shots at me before I found Tommy Delcamino's body. I don't have last names for you, but I know how you can find them."

He took out his notepad and a pen. "Go ahead."

"One guy's name is Jamal. African-American. Light-skinned. Twenty-five. Five eight. Maybe a hundred sixty pounds. Cold eyes. Rugged face. The other guy's named Antwone. African-American. Dark-skinned. Twenty-five. Six seven, six eight. Three hundred pounds. Head as big as a house. Both of them are strapped."

"And you know this how?"

"How I know it isn't important," I said. "I know it. The thing is that they are connected to a former boxer, gang enforcer turned big-time drug dealer named Kareem Shivers. He lives over in Melville. You know Alvaro Peña?"

"Sure."

"He can fill you in on this Shivers guy."

"I'll check with him," Roussis said.

"This Shivers guy is a stone-cold piece of work, Al. Watch out for him."

"Sounds like you've got some firsthand experience with the man."

I half smiled, unconsciously rubbing my abdomen where K-Shivs had punched me. "Some."

"You think this Shivers' guys killed Tommy Delcamino?"

I shook my head. "I don't think so, but I can't promise you that for sure. As far as I know, neither one of them carries a .357. I'm not saying they wouldn't've killed Tommy D. if he wasn't already dead. They strike me as men very capable and willing to do violence."

"But you're sure they were at the scene?"

"They were there. I think they're the ones who tore the place up. I think you'll find their prints were all over the place at Tommy D.'s trailer."

"You tear a place up, you're looking for something," he said. "But what?"

"Ask them, Al."

He shrugged. "Seems pretty simple to me. You say these two are connected to a big-time dealer. They were probably looking for—"

"Drugs!" I slapped the sides of my head with my palms. "I'm an idiot."

"If you're waiting for an argument from me, Gus, don't hold your breath."

"Listen, Al, do me a favor."

"If I can."

"If you pick up Shivers and his crew for questioning, let my name slip."

He made a face. "You got a death wish or something? You just got done telling me these guys were bad news."

"Not a death wish. Just a wish to set things right for a guy who didn't have much go right in his life."

"Delcamino? I talk for the dead, Gus, so he's my responsibility. What's your stake in this? Why do you care?"

I thought about it for a second, and the last two years came rushing back to me so that I was light-headed. But in particular, my last few sessions with Dr. Rosen came back to me.

"I guess I'm not doing it for Delcamino. Not if I want to be honest about it. I'm doing it because there has to be a reason why Tommy and his kid got murdered. I need to know that at least sometimes there is a reason why. I need to know why because sometimes, Al, there is no reason why. I need to do it because I need to know there are some answers sometimes."

I looked around and saw the guys behind the counter were staring at me and that Al Roussis had his hand on my shoulder.

"All right, Gus, no need to let everyone in Suffolk hear you."

"Was I being loud?" I asked, noticing that my hands were shaking and that I was breathing heavily.

"Pretty much, yeah."

"Sorry."

I waved sorry to the guys behind the counter. They nodded back, seeming to understand.

"I'll drop your name when I pick up this Shivers guy for questioning, if that's what you want."

"It's what I want."

Still trying to calm myself down, I stayed seated a few minutes after Al had gone.

Outside, my hands were still shaking a little and I dropped my keys into the slush in the parking lot. When I got down on my knees to look for them, the air above my head whistled. I heard the squeal of brakes and the rapid *crunch, crunch, crunch* of one car hitting another hitting another hitting another. It was a few seconds before I heard the screaming woman.

There's screaming and then there's screaming. Street cops learn to differentiate between them pretty early on in their careers. This was the latter, that hysterical, high-pitched scream of raw terror and disbelief and panic. And it didn't let up. So I scooped my keys out of the slush and ran as fast as I could, given my wounded leg. When I got out onto the street, there were three damaged cars lined up. The back two had battered front ends. The lead car had veered sharply left, its nose blunted against the center median. It was still running and the car was in drive, the engine straining against the median. It was outside the lead car, a pearl-white Cadillac, that the woman stood screaming. She was sixty if a day, heavy, her nose bloodied, her red eyes tearing and unfocused, cheeks swollen. She was well dressed. Her camel-colored overcoat was covered in blood. Only some of it was hers. And when I looked past her, through the smashed passenger's side window, I understood.

Inside the Cadillac, slumped forward against the now-deflated air bag, was a dead man. Blood and brain tissue were splattered all over the air bag, the driver's side window, the windshield, and the interior of the car. Not very much of his head was left intact. It looked as if his head had exploded. But heads don't just explode of their own accord, not without a helping hand. A crowd had formed around the screaming woman, and drivers and passengers from the other cars were becoming aware of what had happened, but not why. Then a Porsche with MD tags pulled over and a dark-haired man popped out of the driver's seat and came rushing toward the crowd. He could rush all he wanted, but unless he'd had experience putting Humpty Dumpty back together again, there wasn't a thing he could do.

As he came toward the crowd, I walked a path to where the skid marks began on the pavement. I turned back to look at where my car was situated in the restaurant parking lot and got a sick feeling in my belly. The Cadillac would have been parallel to where my car was parked when I'd dropped my keys in the snow. I recalled the whistling air above my head and realized the bullet that had killed the driver of the Cadillac had been meant for me.

(MONDAY NIGHT)

Things had gotten very serious very suddenly. Bullets made things much more real than vague threats, planted evidence, and a night in a smelly jail cell. Someone had tried to kill me and had killed an innocent civilian instead. That stank of desperation and it meant that they had little to lose by trying again. So I did what I should have done days before and retrieved my off-duty Glock 26, the gun that had been cleared by ballistics from the scene of Tommy Delcamino's murder. I would have felt better if I could have gotten my old service weapon back, too, but that was unlikely to happen, as it had been taken from me the night I got pulled over on the Sag. I doubted I would ever see that gun again.

And because things had taken this bloody turn, I had choices to make. Slava and I had set up our payback meeting with Milt Paxson for tonight, but I was no longer sure he was worth the time or effort. I wasn't sure how much he knew. I wasn't sure of anything anymore. I had two seemingly parallel lines of inquiry going on in terms of the Delcamino homicides: Regan and K-Shivs. Both threatening, power- ful, and dangerous men with lots of resources at their disposal. All weekend long, I had been leaning toward Regan. Although I couldn't figure out why he would mean Tommy and TJ Delcamino harm, he had acted so guilty. And then there was his misconduct on the job, paying hush money to Furlong. Look, I was never a detective, never wanted to be one, but I could smell the rot. The floorboards were collapsing under Jimmy Regan. I knew it. He knew it. I even think Father Bill knew it. I'd thought if I could just press a little harder . . .

Yet now that it seemed this was all about missing drugs, it was far easier to imagine any number of scenarios that would explain why Kareem Shivers looked better for the Delcamino homicides. All that information that didn't amount to much before suddenly added up perfectly. The drug deal with Lazy Eye that had gone wrong. TJ turning up sick and strung out at Frankie Tacos', then, only a few days later, turning up at Ralph O'Connell's high as a kite, flush with cash and promises of more to come. TJ had somehow managed to steal a shipment of K-Shivs' product. He'd sold some off, used some himself, and stashed the rest of it. Shivers had traced the missing shipment back to TJ and had him tortured to force him to tell where he had hidden the remainder of the drugs. TJ had either stubbornly refused to talk or had died before he could reveal where the drugs were hidden. Months later, K-Shivs figures that TJ must have told his father where the product was stashed or had the goods himself.

There was still some stuff that I was sketchy on and some stuff at the edges that I didn't get, like why had it taken so many months for Shivers to go after Tommy? Why would anyone assume I had the stash? Why wreck my house? And the big question mark was still Jimmy Regan. Why would the cops, especially detectives I had known for decades, protect a suspected murderer, a gang enforcer turned heroin dealer, from a homicide investigation? Sure, law enforcement agencies often shielded important informants from things, but not usually active murder investigations. And if the SCPD was protecting Shivers because he was an informant, he was a shitty one. There was a flood of heroin on the street, and according to Jimmy Regan himself, kids were OD-ing left and right. There was something I wasn't seeing.

Then, as I was headed downstairs to the lobby to tell Slava that we might as well go ahead with our plans to have a chat with Milt Paxson, I got a bad feeling. A very bad feeling. I told him to forget it, that Paxson wasn't worth the risk, not with what was going on. He didn't question my change of heart, nor did he flinch when I asked for the keys to his car.

(MONDAY NIGHT)

On the island, it's easy to know who pays property taxes and who matters to the politicians. You can measure it by the unplowed snow on the streets of places like Brentwood or Wyandanch. At least that was the way it used to be before I put in my papers. I didn't know if that was as true any longer, because for two years I hadn't paid attention to the unplowed snow or to politics or to life on earth. For two years, it was one foot first then the other then the other, and then only most of the time. It was inhale exhale inhale exhale. It was trying to stay human in spite of my instinct to bury myself alive. As I drove to North Bay Shore, I couldn't stop thinking about the black chick at Malo. I had no memory of her face at all, only of her movements. All dark skin and sinew, one wet naked leg before the other.

I tried not to think too much about the last time I'd been on Fifth Avenue, but it wasn't working. Less than a mile south of where I was on Fifth Avenue sat the Third Precinct. And it was off Fifth Avenue that Smudge lived. Problem was, I couldn't remember which street off Fifth. It had been dark the time I picked Bill up from Smudge's terrible rental and I hadn't paid all that much attention. I remembered the house well enough. Half its windows boarded up, the wilt and exhaustion of the place. And as I cruised around Anna, Bancroft, Marvin, and Dalton roads, I listened to the reports on news radio, trying to decipher if the SCPD had made any progress in the shooting earlier that afternoon. So far, the cops had put it down to a twisted act of violence, some lunatic sniper with a rifle who had killed at random.

It wasn't the first time that had happened in Suffolk County. Only a few years after I got on the job, some idiot named Peter Sylvester shot several people through store windows at night with a .35 Marlin hunting rifle. He'd killed one man who had been seated near the front window at a Commack diner and had wounded others in the same general vicinity. So it was natural for the cops to assume that what had happened once could have happened again. They also assumed it because, as yet, they could find no reason for the victim, a retired dentist from Queens, to have been murdered. It seemed the only thing he was guilty of was a terminal case of bad timing.

There it was, Smudge's ugly house on Eden Road. Eden Road, yeah, right. The house was dark and lifeless and as welcoming as a septic tank. Not even snow and the cover of night could improve its appearance. Maybe it was all Smudge could afford or maybe he thought it was what he deserved. I hoped to ask him and hoped he'd be alive enough to answer. That was the thing, now that I was pretty sure of what TJ Delcamino had stolen and just how far the people who wanted it back were willing to go to retrieve it, anyone connected to Tommy Delcamino or his son were in danger. And no one was more connected to Tommy D. than Smudge.

I'd get around to warning Richie Zito in person later. Crippling arthritis or not, Zee was a guy who knew how to handle himself. You don't rise through the ranks of the Maniacs and stay alive as long as he had without being a dangerous motherfucker. I had already tried calling him a few times on my ride over to Brentwood, but he'd refused to get on the phone. The fourth time I called, the guy who answered the phone just hung up. Smudge, on the other hand, was no tough guy, and the man who had protected him and befriended him in prison was dead. I didn't have Smudge's phone number and the only way I had to get in touch with him was to go knock on his door.

I was encouraged to see that there were two sets of footprints in the snow, but just as quickly discouraged by the size of those tracks. Smudge was a little guy with small feet. The prints before me in the snow belonged to bigger, heavier men whose bulk had displaced the snow so that the soles of their shoes reached down to the walkway. I couldn't tell much beyond that because I'd left my Maglite in the trunk of my car, so I used the flashlight setting on my phone. I stood in place at the edge of the house's postage-stamp-sized lot, listening for any sounds coming from inside the house. There were none that I could hear, but there was enough ambient traffic noise coming from Fifth Avenue that I couldn't be at all sure about what I was or wasn't hearing from inside the house.

I took out my little Glock, keeping it down at my side as I approached the house. There were several other houses on the block and I didn't want to attract unwanted attention by waving my gun around. I walked slowly, carefully, up to the front door and tried the knob. It resisted my efforts to turn it. That was something, at least, a locked front door. I crept around to the side of the house, shined the light through a window into the dark kitchen. The kitchen was a mess. It had been tossed much as the trailer at Picture Perfect Paving and my old house in Commack. My heart sank all the way to the bottom when I walked around back and saw that the rear door was flung wide open. There was no good way for me to spin optimism into the sight of that, and when I got to the stoop, the stench that came at me from inside the house removed any stubborn sense of hope I might have clung to for Smudge's survival. The smell of death is unmistakable.

Two weeks before, I wouldn't have hesitated to call 9-1-1, but I couldn't pretend that the last two weeks hadn't happened. It was hard for me to accept that I couldn't trust the very people who had been my brothers and sisters, people to whom I had, on hundreds of occasions, entrusted my life. As hard to accept as it was, I didn't waste any time denying my distrust. I'd almost been killed once already that day and I wasn't going to let hesitation give somebody a second chance. Smudge's body would get found by someone else eventually, but now I had to see for myself.

I walked into the back of the house, gun sweeping before me, and cautiously followed my nose to the source of the stench. You might have thought the house should have been ice cold because of the back door being wide open, but the opposite was true. The cold had caused the thermostat to keep the oil burner churning up heat. Except for the small alcove leading away from the back door into the rest of the house, the damned place was like a sauna. The heat made the nauseating, slightly sweet stink of rotting human flesh and feces even more intense. I found the body in an unfurnished bedroom off the main hall from the tiny living room. In spite of the overwhelming smell and the presence of a man's body at my feet, I smiled when I saw the body wasn't Smudge. This man was way too big to be him, but that was about all I could make out about him, since he was facedown.

As this was one of the rooms with a boarded-over window, I felt fairly safe in turning on the overhead light. When I flicked on the switch, that glad expression on my face went to the place where smiles go to die. The dead man wasn't Smudge. I'd gotten that much right, but I wasn't happy to see whose body it was. The detective who had pulled me over on the Sag was sprawled across the worn, shiny carpeting in front of me with two bullet holes in the fabric of his khaki-brown trench coat. Those two shots had probably gone right through his heart. There was a pillow on the floor there next to him, its yellowed linen case badly charred by contact with the muzzle of the weapon that had fired the two bullets into the dead man's chest. I had to get out of there, but not before I did a quick check to make sure Smudge wasn't dead somewhere else in the house.

He wasn't anywhere in the house, but I couldn't be sure he wasn't dead someplace else. I chose to believe he had gotten away or hadn't been home at all. I didn't want to think that he had killed the detective in the bedroom. I didn't have time to stand around contemplating the possibilities. It seemed to me that someone was as busy tidying up his loose ends as he was trying to retrieve his stolen drugs. I was a loose end. Richie Zito was another. Maybe Frankie Tacos, too, if he wasn't in the middle of this himself. But when I pulled away from Smudge's house, headlights off, I headed to Wyandanch.

I drove past Lazy Eye's house. It was as dark as Smudge's had been. There was no car in his driveway. There were no cars anywhere near his house that I could see. I didn't figure Slava's beat-up old Honda was likely to be associated with me or be on anyone's radar. Well, the only person who might be able to connect Slava's car to me was in a shitty little house in Brentwood with two bullet holes in his chest. So I parked down the block, facing Lamar English's house, and waited. I intended to wait as long as I had to wait or, in truth, as long as I could last. It was cold out and I hadn't stopped for coffee or to take a bathroom break.

I listened to the radio and quickly got bored. The music was all either music my parents had listened to or as interchangeable and disposable as plastic razors. The news stations repeated the same stories over and over and over again without adding a single new detail. But the worst by far was sports talk radio, listening to Riley from Toms River complain about the Knicks to an arrogant host who seemed far more interested in condescension than discussion.

I sat there remembering how, as a cop, I had such mixed feelings about the cold and the snow. How bad winter weather was great at tamping down crime, sometimes even bringing it to a complete halt for days at a time, but how it created other problems and nightmares, nightmares often as terrible and as tragic as murder. There were the traffic accidents, of course. The fools in the big SUVs who forgot that four-wheel drive helps you get through the snow, but doesn't help you stop in it or help you survive collisions with trees. The church vans hitting patches of black ice, speeding up their passengers' reunion with their creator more effectively than any prayer service ever could. The worst were the house fires, though. The poor families using the range or kerosene heaters in enclosed spaces. The smell of fire-ravaged human flesh and hair. The stink of melted plastic. The burnt baby bodies I would never get out of my head. I remembered the fireman's mantra: *Probably smoke inhalation. They almost never burn to death.* As if that was of any help.

And then, about two hours after my vigil had begun, just as I was about to run the engine again to get some heat into the car to prevent my feet from going totally numb with cold and inactivity, a pimped-out Chrysler 300 appeared at the corner of the street. Ground-shaking hip-hop, window-buzzing bass destroyed the silence of the night as it rolled down the block and pulled into Lazy Eye's driveway. I waited in my car until I was sure it was the man I was waiting for. I wouldn't be able to clearly see his face, certainly not his eyes, from where I was parked, but I figured it was a safe bet that if he had a key to the house, it was him.

The car door flew open and the music stopped. Silence returned to the night. A short, almost two-dimensionally thin African-American man got out of the Chrysler. He was dressed in a hoodie over a flat-billed baseball cap—I couldn't make out the team logo—baggy jeans and boots. He reached back into the car and pulled a nickel-plated Desert Eagle, a ridiculous weapon that looked foolish even in the hands of a big man, and stuffed it down the front of his pants. He folded the front of his hoodie over the handle of the weapon. Christ, I thought, if this was Lamar English, he was doing everything possible to call attention to himself. He scanned the night as if to make sure there were no threats close by. He didn't seem to take note of Slava's Honda, or if he did, he didn't seem to care. He took some keys out of his hoodie pocket and popped the trunk. He scanned the night again. Satisfied, he reached into the trunk and removed two densely packed, black plastic garbage bags. He leaned them against the rear bumper of the 300 and closed the trunk.

I was satisfied, too. This had to be Lazy Eye and my bet was there was a good sixty pounds of marijuana in those garbage bags. As I threaded my fingers through the Civic's door handle, a new set of headlights appeared at the corner. There was nothing particularly threatening or noticeable about them, but if a car came down the block as I was approaching Lazy Eye, he would spot me coming. I didn't want him to see me coming, especially if he had any skill with and willingness to use the Desert Eagle stuffed down his pants. As silly a weapon as it was, it had bullets the size of a grown man's thumb. Even an off-center hit could tear you apart. Sorry. One bullet wound at a time was about all I could deal with.

I unthreaded my fingers from the door handle and waited for the car to pass, but that's when things went to shit. The headlights turned off. An engine revved. Tires squealed. I wasn't the only person to notice trouble was coming. Lazy Eye yanked up the front of his hoodie and stuck his hand down into his pants. He was nervous, though. Fumbling the handle of the Desert Eagle, he couldn't get a grip on it until it was way too late to do him any good. I'm not sure it would have done him any good anyway. As the other car approached him, the night exploded in artificial thunder and very real fire. One second Lazy Eye was upright. The next second he wasn't.

I waited a beat to make sure the car wasn't going to make another pass at its target. When I was sure, I got out of the Honda and raced over to where Lazy Eye was. It was him, all right. His left eye aimed at a very different angle than his right. It wouldn't matter now or ever again. Death was an equitable master. Once you crossed the threshold, no man or woman was more dead or less dead than another. And that threshold was one Lamar English had most definitely crossed. He'd been hit in every part of his body, including the face. Bits of his shattered teeth poured out of his wrecked mouth in a stream of blood and saliva. The coppery, metallic scent of blood was still heavy in the air, as was the intense smell of burnt marijuana. The hot lead had ripped through the bales of pot as well as the dead man's flesh.

I ran back to Slava's Honda and got out of there as quickly as I could. There was no doubt anymore about loose ends and inconveniences being tidied up. For me it was no longer a matter of if, but when. I suppose it had always been so. Death is never a matter of if. Murder was more a question of when.

I was lucky Harrigan's was empty when I stuck the muzzle of my Glock under the barman's Adam's apple and told him I had to see his boss for Zee's own good. I had tried asking politely to no good effect and my threshold for bullshit was at a record low.

"The last people you wanna call are the cops," I said to the bartender when he told me Zee was in his office waiting. "Believe me when I say if I hear a siren coming this way, I'm gonna come back out here and beat the piss outta you."

He shrugged, but I couldn't tell if it was that he was unafraid or if he just didn't care. The net result was the same.

Zee was where he was the first time I'd come into his office, seated behind his desk, the haze of a recently smoked bowl hanging in the air like a disoriented ghost. It was the second time in less than a half hour I'd smelled the earthy burn of high-quality marijuana. There was something different about Zee this trip, and I didn't mean the unwelcoming expression on his weathered face. Only his gnarled left fist was atop his desk. My guess was his right hand was in his lap, aiming a sidearm at me. *Probably a .45,* I thought. Something with a lot of stopping power, but nothing as ridiculous or unwieldy as a Desert Eagle. No, that wasn't his style. Besides, there was no way in his condition that he'd be able to handle a weapon as heavy as an Eagle. I didn't blame him for being leery. He'd kicked me out of the place during my last visit and I'd just forced my way in here by sticking a gun in his employee's neck.

"I come in peace," I said, raising my hands above my head as I entered. "All I wanna do is talk."

"First put your piece on the desk, then we'll see about talking."

I did as he asked, laying the little Glock on the desk in front of him.

"I thought I kicked your ass outta here for good."

"You did."

"So why the fuck are you back?"

"If you'd bothered taking one of my calls, I wouldn't be. You mind if I sit?" I asked, throwing my thumb at the chair facing his desk. "It's been a long, strange night."

He nodded. I sat.

"You don't need to be holding that piece on me, you know?"

He smiled a malevolent half-smile. "That's kinda not up to you, Gus."

"What is it, a .45?"

"Something like that. Whatever the fuck it is, just know it's big enough to blow a nice hole in you if you do something stupid."

"Look, Zee, I came here to warn you to watch your back."

He sneered at me. "I've been watching my back since I come out of my momma's pussy."

"Should've been a poet."

"Lotsa shoulda beens and shoulda dones in my life, Gus. Poet was never one of them. Used to play me some guitar when I was young, though." He held up his misshapen hand. "Good thing I didn't chase that career, huh? Tough to play with my hands all fucked up the way they are. Maybe when I get out to the desert I'll have a go at it again. Have someone break my bones and cut my tendons, then have them reset and sewn back together in the shape of an F chord. That chord's a real pain in the ass."

"You gotta live long enough to make it out there, Zee."

"All right, say what you've come to say. I'm in a charitable mood 'cause I'm outta here by the end of the week."

"I know why TJ and Tommy were killed."

Zee's eyes got big in spite of himself, and there wasn't a hint of skepticism in them. He knew I wouldn't have come here if I was just talking out my ass.

"I'm listening."

When I was done explaining to him about TJ and the stolen drugs, the retired dentist with the mostly missing head, and the dead men I'd come across earlier, he told me to come collect my gun off his desk. And I heard the thud as he dumped his weapon into one of the drawers. Afterward, I saw his right hand for the first time since I'd walked in. As he lifted it up, he flexed his fingers and grimaced. It hurt to witness it. I could almost hear his bones crackle and creak.

"That's fucked up. So you think the kid stole a load of heroin and now it's payback time?" he asked, sitting back in his chair and lighting up another bowl. "But why now, four or five months after it happened?"

"Good question. I haven't worked that out yet. I think that maybe the party TJ took it from had given up on the shipment as a lost cause and written it off. Then, for some reason, that party got renewed hope of recovering it." I shrugged. "But what do I really know? Christ, Zee, I'm not even sure who's killing who or why exactly, but all I know is somebody's busy tying up loose ends and that anyone connected to the Delcaminos seems to qualify. That means you qualify."

"How about that asshole friend of TJ's?"

"Ralphy O'Connell?"

"Him, yeah."

I scratched at my cheek, thinking about it. "Good catch. I'll give him a call when we're done here."

"You think TJ mighta told the O'Connell kid where he stashed the drugs?"

"Good question, Zee. O'Connell says no, but who knows? TJ and him were tight."

"Maybe you better go see the kid instead of calling, you know," Zee said. "What I remember of him when he came around here with TJ, he wasn't too bright."

"Yeah, you're right. Seemed like a real loyal guy, but no Einstein. If he's at work, I could see him on my way home," I said, as much to myself as to Zee. "This thing, whatever it is, is coming to a head and fast, but you'll be outta here in a few days anyway."

"A few days. That all you think it'll be?"

"Violence has a certain kind of internal momentum. It's like an unwinding watch spring. Once you release some of the tension, you release it all."

Zee raised his eyebrows, like maybe he was considering what I'd said. "Is that what you think's going on here?"

"The killing's already begun and I don't think it's gonna stop. I better go have that word with Ralphy now," I said, getting up out of my seat.

"Sorry about the harsh words last time. It was a good thing of you to come here and gimme a heads-up." He stretched out his right arm and unfurled his knotted right hand. "I appreciate the help."

I shook it. "If I don't see you again, good luck out west. Hope it helps with the pain."

"Just getting the hell outta here will help with that. Adios, Long fuckin' Island."

And that was that.

I apologized to the barman on the way out, but his reaction was pretty much the same as it had been before. His expression was inscrutable. He looked like a man who had given up. The way I used to look every single day until Tommy Delcamino walked into the lobby of the Paragon.

(TUESDAY, EARLY MORNING)

By most social standards, Ralph O'Connell was a man, but the reality was that he was Ralphy, just a big dumb kid who loved his damned car and missed his best friend. It was hard not to feel sorry for him. Feeling sorry for him wasn't going to save his ass.

"I don't know nothin'. I didn't do nothin'," he kept repeating when I stopped by the Northport Manor.

"Well, kid, if you are holding anything back about the drug deal that went bad or that night last August when TJ came to see you with the money, now would be the time to tell me."

"I swear on my mother," he pleaded, as if swearing on your mother mattered. As if swearing mattered at all. As if it ever had.

I couldn't count how many times guilty shitbirds with bloody hands protested their innocence to me by swearing on the souls of their children, their mothers, or their dead grandmothers. Those lies were then usually accompanied by invoking God and Christ as false witnesses. But for some reason, I believed the poor schmo.

"TJ didn't tell you about any stolen drugs or where he got the money he gave you?"

"Nope. I'm tellin' you, I don't know nothin'."

"How about the black eye and the swollen cheek, did he tell you where he got those?"

Ralph shook his big empty head. He was plenty scared. He had a lot to be scared about. I didn't like doing it to him, but he needed to know he was in danger.

"Okay, Ralphy, get gone right now," I said. "Get in your car and go visit some relative out of state or something. Don't go back home to pick up clothes or anything. Just go."

"But my folks will get all worried."

"Call them from wherever, but don't tell them where you are. If you check into a motel, don't use your real name and pay in cash. Understand?"

I handed him three hundred dollars of Tommy D.'s bankroll.

"Yeah, I understand. I'm not that stupid. But I've got a few more hours of work."

"Don't worry about that. I'll go talk to the boss and it will be okay. I promise you. Freddy and I go back a long way. You'll have a job when you come home."

The only part of what I'd told him that was true was the part about Freddy Guccione and me going way back. For all I knew, Freddy might have a cow when I told him that the kid had split and wouldn't return for at least a few days. I just had to get Ralph out of town.

"How long will I have to stay away?"

"I don't figure too long. Maybe you'll be back by Christmas."

That put a smile on his face. Good, I thought, maybe he'd come around to think of this as an adventure and not focus on the danger he was in. And maybe for a few seconds, it even worked. Then the smile vanished. The fear and second thoughts were making him freeze up on me.

"Go!" I shouted at him, grabbing him and shoving him toward the door. "Go. I'll tell you all about how it turns out when you get back."

Once I'd left Northport Manor and made it safely back to the Paragon, I took the added precaution of switching rooms again. I left everything except the clothes on my back, my framed photo of John Jr., and my gun where they were. I didn't have it in me to move all my things at that hour. Besides, I only needed a place to sack out until the sun came up. I didn't figure anyone was ballsy or stupid enough to try something in the hotel once day broke. I was wrong.

I don't know what it was I thought I'd heard, but whatever my sleeping brain perceived it as, I knew it wasn't good. I swiped my gun off the nightstand even before I opened my eyes. Then I heard it again, again, and again. This time I didn't have any questions about the sound or my muddled perceptions. Gunshots, even muffled, distant ones, have a distinct quality about them that distinguishes them from fireworks or engine backfires.

Still in my clothes, I tripped out of my room barefoot, ran down the hall, and stumbled down the cold stairs to the second floor, trying to shake the sleep out of my head as I went. I turned left out of the stairwell door, running toward my old room. The glut of snowed-in guests we'd had over the weekend had thinned out so that we were now nearly empty, though a few nervous heads popped out of their doors to see what was going on.

"Get back in your rooms," I shouted at them as I ran.

And even before I turned the last corner, I could smell the acrid tinge of gunsmoke in the air. I pressed my back flat to the wall and listened. Nothing. No gunfire. No footsteps. Nobody's breathing but my own. I peeked past the corner of the wall around the bend. Again, nothing, though the last remnants of smoke hung in the air. Then, just as I was stepping out, turning to go to my old room, I heard footsteps coming up behind me. I spun, my gun out in front of me.

"Is Slava, Gus," he said, coming at me. "Don't shooting. Don't shooting."

He held that Russian pistol in his hand as he came.

"The guests are all calling desk to see what is the noise. I'm hearing it from downstairs."

"I heard it, too. Cover me."

He understood and struck a pose with his Makarov aimed right at the door to my old room. As I moved flat along the wall, my gun before me, Slava moved, too. We both inched toward what was left of the door to my old room. Someone had blasted the lock and hinges with shotgun slugs, then kicked the door down. Enough ambient light from the hall leaked into the room so that we could both see the room was empty.

"Clear," I said, as much out of habit as anything else.

When Slava and I finished double-checking, we turned to look at the ruined bed. The comforter was peppered with little buckshot holes around one large central blast that would have cut a tunnel through my midsection and soaked the mattress with my blood and intestines.

"Mixed load," I said to Slava. "Buckshot and slugs."

He nodded at me. He knew it before I said it. Even in the midst of this I could not help but wonder about who Slava really was and how he came to be standing in this hotel room with me.

Slava said, "I was late to come because one of guests using his key card to get in north side door from parking lot entrance was attacked by man with black hoodie. But guest was not robbed."

"No, the guy just wanted to get in without coming through the front entrance. And we know why he wanted to get in."

"This man in hoodie, he is serious to kill you, Gus."

I nodded. "Listen, Slava, I have to get outta here."

He understood and pulled his car keys from his pocket. I told him I'd gotten rid of the tracking device, but that my car might not be safe.

"Don't worry. I will take cab. You go," he said, pointing at my bare feet with the muzzle of his gun.

I thought about running back upstairs to get my leather jacket, socks, and shoes, but the sound of sirens made me rethink that. Instead, I grabbed my gym bag and filled it up with whatever I could yank out of my drawers. Found an old pair of Nikes and stuck them on my feet. Then I did what the Nikes had been designed for: I ran.

'd slept in car seats more comfortable than Bill Kilkenny's couch, but I wasn't about to complain about a man who had opened his door to me at four in the morning without so much as a second look. It was as if he had expected me to show up there sooner or later. Only he knew if it was the former or the latter. All he'd said to me was "You can sleep on the couch and we'll talk later in the morning, the two of us."

Later was now, but Bill was nowhere to be seen when my phone buzzed in the pocket of my jeans. The jeans I'd slept in. And I'd slept lightly, even nervously, and was easily stirred. The sun was up and the basement apartment was alive with the angry hum and rumble of the oil burner. Still, I could see how Bill might find comfort in this basement-dwelling life he'd carved out for himself. It was alive with things: noises and smells that wouldn't permit a man to be numb. I didn't have time to search for Bill, answering my phone instead.

"I got something for you, *jefe*," said Alvaro Peña, his voice full of pride.

I was glad that someone had something for me other than a death wish.

"What you got, Alvaro?"

"I couldn't find nothing on Ilana Little, but I remembered you saying that you weren't so sure on the last name. So I called around to some of the guys who worked Wyandanch back in the day. I think I found the woman you were looking for. She went by the name Ilana Smalls, not Little."

I could hear that Alvaro was still talking in my ear, but I couldn't make out the words he was saying. Somehow the droning of the furnace was more distinct. A flurry of images, of red hair and green eyes, of an old cop and a pretty young girl, flashed through my head. And suddenly things had fallen into place. Not completely, not yet. There were still a few ingredients missing from the stew, but not many. I was almost there. I just had to keep myself alive long enough to get those last few missing pieces to put it all together.

"Are you even fucking listening to me, *pendejo*?"

"Sorry, man. I had a rough night. What were you saying?"

"Starting from where?"

"From the beginning."

"So this Ilana Smalls was really something, Gus. All the guys said she was smoking hot, but that she could be one mercenary bitch. Word is she was connected all around, Mob ties and gang ties and . . ." His voice drifted off.

"And cop ties, too, huh?"

I could almost hear his shoulders sag on the other end of the line.

"Yeah, maybe. That's what the old-timers said. Rumors, you know, that she did favors and got favors in return. But there was nothing anyone could prove. And who wants to prove that kind of shit, anyways?"

"You got a current address for her?"

"Depends, bro."

"On what?"

"On whether you believe in hell, because that's as close to a street address as I can give you."

"Deceased?"

"With a capital D, my man. About eighteen months ago. Somebody in Kings Park used her head for batting practice and dumped her body over on the grounds of the old psychiatric center. Story was all over the media. I'm surprised you didn't hear about it."

I let that pass. I didn't want to go into why the world had been a vacuum and void for the last two years. For all I knew or cared during that time, the Asian continent might have been swallowed up whole or Atlantis could have been discovered. What would any of it have mattered to me?

"Catch the guy who killed her?"

"Nope."

"Thanks, Alvaro. I owe you."

"You bet your ass you do," he said with a laugh in his voice. "Nah, Gus, we're good, man. But I got a bad feeling about all this. Watch your back."

"I will." I was about to say my goodbyes when another question occurred to me. "One more thing, then I'll let you be. You have any idea who caught the Smalls case and who worked it when it was turned over to Homicide?"

I heard his fingers tapping at the keyboard.

"Pete McCann caught it first and it wound up with . . . Paxson and Carey."

"Thanks, Alvaro."

He clicked off.

I swung my feet over the edge of the couch and tried stretching the bad sleep out of my bones. It helped some. I threw on my old Nikes and walked around to the side of the house where Bill did his smoking and thinking. There was no sign of him other than some ugly shoeprints in the hardened snow that remained from Saturday's storm, so I went back into the house. When I got out of the shower, I shaved with Bill's old-fashioned blade razor, and used a little of his mouthwash. Even that was old school. The kind of stuff that tasted more like Lysol than cool mint.

I threw on some fresh clothes and put in a call to Al Roussis. He thanked me for putting him onto Jamal and Antwone. As I'd suggested, he picked them up for questioning. Said that I was right, that there'd been plenty of forensic and ballistic evidence tying them to the Delcamino crime scene, but not to the homicide itself. He was sweating them on the homicide anyway. For leverage, he said. Al was smart that way. If K-Shivs' boys thought they were facing first- or second-degree murder charges, they might cough up all sorts of information to save their own necks. Might even roll over on their boss and put a major-league feather in Al's cap. So far, he said, they weren't talking. My guess was they wouldn't give up their boss, murder charges or no murder charges. With K-Shivs' gang connections, neither Jamal nor Antwone would live to see a month in prison if they rolled over on Shivers. Gangs didn't abide by New York State's ban on executions, and their appeals process was fairly nonexistent.

Bill came through the door as I was hanging up with Al Roussis. He had a brown bag in his hands that might just as well have been a magic hat. For out of that bag he produced two large coffees and two heart-attack specials: scrambled eggs, bacon, and cheese on buttered rolls. The aroma of the coffee and bacon were almost enough to make me forget that somebody, maybe more than one somebody, was anxious to kill me.

"From the look of you in the wee hours, I sensed you might be in need of this," Bill said, spreading the food out on his table. "You can explain as we eat."

I sat down at the table, fixed up my coffee the way I liked it, and demolished the egg sandwich in a few big bites. Bill ate more like a human being, patiently waiting for me to begin the conversation. And when I did, I don't think what I said surprised him.

"When you and Jimmy Regan came to see me the other night and he swore his innocence to me, I saw the look on your face, Bill. You didn't believe him, did you?"

He shook his head. "I did not. Not a word of it, I'm afraid."

"I don't know if he killed either TJ or Tommy Delcamino, but he's involved in some bad things."

"I feared as much."

"You do realize he tried to buy me off with that bullshit about his door always being open to me."

"That was uncharacteristically ham-handed of Jimmy."

"Desperate people do clumsy things. I think he senses the walls are caving in around him and he's flailing about trying to keep me off his case at any cost."

"I have to say I think you're exaggerating a bit there, Gus. It's quite a stretch to describe a vague offer of a job as a desperate attempt to keep you quiet at any cost."

"How about two attempts on my life in one day? Would that qualify?"

Bill swallowed hard and went pale. "Jimmy tried to have you killed?"

"I'm not sure it was him, at least not directly," I said.

I told him about the retired dentist who'd taken the bullet meant for me and the shotgun blasts in my mattress at the Paragon. I told him about the dead detective I'd found at Smudge's house and about how I'd seen Lazy Eye gunned down right in front of me.

He crossed himself. Shook his head in disbelief.

"Gus, while I don't doubt a word of it and I'm sure Jimmy was lying about some things the other night, what has he to do with a dead drug dealer?"

"Remember when Regan denied knowing a Kareem Shivers?"

"I do."

"The guy I saw gunned down last night worked for Shivers, and if what I'm thinking is correct, Jimmy Regan has a pretty direct connection to Kareem Shivers."

Bill made a face. "And that would be?"

"Not until I'm sure, Bill. Not until I'm sure."

"Don't you trust me, Gus?"

"With my life." I raised my palms to him. "I think I trust you more than anyone else alive, but I also think you still trust Jimmy Regan in spite of what I've said and what you've seen for yourself."

He tilted his head and nodded. "I suppose I do. My trust is a persistent thing, not so easily shaken. Sometimes you have to want to believe in people, and I want to believe in Jimmy as I would always want to believe in you, Gus Murphy."

"I'm lucky to have you in my corner and so is Jimmy Regan."

I walked over to the couch and threw on my blue work jacket, the words "Paragon Hotel" emblazoned on the back. I collected my things and tossed them into the gym bag.

He seemed surprised. "Gus, you know you're welcome to stay with me as long as need be. There's no reason for you to leave."

"There will be people looking for me, Bill, and it's better for you and safer for us both if you don't know where I'm headed or what I'm doing."

He didn't say anything to that. Instead, he put out his bony and brown-spotted right hand to me. When I went to shake it, he slipped a small gold crucifix onto my palm and folded my fingers around it.

Anticipating my reaction, he said, "I know you don't believe, but take it and keep it close . . . as a favor to me. And whether you like it or not, I'll pray for you."

He smiled a devilish smile because he knew he had me. I slid the crucifix into my jacket pocket.

"While you're at it, Bill, pray for him to turn my skin into Kevlar."

Bill laughed, shaking his head. "You are a cynical bastard, Gus Murphy."

"I didn't used to be. Not even twenty years on the street could do that to me. I suppose I have God to thank for that. Him and his secret plans for my son."

"You still have the rage in you, Gus."

"Always."

"Do you realize, I wonder, that all that rage and fury is aimed in the wrong direction?"

I felt that heat rising beneath my skin, bubbling up to the surface. "What's that supposed to mean?" I slammed my gym bag to the ground.

"That you're not angry at God."

"Bullshit!"

"It's the truth, and what's more, you know it, Gus."

"For chrissakes, Bill, if not God, then who?"

"Your son."

I opened my mouth to speak, but only barely human noises came out.

"Abandonment is a very special kind of hell, and no abandonment hurts so like the death of a child."

He turned his back to me and retreated to the bathroom. This wasn't up for discussion, at least not between Bill and me, not now. I patted the jacket pocket where I'd put the crucifix and left.

(TUESDAY EVENING)

Before saying a word, I waited for Pete McCann to step fully into the motel room and shut the door behind him. I almost hated to ruin it. He had that smug look on his face, the one I remembered from the times we were out after work and he would target his prey. A really beautiful woman, expensively put together, who had come into the bar or restaurant on the arm of a bored-looking man or a man who looked overanxious. You see, for Pete it was as much about the man as the woman, maybe more so.

He'd give a slight nod, jut out his chin, and say, "Over your left shoulder. That guy's in way over his head with a woman like that. He thinks she's too hot-looking for him. And the fucker's right because she'll be going home with me tonight."

Pete wasn't always right about that. They didn't always go home with him, but they often did. He hit it out of the park enough times to let himself live comfortably with his swings and misses. And that's why I knew he'd show if Annie called. She was reluctant to play the part at first, but she relented. He had crushed her. People hurt each other all the time. That's what we do. But there are times when there's nothing left inside you. No cushion for the fall. Nothing to fight back with.

Sure, part of sleeping with him was about blowing our marriage up beyond repair. That might even have been most of it. I'm sure another part of it was curiosity and desire. Annie and I were married young and we were both pretty wild and not inexperienced. Let's just say she must have been intrigued by the stories she had heard about Pete from other cops' wives. That, and he was a good-looking son of a bitch. Did she harbor secret hopes that their affair in the wake of John's death might turn into something else? I don't know. But as angry as she was at me, it didn't compare to the sting she felt for how Pete had tossed her away like an empty soda can to the side of the road.

I knew he'd show up because the other thing he got off on was the kicked dog coming back for more. Those were the stories he loved to tell most, the ones about the women he'd parted ways with who'd been so furious with him, but who couldn't stay away. It always took a little time for them to get over the first wave of anger, to show him that he didn't matter to them, he used to say.

"Some of them, they just can't help themselves. They either like the sex or they like the abuse, but who cares why they come back as long as they come back?"

I knew he'd come because Annie had been such a big conquest to him and he'd dumped her so abruptly. I knew because I was back on his radar screen again.

"Hey, Annie, I'm here. I bet you're already wet," he said, coming through the door I'd left open for him. "You in the bathroom?"

I had seated myself in the darkest corner of the room and kept the lights off.

"Annie's not coming, Pete," I said. "Turn on the light. It's on the wall right next to the door, but you'd know that. Annie told me you took her here a few times."

When he turned the light on, he saw I was aiming my gun right at his belly. Only his eyes hinted at being scared. The rest of his face was pure cool.

"Have a seat on the bed, Pete, but take off your jacket and coat.

Throw them on the bed, slowly. Put your weapon on the floor and kick it over here."

He did as he was told. I made him lift up his pants legs to show me he wasn't wearing an ankle holster. When I was satisfied he was clean, I removed the clip from his Glock, popped the round out of the chamber, and tossed the gun back to him. He sat on the bed, facing me.

"What's this about, Gus?"

"Took you a long time to ask me that question," I said. "Too long. I think you know exactly what this is about."

"I heard that somebody tried to kill you in your bed at that shitbox hotel of yours. Wasn't me."

"I didn't think it was. Shotgun's not your style. You know about that retired dentist on 454 yesterday?"

"The one that got his brains blown out?"

"That bullet was meant for me. I had lunch over at Mazatlan. Dropped my keys in the snow, knelt down to get them, and . . . *Bang!* Dead dentist. Somebody wants me dead pretty badly, Pete. And as I recall, the last time we spoke, you were pretty fucking threatening to me."

He gave me that charming half-smile of his. "I don't suppose saying I was only following orders will ease your mind."

I shook my head.

"I didn't think so, but it's the truth."

"Jimmy Regan's orders?"

Now it was his full-on smile, the one that dazzled women and men alike. "You should've made detective before me, Gus. You're a smart bastard. Yeah, I was following Regan's orders. He's got a real hard-on for you."

"Why?"

"Don't ask me a question you already know the answer to."

"He killed TJ Delcamino."

The dazzling smile disappeared. "No, no, no. The chief didn't kill the kid. You got that wrong. He smacked the kid around a little, sure, but he didn't kill him."

"C'mon, Pete. You got a pretty loose definition of smacking around. TJ Delcamino was tortured to death. His body had crushed bones, burn marks—"

"Stop! Stop! Regan smacked the kid around a few days before the kid turned up dead. As far as I know, one thing had nothing to do with the other."

I said, "You expect me to take your word about this?"

"Suit yourself. It's the truth. Whether you believe it or not is your headache. And put the fucking gun down unless you really are going to shoot me."

I pointed the gun away from Pete, but didn't put it away. I knew better than to completely lower my guard around him no matter what he said or did. *Fool me once . . .*

"Explain it to me, Pete."

He didn't hesitate. "Last August, someone busted into the chief's SUV and stole a duffel bag. He put out the word to us that when we caught the guy who did it, that we were not to touch the bag and that we were to call him to the scene before we did anything else. Soon enough we got a tip from a snitch that led us to the Delcamino kid. I arrested him. We got the kid, but—"

"But the duffel bag was gone."

"Exactly," Pete said. "That's when shit got weird. Regan demanded to be part of the interview. I mean, that's strange, right? The chief of the department demanding to do the preliminary interview on a kid that had broken into a car. So like ten minutes into the interview, Regan loses it and starts slapping Delcamino around. We had to pull him off before he did real damage to the kid."

"Did you know what was in the duffel bag?"

"Nope. I didn't wanna know. Still don't. But whatever's in it means a lot to Regan. When the kid wouldn't spill, Regan told us to kick the kid loose and not to discuss any aspect of the incident with anyone ever. The chief tells you to do that and you do it. I think he hoped once the kid was set loose that he would lead him back to that stupid duffel bag. I guess that didn't work out so well, and when the kid turned up dead—"

"Regan couldn't risk anyone putting two and two together because he would've been the prime suspect."

"Bingo. He didn't want anyone digging too deep because the whole thing with his SUV, the duffel bag, and his knocking the kid around would've come up. Even if he was cleared of the kid's homicide, his career would have ended in disgrace. For a man like Jimmy Regan, that's not an option."

"That's why Carey and Paxson didn't work the case very hard and why Tommy D. came to me for help."

Pete shrugged. "I guess so."

"But you don't think Regan killed the kid?"

"I know he didn't. I was with him that night at dinner at a Turkish restaurant in Setauket. It was a way for him to thank me for keeping my mouth shut about what had happened the week before with the kid."

What McCann was saying made sense up to a point, but an alibi from him wasn't exactly like getting one from Abraham Lincoln.

"You come cheap these days, Pete. I thought you'd want more than some hummus and a falafel platter for your silence."

He laughed. "You know me pretty well, Gus. No, the dinner was a negotiation for what me and my old partner would get. My partner was easy and the schmuck took the first thing Regan offered. Me, I was smarter than that. I left it open-ended. I didn't figure this would go away and that he would need some more favors."

"You should've taken what he offered you, Pete. Regan's going down."

And maybe for the first time in all the years I'd known him, he got a hangdog look on his face. He had cried at John's funeral, but this was different.

"I know it. Regan's getting stupid and sloppy and he's drinking heavy these days. Something's going on with him. I think it's time to cut my losses."

"I need something from you," I said.

"What?"

"I want you to set up a meeting with Jimmy Regan and me."

He laughed, not a happy laugh. "Why would he agree to that? He hates your guts and you've been nothing but a pain in his ass for the last two weeks."

"Because I know what was in the duffel bag and I think I knew where his car was when it got broken into."

Pete's mouth hung open. Then he caught himself. "Yeah, but still, if you're gonna fuck him anyway, why would he bother? And why would you risk it?"

"I have some questions only he can answer and I need them answered. Besides, there's something I know about him that doesn't need to come out in the midst of all this other shit. Believe me, he'll do almost anything not to have it come out."

"You gotta do better than that, Gus. You gotta give me something to work with instead of vague promises. He'll want to know what you know and that you're not just blowing smoke up his ass. I need to be able to convince him."

"Katy."

"Katy?" he repeated.

"Katy."

"Katy what? Katy who?"

"Just Katy. He'll understand."

"If you say so. Listen, Gus, before I go, I need you to tell me something."

"What?"

"Annie set me up to come here. Why'd she do it?"

"Because you hurt her and because I asked her to."

"But she can't stand you most of the time. I mean, Christ, she fucked me to ruin you. Why would she help you?"

"Because of things you'll never understand."

He shrugged. "Whatever. I'll call you."

"Don't call me," I said.

"Then who?"

I gave him Bill Kilkenny's number. "You can call that number. Now get the fuck outta here, Pete. Don't worry, I'll try and keep your name out of it as best I can."

I didn't expect him to thank me and he didn't. I watched out the window of the motel room to make sure he didn't hang around. And when I was certain he was far enough away, I shut out the lights and left. Now I needed only to wait.

I'd checked in with Bill from pay phones every few hours until the meeting was set. Finding pay phones on the island to check from was a pain in the ass, but a necessary one. I couldn't risk anyone finding me beforehand. There was another problem. Bill wouldn't tell me where the meeting was to take place unless I promised to bring him with me.

"I'm your insurance, Gus. Jimmy Regan would want me there and he won't raise a hand to you in my presence. And the thing is, I'm coming one way or the other, boyo."

He was probably right about Regan, so that was that.

It was pretty obvious that Pete McCann had worked his magic with Regan, not only because the meeting was going to happen, but because of where it was to happen. Only this time when I walked through the unmarked steel door into Malo, there was no big Polynesian guy waiting on the other side. No rollaway bar. No temporary stage. No Magdalena. No nude black chick bathed in sweat, glitter, and boredom. No tables. No dance floor. No carpeting. Nothing. This was Malo as it was during the week: spare warehouse space for a packaging company in the middle of a huge executive park in Hauppauge. The walls and floors were unadorned concrete, the ceiling corrugated steel, and the lighting reminiscent of a high school gym.

The scrape of our footfalls against the rough floor echoed as we entered the building. I knew things were going sideways the second we stepped into the heart of the warehouse and saw a bloodied and semi-conscious Kareem Shivers lying at Jimmy Regan's feet. There was that and the old-style nightstick Regan held in his right hand. There was something else, too. Regan was in his full dress blues, white ceremonial gloves and all. His white gloves were flecked with wet blood. K-Shivs' blood. On the floor to the other side of Regan was a thick brown shipping envelope.

He frowned at the sight of Bill Kilkenny. "For fuck's sake, Murphy, what did you bring him for?"

Bill answered for himself. "I wanted to be here for you, James."

Regan laughed a jangly, almost manic laugh. "James is it? I know it's a serious matter when you call me that."

Shivers moaned. And without a second's hesitation, Regan slammed the nightstick into his ribs.

"Shut the fuck up! I told you to mind that mouth of yours."

I didn't pull my weapon for fear of starting a chain reaction, one that might escalate and get Bill caught in the cross fire. And truth be told, I had no love for men like Kareem Shivers.

"Jimmy," Bill said, "what do you hope to gain by beating the man this way?"

"Oh, we're back to Jimmy now, are we? This is no man, Bill." He reared his leg back and kicked Shivers in the back. "This blackmailing piece of shit helped send me to a place from which I will never return. He made me betray the badge and the people I've fought so hard to serve and do right by."

Bill was confused. "What are you talking about?"

I asked, "Should I tell him, Chief, or should you?"

"You do it, Murphy," he said. "Let's see if I should've forced a detective's shield into your palm at some point along the way."

"Bill, your friend Jimmy Regan, the chief of the department, the cop's cop, has been a drug mule for that man there." I pointed at Shivers. "His name's Kareem Shivers, a boxer and gangsta who moved up the ladder to major drug dealer." I turned to Bill. "Remember when you and Regan came to see me the other night and the chief denied knowing Shivers? Well, I think it's safe to say he was lying about that. How'm I doing so far, Chief?"

"Batting a thousand, Murphy. But we're only in the early innings. There's a lot of game yet to be played. Carry on."

"Last August, Chief Regan was carrying a duffel bag in his SUV, and in that duffel bag was a large amount of heroin in tiny packets. How many packets and how much they were worth, I can't say, but it must've been considerable."

Regan laughed that manic laugh. "Quite considerable."

"Problem is, the chief parked his SUV out in front of a house in Wyandanch. Foolishly, carelessly, he left the bag in the SUV while he went to check that Lamar English, aka Lazy Eye, the guy who sold the drugs, was home. See, what the chief didn't know was that good old Lazy Eye and Mr. Shivers there had screwed two stupid white boys out of about twenty grand in a drug deal. One of those two stupid white kids was named Ralph O'Connell and the other one was—"

Regan interrupted. "Did you say Ralph O'Connell?"

"I did. Why?"

"Dead," Regan said. "Found him in a Plymouth Neon on Daly Road early this morning. Shotgun blast to the head."

"Fuck!" I felt sick and angry and a fool, but I couldn't lose my focus, not now. I took a deep breath and continued. "The other kid's name was TJ Delcamino," I said, my voice a little unsteady. "And what no one realized was that Delcamino's only skill in life besides getting high and fucking up was that he was great at boosting cars. I have that on no less an authority than Frankie Tacaspina Jr. I'm guessing about this part, but I think that what the kid wanted more than anything was revenge for the bad drug deal and to repay his buddy the money they'd lost.

He'd probably been staking out Lazy Eye's house for days, maybe weeks. And when the chief showed up and TJ made off with the duffel, he must've thought God was smiling down on him. Too bad the dumb schmuck didn't realize whose SUV he'd broken into. Am I still batting a thousand, Chief?"

"You're putting up Hall of Fame numbers, Murphy. Hall of Fame."

K-Shivs got to his hands and knees, but stumbled forward as he tried to get up and get away, landing face first on the concrete. It ripped his cheek open and blood poured out of him so that a red puddle formed around his face. Regan whacked him across the back of his head with the baton. The hollow sound the wood made against Shivers' skull bounced off the walls and echoed. It got to Bill and his knees buckled. I clutched his thin arm and steadied him. Regan raised the stick again.

"For the love of God, James, leave the man be," Bill screamed at Regan.

But Regan was already beyond reason or guilt, though he did lower the nightstick back down by his side. That was my cue. As long as I could keep Regan engaged, I didn't think he would do anything too crazy.

"So TJ got high, sold some of the product, and ditched the drugs somewhere. That's when your snitch told you it was the kid who'd busted into your car. You picked him up and knocked him around, but he wouldn't talk. So you let him go in the hope that he'd lead you to the stash, but he didn't. Pete McCann swears to me you didn't kill the kid, but I'm not buying it, Chief. You've got quite a temper there and with your drinking . . . I think you tried torturing it out of the kid and he died before he could tell you where the drugs were. You showed up on the scene so quickly because you knew where he was. You put him there."

"Ah, Murphy," Regan said, shaking his head in disappointment, "you were doing so well, but now your batting average has gone to shit. As Christ is my witness, I didn't kill the kid."

"Every perp I every arrested said the same thing to me, Chief."

Regan turned to Bill Kilkenny. "Bill, you look me in the eye and tell me I'm lying. I've told you things that would have ruined me long ago. There's nothing for me to gain by lying about this. I didn't kill the kid. And as little regard as I have for this scum here"—he pointed the nightstick at Shivers—"I don't think it was him that did it, either. We both had everything to lose and nothing to gain by killing the kid. If he was dead, we'd never find the drugs. He was a fucking junkie. We knew he'd lead us to the stash eventually."

Bill didn't address Regan's story, but asked the big question instead. "Why, James? Why all of this?"

"His daughter," I said.

Regan smiled with approval. "You *are* good, Murphy. You're back on a Hall of Fame pace."

Bill was confused all over again. "Wait a second. I know Jimmy's girls and—"

"Not all of them," I said. "Not Katy. Not the girl he had with Ilana Smalls."

I could see in Bill's expression that he knew who Ilana Smalls was. He knew all about what had gone on with Regan and Neil Furlong back in Wyandanch in the '90s. These were the things that Bill wouldn't share with me, the things that could have ruined Regan's career and reputation. Then I saw something in Bill's face I'd rarely seen—anger.

"Why did you not tell me about this, James? I'd borne all your other sins. We could have gotten through it together."

I answered for him. "Because until about eighteen months ago, he didn't know about her. Right, Chief? That's when he bashed Ilana Smalls' head in and had her body dumped on the grounds of the old Kings Park Psychiatric Hospital."

Regan exploded. "That lying bitch. I loved her. Christ forgive me, but I loved that woman more than anyone I'd ever loved. More than my own wife and girls. I was crazy with love for her. Stupid with it. For years I ate my heart out over losing her. I rolled over on my partner to protect her and she repaid me by hiding my own flesh and blood from me."

"Then why not just acknowledge her?" Bill wanted to know.

"He couldn't," I said. "It would have blown up his career because everyone would have connected the dots back to Wyandanch in the '90s. He would have been known as a rat, a guy who had an affair with a whore, a whore he had given up his partner to protect. But even if he'd been willing to endure that, it would have ruined his marriage and risked his relationship with his other daughters. When Shivers hooked up with his girl by Ilana Smalls, Regan was in an impossible position. And they used that to turn him into the perfect drug mule. What cop was gonna search the chief's car?"

Jimmy Regan was crying now, his chest heaving so that he might shake himself apart. He dropped the nightstick, but any sense of relief I might've felt at that was short-lived. For Regan replaced the baton with his sidearm.

"It's all in there, Bill." He pointed at the envelope with the muzzle of his gun. "Everything. I confess to all my sins, though I am well beyond redemption."

I reached for my weapon, but Regan anticipated the move. His tears came to an abrupt stop and his eyes turned suddenly cold.

"Put it down and kick it away," he said, aiming his gun at me. "I won't miss from here and I've nothing to lose. Do it now!"

I did as I was told. When he was satisfied I was no threat, he half turned to Shivers and shot him three times, the third round into his head. Then he swiftly put the still-smoking muzzle under his chin.

"See ya in hell, Murphy," he said and squeezed the trigger a fourth time.

Regan's crisply uniformed body flopped down on top of the body of the man he had just murdered in cold blood.

A woman shrieked. Bill and I looked up from the bodies to see Pete McCann, a 9mm in his hand, shoving Katy Smalls to the ground so that she landed in a puddle of blood that had leaked out of her dead father and her murdered boyfriend.

Bill and I lifted Katy out of the blood, but she had lost it. Her coat, face, hair, and hands were covered in blood and she was screaming her head off.

"Shut her the fuck up or I'll kill her now and add her body to the pile," Pete said, his voice as cold and steady as the concrete walls.

Bill wrapped his arms around her, stroked her blood-wet hair and whispered to her, "Shhh. Shhh. It's horrible but you've got to quiet down, darling. Shhh. Shhh." She quieted down some almost immediately. Bill was magic that way. Then he lifted his head and asked Pete, "Can I walk her away from this? It will help."

We all understood what *this* was.

"Sure, but don't go too far and don't try anything stupid, Father Bill."

Bill bowed his head to Pete and walked Katy away from the bodies.

"What the fuck is a priest doing here?" Pete was red-faced with anger, his cold voice heating up.

If Pete didn't know that Bill had left the church, I wasn't going to tell him, and I knew Bill was wise enough not to tell him, either. He was probably going to kill the three of us soon enough regardless, but anything that made him hesitate was something to hang on to. Even calculating bastards like Pete McCann had to swallow pretty hard to kill a priest and a twenty-year-old girl.

"He came for Regan," I said. "They go back. Old friends. Nobody was planning on you showing up, Pete."

"Too bad for you."

"I guess." I asked, "So how much did you and the girl see?"

"Enough to freak her out. Throw down your weapon, Gus."

I laughed.

"I say something funny? I must've missed it."

"No. It's just that Regan already made me toss it away." I nodded to my left. "It's over there. You can see for yourself."

He looked, saw the baby Glock on the floor, and it was his turn to laugh. Only he meant it.

"Everybody's being so helpful. First, you want a meeting with Regan that gets the both of you in the same place and he brings Shivers with him and kills the bastard. Then Regan disarms you. Too bad about the chief killing himself with his own weapon."

"How's that?"

Pete reached his left arm behind him and beneath his jacket. When I next saw his left hand, it was holding another 9mm.

"Look familiar, Gus?"

"It's mine, right? The asshole took it off me Friday night when I got pulled over on the Sag. I never thought I'd see it again."

He gave me the half-smile. "Very good. See, if the chief didn't already do himself, you were going to kill him and then I was going to have to kill you before you killed me, too."

"You might've been able to sell that if it was only you, me, and the chief. Now things are a lot more complicated. You're going to have to kill the girl and a priest. Too many loose ends to tie up. Too many bodies to explain away while you walk away unhurt."

"Let me worry about that, Gus."

"No, no, no, Pete. Too many people for you to kill."

He shook his head, that smug look on his face. "Uh-uh, old pal.

You're confused. Not me. You're going to kill them and I still get to kill you. Then at your funeral, I'll hook up with Annie again. A sympathy fuck is good for the soul. You shoulda tried it sometime. Too bad that favor she did for you turned out to be a favor for me. The way I see it, I owe her for that."

I bit the inside of my cheek so hard, I tasted the metal of my own blood. I couldn't let him fuck with me, so I changed subjects.

"That charade on the Sagtikos the other night, that was your doing, not Paxson's?"

"Milt Paxson's an ass. He couldn't find his own dick with a road-map. Milt! What a ridiculous name. Who names a kid Milton? Of course it was me."

"The dead cop in Smudge's house and Lazy Eye, that was you also?"

He nodded, said, "I pulled the trigger, but it was your gun." Then he looked over to where Bill was walking Katy Smalls. Katy had calmed or gone completely into shock and was nearly silent, her supple body rigid under Bill's arm.

"You've got another minute, Father, to say your prayers or to do whatever it is you gotta do," he said, his voice fractured and nervous. Pete may have planned for me to kill Bill and the girl, but he'd gone through too much Catholic schooling and still believed enough to feel the weight of what he was about to set in motion.

I took a peek at where Bill and the girl were walking and decided to piss Pete off in the hope that Bill would take the opportunity present-ing itself.

"You're gonna kill a priest and a girl, Pete? Really? Are you that much of a coldhearted prick?"

"Grief make you deaf or something, Gus? Not me. You."

He was too far away from me or I would have spit in his face. Instead I did what I could, shuffling a foot or two to my right to make his eyes follow me, and then I spit at his shoes.

He laughed. "You missed, pal. Maybe your throat's a little dry from fear, huh?"

"Fuck you, Pete! You cowardly piece of shit. You wanna kill us, do it yourself. The same way you killed Tommy Delcamino."

But instead of rage, confusion washed over his face. "I didn't kill that loser. We didn't kill him. Why would we kill him? When the missing heroin started showing up on the street, we figured we'd keep an eye on him and he'd lead us to it. When he didn't, Shivers got impatient and sent his crew over there to see if he had it stashed in the trailer. When they showed up, Tommy D. was already dead."

"You're full of—"

"Enough!" he screamed. "Enough stalling. Father, get over here and don't do anything stupid."

When they were close to us, Pete waved my old service weapon at me. He placed it on the floor at his feet and toed it over to me.

"Go ahead. Pick it up. There's two in the clip, none in the chamber, so don't get any dumb ideas, Gus. The three of you would be dead before you could chamber a round and aim it at me. Pick it up. Rack that slide in super slow motion and aim it at the girl while you're doing it. Understand?"

"Fuck you!"

Pete stepped close, whacked me across the face with his gun, and stepped back. I went down to my knees, a little dazed.

"That was your only chance to be a hero, Gus. You say something like that again or flinch and I'll put one in your belly. Now get the fuck up and do what I say."

"Okay, okay!" I raised my hands up. "Too bad I didn't wear my vest, then you'd have to put one in my leg or head."

He sneered at me. "Who you think you're talking to? I'm not a fucking rookie. Now pick up your nine and shoot the girl first. I want the drama over with. Remember, slower than slow."

I grabbed my old gun. There may not be any atheists in foxholes, but I knew better than to pray. I stood, keeping the Glock down at my side.

"Do it! Do it now," Pete screamed, pointing his weapon at my head.

I lifted the gun up with my right arm, placed my left hand over the slide and racked a bullet into the chamber while pointing it at Katy's head. She was weeping a steady stream of silent tears, her body shaking violently, but she didn't cry out. I wish she had or had dropped to her knees, anything to distract Pete McCann. Now it fell to me.

"No!" I shouted out and wheeled toward Pete. As I squeezed my eyes shut, I thought of John's face and waited to feel the bullets rip through me.

I heard the shots, but felt no pain. Opening my eyes, I saw shock flash across Pete McCann's face, then a flash of utter confusion. I answered his confusion with a bullet. The shot tore a path through his neck, opening his arteries and spraying the air with his blood. His eyes rolled back in his head and he toppled backward. Bill was still firing the gun he'd retrieved, as I'd hoped he would.

"Stop, Bill! Stop!" I shouted at the top of my lungs, but it was no good. We were all a little deaf from the gunfire.

Finally, I grabbed for the gun in Bill's hand, but he would not give it up. Instead he was trying to squeeze the trigger, though the slide was locked out.

"Bill! Bill!"

He relaxed his hand and let me take it from him. He turned to stare up at me, a look of distant horror in his eyes. It was Vietnam all over again for him. Vietnam, where he'd picked up a dead GI's rifle and shot a girl who had tossed a grenade into the tent of a field hospital where he was serving as a chaplain.

"Christ forgive me, but she couldn't've been more than fifteen. She was about to toss another grenade and I had no choice, Gus," he had confided in me during my mourning for John. "What merciful God could put that on me?"

I was remembering those words when Bill moved his lips. Nothing came out of his mouth at first or maybe it was that I just couldn't hear him for the ringing in my ears. I focused on his lips.

"The girl. The girl." He mouthed over and over.

Oh, shit!

The world didn't exactly slow down or tilt on its edge, but the things that filtered into my eyes came at me as flashes of a strobe light. My adrenaline-fueled tunnel vision only enhanced my weird sense of things as I scanned through the smoke and gore. I found Katy Smalls on her knees, rocking back and forth, holding Kareem Shivers' dead hand in hers. She was so covered in blood that I couldn't tell if she was hit or not, but she seemed okay. I turned away from her and back to Bill, who was crossing himself, a rosary in his hand where the gun had been, his lips moving in prayer. I looked at Pete, his eyes open, staring blindly into oblivion. My bullet had finished him, but his legs were bloodied, chewed-up messes. Bill had emptied most of the clip where I'd hinted to him to fire, below Pete's vest and into his thighs. One of the shots, I thought, had to have hit a femoral artery. Several shots had hit and his pants were soaked with his blood. I stepped over to his life-less carcass and kicked the gun away from his hand. I don't know why. I just did. I looked to see if the brown shipping envelope was still there on the floor. It was. I picked it up, cradling it in my arms as I had Krissy and as I had John before her. Then, behind me, in spite of the still overwhelming ringing in my ears, I thought I heard something. When I turned, I saw that Katy had taken up her father's nightstick and was pounding his body with it. I was frozen and stood there for what felt like an hour, watching her. She tired of it eventually, dropped the stick, and curled herself into a ball next to the bodies of the men who had betrayed her, each in their own way.

I found my cell phone in my hand, though I don't remember put-ting it there. It also seemed I had dialed 9-1-1. I couldn't hear the oper-ator very well and I kept repeating the address. I left the line open, but I put the phone down. I found a quiet corner in the warehouse, far away from Bill and Katy, far away from the three dead men and the blood and the pain, far away from the world. I got as far away as I could and just waited.

(FRIDAY NIGHT/CHRISTMAS EVE)

xpediency Above All is the hidden motto of all police departments. Do they want to get to the truth of things? Do they want justice for victims? Of course, but they also want to clear cases. Closed cases make for pretty statistics and good politics. Police work is just as much sausage making as anything else. Deals and compromises are part of the job. So between the detailed confession Jimmy Regan had left behind, my statements, Neil Furlong's testimony, and the available evidence, you could see it coming down the road. The homicides of TJ Delcamino, Tommy Delcamino, and Ralph O'Connell were going to get hung around the necks of Regan, McCann, and Kareem Shivers.

Even if all of them had denied those killings to me or implied as much, and the missing heroin was never recovered, they were probably going to take the blame. Dead, disgraced cops and murderers make easy fall guys, and I couldn't foresee anyone standing up to defend them. It made for a nice little Christmas gift, all neatly wrapped and presented with a silken bow. And when the DA chatted with Carey and Paxson, you just knew they would say anything to save their own skins. Their statements would follow whatever narrative suited the department and the politicians.

Me? I was unconvinced, but no one cared about what I believed. For the moment, Bill Kilkenny and I were being portrayed in the media as heroes, though neither of us felt remotely heroic, most especially not Bill. The media were as big a fan of expediency as the police and politicians. Bigger fans, maybe, and with fewer scruples. Because they hid behind the banner of the truth, their sausage making was uglier. Their expediency was in the name of entertainment and the lowest common denominator. And there was nothing like a lot of blood and scandal to get people's attention. Bill and me, we were the convenient counterweights, and by New Year's, all of it would have been forgotten. Suffolk County, all of Long Island, the city, and the world would have moved on to new blood and scandal. There was never any shortage of that.

For the moment, I was concentrating only on the woman in the passenger seat. Magdalena looked amazing in a white satin blouse, black slacks, and black heels. The whole car smelled of that perfume she had worn when we first met. Was I bringing her to make Annie jealous? You bet your ass that was part of it, and I'd told Magdalena as much. She didn't seem to mind, but that wasn't all of it. I was a different man than I once was. The toll John's death had taken, the two years since, and the events of the last two weeks had changed me. I was damaged goods and, by her own admission, so too was my date for the evening.

Magdalena and I were testing our friendship, and maybe that wouldn't last very long. We'd find that out eventually. What I knew was that women like Casey, as attractive and kind as she was, were too safe for who I was now. I couldn't fit in a nice little house in Nesconset, into the kind of life I had once so happily lived. I didn't want that because it would be only an empty parody of what I once had. I had no desire to live like a silhouette: the shape of the shadows just right, but without substance or fire. Maybe Magdalena could offer substance and fire, or maybe not.

I think the thing that saved the evening was that my mother-in-law recognized Magdalena from one of her soaps and was too starstruck to bust my chops for bringing another woman to the party. Even Annie and Krissy were kind to Magdalena and, more surprisingly, they were kind to me. I guess maybe my liking Rob, Annie's new beau, didn't hurt. He was a really nice guy and bent over backward to have talks with me. And I suppose it didn't hurt that I was being run up the flagpole as a hero. Besides his trying so hard to put me at ease, there was something about Rob I couldn't help but like: the way he looked at Annie. It was clear that he had a deep, abiding love for her, a love so deep he had carried it around with him for over twenty years. A love so deep he had never married because he knew he could never love anyone else the way he loved Annie and wouldn't hurt someone by giving less than his all. There was a lot to admire in someone like that and a lot to like about him.

The only really awkward moment of the evening came when Annie's mom took out some old photo albums. Annie and I wound up next to each other on the couch, pointing at pictures, laughing, and saying things like, "Remember how sick you got when . . ." or "Remember how cute John and Krissy looked when . . ." When the room got really quiet except for Annie and me, we looked up, and there were Rob and Magdalena standing together staring at us. I don't know what Magdalena was thinking, but it was easy to know what was on Rob's mind.

"Hey, Rob," I said to him after coffee, "come on, let's go for a walk. It's a little crowded in here."

Once we were outside, I put his fears to rest.

"We'll always be connected, Annie and me, but you've got nothing to fear from me. Annie deserves to be happy again. I can never give that to her now, not after the last two years. Maybe you can. I hope so." I shook his hand and clapped him on the back. "I mean it."

He asked me about Magdalena and all I could do was shrug my shoulders. She was easy enough to desire, but I wanted more than to desire someone. I had to relearn how to like the world and the people in it.

(EARLY CHRISTMAS MORNING)

Magdalena asked me to stay after a kiss or two or three, but like I said, I'd been through too much to just cave to desire. Instead, I asked her if she'd like to do New Year's together.

"Can't," she said, a sigh in her voice. "I've got a bartending gig in the city. That's big bucks I can't pass up. How about Christmas dinner here later?"

"Christmas dinner, yes. Here, no." I winked. "I'm a sucker for a woman cooking me dinner. Might get me in all sorts of trouble. I'll call you later. Have a restaurant picked out and I'll come get you."

"All right," she relented, but with a smile. "You really are an okay guy, Gus Murphy."

"I'm getting there."

For a great deal of its length, Route 25A skirted the Gold Coast and the northernmost towns in Nassau and Suffolk counties. At most points along the way, you weren't more than a mile south of Long Island Sound. Back in the day, before Robert Moses built the LIE and the Southern and Northern State Parkways, it had been a major east-west road. But it was a narrow road, winding and tree-lined and hilly and dark, and I would hate to think how long a trip from the Nassau border to Orient Point would take these days.

At one a.m., though, traffic was light, and at one a.m. on Christmas morning it was fairly nonexistent. So I had the road all to myself. It must have been the lack of traffic and that I was alone on the road with only my thoughts for company that helped make it happen. That and the shock of the fat biker dressed in a Santa suit zooming past me in the opposite direction out of the darkness, his Harley done up in red, green, and white Christmas lights. But all I know is that when it hit me, it hit me all at once. I went from knowing nothing to knowing everything. It was as if my unconscious mind had broken a code without me even knowing it had been trying to decipher one.

Yeah, there had been some things irking me, like about Ralph O'Connell getting murdered. I didn't understand what the upside was for Regan, McCann, or even Kareem Shivers in killing the big dumb kid. Ralph was no threat to any of them, not really. His only contact had been with Lazy Eye, Jamal, and Antwone. Lazy Eye was dead and the other two were in custody. And I wasn't buying that Pete or Regan would have dared shotgunning me to death in my bed at the hotel. That was real outlaw shit with the risk of too much going wrong. And where was the missing heroin? The fact was, it wasn't actually missing. Its showing up on the street was what had started this whole second round of violence. Shivers was looking for it. Regan and McCann were looking for it. Someone was selling it, and I suddenly knew who it was.

The thing was, what to do about it? You can't call 9-1-1 with suspicions, especially when they're messy and contradict the official narrative of events. There were other factors, too. Although Bill and I were still wearing the white hats, Jimmy Regan's suicide was too fresh. The details and full extent of his crimes hadn't yet hit the street. Whatever facts had made it into the press were vague and, as always, less than accurate. Some of the media were framing Regan as a tragic figure, a martyr, a victim even. Maybe more details would surface in the coming months. Maybe the whole ugly story would come out someday, but I doubted it. The whole truth would be an embarrassment to a lot of powerful people. Then again, everyone who knew Pete McCann knew he was capable of all sorts of sins. He was the easy villain. No one would have trouble believing the worst of him. His bad rep and the fact that he was too dead to defend himself would come in handy when it came to scapegoat-picking time.

I thought I had one card to play and one man to play it with: Al Roussis. Tommy Delcamino's homicide was his case and I had the answers I hoped he was still looking for. I was depending on his bull-dog nature not to swallow the official bullshit story whole. But as I was fishing my cell phone out of my pocket, I noticed three headlights in my rearview mirror and they were closing in on my rear bumper fast. Those headlights made me realize that I was totally vulnerable. I didn't even have a weapon. Both of my guns had been seized as evidence. I stepped hard on the gas, trying to put some distance between me and the headlights racing in on my tail. Suddenly I felt much more alone than I had only two minutes earlier. I wasn't alone for long.

Under any other set of circumstances, I don't think I would have seen those closing headlights as a threat, but three headlights across meant three motorcycles. And when you were thinking what I was thinking, three motorcycles on your bumper felt pretty fucking threat-ening. When they rode up behind me, in spite of my attempt to put distance between us, my throat got drier with each thump of my heart. I stared into the rearview, trying to see if I could recognize anything about the bikers. It was a waste of time as the glare of their lights pre-vented me from making out any details at all. Then their left turn sig-nals came on at once and they passed on my left in single file. The hoarse rumble of their engines filled up the night as they went. All were dressed in black from neck to toe, with red bandannas across their faces. They all wore goggles and matte-black Nazi-style helmets. Nothing says peace on earth and goodwill toward men like a Nazi hel-met. There was nothing familiar about any of them. The last biker to pass turned to look at me and then gave the thumbs-up as he sped by.

Just as suddenly as they had rushed up behind me, they disappeared over the next hill.

I calmed down some because when I came up over the hill, I didn't see them ahead of me. My moment of relaxation lasted only as far as the next bend in the road. For when I came over the hill and the road curved right, there they were, riding slowly, three across, as if waiting for me to catch up. And when I noticed that none of the bikes had license plates, I knew I was in trouble. I knew that the thumbs-up guy had stared at me as he passed, not to make nice, but to make sure I was who they were looking for.

Once I came up behind them, things went bad in a hurry. The biker in the middle waved his arm and the two bikers on either side moved out wide, then decelerated so that they flanked my right and left fenders. The middle biker weaved his bike in front of me as if to keep my focus on him, but I forced myself to look away, to look right and left to see what the other two were up to. I thought I saw a reflection off something metallic that appeared in the hand of the biker on my left fender. The dark and the distractions made it impossible for me to make out what it was, but I got the sense that whatever it was, it was trouble. The guy on my right thumped my fender with his boot and swerved away. Then did it again and again. Reflexively, I turned my head to the right. When I refocused, I saw that the guy on my left had decelerated so that he was now riding parallel to my door. I looked to see what was in his hand, and even before I could make out the meaning of its shape, I sped up.

The window behind me exploded, little beads of glass pelting the backseat, some hitting my neck through the gap between the bottom of the headrest and the top of the seat. I felt the back of my neck. It was wet with sweat, a lot of it, not blood. The quiet in the car was as shattered as the glass. The wind howled as it whipped through the car, and the deafening noise of motorcycle engines filled up any empty spaces the wind had missed. And it got cold, very cold. The time for reaction had passed, so I sped up and tugged right on the steering wheel. The biker on that side of me had no choice now but to lay his bike down or get pinned between my front fender and a stone wall. But as he made to lay it down, he ran smack into a metal mailbox pole. His bike sparked like mad against the pavement as it skidded out from under him. He skidded along behind it, his head bouncing off the blacktop, his limp body flopping as it went.

Then, up ahead of me on my left, there was another burst of smoke and of fire. My left headlight exploded, metal pinged off metal, my windshield cracked in five or six places, and spiderwebs spread out from where each buckshot pellet had hit glass. I floored it, swerving hard left, really hard left, and clipped the back wheel of the bike ridden by the shooter. He dropped the sawed-off and tried desperately to regain control of his machine. And for about a hundred yards he looked like he might pull it off, but in the end, he lost it and slammed into a guardrail at a curve on the westbound shoulder. The shooter flew off the bike headfirst and into a tree. I didn't know about the first guy and the mailbox pole, but I was pretty sure this guy was dead.

I forced myself to turn my focus away from my sideview mirror and saw that the middle biker, who had been weaving in front of me, was now so far ahead that his taillight was barely visible. I knew better than to think I was safe, so I slowed down as quickly as I could and swung over to the westbound lane. I drove on, looking for a place to hide out. There weren't many straightaways on this part of 25A and I didn't want to risk killing anyone who might be out on the road. Too much blood had lately been spilled on Long Island, and I didn't want to be the reason innocent blood got added to the reservoir. Then again, I had even less desire to add mine to the mix. I drove past the first two accident scenes. Neither of the bikers was moving. I found a hidden driveway at the end of a curve in the road, backed far enough into it so that the nose of my car would be impossible to see. I shut off my one working headlamp and waited for the third biker to double back. I had no doubt that he would. I didn't have long to wait.

The last biker was no fool, though. He didn't come screaming down the road or through the curve. No, he took the curve very slowly, his head scanning left and right. I shut my engine off, fearing he'd do the same. Just because he couldn't see me didn't mean he couldn't hear me. And when he was fully through the curve, he pulled to the narrow shoulder and did what I thought he might. He shut off his engine and the night went silent again. He hopped off his hog, took off his helmet, gloves, and goggles. He slid the bandanna down off his face onto his neck. He moved cautiously forward. I could see him pretty clearly through the bare hedges and under the glow of a garage-mounted spotlight that popped on because he had parked within range of a driveway motion sensor. I didn't recognize him at all. As he moved, he reached under his leather jacket and pulled out a revolver, a big revolver. He was listening for the ticking of my engine as it cooled, the same sound that had gotten my attention at the paving yard the night I found Tommy D. murdered.

It was harder for him to see me than for me to see him since my car was camouflaged in darkness and its shape was broken up by the maze of leafless hedge branches that lined the driveway. He kept moving forward, then stopped in his tracks. He tilted his head in my direction and froze, squinting, trying to peer through the darkness. I don't think he saw me, but he had heard something. He ran straight toward the entrance to the driveway. I was as good as found, but didn't start my engine, not yet. If I had any chance, it was to wait until it was almost too late. Then I saw his silhouette in the middle of the driveway. He turned, raising up his arm up to shoot. I turned the key, dipped my head as low as I could, and put the car in drive. *Bang!* My windshield shattered, a spray of glass beads bouncing off the top of my head. *Bang!* The rear windshield cracked. The next sound was the thud of my bumper hitting the biker flush and of his head connecting with the pavement. I stood on my brakes.

I rushed out of my car, brushing glass beads off my jacket, cutting my hands on their edges, and got to the gunman, who was screaming and writhing in pain in the middle of the road. His gun, a Smith &

Wesson .357, had fallen about ten feet farther across the street. I gave him a quick once-over. His left leg was broken for sure and his right wrist was bent at an angle that wrists didn't make on their own. I felt his abdomen to see if it was hard from internal bleeding. It wasn't, though when I touched his side he wailed and went rigid with pain. My guess was he had a few broken ribs. He was hurt pretty bad, but I thought he'd probably live. I knelt down at his side and took a close look at his gun hand. There was a very vivid tattoo on the back of his hand. It was of a half clown face, half bloody skull. Zee had one just like it on his right hand. It was the gang tat of the Maniacs Motorcycle Club.

"You'll live," I said, picking up the .357. "Don't be a schmuck. When they ask you about Zee, give him up or you'll be spending the rest of your fucking life in prison."

Then I got in my car and headed back toward Huntington Station. As I went, two SCPD cruisers screamed past me, their sirens blaring, their light bars flashing madly. Their drivers too busy to notice the car with one headlight and no windshield driving too quickly on the opposite side of the road.

(EARLY CHRISTMAS MORNING)

arrigan's was still packed fifteen minutes before closing time on Christmas morning. Where else would losers celebrate the birth of Christ: the savior who had failed so miserably at saving them from their own lesser angels? There was always hope, I thought, laughing at myself for thinking it. No there wasn't. Karl Marx had it wrong. Religion wasn't the opiate of the masses. Hope was. Most of the bar crowd were so shitfaced, they didn't notice my bleeding hands or the glass beads I was still brushing off my clothes. Nor did they notice me make a gun of my thumb and index finger and point it at Zee. Zee noticed and that was what mattered. But instead of looking scared or even surprised at the sight of me, he smiled like a man who had it all figured out. We were about to find out if he did.

I tilted my head to where his office was and then pointed at my pocket. When he looked at the pocket, I showed him the handle of the Smith & Wesson. That seemed to concern him some, but not any more than if a fly had landed on his steak. Annoying, off-putting, but nothing more. He was a cold-blooded son of a bitch. Then again, that was the nature of lizards.

Inside the office, I locked the door behind us and pulled the revolver fully out of my pocket. Before I let him sit down at his desk, I checked the drawers. I'd been right about the gun he'd been holding on me the last time I was there. He had an old army-issue Colt .45 in a side drawer. I stuck it in my belt and waved for him to sit down. He moved slowly, painfully, but this time I kind of enjoyed it. He deserved all the pain available to him.

"You shouldn't've killed the O'Connell kid," I said. "If you didn't have him killed, I probably wouldn't have put it all together."

The corners of his droopy, dull gray mustache lifted up in a smile. "The O'Connell kid . . . that's on your head, Gus. You were the one who pointed out that TJ had gone to visit him before we . . . before he died. And then you led us right to him. That was stupid of you."

I wasn't going to debate the point. "I should have known it was you the second I came in here the first time. Tommy D. trusted you. TJ trusted you. Of course the kid would come to you and not his father to stash the drugs."

He laughed. "Maybe it's my sweet face or that the arthritis makes me seem older than I am. People trust the elderly for some stupid fucking reason."

"You saw the opportunity the second you looked in the duffel bag, didn't you? It was your way out, your deliverance. You gave the kid a cash advance on the dope and told him there'd be plenty more to come because you'd be able to get rid of it, all of it. That part, at least, was the truth. The Maniacs have a distribution network that stretches from here to Maine and back.

"Then you let him take enough product to keep him out of it for a few days. What'd you tell him to do if he got picked up? You tell him to keep his mouth shut no matter what, that you'd take care of everything? You took care of everything, all right. You snitched him out to someone in the Second, who alerted the guys in the Fourth. You took any possible stink on you and put it all on the kid. You may be a low-life scumbag, Zee, but not a stupid one."

"Thanks, Gus. I'll have that put on my headstone."

I smiled at the thought. Zee noticed.

"Don't get your hopes up," he said. "I'm not dying just yet."

"There are all sorts of ways to die." I waved the .357 at him. "Only some of them are naturally occurring."

He shrugged. It hurt him to do it.

"But you knew you couldn't trust a junkie like TJ for very long. You had to let him live long enough for the cops to follow him around a little while, but not long enough to trace him back to you. And you knew it was only a matter of time till he came back to you for more dope and more money. Here's the part I haven't worked out yet. How did you know that killing him so brutally might implicate Regan and Shivers?"

"You don't really think I'm gonna answer that, do you, Gus? Not that it matters, 'cause you can't prove a thing."

"For now I'm not worried about proving things. I'm in a locked office with you and I have two loaded guns. Maybe I'm just interested in blowing your balls off."

That shook his tree a little. He tried not to show it, but he couldn't quite pull it off.

"Once you got rid of TJ, you probably thought you were home free, huh? You let Tommy D. cry on your shoulder. Maybe you even paid for the kid's burial. But Tommy couldn't let it go and that was gonna be a problem for you eventually. Who knows, maybe if the cops had worked the case harder, Tommy would have found a way to live with it."

Zee said, "There were times I almost had the poor bastard convinced to move on, but that wasn't Tommy D.'s way, moving on. Then he went to you. I knew that was trouble."

"In a way, but the real trouble was that the stolen heroin started showing up on the island and kids started dying from it. That got all sorts of attention from all the wrong people."

He reached for his top drawer. "I gotta smoke a bowl. The pain's bad."

I walked around the desk and slammed his hand in the drawer.

Then I held the muzzle of the .357 to his temple. "Fuck you! The pain is bad. Good. Good. Just keep talking and I'll think about it."

"You made your point," he said, doubling over in agony. He used one gnarled hand to rub pain out of the other, wincing as he did so. "You made your point."

"Why'd you let the Maniacs sell the shit here?"

"It wasn't a matter of let. I sold it all to them for a lump sum instead of a percentage. I asked them not to sell it here, but they get better prices in suburban New York, Connecticut, and New Jersey than in the 'hood or trailer parks. You think they give a shit about what I want?"

"Why'd you kill Tommy? He was your friend."

"I didn't like having to do that. Christ, I didn't like it at all, but it seemed to me he might've been working his way around to the same conclusion you got to. That somehow I was involved in TJ's murder, and I also needed to distract the cops again once the heroin started killing kids on the island. Maybe it was easier 'cause I didn't actually have to pull the trigger."

I stared at the revolver in my hand and got a sick feeling in my belly. "You were wrong about Tommy."

"What do you mean I was wrong about him?"

"He never suspected you, not for one second. He trusted you."

Though Zee's face went blank, all he could say was "Price of doin' business, I guess." But I could see it in his eyes that not even a lizard like him believed it.

"Tonight on the road and trying to shotgun me in my bed at the hotel, that was you, too?"

"I shoulda had the Maniacs do you after your first visit."

"Why didn't you?"

"I didn't know where all the loose ends might be. I couldn't be sure Tommy D. had told me everything. Now they're all tied up but for you."

"Well, Zee, unless you got a secret weapon in here, that's not gonna happen."

He got a smug look on his face reminiscent of Pete McCann's. "No need," he said. "You can't prove a goddamned thing. Heroin's gone. The money's hidden where nobody but me can find it. There's no evidence connecting me to any of the killings and nobody to testify." He picked up the cordless phone off his desk and waved it at me. "You wanna call 9-1-1, be my guest."

I smacked the phone out of his hand with the revolver and it crashed to pieces against the wall. I didn't mind that the barrel of the gun made solid contact with Zee's knuckles.

"You're almost right, Zee. Almost. One of the three guys who tried to kill me tonight is alive. He's in rough shape, but alive."

Zee got that Pete McCann look about him again and laughed at me. "Man, Gus, you don't understand, do you? He won't testify against me or against anybody else."

"You think he's gonna eat a few murder raps and two attempted murder raps just to save an ex-Maniacs' ass?"

"I don't think it. I know it. And all that shit's got to get proved in court. Let's just see what happens between here and court. The Maniacs got plenty of money for good lawyers and they can make life pretty good on the inside if one of their own goes down."

I'm not sure exactly what set me off—his smugness or the fact that he was right. Whatever it was didn't matter, because I backhanded Zee across the face and knocked him off his throne. I yanked him back into his seat by his hair. Then I pushed the cylinder of the .357 out and dropped the three remaining bullets into my palm. I tossed two away. I put one back in the cylinder, spun it, and flicked the cylinder back into place.

"You think you're gonna scare me with a little Russian roulette?" he said, his voice thin and brittle in spite of his bravado. "I played it once or twice before."

"Yeah, I bet, but the last time you played, you weren't this close to getting out from under. What did you get for the dope, a quarter of a mil, half? The last time you played, you couldn't taste that much money." I held my left thumb and index finger barely apart. "If what you say is true, you're this close to being gone. This close to living the rest of your miserable scumbag life in the warmth of the desert sun. Let's see how much fun you have with it now."

I yanked his hair again, and when he opened his mouth in pain, I shoved the barrel of the Smith & Wesson so far down his throat, he gagged.

"Say goodbye, motherfucker."

His eyes got very big as I thumbed the hammer back. He started to choke with panic when it clicked into position. As I put my finger on the trigger, he pissed himself. It wasn't much of a price to pay for what he had done, but it was something he would have to live with. A guy like him, it would eat at him till the day he died. I pulled the trigger. Empty. I pulled the hammer back again, but there was a knocking at the office door.

"Suffolk County Police, open the fucking door. Now!"

I guess somebody in the bar noticed the gun in my jacket pocket or my bloody hands or that Zee had been missing for a while. I pulled the trigger again anyway. Empty again. Would I have kept pulling the trigger if there wasn't a cop outside the door? I don't know. Maybe. I wiped my prints off both guns and laid them on the desk before opening the door.

Both Zee and I were led out in cuffs. The parking lot outside was alive with the whirling and flashing of blue, red, and white lights. I looked up into the sky, but there was no Santa. There were no reindeer. There never were. I thought of John's face the first time he opened a gift on Christmas morning and the first time he helped Krissy open gifts. I smiled. I thought of the rude display atop Mr. Martino's house and the baby Jesus with the blue doll eyes in the manger on his neighbor's lawn. I thought of Bill reliving his loss of faith and of Katy Smalls beating her father's body with his nightstick. I thought of all the pain and needless violence that came of greed and revenge. And I thought that with each drop of innocent blood spilled, I understood the world less and less.

EPILOGUE

I'd just dropped off four guests from the hotel at the Ronkonkoma station. I wasn't scheduled to do another pickup all night, so I parked the van in the designated spot and went for a stroll. It wasn't spring yet, but it sure felt like it. It had been one of those Marches, one that came in like a lamb and seemed to be staying that way. The sun in the sky was telling the truth again, its warmth on my skin matching the intensity of its color. The trees were budding early. Maybe the grass was greener sooner than usual. Maybe not. Somehow it even smelled right, like there was honey in the air. And I was restless, an old symptom of spring I hadn't been afflicted with for years.

As I strolled the less than scenic area around the train station, I scrolled to Magdalena's number and tapped the screen. The call went to voice mail. I didn't leave a message. We were in a good place, the Mag-ster, as I now sometimes called her, and me. While we had progressed beyond the "just friends" stage, we hadn't gotten to making promises or commitments. We didn't ask each other too many questions and just tried to enjoy each other's company when we were together. One of the few rules we had was that there was no bitching about our exes allowed.

Frankly, I didn't have much to complain about in that area. Annie seemed to have gotten her life back in order. She had moved out of her brother's place and gotten an apartment in Stony Brook to be near Krissy. She and Rob were doing fine. Even if she could never manage to love Rob the way he loved her, she had learned to love him back enough so they could both be happy. We spoke on the phone occasionally, mostly about how Krissy was doing at school. The conversations were always cordial if not downright friendly. I won't lie to you, as incredible as Magdalena looked naked, as good as she smelled, and as intense as the sex was between us, I sometimes missed Annie that way. I suppose I always would.

Magdalena hated her ex, so there wasn't much point in bringing him up, ever. She sold the old Mercedes for a nice price, given its condition, and had thrown out the rest of her custom-made perfume. She was taking acting classes again and doing at least one audition a week. I admired the hell out of her for that. Took more courage than I had. Malo never reopened after the bloodbath that had happened there, but Magdalena got a few bartending gigs at other places. One at a fancy steak restaurant in the Huntington area, a million miles away from Harrigan's.

Speaking of Harrigan's, Zee was right: the cops and the DA's office never laid a glove on him. It wasn't like they didn't try. They did. Al Roussis knew it was true and didn't question any aspect of my narrative when I explained it to him. The ADA also knew the truth when she heard it, but just as Zee had bragged last Christmas morning, there was no evidence of any kind tying him to the homicides or the drugs. The fact was that from all appearances, Zee looked like Tommy Delcamino's best friend and a second dad to TJ. The third biker survived, but, again as Zee predicted, he refused to talk to the cops or the ADA no matter what incentives they put on the table. He's facing about sixty felony counts ranging from first-degree murder to illegal possession of a firearm to . . . I think the only thing he's not charged with is stealing nuclear secrets. His trial is set for some time this summer.

Zee will never face trial, not because he's above the law, but because he's below the ground. He made it out to the desert a few weeks later than he had planned. Still, he made it west all the same. I hadn't really given him much thought because I'd had more than a month of legal entanglements to deal with myself, some stemming from what Bill and I had been forced to do at the warehouse and others from the encounters I'd had on Christmas morning with the bikers and with Zee. Eventually, Bill and I were cleared of everything. About a month ago I picked up a newspaper one of the guests left behind in the van. I skimmed it to kill some time until the next train from Penn Station got in.

After the sports pages, I flipped the paper around. On page five there was a picture of Richie Zito in his younger days, wearing his Maniacs colors. When he wasn't a hunched-over bastard and his mustache wasn't the color of two-day-old snow. I think the headline was something like "Ex-LI Bar Owner Murdered in Arizona." Zee had been caught in a shootout in a small border town. The shootout was between members of a Mexican drug cartel and a motorcycle gang. The writer described Zito as an innocent bystander. In the history of innocent bystanders, there had never been a less innocent one. The levels of irony involved were so varied that it was to laugh. But I didn't laugh because poetic justice wasn't justice at all. I was just happy he was dead and I hoped to Christ it took him a long time to die.

As I suspected, the whole story about Jimmy Regan never made it into the press. Not yet, anyway. Enough was leaked inside and outside the department so that no one made a stink about defending his reputation or building him a statue. Although the O'Connell and Delcamino homicides were still technically open cases, there was little doubt that down the road the cases would go before a review panel and they'd be attributed to Pete McCann or Kareem Shivers. Pete was already guilty of at least two killings. Who knew how many K-Shivs was responsible for? What were a few more bodies to throw their way? No one was going to defend their honor or build them statues, either.

Smudge reappeared after New Year's. He showed up at the hotel to let me know he was all right. Guys like Smudge possess a developed knack for survival. They have to. I explained to him about the differences between the official story of Tommy D.'s murder and the truth. He accepted it without a word of protest or bitterness. That was another thing about guys like Smudge. They didn't open the door to bitterness for fear of it eating them alive.

I have no idea what happened to Katy Smalls after that night in the warehouse. I sometimes think I should drive to the house in Melville to see if she still lived there with her puppy. Whether she was or she wasn't living there, I was pretty sure the events of that night last December had beaten all the residual girlishness out of her. And as far as I know, Jamal and Antwone are still in the system and I hope to steer clear of them when they get out.

Slava and I have gotten into the habit of having breakfast once a week, usually on Saturday mornings. Sometimes we discuss going into business together as kind of unofficial PIs. You know, doing favors for people for a price. Technically, I guess we'd already had a case, and Tommy D.'s three grand—minus the money I'd given to Ralphy O'Connell and to Smudge to help him find a new place to live—was ours. It was something to think about, at least. Slava still refused to discuss his secrets or his shame, but I'd come to know he was a far more thoughtful and serious man than the image he presented to the people for whom he opened doors and carried luggage.

Oh, yeah, Casey started showing up at the club again, but has turned her attention to other men. At first we'd say our hellos and leave it at that. One night, when I went to get a glass of water at the bar, I wound up standing right next to her. It was pretty awkward there for a minute. Then I said, "Don't worry, Jocasta, your secret's safe with me." When she stopped laughing, the awkwardness was gone.

Bill is doing okay and claims to be fine, though he's smoking more and the distance in his stare has lengthened. He's been doing a lot of reading lately on Eastern religion and philosophy. I wonder if his shooting Pete McCann has scarred him or if it has become an extension of what he'd done all those years ago in Vietnam. He won't talk about it. I tried to get him to go to Dr. Rosen, even offered to help him pay for it.

He wouldn't hear of it. "It's not my way," he said. I respect that. And though I can tell he's suffering, I lack his magic for taking away other people's pain.

Yesterday, Bill and I went to visit John Jr. It had been a long while since I'd been to the grave and Bill kind of pushed for me to go. I think he saw the guilt in me. I know he did.

"It's no sin to be happy again, Gus Murphy," he said. "Your having found a way back to the living is no disrespect to John. It doesn't mean you loved him less. Wouldn't the lad want you to live again? Wouldn't *he* want to live again?"

Argue that.

As Bill laid some flowers at the foot of John's headstone, I said, "Do you know why I got involved at all with the murder of TJ Delcamino?"

"You wanted answers, as I recall from your first visit to me."

"Answers," I repeated. "When John died, there were no answers. He had a hidden heart defect. One second he was living and the next he wasn't. There were no answers, no deeper truths, no mystery, no one to blame. I thought if I could get some answers, any answers, about TJ's murder, it would give me purpose and some meaning to John's death."

"I remember saying that some answers had to be discovered for themselves. Well, Gus, you've had your answers. What do you say?"

"That I was wrong. That answers don't give meaning to anyone's death. TJ and John are just as dead today as they were before Tommy D. came to see me last December. The answers didn't bring them justice, and even if I'd managed to get some small measure of justice for the kid, so what? He was beyond it. Justice is for those of us left behind."

He didn't say another word. We just stood there for a while until the caretaker came over and stood with us.

My cell phone buzzed as I was nearly back at the van. I hoped it might be Magdalena, but it was Felix, working a rare night shift. He told me that I had a late pickup at the airport and another one back at the station. It was going to be a longer, harder shift than I'd anticipated, so I went into Dunkin' Donuts for a cup of coffee. Khalid, the night manager, was there as he always was and eyed me with disdain as he always did. But Aziza, the countergirl, was nowhere to be seen. Instead, a new Pakistani girl in a fresh, clean uniform and a shy demeanor was working the counter.

"Where's Aziza?" I asked Khalid.

He smiled at me for the first time in all the months I'd been coming in to get coffee. "Oh, Aziza has gone." He waved his hand.

"Gone?"

"Back to Karachi to be married." He waved his hand again. "She will be here no more."

"Can I help you, sir?" the new girl asked.

Khalid answered for me, barking at the girl. "Small coffee, half-and-half, two Sweet'N Lows."

I paid, dropped the change in her tip cup, took the coffee, and left.

Back in the van I stared at the coffee cup, looked up at Bill's gifted crucifix dangling from the mirror, and cried quietly for Aziza's gap-toothed smile. A smile I would never see again.

AUTHOR'S NOTE

I have lived in Suffolk County for the past twenty-seven years. During that time I have had the honor and pleasure of getting to know several members of the Suffolk County Police Department and of the Suffolk County District Attorney's office. To a person, they are honest, upstanding folks who often perform their duties under difficult and dangerous circumstances. None of them, in any way, resemble the cruel and corrupt characters depicted in this novel. Good-hearted, diligent people make for a safe and stable environment in which to raise a family, but they make for boring crime fiction.

ACKNOWLEDGMENTS

I owe a large debt of gratitude to Chris Pepe, Ivan Held, and David Hale Smith. It is a revelation to have the support of people who believe in you and your abilities even while you doubt yourself.

Thanks to my first readers for this book, Kathleen Eull and Ellen Weiler Schare.

But I could not have come this far without the sacrifices my family made for me. I have gotten to pursue my dream often at their expense. So thank you, Rosanne, Kaitlin, and Dylan. Without you, none of this would be possible or worth it.